THE KREMLIN CONTROL

OWEN SELA is a British author, who lives in London. Celebrated for his fast-paced, authentic thrillers – both *An Exchange of Eagles* and *Triple Factor* were highly successful – *The Kremlin Control* is no exception. A story of compulsive suspense, set inside Soviet Russia today, it confirms Owen Sela as one of the best British thriller writers working today.

OWEN SELA

The Kremlin Control

FONTANA PAPERBACKS

First published by Fontana Paperbacks in 1984
A continental edition first issued in Fontana Paperbacks 1984
This edition issued in Great Britain by Fontana Paperbacks 1984

Made and printed in Great Britain by
William Collins Sons & Co. Ltd, Glasgow

for
SMITA
1010k is a lot

CHAPTER ONE

May. Unexpectedly and unseasonably, the temperature soared. Suddenly, the earth was flooded with soft shoots and walls came alive in a patchwork of yellows, blues, pinks and greens.

As summer cascaded briefly, Moscow became a sweltering island in a sea of torrid air. KGB Headquarters, which could talk to satellites, had no airconditioning. In the Emergency Centre, Captain Yuri Raikin, recently involuntarily repatriated to Moscow, and compulsorily assigned to the Second Chief Directorate's Political Security Service – the Sluzbha – sat before a flagged map of Moscow and sweated.

Red flags for arrests, green for surveillance, yellow for patrols, purple for reserves. That afternoon Moscow looked as if it was innundated with greenfly.

Yuri Raikin was twenty-six years old, with a high cheek-boned Russian face and narrow, close-set eyes that he thought made him look like a bandit. His body was uncharacteristically lean, fined down, not underfed, the leanness emphasizing a swimmer's breadth of shoulder. Like the face the body tapered. It was clad in a grey Marks & Spencer suit. From its lapel there dangled the ribbon of the Order of the Red Banner.

He brushed a strand of damp hair from his eyes and looked across the desk to where Sergeant Pavel Pashchenko sat before banks of radio switches and a console that could be used to reroute Moscow's traffic, direct fire brigade and army units, and control the airspace for forty miles around Moscow. Sergeant Pashchenko, or Pasha as he wanted to be called, had been assigned to teach Yuri the ways of the Sluzbha.

Pashchenko was built like a lead mattress, with a large stomach that drooped and massive shoulders that didn't. He wrestled for a KGB team and was entitled to extra shopping privileges. That morning he had bought three kilos of prime steak, a rare enough commodity even at a KGB store for him to worry about it mouldering in an office without aircondi-tioning. 'We should at least be allowed to open the windows,' he grumbled.

'If we open the windows all our secrets will fly out in Dzerzhinsky Square.'

'What secrets?' Pasha inquired.

Despite its title, work at the Emergency Centre was routine; routine calls from men on the beat, the dispatch of patrol cars and surveillance teams, the arranging of reliefs, the farming out of queries from local KGB offices, the direction of agents to assignments and, most important, the clearing of traffic for the Politburo. Pasha had told Yuri that only once in his seventeen years at the Sluzbha had all the facilities of the Centre been used. That had been on the first day of the Moscow Olympics when CIA sponsored riots and an American bombing raid had been feared, and they had closed all Moscow's airports, cleared its airspace and pulled out troops to stand shoulder to shoulder on Moscow's streets.

There was no such excitement today. Today radios crackled routinely. Phones rang. From time to time Yuri and Pasha moved flags. Between calls Yuri read Kafka.

'A new book?' Pasha asked.

'It's about sixty years old.'

'Russian?'

'No. Czech.'

'What does he write about?'

'Well there's this story about a man who finds himself turned into an insect, and another story about a commandant in a penal colony who runs it so his successors cannot change it.'

'Sounds modern,' Pasha said.

The phone rang. Yuri and Pasha eyed each other, thinking the same thought. Argayan, the trainee from distant Erevan was lost in Moscow again. Pasha reached into his pocket and took out a coin in his clenched fist.

'Tails.'

'Wrong again.'

Yuri grimaced and picked up the phone. It wasn't Argayan. It was a frightened KGB chauffeur called Vasili Frolov. Yuri gestured to Pasha to pick up the extension. Frolov had just killed an intruder in the apartment of General Vyssorian Dolgov.

Yuri said, 'You want the Militia. This is State Security.'

The chauffeur said Dolgov too was dead. 'Dolgov is Red List. My orders are—'

'I know,' Yuri said. The Red List consisted of the most important people in Russia, members and the immediate familities of the Politburo, Chiefs of the Armed Forces, the Directors of State Security. Anything that happened to anyone on that list was of total and immediate concern to the Sluzbha. Yuri had never heard of General Dolgov. But Dolgov was Red List. And Dolgov was dead.

'Stay there,' he said. 'Do nothing. Touch nothing. Speak to no one, till I get there.'

Pasha was lumbering to his feet. 'You take over here. This needs experience.'

Yuri pressed down on Pasha's shoulders. It was like holding down an elephant. 'That also calls for experience.' He nodded towards the console. Yuri had been with Sluzbha nearly three weeks, and Pasha had yet to show him how the console worked. Yuri said, 'I might just direct two convoys of Party bigwigs into the same traffic lane.'

Pasha blanched at the thought. 'Fuck,' he said. A frown turned his face into seamed rock. 'You're sure you can handle this dead general?'

Yuri fingered the decoration in his lapel. 'I got this for handling armies.'

'This is security work,' Pasha growled, 'not a fucking war.' He looked uncertainly around the room.

Men spoke softly into telephones and intercoms. Typewriters and telexes chattered. That day, Pasha had charge of the Emergency Centre. He couldn't leave it, not even for a general who was Red List. And Pasha was choosing someone else, Yuri thought disappointedly. He wanted to take charge of a murder investigation. Compared to the normal work of the Sluzbha, murder was clean.

Finally, Pasha said, 'All right. You better go over there and establish our interest in the case. Find out from this man Frolov what happened. Then inform Director Popov.'

Pasha was very close to Director Popov. Yuri believed Pasha reported on him to Popov.

'Do nothing else,' Pasha ordered.

Yuri saluted with two fingers, mockingly. 'Aye, aye, Comrade General.' Pasha had refused four promotions and remained a sergeant for eleven years, because he felt policemen shouldn't sit behind desks, and he'd told Yuri, there wasn't a chair in Dzerzhinsky Square big enough for his ass.

'Captain, sir,' Pasha hissed, dangerously. 'Get your ass over there, now.'

By the time Yuri reached the ground floor a KGB Volga was waiting, its blue roof light revolving urgently. He leapt in beside the driver. KGB gatemen froze traffic. They roared out onto Kirov. By courtesy of the Emergency Centre, the traffic remained frozen all the way to Kropotkinskaya.

The apartment house was new, bright yellow and highly security conscious. Yuri had to produce his bright red work pass with the embossed gold sword and shield emblem of the KGB three times before he reached the floor on which the General had lived. The frightened chauffeur, Vasili Frolov admitted him into a dim lobby.

Frolov was small and slope-shouldered, with an oval, unmarked face and a tiny patch of dark hair on the crown of his head. His eyes were dark and artless, his shoes and uniform buttons highly polished. Chauffeurs in their way, Yuri thought, were as vain as generals.

The General lay in the doorway behind Frolov, splayed legs and barrel chest covered with a tracksuit of episcopal burgundy, striped training shoes with black, ribbed soles pointing into the air. From behind a sofa in the sunlit living room, a bloody head gaped.

Yuri looked hurriedly back to Frolov. 'What happened?' He held out his hand for Frolov's work pass and gun.

The work pass described Frolov as age twenty-six and a Grade 2 chauffeur with the KGB Motor Pool on Chkalova Ulica. The gun was a standard issue 9 mm Makarov. Yuri snapped out the magazine. One bullet had been fired. A faint smell of burnt powder hung in the air.

Frolov said he had been with the KGB eight years, trained

in the use of firearms and entitled to chauffeur anyone below Central Committee status. Dolgov was a regular user of the KGB Motor Pool; Frolov his almost regular driver. Every Monday, Wednesday and Friday afternoon he collected Dolgov from the apartment and drove him to the Druzbha Gymnasium, where for an hour and a half the General worked out with weights.

That day, Frolov had been held up by an out of town truck that had balked him all along Chernycevskogo. Frolov had been ten minutes late. Yes, he said, in answer to Yuri's question, he always kept to the same route.

When he'd reached the apartment he'd been surprised to find another chauffeur had been sent for. Not suspicious then, but nervous and a trifle peeved, he'd gone up to the apartment to make his explanations. The apartment door had been ajar. He'd glimpsed the General lying on his back across the entrance to the living room. He'd drawn his Makarov and entered.

The intruder had been standing by the bookcase, casually throwing books and papers to the floor.

Frolov had levelled his gun and called, '*Stoi!*'

The intruder had turned. He had shown no surprise, no fear. He'd simply stood there, silently contemplating Frolov. Then slowly, almost mechanically, he'd reached into his pocket and taken out a gun.

Frolov had fired.

'I was lucky with the head shot,' Frolov said, rolling a cigarette between his fingertips and fidgeting with a lighter. 'I didn't think, I didn't aim. I simply pulled the trigger.' Frolov's mouth trembled. A thin sheen of sweat laminated his forehead.

'Smoke if you want to,' Yuri said and walked past Frolov to examine the bodies.

Dolgov lay on his back, florid, white haired, unusually smooth complexioned. He had the heavy shoulders, short neck and deep chest of a weight lifter. He'd been a handsome man, with a straight, patrician nose, a large, sensual mouth. His eyes were frozen in an expression of surprise, and the flesh around the jowls had sagged in death. Beneath the ruddiness there was a tinge of blue.

A glass Dolgov had been carrying had shattered, and lay now

in bright slivers about the inert head. There were tiny nicks on the left cheek, which had scarcely bled. Yuri looked carefully at the General's body. There was no sign of the intruder having used his gun.

He walked into the living room, its walls decorated with scenes of battle and a reproduction of Repin's 'Remorse of Ivan.' Dolgov had lived well, among imported, pale wood furniture, low, elegant and modern. Behind the angular sofa a waist-high bookshelf separated the living area from a neat dining room in the same modern style. The intruder's body lay between the sofa and the bookshelf.

Yuri forced himself to look. The bullet had exploded into the man's forehead with the force of a grenade, lifted out skull and skin and hair and left a jagged, red, pulpy opening from which insect-like shiny grey matter trailed. The body was dressed in a KGB chauffeur's grey uniform. A cap and a gun lay on the floor amid blood-spattered books and papers. The edge of a red work pass peeked out of the man's top pocket.

Yuri's stomach surged on a great wave. As Frolov watched nervously from the doorway, he breathed deeply and forced himself to kneel beside the body. With finger and thumb he extracted the work pass.

It described the dead man as a chauffeur attached to the KGB Motor Pool since 1974. But Yuri noticed the computer tracing on the work pass was printed, not magnetically stamped. It was a forgery.

Dolgov's apartment had no air conditioning, and already there was a faint, raw odour of putrefaction about the body. Keeping his eyes on the red-piped coat lapel, Yuri slipped his hand into the man's jacket. Fifty roubles in notes, and as he'd suspected, the man had been Russian enough to carry his own work pass, giving details of his birth, parentage, ethnic origins, residential registration and lifetime employment record.

His name was Sergei Kronykin and he'd been born in Moscow in 1950. He'd received his work pass at the age of sixteen in Smolensk, attended school there, done his national service with 426th Infantry and transferred to Special Task Forces. He'd spent two years in Afghanistan, and on his return had left the Army. For the past year he'd worked at the Martov

Chemical Factory in Smolensk. Kronykin had been married, with a son aged nine, and a daughter aged seven.

Yuri carried the documents to the phone. He had, as ordered, established the KGB's interest. He had ascertained what had happened. Yuri dialled and asked for Colonel Director Popov. He had been brought back to Moscow after all, to learn to do what he'd been told.

'Do nothing,' Popov rasped. 'Touch nothing. Don't even breathe till I get there.'

CHAPTER TWO

Popov came bustling vigorously in, calf-length rain coat belted against the sun. A brown fedora was jammed over his bald head. Squat, bandy legged and aggressive, he reminded Yuri of a tug battling ice floes in the Moskva.

'Where's Pashchenko?'

'At the Emergency Centre, keeping the proletariat in line.'

Beneath the brown fedora, Popov's ballbearing eyes took on a metallic sheen. 'Don't get smart, Raikin.' He bared his lips as he spoke, revealing nicotine stained steel teeth. 'The last time you got smart you got shifted from London to Moscow. Next time . . . ' Leaving the threat unfinished Popov shouldered his way past Yuri into the living room.

Popov was a typical Sluzbha ballbreaker, Yuri thought, crafty, arrogant, a sonofabitch and a bully. In London he'd suspected Yuri was a CIA agent and had him injected full of scopolamine. Now, he questioned Frolov about the shooting, then Yuri about the call to the Emergency Centre and what he'd done after that. He examined Kronykin's documents, strode into the living room and hissed tobacco smoke over the bodies. He flung open doors, looked cursorily into rooms, then shut himself in Dolgov's bedroom. The phone in the living room tinkled sympathetically as he dialled on the extension.

Yuri counted six calls before Popov emerged from the bedroom, raincoat unbelted, a gleam of sweat on his pink forehead.

'I have spoken with Professor Andronov of the Botkin Institute,' Popov said. 'It is essential that the General's body be examined immediately.' The tiny eyes slid and fastened themselves on Frolov. 'You will take the General's body to Municipal Hospital Number 11 on Dovato Ulica.'

That didn't make sense. The Botkin Institute and Professor Andronov were located near the Hippodrome to the northeast of the city. Municipal Hospital Number 11 was near the Lenin Stadium to the south. 'You really mean the body should be taken to the Botkin?' Yuri asked.

Popov's eyes had an angry, metallic glitter. 'I mean the Municipal Hospital on Dovato Ulica,' he snapped. 'They have already made arrangements for the examination.'

'What's Professor Andronov looking for?'

'What professors usually look for in cases of sudden death.' Popov's eyes danced and shifted as he spoke. 'Captain Raikin, help Comrade Frolov get the General's body to the car. Hurry. Time is vital.'

Hurrying, when the General was already dead didn't make sense either. Besides, it was usual for bodies to be examined where they were found. And if Dolgov's body had to be transported, why not send for an ambulance? And what good was a professor, however eminent, when the patient was dead? Yuri said, 'The body should be examined here.'

'There are no facilities here,' Popov rumbled.

'And if it is a question of urgency, it would make more sense to rush Professor Andronov to the body.'

A wash of red flooded Popov's face. 'It would also make more sense if you learned to do as you're told. That's why you were transferred to Moscow and committed to my charge. So stop asking stupid questions and help Comrade Frolov get the General's body to his car.'

Yuri didn't move. Popov was acting as if Dolgov were still alive. By transporting the body by car to the Municipal Hospital, Popov was deliberately obscuring the circumstances and manner of Dolgov's death.

Yuri considered alternatives. Be a robot and do as he was told or . . . . There were no alternatives. In London, he'd been committed to Popov's supervision. 'Is that a direct order, sir?' he asked.

Popov stared at him challengingly, little pig eyes narrow slits in folds of far. 'It's certainly not a request, Captain.'

Yuri picked up the General by the shoulders. The body was still pliant. The chill of dead flesh seeped through the track suit onto his fingers. As they raised him, the General's head lolled back. A shard of glass fell out from beneath his nostrils.

Popov held open the door as they backed into the corridor. The corridor was empty, the doors of the other apartments sealed like fast shut eyes. They manoeuvred the body, lurching sideways towards the elevator. The elevator was waiting for them. They lowered the General onto the floor and Frolov pressed the button plunging them downwards. Accompanied by the dead they rode in deathly silence.

The metal doors slid open. Yuri stooped and picked up his burden. The lobby was deserted. Frolov directed him toward the back of the building. They went out through an unguarded rear entrance into an empty courtyard. Popov's arrangements had obviously included temporarily clearing the building of security personnel. There were to be no witnesses to the transfer of Dolgov's body.

'Boot or rear seat?' Yuri asked, by Frolov's Volga.

'The seat will be easier.'

Frolov dropped the General's legs and opened the door. Yuri backed into the car dragging the body after him and arranged the General upright on the rear seat. As Frolov drove away, the body lurched sideways. An arm raised itself against the side window in a grisly goodbye.

Yuri waved back and told himself, don't get smart. Next time, the fact that Popov knows your hero father, that you're something of a hero yourself, won't save you from Siberia. So don't think about inconsistencies and don't look for explanations. This is Moscow, not London, and besides, this General Dolgov is beyond help, already dead.

In London, a life had been at stake.

Four weeks ago, Yuri had been in London. He'd met Charlie Simmonds on the embankment opposite the Royal Festival Hall. A thin drizzle had studded watery pinheads on the synthetic fur collar of Simmonds' coat. Across the Thames, office towers had gleamed with damp, smaller, lighter and less grandiose than Stalin's Moscow.

Charlie Simmonds was a journalist, a sagging sack of a man, with a pear-shaped head, a petulant mouth and defensive blue eyes. Thirty-eight years old, he'd worked for an agency specializing in East European affairs, and a year previously, had achieved prominence by being the first Western journalist to interview Russia's new leader, Pyotr Deryugin. Yuri had been running Simmonds for ten months.

Charlie Simmonds had said, 'I'm going to defect to the Americans.'

'Why defect?' Yuri has asked. 'And if you are going to defect, why tell me?' Simmonds had only recently returned from a second visit to Moscow.

Simmonds had placed an arm around Yuri's shoulder. His breath, Yuri remembered, had been yeasty from the beer he'd drunk with his lunch. 'Yuri, you're my control. You're also my friend, and I trust you. I want you to tell Moscow I haven't really defected. Not from here.' He'd placed a grubby palm across his heart. 'Tell them I am still and always will be loyal to the cause. Tell them all I've done is seek sanctuary.'

'Sanctuary? From whom?'

Simmonds had said, 'Your chaps want to kill me.'

Simmonds was a romantic. At Cambridge, he'd read John Reed's melodramatic account of the October Revolution and been converted by a professor who'd served in Spain with the International Brigades. Yuri believed Simmonds thought of himself as another John Reed. His father was a well-known barrister. He had a small, independent income. Not working class, he demonstrated his solidarity with the proletariat by wearing sports jackets, scuffed rubber-soled suedes and red flannel ties. Even the name Charlie was an affectation. His real friends called him Charles. There was no reason on earth why anyone would want to kill him, least of all the KGB. 'You're a valuable and trusted agent,' Yuri had said, soothingly, thinking that Simmonds had finally gone ape.

Simmonds had released Yuri and turned to stare at the river. 'Not any more,' he'd said, disconsolately.

'For heaven's sake, Charlie, what have you done?'

Simmonds' face had clouded with worry. 'They say it's because of the LASM-Two leak.' His tone was bitter.

'That's bullshit!' The LASM-Two was a laser-based offence-defence system, and Yuri had been authorized by Moscow Centre to have Simmonds give details of it to the Americans. 'The LASM-Two leak was authorized. It's all on the record.'

15

'You checked the record, recently?' The fear in Simmonds' eyes was very real.

'Charlie, what the hell are you talking about? I *ordered* you to leak that information to the Americans. I was ordered to do so by my Moscow control, Alexei Zamyatin. Zamyatin was ordered by Comrade Director Suslov, and Suslov's orders came from the very top.'

Simmonds had said, 'They still mean to kill me.'

Yuri remembered a barge cutting a muddy swathe on the pimpling water, a white pleasure steamer pitching against its mooring by the Strand. Stabbing a hand into a pocket Simmonds had brought out a newspaper clipping. 'It's really because of this.' He'd thrust the clipping at Yuri.

The article had been datelined four days previously. There was a picture of Charlie Simmonds beneath the headline. Since his interview with Deryugin, Simmonds' freelance income had trebled. The headline questioned if Deryugin would last. Curiously, Yuri read.

A not-so-secret scandal following the arrest of an underground businessman, Solomon Lazar, threatens not only to bring down Deryugin's government, but to alter permanently the machinery of political power within Russia.

Solomon Lazar, 62, was arrested two months ago, after a bizarre series of coincidences including the discovery of his KGB file in the offices of the militarist magazine, *Young Guard*. At his trial Lazar not only admitted to lavishly bribing officials of the KGB but to owning no less than 64 illegal factories, and a fortune of over 300 million roubles.

What makes the matter of vital political interest is that Moscow is full of impossible-to-authenticate rumours that Lazar was protected throughout his career by influential people, including Second Secretary Deryugin himself.

These rumours are given some credence by a statement from Lazar's brother, that Lazar was not simply a black marketeer, but had, especially in the years immediately after the war, used his contacts to help rebuild the Ukraine. General Secretary Deryugin was at the time responsible for the economic redevelopment of the region, and it was his successful work in the Ukraine that brought him recognition by Moscow and the position of Controller of the State Bank.

In order to combat the rumours, Deryugin has created a Commission under Soslan Zarev, 52, First Secretary of the Leningrad Party and a known opponent of Deryugin's laissez-faire policies. So far, the Zarev Commission has concerned itself with investigating corruption within the KGB's Second Chief Directorate, the principal arm of Russia's internal policing.

There is concern however, that Comrade Zarev may be taking his responsibilities too seriously, that his investigations have become so far-reaching that the KGB itself is walking in fear.

It is rumoured that Colonel Turayev, the former deputy head of the Second Chief Directorate, committed suicide after a stormy inverview with Zarev, who had apparently accused Turayev of corruption and suppressing the names of influential persons involved with Lazar.

And in a secret interview with a high-ranking KGB official this reporter learnt that the KGB itself has been investigating Zarev, and was shown evidence that Zarev is being supported by an elite within the KGB called the Krasnaya Dela.

The Krasnaya Dela was originally formed in Leninist days, to distinguish between revolutionary members of the Cheka and former members of the Tsarist Okhrana. Under Stalin and Beria the Krasnaya Dela accumulated considerable power, and it was to prevent its emergence as a political force that, in 1959, Khrushchev split the domestic section of the KGB into separate Directorates – a policy his successors have prudently followed.

It now appears that in return for a promise to unify the KGB, certain members of the Krasnaya Dela are combining with Deryugin's opponents within the Politburo, to bring down the Deryugin government. Informed sources stated that Zarev's zeal was directed, not at eliminating corruption within the Second Chief Directorate, but in tearing the Second Chief Directorate apart.

Which raised the interesting question of why Zarev, no stranger to the means through which the Politburo and the Party control the Russian people, should seek to destroy the prime means of that control. And who is behind Zarev and why?

Comrade Zarev is undoubtedly familiar with the work of Nechayev, the 19th century anarchist, who had a profound influence on both Lenin and Stalin. In 1872, Nechayev wrote, 'Before you can create meaningfully, you must destroy completely.'

Yuri had read the article twice before he'd said, 'No wonder they want your ass. Why the hell did you write this, Charlie? If you couldn't get to Deryugin this time, why did you have to think up this sensational crap?'

'Because every single word of it is true,' Simmonds had cried. 'My source was impeccable, and I double-checked where I could.'

'Who was your source?' Yuri had asked.

'I can't tell you that! I can't tell; for Christ's sake, man, they murdered him' He'd grabbed Yuri by the lapels. 'And now they want to murder me!'

Yuri had eased himself from Simmonds' grasp, snapped his fingers in front of the man's face. 'Charlie, wake up! You're imagining all this.'

Simmonds' fleshy cheeks had glowed red. 'I swear to you everything I've told you is true.' Lips whitening, he had turned away from Yuri. Then, lowering his voice, he'd asked, 'Yuri, can you get to Deryugin without going through intermediaries?'

'I can't even get to Moscow without intermediaries.'

'What about your father? He's a famous hero. Can he get directly to Deryugin?'

Yuri fought back his annoyance. His acquaintances were divided into those who believed it was nice to be the son of a hero, and those who wondered what he'd done to deserve the privilege. 'My father is a soldier,' he'd said, shortly. 'He doesn't involve himself in politics.'

Simmonds had looked down at the rain spitting on the concrete. 'Then there's no help for it, I suppose, but the Americans.' The downpour darkened his sandy hair, glistened on his scalp. He forced a brave smile. 'Do this, then. Get to Deryugin, the best way you can. Tell him that I have the names of the politicians behind Zarev and the Krasnaya Dela. I know what they mean to do. Have Deryugin make contact with me through someone he trusts absolutely. Have him send you to me in Washington.'

'Give me the names,' Yuri had said.

'No.' Simmonds had smiled wryly and shaken his head. 'It's not that I don't trust you, Yuri. It's just that you might reveal the names to the wrong people. Get a direct line to Deryugin and . . . ' He'd held out his hand. 'I must go now. George Carpenter is expecting me.'

'Do I contact you through Carpenter?'

'I expect so.'

Yuri ignored Simmonds' hand. 'Charlie, you're being foolish. If what you're saying is true –'

'It's true. The man they've sent to London to kill me is Georgi Vilna.' Simmonds' eyeballs, ringed with white, had seemed to protrude.

Yuri's breath caught. Georgi Vilna had arrived in London two days ago, spent his time since closeted with Viktor Serov, the London KGB Resident. But Simmonds belonged to Yuri. They wouldn't liquidate Simmonds without checking first . . . they wouldn't kill an agent, even if . . . . Yuri had realized, they would.

Simmonds was already hurrying past the rain-splattered tables of an open air café, toward a concrete apron that led to gloomy arches supporting a terrace and a parking lot beyond. Suddenly, on the terrace above the arches Yuri had seen Georgi Vilna move, transferring a brown paper parcel from his left hand to his right as he hurried to position himself behind Simmonds.

Instinctively, Yuri had shouted. 'Charlie! Run! For God's sake man, run!' But the breeze snapping up from the river had carried his voice away, and Yuri had himself begun to run, sprinting past the café and across the open expanse, into the darkness underneath the terrace.

Vilna had already been there, his body braced against, half

hidden by a stone column. At the far end of the passageway, Simmonds had walked, head thrust low between his shoulders.

'Don't do it, Georgi!' Yuri had shouted. 'Simmonds is mine!'

Vilna had been cradling the gun in both hands and sighting carefully along the barrel. 'I've completed my investigation,' he'd said, softly. 'I have my orders.'

Yuri had hit him in the stomach.

Vilna had gasped and bent double, staggered in a semi-circle to face Yuri. 'Keep out of this, Raikin. I'll take you, too, if I have to.'

Yuri had lunged for the gun. He was bigger than Vilna, but there was a steely wiriness about the gunman. Vilna had clung desperately to the gun, as if realizing it was his only advantage and tried to bring his knee into Yuri's crotch. Yuri had bounced him against a pillar. Vilna had gasped and thrust the gun into Yuri's shoulder. Yuri had twisted his shoulder away and kneed Vilna in the stomach. He'd grabbed Vilna's coat and moved him sideways. Vilna had thrust the gun barrel against Yuri's chest. Yuri remembered Vilna's finger whitening on the trigger.

He had pivoted on his left foot and turned away from Vilna, lowered his body and pulled Vilna onto his right hip. He'd lifted upwards and forwards. Vilna had curled over Yuri's hip.

Deliberately, Yuri had let him go.

Vilna had wheeled to the floor, with a clatter of metal across concrete, and the sharp crack of bone snapping.

Yuri had scooped up the gun and turned. By then, Simmonds had disappeared and Vilna was sitting up cradling his wrist.

'You bastard, you've broken my hand,' Vilna had hissed through pain-twisted lips. 'Moscow will fry you for this.'

The apartment was hazy with cigarette smoke. Popov stood where Dolgov's body had lain, looking like a malefic gnome who had popped out of a magic bottle. He threw Yuri a cordial, if stubby wave. 'I've decided to give you a chance to redeem youself,' he announced. 'I am putting you in charge of investigating this burglary.'

'Burglary?' Yuri was instantly suspicious. The last time

Popov had helped him, he'd ended up drugged and babbling. This time it could be complicity in suppressing a murder. 'Two men were killed here,' he said, sternly.

Popov's grin glinted through the smoke. 'One,' he said, holding up a finger to emphasize the number. 'Sergei Kronykin was killed by Comrade Frolov in the lawful execution of his duty. Comrade Frolov will in due course be commended for his courage and exonerated from all blame.' Popov lowered his upraised finger and squinted closely at Yuri. 'We do not know yet how General Dolgov died. So until we receive a report from the eminent Professor Andronov, this is a case of burglary.'

Technically, Yuri supposed, Popov was right. But what if Dolgov had been murdered? Proper procedures had not been observed. Vital evidence might have been destroyed in transporting the body to Municipal Hospital No. 11. Was that why Popov was putting him in charge of the case?

'First of all,' Popov was saying, 'I want you to find out everything possible about this man Kronykin. I want to know who he was, what he was doing in Moscow, who his associates were, and what he was looking for in General Dolgov's apartment.

I have arranged for the body to be taken to the Militia Pathology Lab,' he went on. 'You will impress upon the examiner that this is a KGB matter and that reports are only to be given to you.' Popov's eyes skidded past Yuri's shoulder. 'You will not discuss it with anyone, except on my authority. You will report only to me.'

Why all the secrecy, Yuri wondered and said, 'I'll need help tracing where Kronykin stayed in Moscow.'

'Sergeant Pashchenko will help you arrange that.' Popov lit another cigarette. 'Now, you'd better get Kronykin's gun to Ballistics.'

Yuri hesitated. He'd read that suspect weapons should never be touched. In Julian Semyonov's books, detectives always picked up guns with handkerchiefs or with pencils inserted through the barrels. Yuri jabbed a pen in the barrel of Kronykin's weapon and transferred it into a handkerchief wrapped hand.

'I see you read Semyonov,' Popov said, and sighed.

CHAPTER THREE

Yuri rode the Metro back to Headquarters, a carrier of bodies and transporter of weapons. He had little choice but to go through the motions. In Russia you were promoted for going through the motions. Yuri wondered if he might earn enough merit points to be transferred back to the First Chief Directorate, which ran all the KGB's foreign operations and which had recruited him in the first place.

KGB Headquarters dominated the north side of Dzerzhinsky Square. In Tsarist days the All Russian Insurance Company had underwritten the Baltic fishing fleet from what was now the Old Building. More significantly, in 1918, Feliks Dzerzhinsky had installed the Cheka there.

The New Building had been erected in 1947, coloured the same pastel yellow, connected to and indistinguishable from the Old. The massive composite spread two whole blocks backwards along Kirov Ulica and Dzerzhinskovo. Beneath its rusticated stone base lay Lubyanka Prison.

Yuri entered through the pedestrian gateway on Kirov, delivered the gun to Ballistics and went over to Technical Services Group in the rear of the New Building.

Technical Services Group produced, maintained and operated bugs, bleepers and devices that recreated conversations by analyzing the vibrations of window panes. They devised cigarette lighters that fired bullets, cameras that took pictures in near darkness and chewing gum that could blow a man's head apart. They forged documents, enlarged microdots and produced code pads so small they could be hidden in the lining of a jacket, and if discovered, eaten. They arranged burglaries and opened letters. Yuri only wanted sixty copies of Kronykin's photograph lifted from the fake KGB work pass.

The technician clucked sympathetically and looked at his

watch. 'It will take at least an hour to get all this logged. Perhaps tomorrow—'

'Tomorrow you'll be wearing an outsize truss,' Yuri warned. 'The photographs in an hour or Director Popov will be dancing on your balls!' Ball-stamping was the current Sluzbha threat.

'You should have said it was for Director Popov,' the technician muttered.

Returning to the Old Building, Yuri stopped by an empty payphone. Payphones were a triumph of planning over reality. Planners insisted that if payphones were available, people would use them. The reality was that no one used payphones if he could help it. Why pay when you could use an official phone for free? Yuri inserted two kopecks, dialled the First Chief Directorate and asked for Major Alexei Zamyatin.

An unfamiliar voice asked, 'Who wants him?'

'An old friend.'

'You have a name, old friend?'

Yuri gave his name.

'Major Zamyatin will call you back.'

Zamyatin had been promising to call him back, since he'd returned to Moscow. Yuri forced himself to replace the receiver gently. Zamyatin couldn't avoid him forever, he told himself as he walked back to his office.

The Sluzbha occupied the entire second and third floors of the Old Building. The walls were a deep green and the floors, parquet. There were partitioned cubicles everywhere and open spaces where typists sat and men shared desks. Lighting that ranged from ornate chandeliers to naked bulbs cast uneven shadows. Men came and went noisily. The floor vibrated to the tread of their boots. Shouts carried along the warren of corridors and clashed with the rattle of typewriters and the cackle of telex machines. There was a continuous slamming of doors and ringing of phones. Kettles boiled. Men swore. The place smelled of sausage, perspiration and sharp tobacco. Yuri thought, working in the Sluzbha was a little like working in a subway station.

His office was on the third floor, a tiny cubicle with green hardboard walls, a strip of lino over the parquet, a battered desk, two surprisingly new chairs, a safe, and an ancient

24

Underwood on a metal trolley. There was a picture of Dery-ugin on one wall, a peeling map of Moscow on the other. A yellowing notice by the window warned against letting papers blow into the courtyard.

The scuffed, half moons of Pasha's shoes rested on Yuri's desk, Pasha himself tilted precariously in the visitor's chair, a weeping parcel of meat balanced just as precariously on the window ledge behind the desk. 'Message from your wife, Rima Aristova,' Pasha said, squinting at a note beside his shoes. 'She wants you home, straight after work. Her father is coming to dinner.'

'Shit!' Yuri exclaimed. He scooped up the note and with the same motion swept Pasha's feet off the desk. When he and Rima had first been married, the Aristovs had sent food parcels, and Aristov had dropped in unannounced, one or more times a day. Then, Rima, sensing Yuri's growing irritation, had told her father not to visit them without being invited. Rima and he had grown apart since, and now Aristov had once again taken to visiting unexpectedly.

Pasha said, 'I'll look after the Dolgov business. For a guest who is Chairman of Party Organs, a member of the Central Committee and an alternate member of the Politburo, you should leave early.'

'The Chairman of Party Organs can bloody well have dinner alone with his daughter,' Yuri exclaimed.

Pasha eyed him curiously. 'What's the point of having privileges if you don't use them?'

'And what's the point of your sitting there staring at your meat when we have work to do?' Yuri went round the desk and sat.

Like the shadows of birds, a succession of expressions flitted across Pasha's massive face – curiosity, puzzlement, liking and a kind of respect. Suddenly he grinned. 'I'm waiting for your orders, Captain. I've already spoken to Pathology. Dr Yedemsky will have a report on Kronykin for you in the morning.'

Yuri said, 'We'd better get some people looking for where Kronykin stayed. Technical Services will be here soon with sixty photographs.'

Pasha picked up an internal phone and began talking to Surveillance and Trainees. Yuri hesitated uncertainly, then called Militia Records and asked for details of any burglary where entry had been obtained with forged KGB documents.

'No one would be mad enough to try that,' a wondering Militia Sergean' said.

Remembering that Kronykin had resided in Smolensk, he called the KGB there and asked for Kronykin's file to be sent by courier.

'That file is already in Moscow,' a records clerk said. It seemed that two months previously, Kronykin had been arrested for spreading scurrilous stories about the war in Afghanistan. He'd been handed over to the Fifth Chief Directorate for rehabilitation, and Kronykin's file was with them.

'Trust the Fifth to take a rumourmonger and turn him into a thief,' Pasha laughed when Yuri told him. According to Pasha the Fifth Directorate was the preserve of intelligents, paranoids, megalomaniacs and faggots, who an otherwise omniscient state had put in charge of all the institutes of psychiatric rehabilitation. 'You'll get nothing from those shitheads,' he warned.

'We can at least ask them for the file,' Yuri protested.

'Only if you want Director Guschin stamping on your balls.'

A messenger brought the photographs from Technical Services. 'Looks like a trouble maker,' Pasha commented, arranging the photographs into neat piles.

While they waited for the search party to assemble, Pasha bought sweet, fizzy drinks from the dispenser at the end of the corridor. He said, 'Popov must think highly of you to put you in charge of this case.'

Yuri sucked sweetness through the top of a can. 'Sheer inexperience,' he said. 'I've heard that Popov was only appointed Director because he's a friend of General Secretary Deryugin's from Dnepropetrovsk.'

Pasha's face coloured. The can buckled in the grip of his massive fist. 'Someone's been jerking your chain, asshole,' he said fiercely 'Popov's the best fucking director we've ever had.' He drank and hurled the crumpled can into the bin.

Yuri studied Pasha carefully. His anger was genuine enough;

Pasha believed what he'd been saying. Also Pasha was no rookie, but a hard-nosed cop who'd been in the force seventeen years. Yuri wondered what it was about Popov that commanded such passionate loyalty. 'Popov was in Special Investigations,' he probed. Special Investigations was the most hated and despised section of the KGB, men who spied on and disciplined their colleagues. 'How come he's suddenly such a good cop?'

'He still remembers what it was like on the streets,' Pasha said. 'And he's on our side, man, not like some of those other fuckers.'

Yuri waited for Pasha to mention names, but he didn't. Instead, he looked keenly at Yuri. 'I'll tell you something,' he said. 'Popov likes you.'

'He knows my father.' Yuri half smiled, and thought, if not for that accident of birth I might have ended up in Siberia.

In London, Popov and a Major General Golovkin from Special Investigations had conducted the enquiry into his assault on Vilna. Golovkin had asked Yuri why he hadn't stopped Simmonds from defecting, and Popov had said he'd found it difficult to imagine that the son of Marshal Gennadi Raikin was a traitor. They'd both suspected Yuri was doubling for the CIA.

When Yuri had told them the reason for Simmonds' defection, Golovkin had been sceptical. Popov however, had become very thoughtful. And afterwards Yuri had found out that he'd had the Marshal intercede, and Yuri had been returned to Moscow to work under Popov's direct supervision in Moscow.

'We need officers with your high moral principles,' Popov had said, at the time.

Yuri hadn't wanted to work for the Sluzbha. He'd felt that Popov should have investigated Vilna. 'Won't those principles be a hindrance when it comes to beating up intellectuals who piss on the flag?' he'd asked, sarcastically.

'You get smart with me,' Popov had shouted, 'and I'll piss on you.' Then, suddenly he had smiled, a brilliant sunburst of gaiety illuminating his face. 'You'll be happy with the Sluzbha in Moscow,' he'd predicted. 'For one with your special talents,

Moscow will be exceptionally rewarding. In Moscow, you will find much to investigate.'

If he started with the Dolgov case, Yuri thought bitterly, Popov would be the one most surprised.

In the large hall on the ground floor that was used for Party meetings on Monday and Friday afternoons, Pasha addressed the men who were to find out where Kronykin had stayed in Moscow. Kronykin, Pasha told them, was a con man, who'd used a forged KGB work pass to warn old ladies of an impending raid, offered to hide their valuables for them and then disappeared with the spoils. Kronykin's activities had given the KGB a bad name.

The hastily recruited trainees and surveillance men all looked severe.

Kronykin had to be found. Pasha issued the photographs and told them to start by checking all the lodging houses within the Sadovaya Ring. He warned them Kronykin could be registered under another name, and that they should not rely on registers, but on physical recognition.

The men left, carefully studying the photographs.

'Now let's get over to Dolgov's apartment,' Pasha said, 'and see if we can find what Kronykin was looking for.'

CHAPTER FOUR

The apartment building was busy with people coming home from work. The elevators whirred ceaselessly. Doors slammed. The corridors smelled of cooking and vibrated with the rumble of television sets and shouted conversation. By comparison, Dolgov's apartment was a tomb.

Pasha put away the key and asked, 'What are we looking for?'

'For whatever brought Kronykin here.'

The lighting seemed unnaturally bright, and whoever had cleared Kronykin's body, had tidied the bookshelf and drawn the curtains. Already the apartment had acquired the anonymity of a hotel room.

Yuri stood in the living room. There was a smudge of powder where Kronykin's body had lain. Pasha padded past him to the open plan kitchen and put his parcel of steak in the refrigerator.

Like all Moscow's modern blocks, the apartment was boxlike, only here, because Dolgov was *nomenklatura*, the boxes were larger and there were more of them. Along one side of the apartment were three bedrooms and a narrow bathroom. The master bedroom was at the back, opening onto the dining room and the kitchen. Yuri went to the dining room and pulled back the curtains. A terrace ran the width of the apartment. Yuri stared at other apartment houses, beyond which were the darting lights of the Inner Ring Road.

He turned and looked about him. That he had such an apartment, that he'd had such furniture, showed that Dolgov had been both influential and wealthy. If he wasn't, he wouldn't have been Red List, and Yuri wouldn't have been standing here wondering where to start looking.

From the kitchen, Pasha cried, 'Holy shit! Just take a look at this fucking freezer! He's got enough meat to feed an army!'

29

The freezer was large, American, and a giant yellow rectangle of light washed over the kitchen floor when it was opened. Like nearly everyone else in Russia, Dolgov had hoarded.

Yuri looked at the books Kronykin had been rifling, standard military works, campaign histories, biographies of generals and General Secretaries. Mixed with them were copies of the *Red Army Journal*, *Newsweek*, *Time*, *The Economist* and *Playboy*. Pasha ceased gloating over the food, lumbered over and started gloating over tits. 'Oh boy, I could hibernate with that all fucking winter!'

'Why hibernate?' Yuri asked.

The television was a massive twenty-six inch Philips in a tasteful teak cabinet. The hi-fi, a Sony, with record player, cassette deck and tuner. Dolgov's taste in music had been catholic and alphabetically arranged from Beethoven and the Beatles through to Tchaikovsky and Wagner.

They went into the bedroom. A king size bed with an imported quilt coverlet. Beside it, attention grabbing, eye snatching, was a framed glass case enclosing the heavy gold and red medallion of a Hero of the Soviet Union and *two* Orders of Lenin. So Dolgov had been tops, and, as if that needed confirmation, a large portrait hung over the bed. Dolgov in uniform looking as if he had just taken Berlin single handed. Yuri studied the heavy, thick set figure. Dolgov had been a weightlifter even then, with a sturdy, brutal physique. The face was a solid wedge, with outthrust jaw and a surprisingly sensual mouth curled in a disdainful grimace. A cap sat squarely on his low forehead and there was a challenging glint in the eyes. A hard man, Yuri thought, a strutting, self-centred, rapacious man. A groin kicker.

Pasha opened the wardrobe which ran the length of the room. Uniforms, one fatigue, three dress, and an orderly parade of suits labelled Austin Reed, Hartford, Simpsons and Jaques Lamar. On the dressing table were mother-of-pearl backed brushes and bottles of Givenchy Male and Brylcreem. In the drawers, Hathaway shirts, silk socks and scarves, underwear from Marks & Spencer. Dolgov had been a collector of imported finery. Above the dressing table another photograph,

Dolgov in full dress uniform being awarded the Order of Lenin by Deryugin; beside it framed letters from Khrushchev, Brezhnev, Andropov and Deryugin, each thanking Dolgov for his good wishes on their respective appointments as General Secretary.

Dolgov's feet must hardly have touched the ground.

There was a bathroom *en suite*. Pasha went into it, emerged reeking of Aramis and pronounced it clean.

The second bedroom was a black marketeer's treasure trove. Cartons of whisky and cigarettes, cases of French wine and champagne littered the floor. There was a cupboard full of canned goods. Drawers held cigarette lighters, bijouterie, exotic soaps, perfumes, contraceptives that promised to be feather light.

'Shit!' Pasha breathed. 'Get this lot to market and we could retire.'

The walls were covered with photographs. Dolgov, Dolgov and friends, picnics, parties, women. Yuri wondered how many Russian girls had spread their legs on the king size bed in exchange for cigarettes or soap or perfume. Not ordinary, impoverished Russian girls either. Some of the photographs were of actresses and ballet dancers. Many of them were inscribed, 'to Vyssorian with undying love.' In one photograph, the film actress Sonya Matsyeva smiled adoringly up at Dolgov.

Yuri felt himself suffocating. Sonya's older brother Nikolai had been his best friend at Psy Math. The Matsyevs had owned a neighbouring dacha in Yevapatoriya and for four consecutive summers the families had spent their holidays together. That last summer, Yuri had fallen hopelessly in love with Sonya.

Suddenly, she'd no longer been the reedy child, with skinny legs and a backside like a boy's, who'd intruded plaintively on him and Nikolai. That summer, the angular lines of her body had been softened by intriguing curves. She'd developed small and perfectly rounded breasts, together with a brittle reserve. There had been a curious sensuousness about her ankles and feet. At the time Yuri had wanted to be a poet, and he'd written they were poised like the claws of a yawning cat.

Her face, with its large, sloe eyes and wide curving mouth

had haunted him. All that summer, Yuri had been tortured by visions of her body, half woman, half child, a dark arrow on the beach, so near and yet so unattainable. When she'd read Mandelstam to him, her copy of this banned work illegally obtained, his captivation had been complete.

Four years afterwards they'd met again in Moscow. Yuri had been completing his cadetship at the Foreign Office and Sonya had recently graduated from the theatrical academy, GITIS. Yuri had pursued her with a manic intensity. He hadn't known many women, and none of them had even approached Sonya's dreamlike perfection. When he and Sonya finally became lovers, Yuri had felt fulfilled and complete.

Sonya had been playing small parts in Chekhov, and somewhat larger parts in modern comedies. At the Taganskaya a director called Kazakov had seen her play Zoya in Mayakovsky's *Bedbug*, and given her a part in a film. She'd fallen in love with film making, and hoped Kazakov would like her work enough to give her a more important part, because she wanted to be a star.

'Why?' Yuri had asked.

She'd given him that impish, heart-stopping grin which was later to become so famous and said, 'Because it's the only way to beat the system.'

He'd asked her to marry him. She'd wanted time to think, time to see how her career went. She was auditioning for the lead in a new Kazakov film, *Red Flowers*.

The afternoon Yuri had come to tell her he had joined the KGB's Foreign Service, he'd found her in bed with Kazakov, and realized that all Sonya wanted was to be a star.

Pasha was saying, 'I've seen all Sonya Matsyeva's films. I took my wife to see *Winter Loves* three times.'

'I was in Africa,' Yuri muttered, thickly. 'In Africa they don't have winters.' The remembered pain was like a needle probing a stab wound. From bedding film directors for important roles, Sonya had graduated to bedding influential generals. For what, Yuri wondered. For imported fal-de-lál? For status and privilege?

Bitch! Whore! There was a lump like a fist in his throat. In Africa, the memory of her face had been like an ikon. Embarrassed by the strength of his feelings, Yuri had forced himself to concentrate on examining the apartment.

Dolgov had used the third room as an office. It was furnished with a small, modern desk and tubular steel chairs covered with vinyl. Filing cabinets lined the walls. Above them were more photographs. Dolgov with the head of the State Planning Commission, Dolgov with the Minister of Foreign Trade, Dolgov with a group of foreign businessmen and Soviet officials signing agreements, Dolgov with other groups on the steps of the Bolshoi.

Dolgov had represented Amrocontinental, a company whose head office was in Zug. Pasha identified John Drasen, the owner of Amrocontinental, among the faces on the wall. Mid-fiftyish, with a square head of crewcut silver hair, an expression as tight as a shut purse and a skin like crinkled leather, Drasen looked unmistakably American.

Yuri asked, 'What's an American doing running companies in Russia?'

Pasha grinned. 'Making the rope with which the capitalists will hang themselves.'

'If that were the intention we'd do better dealing with General Motors.'

'We already do,' Pasha said. 'That's the kind of thing Drasen fixes. He's been here since the war. And he's close to everyone important. People say he used to advise Deryugin, when Deryugin was running the State Bank. Drasen's been here so long, he's one of you.'

'One of us? What do you—'

'*Nomenklatura*,' Pasha said, '*Vlasti*, Party bosses and Army chiefs, heads of the KGB and militia generals, the top thousand families.'

'We are a socialist democracy,' Yuri said, heatedly.

Pasha held up his hand.

They went through the filing cabinets. Dolgov's files were divided into Ministries and Projects. The General had been involved in chemical plants from Irkutsk to Kiev, in truck building plants along the Kama River, in producing textile machinery in Tashkent and soft drinks in Omsk. Together with

Amrocontinental and Drasen, Dolgov had brought capitalism to the Soviet Union.

A hero!

The phone on Dolgov's desk rang. It was Headquarters. Argayan, the perpetually lost Armenian, had located Kronykin's lodgings.

CHAPTER FIVE

Kronykin had lodged in the Old Arbat. They took the Ring Road to Povarsky Street where the Tsar's cooks had lived, and which was now called Vorovskovo after a revolutionary diplomat who had been assassinated in Lausanne in 1928. Yuri drove.

Pasha said, 'So now we know what Kronykin was looking for. The General's *defitsitny* goods.'

'Not the goods,' Yuri said. 'To take cases of whisky and crates of canned goods out of the apartment, Kronykin would have needed accomplices. He would have needed a truck.'

'Perhaps he was just reconnoitering.'

'Perhaps.' Yuri remembered Kronykin had been standing beside the General's bookcase when he died. 'Or looking for something smaller.'

Yuri turned into the Arbat. Centuries ago, Ivan the Terrible had driven out the original inhabitants and put his retainers here. Later, merchants and aristocats had moved in. Gogol had lived here. Dostoevsky had lodged in these winding streets and Tchaikovsky had resided here in somewhat grander style. Along Khlebny Pereulok, where once all Moscow's bread had been baked, Yuri stopped outside a shabby apartment building. A single electric bulb illuminated a faded sign: *HOMepa*.

They entered a monochrome lobby where Argayan and the manager waited. The manager's porcine cheeks were covered with stubble and the collar of his striped shirt was ringed with dirt. They followed his fat buttocks up a narrow stairway to the fourth floor.

Kronykin had lodged in a narrow triangular room near the roof. The walls were damp and stained, the threadbare carpet mottled with ground-in food scraps. A narrow bed stood against one peeling wall, and a heavy oak dresser under the eaves, with a mirror angled precariously on it.

Kronykin had arrived the previous evening, the manager wheezed. He had produced papers showing he'd been recently discharged from the Army. He'd wanted to spend two nights in Moscow before returning to Smolensk. All the details were filed with the Militia. The manager ran a law-abiding establishment.

Yuri wrinkled his nose at the smell of stale food, stale bodies, stale sweat. The heat brought out all the odours. Did Kronykin come alone, he asked. How had he spent the previous evening?

He'd gone out, the manager said, and returned about eight o'clock. Later, Kronykin had asked for a mirror and for writing paper. He'd stayed in his room till lunchtime, when he'd gone out for food. In the afternoon there'd been a phone call. Kronykin had taken it by the desk in the lobby. He hadn't said anything, only listened. When the caller had finished he'd put the receiver down without a word and gone back to his room. The manager hadn't seen him leave that afternoon.

Yuri saw that Pasha and Argayan were taking notes. A battered suitcase stood by the foot of the bed.

From the way the bed was made you could see Kronykin had been a soldier, the manager said.

Inside the suitcase was a shabby suit, a spare shirt, socks, a paper bag of soiled underwear. Very neat. Very soldierly. Kronykin had been ready to leave, but where had he been preparing to go?

Face down on the dresser was a photograph of a little girl. Beside it an untidy pile of paper, covered with scribble.

Yuri read, 'I do this for you, Tanya. I do this for you, for my whole family. Family. Family.'

The scribbles went on endlessly, the ravings of a lunatic. 'Pay to me, pay to ME, Sergei Anatolevich Kronykin. Pay money. Pay money to me.'

The man was mad, shell shocked perhaps, from the war.

'The snow comes to Tsaritsyn. The snow, it is bad. The snow is bad for the General.'

Yuri froze with shock.

'The General must be disposed of. For my sake, for your sake, Tanya, for the sake of my family, the General must be disposed of. The General is responsible for what happened to me. He was responsible. He. The General. Responsible.'

THE GENERAL MUST DIE!!!!

They took Kronykin's suitcase and scribbles back to Headquarters. Pasha arranged for a forensic team to check out the room. From his office Pasha brought vodka and two dusty glasses.

'We're on duty,' Yuri protested.

'We're on our own time,' Pasha said. 'Drink up and console yourself for being late for Comrade Aristov.'

Yuri drank. 'Looks like we have a murder case,' he remarked.

'Murder?' Pasha's tone was oddly challenging.

'Murder,' Yuri repeated. He patted Kronykin's scribbles lying neatly on his desk. 'It's all here in black and white. Kronykin came to Moscow to kill Dolgov.'

'Kronykin came to Moscow to kill someone,' Pasha corrected. 'I haven't seen Dolgov's name anywhere in those notes.'

'Dolgov was a General. Kronykin went to Dolgov's apartment.'

'To steal.'

'To murder.'

Pasha said, 'We don't know yet how Dolgov died. We don't know yet if Kronykin came to Moscow to kill Dolgov or someone else, if the burglary was incidental to another killing, or to something else.' He picked up his parcel of meat from the floor, and slipped the bottle of vodka into his pocket. 'Let's wait till all the information is in. We'll have Professor Andronov's autopsy report on General Dolgov tomorrow. And tomorrow, we'll pull Kronykin's and Dolgov's files from Army Records and see if there was a connection between them, if there was a motive.' Pasha stood up. 'Without a motive, there is no murder.'

Yuri felt Pasha was being unduly cautious, but he didn't say anything. After Pasha left, he called Zamyatin.

'Zamyatin here,' the voice at the other end said. 'Who is that?'

'Yuri Raikin. I've been calling you every fucking day for two weeks.'

There was a confused spluttering on the end of the line, and for a moment, Yuri thought Zamyatin would hang up. Then, 'Yasha, I've been meaning to call you. It's just that there have been problems.'

'I've had problems too,' Yuri said, angrily. 'Why the fuck did you tell Popov and Golovkin the LASM-Two leak wasn't authorized? Why did you lie, Alexei? You met me in Geneva and—'

'Yasha, Yasha, we can't discuss this on the phone.'

'So let's meet.'

Hesitantly, Zamyatin suggested the Yunovst bar in forty minutes.

CHAPTER SIX

In Moscow, the rich drink at home, the poor drink in bars. Consequently, Moscow's bars are sordid places, reeking of stale food, urine, tobacco smoke, spirits, never more than a hundred grammes away from violence. The Yunost on Mayakovsky Square was better than most. Close to the Tchaikovsky Concert Hall and the Mossovets Theatre, it was considered safe enough for the occasional tourist to drop in to absorb the local atmosphere. Tonight the local atmosphere consisted of three clerks in worn blue suits huddling away from a crowd of workers in sweat-hard leather jackets. Yuri carried a bottle and two glasses to a table from which he could watch the electric advertising sign that was Moscow's answer to Broadway.

Green dots danced, formed letters. TAKE TAXIS – ALL STREETS ARE NEAR. A rapid, jumbling of dots, then – BRING LIFE TO THE RESOLUTIONS OF THE TWENTY NINTH PARTY CONGRESS. Despite the chill, a small crowd stood in the square, watching the dancing lights in silent wonder. WORK, STRIVE, INCREASE OUTPUT! HELP ACHIEVE TRUE COMMUNISM!

Yuri thought of Piccadilly with its brighter, more varied, more garish lights, realized his senses were starved of the glittering display of signs and billboards and advertising jingles, so starved that he was probably the only person in Moscow who read the slogans and banners draped across the streets and buildings, half expecting a ravishing blonde to pop out from behind the rows of heroic workers and the exhortatory visages of Deryugin and Lenin, and offer Pepsi-Cola.

Zamyatin came, a series of glints, large spectacles, damp skin, large teeth, a bulging briefcase of artificial leather. He put the case down breathlessly and sat. 'Yasha, Yasha, it's so good to see you!'

'You certainly took your time,' Yuri said, sourly.

Zamyatin looked carefully around the bar. Apparently satisfied, he leaned his elbows on the table and thrust his head close to Yuri's. 'There were problems.'

'You said that before. What problems?'

Without moving his head, he gulped the drink Yuri had poured, sighed comfortably all over Yuri as the vodka bit. 'I had to get clearances.' He stuffed salted herring into his mouth and looked round again. 'The Ministry of Defence, for one.' His smile was like that of a dealer in contraband watches, friendly, nervous and archly conspiratorial.

'What's the Defence Ministry got to do with this?' Yuri asked angrily.

Zamyatin leaned forward confidentially and lowered his voice to a whisper. 'This is absolutely secret. One word and we're both building power stations in Bratsk.' Zamyatin's thin, brown hair was stuck to his forehead. His forehead gleamed. Yuri wondered if it was only the heat in the bar.

Zamyatin said, 'The LASM-Two weapons system does not exist. The information you gave Simmonds was a blind, a mixture of fact and calculated guesswork, designed to make the Americans believe we are much further advanced in satellite laser weapons systems that we in fact are.' He popped a piece of fish into his mouth. Large teeth clamped down with brutal suddenness. 'Let me get a bottle.'

'There's enough for two. Keep talking.'

Zamyatin said, 'We hoped that faced with the alternative of spending billions of dollars on a new defence system or talking, the Americans would choose to talk. That's why we authorized the Simmonds' leak. It was only afterwards we learned that Simmonds was already working for the Americans.'

'So you decided to kill him,' Yuri said. 'Shutting his mouth and at the same time convincing the Americans that the information he gave them was authentic.'

'Right, Yasha,' Zamyatin yelped. 'Sharp as ever, Yasha. You haven't changed one little bit.'

'No,' Yuri said. Then, he snapped, 'What proof do you have that Simmonds was working for the Americans?'

Zamyatin's smile faded. He blinked rapidly, as if a speck of dust had entered his eye. 'The – the evidence is undeniable.'

'What evidence?'

Zamyatin's tongue shined rubbery lips. 'I – I don't know if I can discuss that with you. After all, Yasha, you're no longer with the First.' He smiled, placatingly.

'Only because you lied,' Yuri shouted. He reached forward and pulled Zamyatin across the table by his lapels. 'You son of a bitch, do you realize that if I hadn't been born lucky, I could have got Siberia!'

Zamyatin wriggled free and wiped the perspiration from his forehead. 'You shouldn't have interfered,' he muttered.

'Damn it, Alexei! Simmonds was my agent. I ran the man for ten months. I knew him better than any of you, better than he knew himself. If you thought he was doubling, you should have told me!'

Zamyatin looked down at the table and shrugged. 'You know how it is, Yasha. An agent is suspect, his case officer is also suspect.'

'But how could you order his liquidation without checking with the person who ran him?' Yuri cried, aghast. Still looking down, Zamyatin lifted his glass and drank. Yuri lowered his voice and continued. 'I knew Simmonds better than any of you. Simmonds wasn't a traitor. And if you're saying he was, if you got me transferred to the Sluzbha because you're saying he was, then I want to see the evidence.' He reached forward and lifted Zamyatin's chin. 'If you won't do it, Alexei, God help me, I'll speak to Aristov.'

Zamyatin brushed Yuri's hand away, his face strangely expressionless. 'The Simmonds file is no longer with us,' he said. 'It's still with Department V.'

'But you will get it back?'

Zamyatin sighed. 'One day. You know how long these things take.'

'Will you let me know when the file is back? Will you let me see it then?'

'If Director Suslov approves.' Zamyatin shifted heavily in his chair, and looked directly at Yuri. 'To be quite frank, Yuri, I don't think he will. You must understand that as far as we're concerned, the Simmonds matter is finished. I'm only talking to you now, because I felt you were owed an explanation, and heaven knows, getting the permission for that was difficult enough.' Zamyatin gulped his drink and stood up. 'I'll talk to Suslov, but nothing may come of it.' He reached down and patted Yuri's shoulder. 'I know it isn't nice working for the Sluzbha, but think of it this way. You're getting unique experience, and in a year or two you could be back with the First Directorate. In a year or two, everyone will have forgotten.'

Never, Yuri thought. This was Russia where nothing was forgotten and everything went on record. If he was ever going to clear himself, he had to get hold of Simmonds' First Directorate file. He had to find out why the First Directorate had wanted Simmonds killed.

And Zamyatin was going to be no help at all.

CHAPTER SEVEN

Yuri walked home through a Moscow of shrouded windows and solitary street lamps. On the corner of Pushkinskaya two motor cycle militia loaded a weakly protesting drunk into a sidecar.

When he'd returned to Moscow, it had still been spring, the season not of hope and flowering buds, but *rasputitsa* – roadlessness. Moscow's streets had been avenues of slush, bordered and divided by walls of muddy snow. There had been craters on the pavements, covered with a treacherous crust of frozen mud. Tyres had hissed a dark, icy spray.

Alternately thawing and freezing, the Moskva had been a reticular lattice of ice forms. Blue lakes surrounded by granite masses of pack ice had formed in the sun. The nights had been white with mist and frost.

Rima's father had found them an apartment in an enclosed courtyard off Gorky Street, overcoming Yuri's protests by pointing out that an apartment like this was one in a million and that any kind of apartment did not happen in Moscow overnight.

Which was true.

Rima had said the apartment was very nice.

Which was also true.

It had a balcony, two bedrooms, a large rectangular terraced foyer overlooking an open plan dining room, kitchen and living room. The former owner had left most of his furniture, not the usual hodge-podge of bargains, presents and family heirlooms, but low leather sofas, a walnut dining table with matching chairs and a marvellous old chest of drawers.

His father had given them a refrigerator, the Aristovs, an electric range. They had bought beds from Univermag and hung the Impressionist prints they had bought in London, in the living room. Yuri had erected bookshelves in the second bedroom.

Aristov had said that even a director of the KGB would have been proud of such an apartment in such a location.

Yuri had felt like a pimp.

When he got home, Rima and Aristov were having dinner, their heads close together, talking animatedly. Candles, appropriately red, glowed over Rima's best dinner service. Rima herself wearing a smart black cocktail dress she'd bought in London. It seemed a long time since he and Rima had dinner like that . . . .

Rima took her attention away from her father long enough to say, 'We didn't know when you'd be back. We couldn't wait.'

'There was no reason to wait,' Yuri said and went to the kitchen. The wondrous cooking pot Rima had bought in London was empty. Usually, each morning before she left for work at the Foreign Office, Rima put meat and vegetables into it. At a preset time it turned itself on, cooked the food and turned itself off. It was like being fed by a robot. Every night they had stew.

But not tonight. Tonight, in Aristov's honour, Rima had cooked pork fillets with apples and eggplant in a coriander sauce. It was the best part of Aristov's visit, Yuri thought.

At the table Aristov was saying, 'The great cultures of the past perished only because the originally creative race died from dilution of the blood.' Aristov was on his favourite topic, the eventual domination of Russia by foreign hordes. The words continued to gush forth as Yuri joined them.

'In any nation where foreign blood enters the national body, that nation weakens and loses its inner self. To save Russia from its present evils, we must rid it of the foreign virus.'

Yuri concentrated on eating. Last Saturday, he'd nearly called Aristov a fascist. According to Marshal Raikin, during the Great Patriotic War Aristov had worked with the Main Administration of Counter Intelligence, known as SMERSH, among whose tasks were the clearing of minefields by driving prisoners through them. Aristov's work for SMERSH had impressed NKVD boss Lavrenti Beria greatly, and Beria had become Aristov's patron.

Aristov came from the Ryazan district, an area riddled with corruption and divided by a gang war between rival Party factions until, after a series of dramatic, midnight arrests by Beria's NKVD, Aristov had emerged from the conflict as First Secretary. Marshal Raikin believed Ryazan was still corrupt, and regarded Aristov as nothing more than a political gangster.

Aristov's large head, with its slab sided cheeks and spiky brown hair loomed in front of Yuri. 'What does your father, the Marshal, say about the fact that in a few years the Red Army will be commanded by foreigners?' he asked.

Yuri thought carefully before he answered. While the Marshal though Aristov to be a political thug, Aristov resented the Marshal's fame, achieved as he believed, by one hasty act of reckless folly. Yuri said, 'My father says that over ninety per cent of senior officers are Russian, as are seventy per cent of junior and middle-ranking officers. Consequently, he does not believe that we will at any time have to rely on our Chinese to fight their Chinese.'

A wash of red flooded Aristov's face, but his small, granite coloured eyes remained expressionless. 'Statistics,' he grumbled, and spoke to Rima about her brothers, Aleksandr who worked for the Central Committee and Valentin, a nuclear physicist in Vorkuta. From behind her aviator glasses, Rima glowered at Yuri.

Then, as if to contrast Yuri's more humble achievements, Aristov asked, 'How are you getting on in the Sluzbha?'

'It is necessary work.'

'I suppose there was a lot of excitement today over General Dolgov's death. It's unheard of, you know, someone on the Red List being killed by an intruder.'

Yuri said, 'Dolgov wasn't murdered.'

Aristov spluttered into his wine.

Yuri added, 'Colonel Popov is treating the Dolgov case as one of burglary.'

'That bloody Ukranian would!'

Aristov hated and distrusted the Ukranians more than the inferior hordes. In the late 1940s Aristov and Deryugin had

45

been considered the brightest young men in the Party. Both men had been brought to Moscow, Deryugin to run the State Bank, and Aristov to effectuate *agrogorod* – Stalin's policy of forcibly converting collective farms into agricultural cities. Aristov had been ten years younger than Deryugin and more successful. He had been spoken of as a future leader of Russia. Then Stalin had died, and Aristov moved back to Ryazan, while Deryugin had stayed on in Moscow and with the help of men like Khrushchev, Kaganovich and the rest of the Ukranian Mafia, had gone on to achieve supreme power.

Yuri asked, 'You have information that Dolgov was murdered?'

'You are a policeman,' Aristov snapped. 'Why don't you look at the facts?' He leaned forward and poured wine into Yuri's glass, a rare and expensive Kinzmarauli, Aristov's favourite wine. 'Dolgov, for all his military titles, was a ten per cent man, who made a fortune selling Russia to the West. He'd been summoned to appear before the Zarev Commission, because of the bribes he had received and paid.' Aristov brought his face close to Yuri's. 'Dolgov knew where all the bodies were buried,' he hissed.

'Whom did Dolgov bribe?' Yuri asked.

'Fine policeman you are,' Aristov sneered. 'Who did Dolgov work for?'

'Amrocontinental . . . I think.'

'You think!' Aristov's lip curled expressively. 'Do you know who Amrocontinental are? What they do?'

'Business,' Yuri said, feeling guilty that he hadn't studied Dolgov's records more closely.

Aristov shook his head in disappointment at Yuri's ignorance. 'Amrocontinental is one of the biggest foreign investors in Russia,' he said. 'They've not only invested hugely themselves, but have helped and encouraged others to do so. They have turned Russia into a capitalist swamp. And how do you think they persuaded Russians to forget the principles of Lenin and Marx? With money! With bribes!' Aristov swirled wine furiously in his glass and drank. 'If you want to find out what really happened to Dolgov, look at his business,' he continued. 'Find out who would go to such lengths to keep Dolgov's mouth shut. If Dolgov testified before the Zarev Commission the shock would have vibrated through the Kremlin.'

'Are you saying Deryugin arranged Dolgov's murder?'

'I'm saying you should examine all aspects of Dolgov's affairs,' Aristov said, tightly. 'And another thing, Yuri. Be careful. This case is very sensitive. Whatever conclusions you reach there will be someone who will come after you, someone who will check everything you have checked. And if he finds that you have diverted from the truth, that you have reached unacceptable conclusions . . . .' Aristov's face froze in a rat trap smile. He drew the side of his hand across his throat. 'Even I will not be able to save you.'

Yuri said, 'At all times I will be following the orders of Colonel Popov. I couldn't be more careful than that.'

Aristov rested his hand confidentially on Yuri's arm. 'Be especially careful of Popov,' he warned. 'Popov and Deryugin have been friends since they were children. Popov was Deryugin's enforcer in the Ukraine. Popov is at the Sluzbha to look after Deryugin's interests. All he's done since his appointment is transfer Sluzbha officers out of Moscow to prevent them from testifying before the Zarev Commission.'

All right, Yuri thought. He wouldn't trust Popov. He didn't trust Popov anyway. But what could he do? He asked Aristov the question.

'Trust only those tied to you by blood,' Aristov said. 'Trust only those who have proved themselves. For Rima's sake I'll give you some advice. Leave the KGB now. I'll arrange a senior investigator's post for you at the Central Committee. You'll have a car of your own, shopping privileges, a small dacha . . . .'

And spend a lifetime beholden to Aristov? No thanks! Besides he'd been sentenced to serve under Popov. 'I'll stay with the Sluzbha,' Yuri said. Aware of Rima's angry glance, he added, 'It won't be for long. They'll soon be transferring me back to the First.' And they would. As soon as he found out the truth about Simmonds.

Aristov's face was set in its customary expression of watchful impassivity. 'In that case you're going to need powerful friends,' he said. 'Come to me if you need anything. More important, come to me if there is anything that troubles you. You're going to need all the help and advice you can get.'

After Aristov left, Rima asked, 'Why won't you take the job with the Central Committee?' They were seated in the living room, sipping Armenian brandy. Rima puffed delicately at a cigarette.

Black made her look even smaller. It heightened the porcelain glow of her skin and accented the precise sculpting of her limbs. Alone on the large sofa, Rima looked lost and vulnerable. Like much about Rima, Yuri knew, that was a sham. He said, 'You know I can't leave the Sluzbha. Not after what happened in London.'

'My father can fix that.' Rima didn't believe there was anything Aristov couldn't fix. And Yuri knew there was nothing Aristov wouldn't fix for Rima.

'I don't want favours,' he said.

'Only a fool has privileges and does not use them.' Rima blew a plume of smoke at the ceiling. Since London, she had taken to wearing oversized aviator glasses which emphasized the fragile perfection of her heart-shaped face. Behind the tinted lenses, her eyes slid away contemptuously.

'Better a happy fool than an unhappy *apparatchik*.' Even though Lenin himself had once decreed that people were to be rewarded according to their standing in the Party, Yuri believed privilege was wrong and was embarrassed by it. 'I wouldn't be happy working for your father,' he said.

'You're talking nonsense!' Rima's voice was shrill with annoyance. Angrily, she stubbed out the cigarette. 'My father is fond of you. He only wants to help.' She looked pointedly round the apartment. 'See how much he has helped.'

'Too much,' Yuri said.

Rima curled herself on the sofa, wrapping her arms round her knees. Staring at the carpet, she said softly, 'It would be nice to have a car and driver of our own. Then I needn't bother you to take me shopping. And we'd have our own access to the Central Committee shops.'

'We have that anyway.'

Her mouth curved in a thin smile. 'Only because of my

father.' She looked dreamily away from him, tousling her fringe of ash-blonde hair. 'Our own dacha would be nice, too. We could get away at weekends. And you could write poetry.'

'I'm not a poet,' Yuri said.

Rima ignored him, lost in her fantasy. 'We could have picnics and parties. We could invite all our friends.'

'What friends?' Yuri demanded. 'Since we've been back, you've avoided all our friends, even Natalya and Gvishani.'

Rima smiled knowingly. 'There will be no shameful things to hide when you work for the Central Committee.'

'There's nothing shameful about what happened in London,' Yuri cried. 'In London, I saved a man's life.'

'A traitor's life! If you weren't so well-connected you'd have been sent to Siberia.'

'Simmonds wasn't a traitor,' Yuri said, angrily. 'You don't know what you're talking about.'

'I know enough.' Rima's smile was triumphant.

Yuri carried their glasses to the kitchen. Recently every discussion with Rima seemed to end in an argument.

From the living room, she called, 'Why were you late? Didn't you get my message?'

'I got the message,' Yuri called back. 'I had things to do.'

She came into the kitchen, her face pinched with anger. 'Like what? Going out drinking when you knew my father was coming to dinner?'

'I had to see Zamyatin.'

'What's so important about this Zamyatin that you have to see him in preference to my father?'

Yuri said, 'Alexei Zamyatin was my control at the First Chief Directorate. He ran me. And I ran Charlie Simmonds.'

Rima stood in front of him, leaning back slightly from the waist, delicate hands on slender hips, her face twisted with rage. 'Enough of this bloody Charlie Simmonds,' she cried. 'What the devil's the matter with you? Isn't being punished and sent back from London in disgrace enough? What do you want to do? Get us all transported to Siberia?'

Yuri said, 'Zamyatin wanted me to get the LASM-Two material to Simmonds. He wanted me to make sure that Simmonds leaked that information to the Americans. Then

49

they tried to kill Simmonds for doing precisely that. And at the enquiry, Zamyatin denied authorizing me to release the LASM-Two material.'

'So what? All that's over now, and you're back in Moscow.'

'It isn't over,' Yuri said, 'I want to know why Zamyatin lied, why they wanted to kill Simmonds. I want to find out why Popov brought me back to Moscow.'

'Why?' Rima asked. 'Why do you always have to find answers? Why do you have to be so curious?' She poured fruit water into a glass and drank it quickly. 'You know something, Yuri Gennadovich? You are obsessive. You should see a psychiatrist. When you get hold of something you never let go.'

'A very necessary quality in a police officer,' Yuri muttered.

'Don't be funny,' she snapped. 'What you're doing is very serious.' Behind the tinted lenses her eyes blazed like headlamps at dusk. 'Yasha, remember you're married to me! That my family could be held responsible for your errors.'

'We can always get divorced,' Yuri said, feeling more serious than he sounded. He hadn't thought it right to abandon Rima in London, but now that she was back amongst her own, he'd been thinking more frequently of ending their marriage.

'Don't talk nonsense, Yuri! You're in Russia now, not America or England. In Russia you have to be practical.'

'And so I am trying to discover why I have been punished.'

'You're a stupid, thoughtless fool,' Rima shouted. 'You'll never get back to the First Directorate this way! Never! Never!'

'All I can do is try,' Yuri said. 'Anyway, let's talk about it another time. We've both had a long day. Let's go to bed.'

Rima hesitated momentarily before she said, 'You go. I'll sleep in the study.'

CHAPTER EIGHT

Sleep wouldn't come. It was the heat. It was impossible that Moscow should be so hot in May. Yuri threw off his blankets and lay on top of the sheets. His body sweated. His brain threshed.

He thought of Dolgov, a General who'd betrayed Russia, of Popov and Deryugin. Leave it alone. It was not his problem. He was in Moscow to learn discipline. Better concentrate on Zamyatin. Find out why they wanted to kill Simmonds. Concentrate on the Krasnaya Dela and other Chekhists. And what to do about his marriage. Sleep. Sleep wouldn't come. The more he tried to force sleep, the further away it drifted. It was too damn hot.

Aristov had hinted that Deryugin had murdered Dolgov, that Popov was covering up that fact. Well, Aristov was right in that Popov was covering up something. What? There was no way he, Yuri Gennadovich Raikin, a captain in the Sluzbha and on probation from Siberia could take on Popov, Deryugin and the whole goddamn Kremlin. So take instead the job Aristov had offered; visit regional offices, investigate philosophical deviations and financial manipulation, terrorize bureaucrats and grow fat on pay-offs and lavish dinners. No, better go to the office and obey orders.

That was impossible with someone as important as Dolgov murdered. Impossible too, if others would check on him afterwards. So investigate Amrocontinental? He knew nothing about business, and it was hardly likely there would be entries in Dolgov's books marked 'Bribe!' So leave it, leave Russia to be governed by thieves and murderers. He couldn't do that. He had sworn to uphold justice, he wore the sword and shield. So investigate and prove Aristov a liar. Or Popov a murderer. Or resign and go and chase fat Party cats in the provinces. Except, he had to know how Dolgov had died and why Popov had behaved so peculiarly. He couldn't simply walk away. Rima was right. He was obsessive.

Obsession was something he'd inherited, something he'd learned. His father had counter-attacked when by all the military text books he should have retreated. His father's sister, Seraphima, had taught him to have the courage of his convictions.

Yuri's mother had died bearing him, and Yuri had been brought up by Tanty Sima in Sarasovo, a village outside Moscow. Tanty Sima had been fearless, outspoken, obstinate and sometimes violent. Yuri remembered how, when a local volunteer policeman had objected to her taking Yuri to church, she had attacked the man with her shoe; how, when the local Party had attempted to convert the church into a meeting hall, she'd organized a picket line of *babushki* who'd remained praying outside the building for two days until the embarrassed Party official relented.

Tanty Sima had told Yuri that God was older than Marx and wiser than Lenin, stronger than Yuri's father, Chairman Khrushchev and the Politburo combined. By her example she had instilled in Yuri a sense of rightness. That was why he supposed, he'd stopped Vilna. Simmonds had been innocent and there'd been no reason to kill him. Yuri remembered that he had acted instinctively. Perhaps, he thought, as he drifted into sleep, the values instilled in childhood were the ones that remained.

He woke trembling, his body bathed in clammy sweat. He'd had the same nightmare three times since London.

In London, Golovkin and Popov had taken turns interrogating him. They had asked him about Simmonds and about Africa. First Golovkin, then Popov. They had asked him about America and about London. Again and again. Golovkin and Popov. Simmonds, Africa, America, London. His whole career a stream of words and paper.

'Why did you join the KGB?'

'To serve my country.'

'Did you make your decision before or after you were

approached by the Americans?' Golovkin's eyes had held the gleam of a cat approaching a squirrel.

'I was never approached by the Americans.'

'In your last year at MIMO you refused an invitation to join the KGB?'

'I did not want to become a Chekhist.'

'What made you change your mind?'

'Mikhail Sudgorny convinced me I could be of more use to Russia working for the First Directorate than being a diplomat.'

Golovkin had accused him of being a CIA agent. He had said Yuri's success in smuggling a microwave surveillance receiver out of America had only been done with the help of the CIA.

Yuri had said he'd done what he'd been sent to do, and the Americans didn't work like that anyway.

Golovkin had shown him a photograph of Harry Snead, the CIA Base Chief in Motumbi. 'When did you last see Snead?'

'In a bar in Motumbi, two years ago.'

'What did you talk about?'

'We didn't talk. In my position I would have been mad to talk to the CIA. I listened to their conversation. They talked about baseball.'

Golovkin had shown him a photograph of Snead and Simmonds taken in Washington. 'Your reports say nothing about this.'

'Because I didn't know they'd met.'

Golovkin hadn't believed him. He'd said Snead was Yuri's CIA control, and asked Yuri to tell them again about Simmonds.

After Golovkin had left, Popov had asked Yuri about America and London. He'd said he could understand Yuri working for the Americans. Yuri had been home only six months in four years, and it was understandable if he'd felt abandoned.

'I'm Russian,' Yuri had muttered. 'I won a decoration for Africa. I'm not a traitor.'

Popov had said the Americans had much to offer. In Yuri's

place and at Yuri's age, Popov himself would have considered defecting.

Yuri had said, 'If I'd wanted to defect, I'd have gone with Charlie Simmonds.'

Popov had been replaced by Golovkin, Golovkin by Popov. Sometimes they'd interrogated him together, and sometimes they'd left him alone in the small room without windows, whose door was made of bombproof steel and secured by a series of levers and locks. High in the ceiling behind a wire grille, a yellow light had burned continuously.

They had only allowed him sleep in brief snatches, food at irregular intervals. He had not been allowed to wash or shave. He had begun to smell his own body.

Golovkin and Popov had covered the same ground over and over again. Africa, America, London, Charlie Simmonds, Harry Snead. Doggedly Yuri had repeated, I am not a traitor. I have no connection with Harry Snead.

In the end they had lost patience, strapped him to a chair and injected him with scopolamine.

Yuri had felt as if he were drunk. He had floated, determined not to talk. Then waves of hot and cold had washed over his body. His brain had boiled under a white hot light. Words had flooded from his mouth.

And they had believed him.

And Yuri felt he had been raped.

It had all been so easy, Yuri thought, remembering his help-lessness, and how simply he'd been reduced to a blubbering, garrulous mess. Then he thought, if it happened to me, why not Kronykin? Kronykin had been rehabilitated. Kronykin had been subjected to drugs, hypnosis, and heaven knew what else besides. Could Kronykin have been compelled through drugs and hypnosis to murder Dolgov?

The records of Kronykin's medical treatment were material evidence, he thought. But if Popov was suppressing the fact of Dolgov's murder, wouldn't he also suppress that evidence? But what if he, Yuri, got those records? Once Kronykin's medical records were part of the official file, the investigation would be thrown wide open. And Popov, the great stomper of balls and adjuvant of scopolamine, would be well and truly scuppered.

But how to approach the Fifth Directorate? Through Aristov of course. Aristov wanted to help. And once Yuri had the truth about Dolgov, neither Popov nor Deryugin would be able to stop him.

CHAPTER NINE

The next morning, Yuri sat at the Aristov's before a plate heaped with kasha, ham, eggs, and black bread, while he told Aristov his problem.

'Simple,' Aristov said. He went to his study and made a phone call, returned and told Yuri, 'Director Guschin will see you at eleven.'

On his way to the office, Yuri stopped off at Militia Pathology in the basement of the yellow, six storied Militia Building on the corner of Petrovka and Stolesnikov Pereulok. A pathologist, Dr Yedemsky, saw him in a tiled anteroom, furnished with a simple wood framed desk and three uncomfortable wooden chairs. A door opened onto a much larger room, also tiled, with a line of body sized, refrigerated metal cabinets along one wall, and a row of chest high platforms in the centre, topped with metal trays. A body lay on one of the trays. Yuri stared at a cranium that gaped like the inside of a large, bloodstained shell, tipped with a fringe of beard. He felt his breakfast rise to the back of his throat.

'Ever seen one of these before?' Yedemsky asked. He was a spidery man with a prominent nose and large, sad, liquid brown eyes. He wore a white surgeon's coat over a shabby grey suit. The coat was streaked with blood stains, the whole spectrum of reds.

The smell of rotting eggs from the large room became overpowering. The body looked oddly deflated, its chest held together by large, jagged stitches. Yuri saw that the beard was actually the top of the scalp pulled down under the chin. Yedemsky explained that they made an incision from ear to ear and pulled the flesh down like a cap before sawing through the top of the skull. Yuri felt sick.

'We put it back reasonably tidily,' Yedemsky said. 'The only way anyone will know what we've done is from the way the head will ride lower in the coffin.'

The cranium gaped.

Yedemsky took Yuri through his report, four closely typed pages that described the body on delivery, its external physical condition, the state of the internal organs, and in highly technical terms, the damage Frolov's bullet had done. There were sketches showing the location of scars, birth marks and the bullet wound.

In non-technical terms, briefly and simply, Frolov's bullet had killed Kronykin.

Yedemsky offered a cigarette. 'It's all right to smoke. There's nothing sacred here.'

'I don't smoke,' Yuri said.

'Funny,' Yedemsky said, lighting up. 'The first time, most people puke or smoke or both.' He studied Yuri carefully from behind the curtain of smoke. 'There's something else that's not in the report,' he said. 'In the lungs and in the stomach, we found traces of sodium thiosulfate and amyl nitrite.'

'Poison?'

Yedemsky shook his head. 'Not necessarily. Sodium thiosulfate is normally used by photographers to fix negatives. It's commonly known as hypo. Amyl nitrite is used for the treatment of certain heart conditions.'

'Kronykin wasn't a photographer,' Yuri said. 'He was an ex-soldier who worked in a factory in Smolensk.'

Yedemsky's gaunt gaze was impassive. 'And his heart was perfectly sound,' he said.

When Yuri got to the office, the report from Ballistics was on his desk. The bullet that had killed Kronykin had, without any doubt, been fired from Frolov's gun.

Kronykin's weapon had been illegally acquired. Its numbers had been filed down and it was of American manufacture, an Iver-Johnson .22. It had not recently been fired.

The sergeant from Militia Records called. In the past year there had been no burglaries where forged KGB documents had been used to gain entry.

Professor Andronov's post-mortem report arrived, all five

paragraphs of it. According to Professor Andronov, General Vyssorian Dolgov had died of a massive heart attack. What Professor Andronov didn't say but implied strongly was that Dolgov had died very shortly before he'd reached the hospital. In fact, it seemed from Andronov's report that Dolgov had been on his way to the Druzbha Gymnasium when he'd been afflicted.

The cover up was complete.

Noting in his diary that he was seeing an informer about Kronykin's gun, Yuri left to see Director Guschin.

The Fifth Directorate had its offices in the new part of Kalinin Prospekt, a fitting location for an organization which believed that crime was a matter of motivational analysis and diagnostics. Kalinin Prospekt had been Stalin's architectural vision of the future, a wide carriageway lined with trees and open air cafes, sweeping triumphantly past skyscrapers and broad pavements. Along one side were five, twenty-four storey apartment buildings whose lower floors were given over to shops and restaurants. On the other side, a two storey high, glass fronted gallery linked five massive chevrons of concrete and glass. The Fifth Directorate's offices were in the third of these.

Its interior was suitably modern. Where Dzerzhinsky Square had parquet flooring, the Fifth had fawn carpets, wall to wall. Instead of furniture that seemed unchanged since Dzerzhinsky's time, there were chairs of tubular steel and desks of pale wood, potted plants and discreet overhead lighting. The offices were partitioned by screens of tasteful grey, and there was a sense of limitless space. It was more like the lobby of the Hotel Rossiya than an office of the KGB, Yuri thought.

Kyril Guschin was an elegant man in his mid fifties. A close curled head of steel grey hair crowned an imperious, finely chiselled face. His office was large and uncluttered, with a fine view of the Intourist Hotel and the USSR Council of Ministers.

A secretary brought coffee and tiny fresh cream cakes. Guschin took a Turkish cigarette from a thin, platinum case and urged Yuri to eat. 'When I was your age, I could eat anything. Now,' he gave a small sigh. 'Alas.'

'Smoking's worse for you than cream cakes,' Yuri pointed out.

Momentarily, the cigarette at Guschin's lips glowed more fiercely. Then he smiled. 'A safe pleasure is a tame pleasure,' he said. 'You are, of course, familiar with Ovid.'

'Like you, only in translation.' Yuri smiled, and swiftly added, 'The fly that prefers sweetness to a long life, sometimes drowns in honey.'

Guschin laughed. 'What a way to go – if you are a fly.' He crossed razor creased knees and tilted backwards in his chair. 'I'm so glad Popov is recruiting graduates from MIMO. The Sluzbha is in dire need of intellectual leavening.' His alert, inquisitive eyes twinkled challengingly.

If the Second Directorate looked on the Fifth as a bunch of science crazy megalomaniacs, the Fifth believed the Second was entirely composed of louts and psychopaths. Yuri was determined not to get involved in their rivalry. He nibbled his cream cake and said, 'Comrade Director, with your permission, I would like to examine the file on Sergei Kronykin.'

Guschin exhaled twin streams of smoke. 'I know you would.' He studied the ceiling thoughtfully, then swivelled forward and looked seriously across the desk at Yuri. 'But that is not something I can allow. In fact, if you were not the son of Marshal Gennadi Raikin, the hero of Kursk, if Comrade Aristov had not requested it, I wouldn't even have agreed to see you.' His smile was genuinely apologetic. 'It isn't that we have anything to hide. But we do have a problem with Director Popov.'

While Yuri sipped tea, Guschin explained there had always been a friendly rivalry between the Fifth and Second Directorates. However, since Popov's appointment as Director, that rivalry had become an undeclared war. It was Popov's fault, he said. Popov resented the division of responsibility between the Directorates. Popov was trying to increase the power of the Sluzbha. He was a careerist and extremely ambitious. He wanted to head not only the Sluzbha but the entire KGB. Now Popov had serious problems with the Zarev Commission. And he was in trouble over Dolgov. 'I'm not giving Director Popov the opportunity to divert attention from his problems by creating trouble for the Fifth,' Guschin finished.

Yuri felt as if an escalator he'd been riding had suddenly stopped. His entire theory had been based on the belief that somehow Popov had manipulated Kronykin's treatment.

Guschin was leaning back languidly and lighting a fresh cigarette. 'As you can well imagine,' he was saying, 'the process of rehabilitation is highly technical and very complex. Psychiatry is art as well as science. It is what gives our work an endless fascination. But,' his tone became waspish, 'put two psychiatrists in one room and you get six different opinions.' He smiled. 'You see the problem, dear boy.'

'So the Sluzbha had no interest in Kronykin's treatment?' Yuri blurted.

'None whatsoever.' Guschin frowned suspiciously. 'Why should the Sluzbha be concerned with the work of the Fifth?'

'All I want to know is what was done to Kronykin and who authorized it.'

'Kronykin's treatment was medically correct.'

'I don't doubt that,' Yuri said, and paused for effect. 'But I can't help wondering why so soon after his rehabilitation, Kronykin went from spreading scurrilous rumours to burglary and perhaps, murder.'

'Are you saying General Dolgov was murdered?'

'We don't know the cause of death yet,' Yuri replied. 'But murder is a possibility.'

Guschin gave him a thin smile. 'And so you perceive the very essence of my problem. General Vyssorian Dolgov was a very well connected man, a friend I believe of General Secretary Deryugin himself. You can imagine the consequences for me and for the Fifth Directorate if it were to be demonstrated, however implausibly, that General Dolgov had been murdered by a former patient of the Fifth.'

'Surely the best way of avoiding those consequences,' Yuri said, 'is by opening your records to examination and showing you have nothing to hide.'

'I would,' Guschin said with a small sigh, 'if anyone but Popov were involved.'

'Who said anything about Director Popov?' Yuri asked. 'I have been given charge of this investigation. My father-in-law has advised me that I should find the truth at all costs. He has also advised me that normal departmental procedures may have to be ignored. He has asked that I come to him with any problems.'

'I see,' Guschin said, thoughtfully, looking down at his desk.

'My father-in-law also informs me that there is a degree of sensitivity about this investigation. I would not wish to inform Comrade Aristov or place on official record that I was denied access to Kronykin's medical records by the Fifth Directorate.'

'You are a doctor?' Guschin demanded. 'You have medical experience?'

Yuri shook his head.

'In that case what can you find in records written exclusively in medical terms?'

Shit, Yuri thought. He'd walked into that one.

Then, suddenly Guschin smiled. 'But we have nothing to hide from an honest investigator, the son of a hero, and the son-in-law of Comrade Aristov. I think, therefore, you should see Dr Drachinsky who treated Kronykin and who will explain his treatment to you. You agree that will be more use than poring over medical hieroglyphics?'

'Agreed,' Yuri said, almost crying out with relief. But as he followed Guschin to the door, he couldn't help wondering if that was what Guschin had intended all along.

Yuri saw Dr Drachinsky in a temporary office with empty bookshelves and a view of Arbat Ulica. Yuri made out the graceful columns of the Vakhtangov Theatre where the avant-garde of Meyerhold had first been combined with Russian realism. Meyerhold, Yuri remembered, had disappeared in the days before psychiatry had been used to straighten hunchbacks.

Drachinsky was a stout man in his mid thirties, with a round face and a balding head. There was a curious immobility about his eyes. He explained that Kronykin's problems stemmed from the loss of his father at an early age. In compensation, he had developed exaggeratedly male characteristics. He had fitted beautifully into the Army. 'The Army, with its authoritarianism and ordered lifestyle became Kronykin's substitute father,' Drachinsky said.

Drachinsky was crazy, Yuri decided. Half an hour of analysis with him, and he'd tell Yuri the KGB was his substitute mother. 'Why did Kronykin leave the Army?' he asked.

'He failed a Special Task Force physical and was too proud to join a less prestigious outfit.'

Drachinsky explained that on his discharge, Kronykin had demonstrated the typical behaviour of a child freed from parental authority. He'd been over-enthusiastic about his work and over-anxious to make new friends. But in the end, like all children, he'd needed authority, needed a father. His scandalmongering had been a cry for help.

'How did you find all this out?' Yuri asked.

'A psychiatrist uses three methods to elicit information,' Drachinsky said. 'Friendship, but that takes too long. Mental or physical pressure. That's dangerous and unethical.' He smiled wetly. 'Or one relaxes the patient with drugs and then subjects him to light hypnosis. It isn't as drastic as it sounds. It's like having a drink with a friend.'

'Do you drink?' Yuri asked.

Drachinsky's smile was bland. He said the same process had been used in reverse to rehabilitate Kronykin. Drugs were used to induce a hypnotically receptive state; Kronykin was given positive statements under hypnosis and taught to react unfavourably to negative statements. Afterwards, Kronykin had been tested with simulated stress situations. When he'd coped successfully, he was pronounced cured and released.

'So what happened? Why did he break down?'

Drachinsky's eyebrows lifted into his smooth forehead. 'Break down? I'm not sure I follow you, Captain Raikin.'

'This model citizen you created was shot and killed while burglarising the apartment of General Dolgov.'

'I don't believe Kronykin was attempting to burgle General Dolgov's apartment,' Drachinsky said. 'I believe he went there for a different purpose. I believe that when we gave Kronykin back his whole personality, we made him remember something that had happened with Dolgov.'

'What?' Yuri asked.

'That, Captain,' Drachinsky said, 'is for you to find out.'

CHAPTER TEN

Yuri returned to Headquarters. The Dolgov dossier on his desk was already an inch thick, its contents reducing Kronykin's death to a series of scientific facts, the trajectory of the bullet, the angle of an entrance wound, the muzzle velocity of a Makarov. There was nothing to indicate why Kronykin had gone to Dolgov's apartment or what the connéction between them had been.

The walls of the cubicle shook. Pasha entered carrying more files. 'What did you find out ·about Kronykin's gun?' he asked.

'Nothing. It was a false lead,' Yuri lied.

Pasha sat down, frowning suspiciously and dumped Kronykin's and Dolgov's army files on the desk.

Avoiding Pasha's gaze, Yuri pulled the files towards him and read.

Dolgov came from an Army family with an impeccable revolutionary pedigree. His father had been one of the first sergeants in the Litovsky to shoot an officer. At seventeen, Dolgov had entered the Frunze Military Academy, graduating three years later and joining an infantry division in the Volga. After four years unspectacular service, he'd been recalled to Moscow for further training. There, he married Amalia Nikolayeva, the daughter of General Vladimir Nikolayev. The marriage seemed to have been a step in the right direction. Dolgov was assigned to Moscow Headquarters Administration and had remained there for the next three years.

At the outbreak of the war, Dolgov had been dispatched to Finland. He'd been wounded in January 1940 and repatriated to Moscow. That was the last time Dolgov had heard shots fired in anger.

In May 1940 he'd resumed duties at Moscow Headquarters Administration, and later helped to organise the evacuation of the government to Kubyschev. From then till the end of the war he'd worked in Beria's Ministry of Economic Reconstruction. After the war he'd been transferred to liaison with fraternal countries and worked in Poland, Rumania and the Balkans. In December 1947, while on holiday in the Crimea, Amalia Nikolayeva had died of typhus.

In June 1948, Dolgov had been promoted to Major and recalled to Moscow Headquarters Administration. In January 1949, he'd been transferred to the Department of Security for the Administration of the Kremlin.

Dolgov's military career seemed to have ended there. Then, in March 1953, he'd been promoted to Major General and transferred back to Headquarters Administration. In December 1953, Lieutenant Colonel and the Order of Lenin. In June 1954, Colonel and Deputy Commandant, Moscow. July 1955, General, and a transfer to command of Strategics and Supply.

Dolgov had retired in 1958 with a full pension and been appointed to the Defence Advisory Committee, from which he had finally resigned ten years later.

Yuri picked up Kronykin's file. Kronykin too had been born into an Army family. His father had been a Major Anatol Kronykin, attached to the Kremlin Security Administration. But while Dolgov's file had shown the rise and rise of an armchair general, Kronykin's showed the pedestrian progress of a rank and file soldier. After fifteen years in the army, Kronykin hadn't made it beyond sergeant. Kronykin had transferred from the 426th Infantry to Special Task Forces. He'd served in Czechoslovakia in 1968 and returned to Russia in 1970. Afterwards, his career had alternated spells abroad with service at home. 1972, the German Democratic Republic. 1974, the Chinese border where he had received a commendation. 1977, the Chinese border again and another commendation. Service in the Ukraine in 1978, Kazakhstan in 1979. Kronykin had been sent to Afghanistan in 1980. On his return, he'd failed a routine medical and been honourably discharged.

Pasha looked across at Yuri and said, 'Well?'

Yuri said, 'Kronykin never even knew Dolgov.'

'Why should Kronykin have known Dolgov?'

'It was Dolgov's apartment he went to. Dolgov was the General he wanted to murder. There has to be a connection.'

Pasha stared at him suspiciously, 'Where the hell were you this morning?' he demanded.

'Talking to an informer about Kronykin's gun.'

'That's a fucking lie! You haven't been in Moscow long enough to know any informers.' Pasha leant across the desk, his massive fists clenched, his face tight with anger. 'Let's get something straight, Captain. If we work on a case together, we're partners. And if we're partners, we don't hide anything from one another. If you want to play it differently, one of us is out.'

Yuri thought, the one out could be him. Also, if Pasha was replaced, his successor could be less experienced and a real *stukachi*. He asked, 'What happens if I want to cut a few corners?'

'Then you cut corners. But you tell me first.'

'And if you cut corners?'

'I'll tell you. We can't always do everything by the rule book, but that's no reason for one of us to get shafted because the other's trying to be a hero. Now, what were you doing this morning?'

'I saw Director Guschin.'

'You're out of your fucking mind!' Pasha cried. 'If Popov finds out he'll —'

'Stamp on my balls?'

Pasha glowered at him. 'Yes. And you'll damn well deserve it.' He took a deep breath. 'We'll have to find some way of telling Popov. If he were to find out —'

'He asked me to find out everything I could about Kronykin. The Fifth had rehabilitated Kronykin, so someone had to talk to them.'

'You should have got approval,' Pasha said.

'There was no time for approvals. Dolgov's being buried on Monday.'

'If Popov asks, we'll tell him that.' Pasha sounded relieved. 'Now what did you find out at the Fifth?'

Yuri told him.

'Those intelligents at the Fifth need a dose of psychiatric rehabilitation themselves,' Pasha grunted when he'd finished. 'They were snowing you, Yuri. All they want is to make trouble for us. There's no connection between Dolgov and Kronykin.'

'It's the only thing that makes sense.'

Pasha shook his head. 'This is how it happened. Kronykin was a soldier who had a strong emotional involvement with the army. He resented his discharge and started getting his own back by spreading malicious rumours about his service in Afghanistan.' Pasha was spraying spittle over the desk in his eagerness to explain his theory. 'Kronykin got picked up by the Fifth and rehabilitated. Whatever the Fifth did to him, didn't work. He came out of treatment more determined than ever to get even with the army. So he comes to Moscow, gets himself a gun, a KGB chauffeur's uniform and work pass. He goes to the apartment of General Dolgov. General Dolgov, the great armchair hero, panics and dies of a heart attack. Kronykin, thinking all his Maydays have come at once, starts to ransack the apartment. Comrade Frolov arrives. *Stoi!*' Pasha pointed two fingers at Yuri. 'Bang! Bang! End of Kronykin. End of case.' Pasha dabbed at his forehead with a greasy handkerchief. His face creased into a self-congratulatory smirk.

'Too simple,' Yuri said.

'What the fuck's wrong with that? Your trouble, Yuri, is that you're over-educated. You want a complex answer to a simple problem.'

Yuri asked, 'Where did Kronykin get the uniform, work pass and the gun?'

Pasha thrust solid elbows on the desk. 'Kronykin was with Special Task Forces,' he said. 'You know who the STF are, Yasha? They're the toughest fucking regiment in the whole Russian army. Those guys will go anywhere, do anything and they'll kick the shit out of anyone who gets in their way. In the army they say that one battalion of STF is worth two of tanks.'

'So they've been in Afghanistan for years fighting natives,' Yuri said. 'Okay, where did Kronykin get his equipment?'

Pasha's huge shoulders heaved. 'Yasha, this is Moscow. You can get any damn thing you want in Moscow if you know the right people. You want a gun, I'll find you a gun. Give me twenty minutes.'

'An American gun?'

'What difference does it make, what kind of gun? Kronykin took what was available.'

'And the uniform and the work pass?'

Pasha's face crinkled. His skin had the texture of an orange. 'More difficult,' he admitted, 'but not impossible.'

'Yedemsky says he found amyl nitrite and sodium thiosulfate in Kronykin's body.'

'So what? Kronykin worked in a chemical factory!'

'We should check the lung and stomach contents of the workers.'

'Check, check, check, what good will that do? The stuff wasn't in Dolgov. Dolgov wasn't poisoned. Dolgov had a heart attack. Who knows what chemicals they'd find in our bodies if they open us up?'

'Nothing fits exactly,' Yuri said.

'So what are you, a watchmaker?'

They paused, staring at each other. Pasha was trying to suppress the fact of Dolgov's murder, thought Yuri.

He asked, 'What about all that scribbling, "the General must die, the snow of Tsaritsyn"?'

'Yasha, you've done judo. Tell me, what do you do just before a bout. No, I'll tell you. What you do is you sit and think, you make yourself calm and tell yourself you're going to smash the other guy. You think yourself into smashing him. You think yourself into hating him.'

'The snow of Tsaritsyn,' Yuri insisted.

Pasha sighed wearily. 'Tsaritsyn became Stalingrad, Stalingrad became Volgograd. The history of post-revolutionary Russia in three names. You know about Stalingrad? A great battle was fought there.'

'Neither Dolgov nor Kronykin was at Stalingrad,' Yuri pointed out.

'The STF were. They were part of the Thirteenth Guards. They were the first in and the last out. "Remember the snow at Tsaritsyn" became their way cry.'

Pasha had become a veritable mine of information. 'Why Dolgov?' Yuri asked. 'If Kronykin hated the army so much, why not take out an STF general? Why not take a gun, hang around the Ministry of Defence and take out a dozen generals?'

'The man was a nutcase,' Pasha said. 'You can't explain every single thing a nutcase does.' He got up and lumbered over to the typewriter. 'Let's get started on our report, and finish this Dolgov business.'

'It isn't over yet,' Yuri protested.

'It's over, finished, complete.' Pasha made a scything motion with his hand.

'I'm not completing a report,' Yuri returned.

Pasha stared at him. 'Let's talk to Popov,' he said.

Popov's office was on the fifth floor of the Headquarters Building. The corridors were lined with the stern faces of former heads of the KGB, Dzerzhinsky, Menzhinsky, Serov, Andropov. No pictures of Stalin's henchmen, Yagoda and Beria, Yuri noticed, or of Shelepin, retired in disgrace.

There was thick, red carpet on the floor, and red flecked wallpaper studded with hammer and sickle emblems in gold, on the walls. Popov's office itself was spacious, with a large tooled leather desk and four leather upholstered, swivelling visitors' chairs before it. Beside the chairs were an ottoman and two armchairs, and the floor beneath the desk and armchairs was covered with a magnificent Kazakh. On the walls above Popov's glistening head were life size portraits of Lenin and Deryugin. More intimate photographs graced his desk. Deryugin and Popov, standing with youthful confidence before the Mikhailov factory in Dnepropetrovsk, an informal, signed portrait of Deryugin, a photograph of a young woman, smooth cheeked and laughing eyed, her perfect mouth parted in a happy smile. Wife, Yuri wondered, then looking at Popov, decided a favourite niece.

Popov smoked two cigarettes while he listened first to Pasha, then to Yuri. His face hardened when Yuri told of his visit to Guschin. When they'd finished, he said, 'Both of you are wrong.' He fixed his gaze on Pasha. 'You, Pashchenko, are trying to close a case by selecting the easiest and most obvious explanation.' His gaze swivelled to Yuri. 'And you, Raikin, are simply selecting facts to justify a dangerous and totally incorrect presumption.' Popov's eyes took on a basilisk glitter. 'The most important fact you have overlooked is that Dolgov was not murdered. Professor Andronov's report confirms beyond all doubt that General Dolgov died of a heart attack. What are you trying to do, Raikin? Become a hero on the cheap? Solve an imaginary murder so you can impress me?'

'Dolgov's heart attack could have been induced,' Yuri said. 'There were shards of glass on Dolgov's face. We should find out –'

Popov slapped his hand on the desk. 'Professor Andronov did not find any glass on Dolgov's face,' he shouted.

Yuri froze. He had seen the glass. He had seen the cuts on Dolgov's face. Popov and Professor Andronov were lying. Yuri forced himself to keep still. There was nothing he could do about it right now. But later.

More calmly, Popov continued. 'So we are satisfied that Kronykin did not murder Dolgov. Which leaves us with the question of why Kronykin went to Dolgov's apartment and who sent him there?' Popov paused and looked at Yuri and Pasha in turn. 'You will concentrate your enquiries on who Kronykin saw in Moscow, where he got the gun and the KGB uniform, who provided him with the fake KGB work pass.' His eyes bored into Yuri's face. 'And you, Captain Raikin, will refrain from utilising the influence of your family without my prior approval. Is that understood?'

His eyes held Yuri's till Yuri nodded. Popov waved dismissively. 'Get on with it then. You'll never solve anything sitting around like a pair of stuffed ducks.'

Pasha leading, they moved quickly to the door.

Popov called, 'Captain Raikin!'

Yuri turned.

Popov's steel teeth glinted ominously. 'While you were hanging around with Director Guschin, I was talking to Director Suslov. It seems your former colleagues at the First feel you were dealt with too leniently.' He thrust his barrel like body over the desk. 'Have you met with Zamyatin since you've been back in Moscow?'

Yuri stared wide eyed. What the devil was Popov up to now? 'I've seen Zamyatin,' he said.

'And?'

'The meeting was inconclusive.'

'I suggest you make it conclusive, Captain,' Popov rasped. 'For your sake, the sooner the better.'

CHAPTER ELEVEN

That night, Yuri dined with his father. He felt a wrench of despair as an unfamiliar subaltern opened the door. For as long as Yuri could remember, his father had been looked after by Igor, a giant Ukrainian who had been with the Marshal since the breakout from Kiev.

'I was just leaving,' the subaltern said. 'Your father's expecting you.'

'I know.' Yuri watched the subaltern leave, with the resentment of a man seeing his home invaded by strangers. Igor had been a second father to Yuri. In many ways he had been closer to Igor than to the Marshal. When as a boy, he had visited his father on weekends, it had been Igor who'd collected him from the Pavelets Railway Station, Igor who had taken him for walks in the Lenin Hills, Igor who had taken him to the cinema, prepared dinner for all three of them, and afterwards sat by Yuri's bed and told him stories of the war. It was Igor, Yuri remembered, who'd taken him to the Kodokan to learn judo, who'd taught him to drive a car, who'd told him never to show fear, because fear encouraged people and dogs to attack. Igor had died while Yuri had been in London, and the Marshal hadn't told Yuri till a week afterwards.

As he did each time he visited his father, Yuri paused before the console table in the hallway and looked at the gold framed photograph of his mother. Yuri did not remember her. In the photograph she was a woman of startling beauty, as finely taut as a violin string. Her eyes were dark as pools shadowed by rock, and she'd had an exquisitely moulded mouth. She'd been an actress, Tanty Sima had said, and told Yuri he'd inherited his mother's sensitive nature. Tanty Sima had always said nice things about him.

The Marshal waited in the dining room, sitting very erect, at the head of the table. On the wall behind him was a divisional flag of the 82nd Army, surrounded by regimental photographs, photographs of tanks in battle, photographs of smiling men posing self-consciously beside shell craters and ruined buildings. On the other walls were oil paintings of forests and the Siberian taiga, photographs of Generalissimo Stalin, of Deryugin looking very much like a civil servant, of Marshal Rodion Malinovsky. On the mantlepiece was a scale model of a T-34 tank made from a shell casing.

The table was covered with dishes of black and red caviar, cold meats, salads, cucumber in sour cream, and three kinds of bread. Conveniently to the Marshal's right was an ice bucket with bottles of vodka and white wine, and to his left, a low kingswood table inlaid with a mother of pearl chess board, and pieces of ivory and jade.

'Where's your wife?' the Marshal asked.

'She's had to see her parents,' Yuri lied. In fact, Rima had refused to come. She hadn't wanted *zakuski* and said the Marshal's apartment with its macabre mementos of past campaigns gave her nightmares. 'She sends her apologies,' Yuri said. 'She'll come next Friday.'

'I don't give a shit whether she comes or not!' the Marshal cried, with more than a hint of querulousness in his voice.

Marshal Raikin was still a vigorous man. He shared Yuri's face, narrow and handsome, with a wild, barbarian flare of cheekbone. His head was a close cropped frizz of silver. Beneath tangled white eyebrows, blue eyes burned fiercely.

Yuri kissed him on the left cheek, then on the right, mottled with dark skin and pink flesh, the result of a blazing tank outside Kursk and botched plastic surgery afterwards. As a child, Yuri had been fascinated by his father's scars, believing he would inherit them as he had inherited his father's tall body, wide shoulders and strong legs. He'd spent hours staring into a mirror, looking for the first sign of charred flesh on his cheek, examining his body for a replica of the thick brown stripe that coiled around his father's body like a snake.

'I don't know what you see in that spoilt little bitch,' his father grumbled. 'You should get yourself a woman with some flesh on her. Someone with something you can hold on to while you're fucking.'

Yuri found himself blushing. Since they'd returned to Moscow, he and Rima had made love only once, and that had been over so quickly, it wouldn't have mattered if there had been something to hold on to or not.

'So she's not even giving you that,' his father jeered. 'You should never have married her, Yasha. Take my advice and get rid of her.'

Yuri sat down without replying. His father may have been right, but his marriage was his own affair.

The Marshal poured out vodka. The backs of his hands were covered with scars, the knuckles broken and splayed. In the Marshal's day, a punch on the snout had been the recognized manner of enforcing discipline in the Red Army. Only once, Yuri recalled, had the Marshal raised his hand to him. That had been when he'd told the Marshal he'd wanted to enter MIMO and train to be a diplomat, instead of joining the Army.

'To the 82nd!' the Marshal cried, raising his glass.

They drank, tossing the vodka straight down the back of the throat. Yuri felt the vodka glow. Since Igor's death, the Marshal had aged. There was a growing softness around his jaw, a new mistiness in the eyes, a sunken look about the mouth that hadn't been there before. His father, Yuri recalled, was older than Igor and Igor was dead. Yuri asked, 'Are they looking after you all right?'

'I can look after myself. Did so in bloody China, can do it in Moscow. Ate frogs, in China. Did I ever tell you that? Igor . . . ' The Marshal trailed into silence.

'Tell me about Igor,' Yuri said.

His father refilled their glasses. 'As your wife isn't here,' he said, obstinately, 'We can play chess while we eat.' Deliberately, he set up the pieces.

His father had always buried his emotions in silence, Yuri thought. He never spoke of Yuri's mother, and though the only remembrance of her was the picture in the lobby, the Marshal had never remarried. When, as a student at Psy Math, Yuri had lived with the Marshal, their conversations had been limited to what he had done at school, and though his father had taken pride in his scholastic and athletic achievements, he'd never shown it. Now, Igor too was being consigned to silence.

'I loved Igor, too,' Yuri said. 'It will do you good to –'

The Marshal silenced him with a glance. 'Play,' he snapped. 'White is on your side of the board.'

Yuri opened cautiously with a king's pawn.

Immediately, his father challenged recklessly with the queen's.

Yuri spread caviar on toast and pondered the next move. His father threw back another glass of vodka in a single gulp. Tiny red capillaries stood out on the sides of his nose, and Yuri thought the old man was perhaps drinking too much. He moved his bishop to knight five. The Marshal began a flanking movement. Yuri remembered that it had been an unauthorized, unorthodox flanking movement that had trapped his father in a blazing tank outside Kursk and forced the Germans to wheel round and open the centre of the salient. Yuri said, 'Tell me about Director Popov. He served under you, didn't he?'

'That's correct.' His father brought out a knight, threatening Yuri's bishop. 'Stanislav Iliodorovich was one of my best officers, honest, courageous, principled and responsible. He may have been a political, but he was a damned good soldier.'

A damned good soldier was the Marshal's highest accolade.

The Marshal heaped cold meat and salads on to a plate and passed it to Yuri. 'Stanislav Iliodorovich was with me on the push down to Rumania. Struck me as a damned fine soldier, then. Never claimed special privileges. Always one with his men. Very important that, for an officer. Sharing hardship with the troops.'

Yuri said, 'To me he seems typical Sluzbha.' He scooped meat and salad into his mouth and looked at the board. His father's unorthodox attack was making nonsense of his strategy. Yuri moved a pawn.

His father studied the board briefly and brought out a bishop. 'You're wrong about Popov,' he said. He speared meat from his plate and followed it with vodka. 'Prague,' he said. ' '68. The politicals were given orders to execute certain high ranking Czech officers. Popov refused. He believed executions would only create martyrs and the Czechs did not need martyrs, but men of principle. So he set about Russifying the men.' The Marshal's cheek crumpled like a brown paper bag as he smiled. 'He had them attend lectures. He screamed at them. He threatened them. He punished them. He begged them. He pleaded with them. He never left them alone until they became ours.' The Marshal looked down at the board. 'Igor Popov is one of the bravest and most upright men I know.'

'There are stories that he was only appointed to the Sluzbha because of his friendship with Deryugin.'

'You've got no business paying attention to stories like that,' Marshal Raikin snapped. 'Remember, you owe Popov a lot. If not for Popov you'd be in Siberia.'

If Popov had investigated Vilna, Yuri thought, he'd still be in London. He brought out a knight. 'Did you know General Vyssorian Dolgov?'

'Yes. I remember him lurking around Headquarters after we got back from Kiev. A very sinister type, very close to Beria as I remember. Of course he never gave us any trouble. We were Vlasov's lot, and at that time, Vlasov was a hero. We were all heroes. The Generalissimo believed we could smash the entire German Army.' Marshal Raikin brought his queen into the attack. The game was only eight moves old.

Yuri said, 'But Dolgov was a hero. He was wounded in Finland.'

His father made a rumbling sound, deep in his chest. 'That wasn't a soldier's wound. That was the wound of a coward and a bully.' Abruptly he crossed himself. 'Shouldn't speak ill of the dead.'

'What happened in Finland?' Yuri asked.

'Man should have been cashiered,' the Marshal hissed in disgust. He told Yuri that in Finland, Dolgov had worked behind the Russian lines, transporting captured partisans for interrogation. Many of the partisans had been delivered badly beaten up, and once a group of them had been found, strangled and horribly mutilated. 'Dolgov got beaten up by a Finn he was interrogating,' the Marshal said. 'The Finn claimed that Dolgov had tried to strangle him, and had in fact strangled others. The Finn's claim was found to be true.'

'So what happened?'

The Marshal shrugged. 'At the time we were trying to negotiate a peace with the Finns. Deryugin was the Political

Commissar in Vipuri then, and he decided that publication of Dolgov's atrocities would have prejudiced the negotiations. So he had Dolgov quietly shipped back to Moscow.' The Marshal shrugged. 'An unfortunate decision, but the right one.' He studied the chess board. 'Your move.'

Yuri moved a pawn. 'Were political reasons the only ones for sending Dolgov quietly back to Moscow?'

The Marshal glared at him, fiercely. 'What the hell do you mean?'

'I mean, was there any personal reason why Deryugin should have protected Dolgov?'

'Not as far as I know.'

Yuri said, 'Despite what he'd done in Finland, Dolgov remained in the Army afterwards. How was that?'

His father moved a knight. 'Beria,' he said. 'The strangler of Vipuri worked for Beria, afterwards. Beria had a need for men like Dolgov. After the war, Dolgov returned to the regular Army, but most people believed he was still spying for Beria.'

Yuri said, 'Dolgov was promoted very rapidly after 1953.'

'Someone up there liked him.' His father's hand could have pointed to heaven or the Kremlin.

'Anyone we know?'

His father shrugged. 'After Beria's death, I expect Dolgov made new friends. Don't ask me who they were. You know I've never involved myself in politics.' A wry smile broke over the older man's face. 'They used to say that when I was Moscow Commandant, I kept my tanks slightly unserviceable, so that no one could accuse me of political ambition.' He crossed his bishop in an outrageous move. Yuri's knight fell. 'Anyway, what's all this about Popov and Dolgov?'

Yuri told his father how Dolgov had died synchronously with the burglary.

His father laughed, a deep, bellowing sound. 'An appropriate fate for an armchair General who lifted weights.'

Too late, Yuri tried to move his bishop into defence.

His father said, 'Son, you're not paying attention.' He moved his knight. 'Check, and I believe, mate.'

Yuri stared at the pieces, and tipped his king over in submission. He told his father of his meeting with Drachinsky and how he suspected that Kronykin's rehabilitation had unearthed memories that had made him kill Dolgov.

'Funny,' his father said. 'Dolgov was involved in a shooting accident near Zvenigorod. A Major Kronykin – I'm sure that was the name – Dolgov's superior officer at the time, was killed. I remember there was an enquiry afterwards, because they'd used army weapons on a bear hunt.'

The shock was like a sudden immersion in ice water. Yuri asked, 'Would the name be Major Anatol Kronykin?'

'It could have been. If it's important, why don't you check with your KGB people at Zvenigorod?'

Yuri stared unseeingly at the chess pieces. If Kronykin's father had been a Major Anatol Kronykin and Dolgov had killed him then it was possible that the Fifth Directorate's rehabilitation process had uncovered deeply buried feelings in Kronykin that had driven him to take revenge.

The Marshal said, 'If there is anything in all of this, I am sure you will find it. You want another game?'

Yuri shook his head. He told his father about Popov's attitude and Professor Andronov's report. 'I feel that for some reason, Popov is trying to suppress the fact of Dolgov's murder.'

His father lit an unfashionable, tubed cigarette, its upper end filled with black, Russian tobacco. In a low voice he said, 'If Popov's bending, he's caught in a storm. My advice to you is, keep out of the storm.'

Yuri wondered if his father's judgment had been affected by Popov's soldiering ability, if Popov himself hadn't changed since he'd fought Fascists and suppressed rebellions.

The Marshal pointed to a picture of Malinovsky. 'That,' he said, 'was the greatest Russian soldier of them all. I went with him to Rumania. For him, I fought the Chinese and the Japanese. I would have died for him.' He lit another cigarette. 'The Generalissimo loved Malinovsky. He offered Malinovsky anything he wanted. Malinovsky wanted the Far East Command. He got it.'

His father swung forward and raked Yuri's face with his eyes. 'Do you know what ruined Malinovsky? Politics! Khrushchev brought him to Moscow as Deputy Minister of

Defence. In four years he was finished.' His father shrugged. 'Same thing happened to Zhukov. A soldier's job is to fight, not get involved in politics. Same thing applies to you. You are a policeman. Do a policeman's job. *Ugadat, ugodit, utselet* – sniff out, suck up, survive.'

'Was that what you did outside Kursk?'

'That was soldiering,' his father said. 'To be a hero you've first got to be right.'

CHAPTER TWELVE

Early the next morning, Yuri left for Zvenigorod. Rima had been furious at his going. In London, she'd had enough of his working all hours and his sudden, unexplained disappearances. She wasn't going to put up with it in Moscow. Besides, that evening, her parents were expecting them to dinner.

If he wasn't there, she'd warned, Aristov would be angry. She'd told him that Aristov had done five times as much for them as the Marshal and that Aristov would think him an ingrate.

She'd smoked four cigarettes while she'd argued, and said his selfishness made her ill. He'd made her sick with worry in London, and was now doing the same thing to her in Moscow.

Abruptly, she'd become tearful. She looked forward so much to their Saturday evening dinners at the Aristovs. She loved listening to Yuri and her father talk. This evening some of her father's influential friends would be present. Who knew what Yuri could achieve if he impressed them.

Yuri had said that revolutions were achieved by hard work and not influence.

Go then, Rima had cried bitterly, go and achieve the revolution single handed! As he'd left, he'd heard an ashtray smash against the door.

He'd met Rima at a party soon after he'd returned from Africa. Her exquisitely tiny figure, and the porcelain glow of her skin had reminded him of a statuette his father had brought back from Dresden. His hosts, Natalya and Gvishani Kirichenko had told him she was Rima Aristova, and that her father was a member of the Central Committee and Chairman of Party Organs. Natalya who had been at school with Rima, had warned Yuri she was not as fragile as she looked.

He'd made his way to her across a room full of *apparatchiks*, and introduced himself.

She'd said, 'They tell me you're something of a hero,' and, with a delightful impulsiveness, touched the medal he had won in Africa.

He'd been charmed by her spontaneity and flattered by her admiration. All that evening he had told her what he'd done abroad, while she'd listened with rapt interest. She'd seen his picture in *Soviet Encounter*, she'd said, and Yuri had been impressed. *Soviet Encounter* was a highbrow literary political magazine, and it was only afterwards that he learned she'd picked it up by accident.

He'd seen her again. And again. And each time he'd found her more captivating than the last. Her wide, grey eyes had brimmed with infectious laughter, and there had been an insouciant gaiety about her that filled him with happiness. She'd enjoyed being with him too, and showing him off to her friends.

When Aristov objected to their relationship, they'd met secretly in Gvishani and Natalya's apartment, and when Yuri was sent to Kamysin, eight hundred miles from Moscow, to train for his American assignment, Rima had waited two whole months for him, passionately loyal. On his return, she'd quarrelled with Aristov and forced him to agree to an engagement.

Immediately afterwards, Yuri had left for America. He'd remained there eighteen months, and it was only later that he discovered that Aristov had persuaded Director Suslov not to allow him any home leave.

A week after his return, they'd got married.

Disillusion had set in almost immediately. Yuri discovered that Rima was no perfect, porcelain figurine, and Rima learned that marriage to a hero was not like the story books said. Which was hardly surprising considering that, despite their long engagement, they'd hardly spent two weeks together before their marriage, and that Aristov's opposition combined with their long separations had given their affair an unreal and melodramatic sense of urgency.

But that was not why their marriage had failed. The problem was Rima. Born nine years after her brothers, she had been doted upon, indulged and hopelessly spoilt. Her charm and vivacity, Yuri had discovered, were attributes she adopted as casually as make-up. She was impossibly wilful, totally selfish and still a child.

In the fifteen months that had passed, Yuri had despaired of her ever growing up.

The ice age had levelled Russia. Spreading almost to the Black Sea it had ground down mountains and created deep depressions into which, as the ice retreated, rivers had dug themselves deeper. The melting ice had left behind scattered ridges and packs of glacial debris. Russia was a country where a few bits were higher than other bits, and a great many seemed to be lower.

Zvenigorod, nine miles north of the main Moscow to Smolensk highway was one of the higher bits. Surrounded by forest it stood over a ravine of the Moskva. A massive earth fortification, the Gorodok, rose a hundred and fifty feet above the town. A stone cathedral stood in its centre, surrounded by rust red roofs and pink and caramel walls. The town had that sense of recent anonymity common to all Russian towns. Along the main street black signs announced, Bakery No.3, Gastronom No.2, Shoes. There was a statue of Lenin, a War Memorial and a Militia station.

The KGB office was just behind the Militia station. At seven o'clock on a Saturday morning it was manned by an apple-cheeked boy whose eyes held a pleasant, peasant shrewdness. But he didn't enquire why Yuri was interested in a shooting accident of so long ago. Asking Yuri to man the phone, he went into the record room and looked.

The phone didn't ring. The boy returned twenty minutes later, blowing dust off a slim, cardboard file. The paper inside was stained brown, as if gravy had once been spilt over it. The typing had faded to a bluish grey. The boy gave Yuri tea while he read the report.

On the 25th February, 1953, five army officers had come from Moscow, hunting for heaven knew what. Even now the countryside around Zvenigorod teemed with wild duck, black-cock and partridge. Then, there must have been wolf, lynx and bear.

Yuri could imagine the five men marching noisily into the

woods, carrying guns, lunch pails and vodka. They had come to be together, to talk, tell jokes, to drink. They had come to be part of the forest, to walk in snow, to feel part of the earth; they had come to fulfil a basic human need, to hunt and to eat the meat they had killed.

According to their statements, in the early afternoon, they had split into two groups. Kronykin, Dolgov and a Lieutenant Velichko had been together. They had shot some duck.

Shortly before dusk, Kronykin had left, believing he'd spotted the trail of a bear. In retrospect, it had been a foolish thing to do. Velichko and Dolgov had waited in a clearing.

Later, in the half dark, they'd heard a rustling and a thrashing and a growling. They'd cocked their weapons. Something had moved massively in the forest. They'd fired.

Moments later, going into the forest, they'd found Kronykin dead.

The coroner's enquiry had recalled many similar accidents. It had sanctimoniously pronounced on the dangers of combining vodka with guns and returned a verdict of death by misadventure.

Yuri wondered if a three year old boy had accepted and understood that verdict. He wondered if that three year old boy, grown into a thirty-three year old fighting soldier had decided to do something about it.

Then he thought, the accident had occurred in 1953, the year in which Dolgov had begun his meteoric rise in the army. There was altogether too much of 1953 in the Dolgov case. Yuri thanked the babyfaced KGB officer and set off for Smolensk.

Smolensk was a hundred and fifty miles away, the highway empty except for trucks. Potholes, left over from the previous winter, bumped the Zhiguli's suspension and jarred Yuri's spine. He reached Smolensk shortly after two.

During the war the city had been razed by the Fascists, most of it reconstructed in grim concrete blocks, amongst which were dotted the gleaming domes of cathedrals. Around the city, factory chimneys belched smoke into the air like cannon. On Temple Hill there was a life sized equestrian statue of Field

Marshal Kutuzov, the man who'd left Moscow to Napoleon, believing in the virtue of losing battles to win wars. A KGB investigator could learn from that, Yuri thought.

Sergei Kronykin had lived in a twin towered, eight storey apartment block on Korolkov Street, which had been built across the old city wall. Yuri walked across the courtyard where children were climbing a life size wooden horse, and went up narrow, concrete stairs.

An old woman opened the door of 617. Kronykin's mother, not his wife. Her head was draped with a black shawl. In a wizened moon crater like face, her eyes were dark pits.

'Evgenya Kronykina?' Yuri showed her his red work pass.

Numbly she stood aside. He entered a cluttered room, with toys scattered on the floor, the remnants of lunch on a wooden table, a sofa covered with bedclothes. Kronykin, his wife, two children and mother had lived in two rooms. In comparison, the crumbling apartment Yuri had shared with Rima when they were first married was a palace. The kitchen and bathroom were down the corridor. A line of washing hung across an open window. In a corner of the room, a samovar bubbled.

Evgenya Kronykina asked, 'You have come about my son?' She spoke hoarsely, with the shrillness of the partially deaf. There was curiosity in her tone, but no expectation. She had trained herself not to hope.

Yuri couldn't bring himself to tell her that her son was dead. 'Your son is being dealt with by another department,' he said. 'I have come to talk about your husband's accident.'

'You have come from Moscow?'

Yuri nodded.

She cleared herself a space on the sofa and sat. 'You are very thorough enquiring into something that happened so long ago.' Her hands, reddened and wrinkled, rested motionless on her lap. Her tone was completely matter of fact.

Yuri pulled a chair from the table and sat opposite her. 'Do you remember what happened?'

'Could I ever forget?'

She remembered the day, Wednesday the 25th February, 1953. She remembered it had snowed the previous night. She had woken early to prepare her husband's breakfast, kasha, because it had been a bad winter and there wasn't much food, and chifir, tea concentrated twenty times over to give him energy for the hunt. The previous night she had packed his lunch, potato pie, some black bread and a small cake. Her husband had got some vodka from the army store.

Dolgov and some friends had come about seven o'clock, driving an American jeep. Her husband had left saying he would bring back a bearskin and promising they would eat fresh meat that night.

'Wednesday,' Yuri asked, 'didn't your husband have to work?'

Evgenya explained proudly that her husband had been Deputy Commandant of Security at the Kremlin. He was on duty that weekend at Kuntsevo, at the dacha of Generalissimo Stalin. So he'd had the Wednesday off. She paused, staring at invisible images that peopled the space between them. At nine o'clock that evening, the Militia had informed her that her husband was dead. She drifted into silence, as if there was nothing more to say.

Yuri asked, 'Do you know how your husband died?'

'Of course.' She'd gone to Zvenigorod for the inquest. 'My husband always worried about this kind of accident,' she said. 'He always wore a red bandana when he went hunting. But I suppose it was dark, and they didn't see it.'

'Your husband and Dolgov were friends?'

Evgenya Kronykina nodded, her entire body moving with vehemence. 'They'd known each other at military school, and they'd served together in Kubyschev. Some years before the accident, Vyssorian Ilyich came to work in the Kremlin. He worked with my husband. He used to eat with us often. We had an apartment in the Terem Palace, and Dolgov lived alone. His wife died when he was serving abroad, you know.'

She told Yuri that after her husband's death they had moved to Smolensk. When her children were old enough to attend school, she'd gone to work in a textile factory. Now she received a state pension, and lived with her son's family. Her grandchildren were at school, she said, and Sergei's wife was at work. She spent most days alone.

'Did Sergei know how his father died?' Yuri asked.

Again the old lady nodded, shaking her body.

'Do you resent Dolgov for what happened?'

She looked at him as if she didn't understand the question. 'Resent? What is there to resent? What good would it do?'

'Did Sergei resent Dolgov for killing his father?'

'Why should he? It was an accident.'

'Have you seen Dolgov since?'

She shook her head. 'Not after we moved to Smolensk.'

Yuri asked if Sergei had a heart condition.

The old lady looked even more mystified. 'That is the disease of an old man,' she said, disdainfully. There was a rich pride in her voice as she told him Sergei had been a soldier like his father. Sergei had been a fine, strong boy. He'd been with a good regiment. He had been healthy until Afghanistan.

'What happened in Afghanistan?' Yuri asked.

'He was wounded. He never told us how, but when he came back, he had bad headaches. And from time to time he would forget things. Not small things like items from the shops.' Her face clouded. 'Sometimes, he seemed to forget where he was or who he was. Sometimes he would stare at me or his wife or the children as if he couldn't remember who we were.' She shifted uncomfortably on the sofa. 'Those stories they say he told, he did that because he was ill. Up here.' She tapped her head. 'Sergei was a good boy, a soldier like his father. He did not mean to harm the State.'

'Did his condition improve after they took him away?'

She shook her head. 'I didn't think so. He was quieter, yes, but he was not well. He didn't have headaches and he didn't forget things as often, but I remember, he didn't play with the children very much after he came back. He seemed remote, distant, as if only his body were here.'

'When did he leave Smolensk?' Yuri asked.

'Eighteen days ago.'

Yuri felt she could have told him the hours and the minutes.

'He said he had been asked to rejoin the army.'

'That must have pleased him.'

'Somehow I don't think it did.'

Yuri got to his feet. 'Was your son a keen photographer?' he asked.

Evgenya Kronykina looked up at him in surprise. 'Photographer! He didn't even have a camera!'

Every factory in Russia has its KGB representative. The office in Smolensk told Yuri that the representative at the Martov Chemical Factory where Kronykin had worked, was a man named Ulyanov.

Yuri found him seated with three other men in the factory canteen, staring suspiciously at a slice of sponge cake.

'Moscow,' Ulyanov said, fingering Yuri's work pass. He picked up his plate and led Yuri self-importantly to a secluded table.

Yuri asked him about Kronykin.

'A good worker,' Ulyanov said. 'No trouble with him until he started spreading those stories.' Ulyanov narrowed fleshy lips disapprovingly. 'I think he was affected by the fighting.' He tapped his close-cropped head significantly.

'What was he like when he came back?'

'Quiet. Too quiet if you ask me. I wasn't surprised when he left to rejoin the army. There are some soldiers who can never adjust to civilian life and a good thing too, I say. Where would we be without our soldiers?'

'Was he ever ill?'

'Not ill. About the time he was spreading those stories, he malingered. I had the factory doctor look at him. There was nothing wrong with him.'

'And after he came back?'

'No illness.'

Yuri asked what the factory did.

Ulyanov told him it produced dyes for textiles. They had the latest equipment, imported from Germany. The factory itself had been built by an international consortium, called Amrocontinental.

Yuri remembered, Dolgov had been involved with Amrocontinental. He wondered if Dolgov and Kronykin had met at the factory, and if that meeting had triggered off something in Kronykin's subconscious that made him spread scurrilous stories, not because of a sudden hatred of Dolgov. Drachinsky would love that, Yuri told himself. But he was a policeman, not a shrink. He asked Ulyanov if the factory manufactured amyl nitrite or sodium thiosulfate.

Ulyanov's eyes never left Yuri's face as he shook his head and said, 'No.'

'Would either be a by-product of any of the processes?'

'Most certainly not,' Ulyanov said.

Yuri asked if the workers were affected by the chemicals, if they were periodically checked.

'That is unnecessary,' Ulyanov said. 'We use the latest equipment.'

It was nearly eight o'clock when Yuri got back to Moscow. He telephoned the Militia and with some difficulty got Yedemsky's home address. Yedemsky lived near the Pavelets Railway Station on the other side of Moscow. Yuri drove there.

The apartment block overlooked the railway; even the front of it was smudged with soot. Yuri went up four flights of stairs. All Moscow, all Russia, was made of stairs. At least it felt like that if you were a KGB man on the hoof.

Yedemsky opened the door wearing a sleeveless cardigan over a crumpled tracksuit whose trousers sagged at the waist and whose narrow, crinkled legs emphasized Yedemsky's spindly shanks. 'Ah,' Yedemsky said, 'the boychik from the KGB.' His wispy hair stood out like needles. His eyes were watery and his nose glowed like a traffic signal. He carried a smouldering cigarette and a glass of vodka.

'May I come in?'

'Yes, of course, of course.' Yedemsky spoke with the geniality of the half drunk. 'I don't know whether you have come on pleasure or business, boychik. But for me your visit is pure pleasure.'

He waved Yuri into a small, crowded room. In an alcove, at the far end, was a washbasin and a small stove; beside the alcove a rumpled bed beneath a row of bookshelves. The wall opposite was lined with books and by the window overlooking the railway line, there was a wooden table, covered with files, papers, magazines, a plate and three dirty cups. In the centre of the room was a worn, leather armchair, beside which there were more magazines, topped with a face down copy of

Dostoevsky's *The Idiot*. A small black and white television mouthed silently at the chair.

Without asking, Yedemsky slopped vodka into a glass, pulled a padded footstool from underneath the television and sat on it.

Yuri felt uncomfortable about taking the man's armchair and the older man squatting at his feet. He sat on the chair's edge and swirled the vodka in his glass. 'I am sorry to disturb you.'

'Nonsense, boy. I was hoping someone would call. Drink up.' He accompanied the word with the deed. 'Do you know the work of Dostoevsky well?'

Yuri drank the vodka and covered the glass with his hand.

'*The Idiot* is the least known of his works. In a strange way, it reveals more about Dostoevsky than –'

Yuri told Yedemsky of his visit to the factory where Kronykin had worked.

Yedemsky lit another cigarette from the butt of the first. 'Working on a Saturday,' he mused. 'You must want to be a hero.'

'The factory produces textile dyes,' Yuri said. 'Nothing they do produces amyl nitrite or sodium thiosulfate.'

Behind the spirals of smoke, Yedemsky's eyes were wide open. 'I could have told you that, boychik. I could have saved you the journey.' He lapsed into a short, silent reverie. Then he said, 'The mixture of amyl nitrite and sodium thiosulfate is the recognized antidote for cyanide. I thought you knew that.'

'No,' Yuri said. He remembered the shard of glass that had fallen from Dolgov's face, remembered a KGB instructor saying one of the most effective and easily concealed methods of assassination, was crushing a capsule of cyanide beneath the victim's nostrils.

Yedemsky said, 'My, you really are a boychik!'

Yuri went home and called Dzerzhinsky Square. Popov, he was told, was spending the weekend at his dacha. They wouldn't give him the address or the phone number.

Yuri called Pasha.

'He'll only bawl you out,' Pasha said. 'Popov hates being disturbed on the weekend.'

Yuri was insistent.

Pasha gave him the phone number.

Popov started off hostile. Yuri could picture his beetle browed, basilisk glower. Then suddenly, he became genial. 'Come tomorrow morning,' he said. 'Come early, around ten. You play tennis, don't you? Bring your tennis things.'

CHAPTER THIRTEEN

From choice or spite, Rima had stayed overnight at the Aristovs. For breakfast, Yuri found an egg, ate it with the remnants of a loaf and left. He was anxious not to be late.

Popov's dacha was in Zhukovka, twenty miles from Moscow, an enclave so exclusive that not even Marshals of the Soviet Union had dachas there.

From the main road, Zhukovka looked like any Russian village, a cluster of wooden houses with timbers cracked and seamed by the weather, decorated with fretted eaves and windows, like wooden lace. It was only as he drove into the village he realized that the houses were larger, the spaces between them wider, and that in the centre of the village there was a large, low, cement building with the darkened windows of an exclusive store.

Yuri drove into the large parking area beside the store, and stopped amongst Volga and Chaika limousines, Mercedes' and Jaguars. All the vehicles bore the MOC and MOII licence plates of the Central Committee.

Pausing to admire the Jaguar, Yuri went to the Security Office beside the store. Four stern faced men wearing the green and red shoulder tabs of the KGB's Guards Directorate, took turns examining his work pass, asking him his business and checking with Popov by telephone, before directing him to drive to a road behind the store.

Yuri drove past raised barriers and scowling guards on to a well made, twin track road, which led into the forest. Within minutes, the forest enclosed him in a tall, dappled blanket of green and brown. The car filled with the cool, sharp odour of pine. After a few minutes, the road rose over a railway cutting. Yuri glimpsed the roofs of more dachas through the trees, before the forest closed in on him again. There was an essential tranquility about Zhukovka, he thought, a special, Russian enchantment.

A few miles further on, he rounded a corner and came to a gateway, with a red and white barrier lowered across the road and concrete pillboxes on each side, a guard house and a tall chain linked fence spreading through the trees. Another aspect of Russian enchantment, Yuri thought, as an unsmiling officer came out, checked his work pass, noted the time of his arrival and gave him directions to Popov's dacha. The barrier was raised. Yuri drove past armed KGB guards, feeling as if he had crossed a national border.

Popov's dacha was five kilometres from the gateway. Long, low, wide and new, built of glass and imported yellow brick, it looked more Laurel Canyon than Zhukovka. A neatly trimmed lawn ran down one side of the dacha to a tangled bluff over the river. In a two car garage on the opposite side, was a Mercedes coupé.

Popov opened the door, malevolently gnomish in baggy white shirt, knee length tennis shorts and ankle socks. His hairless calves were like bottles.

Yuri changed in a small washroom by the door, while Popov impatiently beat the strings of his racquet against the heel of his hand. The court was a few minutes walk away, at the dacha of Deputy Foreign Minister Krasin. Krasin, Popov told Yuri as they set off, was his regular partner. He'd been trying out a topspin forehand and given himself tennis elbow. So Popov had been delighted when Yuri had called.

'Comrade Director,' Yuri said. 'I have some important new information concerning the death of General Dolgov.'

'Later,' Popov snapped. Then, in a more conciliatory tone, he added, 'We must give such an important matter the time it deserves.' He talked about the store in Zhukovka village. Before it had been built, everyone had to bring supplies from Moscow. Khrushchev had ordered the store built. 'And now,' Popov continued, 'more people remember Khrushchev for that store than for building the Moscow Metro. Such is the lesson of history. Such is the fate of those who try to achieve too much, or set themselves up above the system.' He darted a shrewd sideways glance at Yuri.

Popov turned down a small path and opened the gate in a green wooden fence. They walked round the back of an enormous wooden dacha whose drooping eaves and carved shutters made it look part of a grizzly fairytale. Popov waved belligerently at a woman in the kitchen. 'Mrs Krasin,' he told Yuri. 'A peasant. She'd like to turn the tennis court into a vegetable plot.'

They spun racquets. Popov opened a new can of balls. After a few booming hits into the back netting, he announced he was ready.

Popov played with an eager ferocity, darting furiously round the court, shaking off sweat like a wet puppy. He tied a handkerchief over his head, which soon became moist and wrinkled.

Yuri held him with steady, persistent drives from the baseline, working on Popov's backhand and giving him slow, kicking services. He took the first set easily at 6–3.

Miraculously, in the second set, Popov found his length. His massive hits cannoning off the baseline, forced Yuri to return short. Popov went into a 4–2 lead before Yuri's jinks and looping topspin lobs broke his rhythm. Yuri won 7–5, and as they touched sweaty hands at the net, told Popov he'd played well.

'Ah, if I were only twenty years younger. If I'd only learned the game twenty years ago.'

A trestle table with cans of beer and a jar of fruit juice had been set up beside the court. A pale, sandy haired man in T shirt, sandals, slacks and elbow bandage stood watching them. Popov introduced Deputy Foreign Minister Krasin. 'Marshal Gennadi Raikin's son. Did you see him play? Isn't he a great player?'

Krasin said coolly, 'You must come again.'

Walking back, Yuri said, 'About General Dolgov.'

'After lunch,' Popov said. 'Relax, boy. Enjoy yourself.'

They lunched on the lawn. Sunlight, more crystalline white than yellow, shot brightly off bottles of vodka and wine. Popov's wife, whose photograph Yuri had seen on Popov's desk and thought to be his niece, laid out bowls of cucumber and yoghurt, brought out a tray full of stuffed peppers.

She was a Czech, vivacious and friendly, with a fine, open face and splendid breasts. She was about fifteen years younger than Popov. 'My third wife,' Popov informed Yuri with boastful pride.

Mariya Popova talked to Yuri about his life abroad, bullied Popov about drinking vodka in the sun, matched Popov's earthy response with one of her own, and told Yuri not to be shocked, that he was in their home and should feel free to say what he liked. She asked him about foreign shops and Western fashions. Popov talked about tennis and had Yuri carefully describe Wimbledon. He spoke of his time under Yuri's father, encouraged Yuri to describe what it felt like living in Moscow again. Mariya Popova repeatedly heaped his plate. Popov continually refilled his glass and told jokes.

He'd once arrested a man who'd called the Economics Minister a fool. The man received five years for slander and fifteen for revealing a state secret.

A group of ninety year old Georgians greeted Stalin on his seventieth birthday and thanked him for a happy childhood. Stalin protested, 'But I wasn't even born when you were children!' 'That's why we had a happy childhood!'

Yuri felt bold enough to tell them of Adam and Eve being Russian. They had no clothes, they had only an apple to eat and believed they were in Paradise.

Mrs Popov brought out a tart filled with plum jam. They had coffee and Armenian brandy. When they had finished, she shook his hand firmly, insisted that he come again and bring Rima.

Yuri and Popov walked across the lawn to the river. A flight of steps led to the river bank, and as they walked down a launch churned by; a typical, formally attired Soviet mother and father seated primly in the stern, two little boys crawling over the seats, and a teenage girl standing aloof on the forward deck, her hair streaming in the wind, her denim jacket covered with button badges.

Popov waved and the father waved back.

'Minister of Foreign Trade Sarasov,' Popov said.

At Zhukovka they seemed one happy family.

They walked beside the river and Yuri told Popov of his

visit to Zvenigorod and Smolensk and his talk with Yedemsky. 'Kronykin had a motive for killing Dolgov,' Yuri said. 'Kronykin killed Dolgov. He took an antidote for cyanide before he went to Dolgov's apartment. No ordinary burglar would do that.'

Popov stopped and stared at Yuri. His eyes bulged as if he would perforate Yuri's skull. Beneath the flush of exercise and alcohol his face had a yellowish pallor. He started back for the dacha. 'Tell me again,' he snapped.

Yuri told him again about his visit to Zvenigorod and Smolensk, about his discussion with Yedemsky.

'Rehabilitation,' Popov muttered. Head thrust forward, hands deep in his trouser pockets, he stepped off the path onto the lawn. 'It all started with rehabilitation. Kronykin didn't murder Dolgov.' Popov seemed to be talking to himself. 'If Dolgov was murdered, Kronykin was only the means.' Abruptly he stopped and turned to Yuri. 'Wait here,' he ordered and hurried into the dacha.

Yuri waited. The furniture on which they had eaten had been taken indoors. There was no sign of Mrs Popov. Yuri strolled towards the dacha. The glassy sheen of the sky had become clouded and there was a caressing sting in the evening air. The heat wave was over. From a clump of trees came a series of whirring sounds. Birds twittered and rose suddenly, beating the air. As he neared the dacha he heard the low rumble of Popov's voice, occasionally raised, intermingled with intervals of silence. Popov was talking to someone on the phone. He seemed to be having an argument. Finally, his voice died in a succession of assenting grunts and moments later, he emerged from the dacha, dabbing at his forehead and squinting suspiciously round the lawn, till he saw Yuri. 'Ah, there you are!' He took Yuri's arm and led him back to the path by the river.

They walked for a while in meditative silence. Then Popov said, 'I don't understand it.' He sounded genuinely puzzled. 'My other officers, they have a day off, they paint their apartments, they dig their gardens, they visit their parents, they procreate. You, you drive nearly four hundred miles at your own expense to carry out a routine investigation.' Popov turned to Yuri as if hoping to find some clarification. 'What's the matter, boy? You want to be as big a hero as your father? You're getting tired of your wife or what?'

The reference to Rima stung. Rima would have said it served him right for trying to achieve the revolution single handed. Yuri said, 'I am simply carrying out orders. After all, that's why I was transferred to the Sluzbha.'

Popov flicked short arms sideways in exasperation. 'I should have let Golovkin have you,' he said. 'I should not have let my respect and admiration for your father affect me. I should have taken notice of Sudgorny's reports.' Abruptly he stopped and whirled to face Yuri. 'Do you know what Mikhail Sudgorny, your controller in Africa, said about you? He said you were over-emotional and over-committed. That you had no sense of the possible and that you allowed yourself to get carried away.'

Yuri didn't say anything. Before he'd made that phone call, Popov had believed him. It was because Popov had believed him that he'd made that call. And now, by reminding Yuri of what he had done for him, he was trying to persuade Yuri to help conceal murder. No way, Yuri decided. Aristov had warned him his investigation would be followed by others. Besides, what Popov was doing was wrong. Wrong for both of them and wrong for Russia!

Popov rumbled, 'To be a bigger hero than your father, you need a war.'

Popov was fudging. The angry bull of the Sluzbha, the instinctive ball stamper, was embarrassed and uncertain. Could Popov really want to find out who had murdered Dolgov? Was Popov, the best fucking director the Sluzbha ever had, the man who had defied Party orders to save Czech lives, being forced to conceal Dolgov's murder? *If Popov's bending*, the Marshal had said, *he's caught in a storm.*

What storm? By whom? Who had Popov phoned? Whoever he had phoned, had the power to compel Popov to act against his own judgment. Only one person could do that. Popov's boyhood friend, First Secretary of the Communist Party and leader of all the Russias, Pyotr Deryugin.

Holy shit!

Popov was saying, 'Sudgorny was right, you know. Anyone

else would have let Vilna take Simmonds. Charlie Simmonds was *brak*.'

'Simmonds was innocent,' Yuri said, tightly. 'Simmonds was my agent. He was my responsibility.'

'And who the hell do you think you are? God?' They turned and walked towards the dacha. After a while, Popov said, 'Your problem is that you have been away from the Soviet Union too long. You are filled with some kind of American enthusiasm for attempting the impossible. Here in Russia, we have to be more realistic.'

Yuri said, 'Investigating Dolgov's death is a realistic ambition for a police officer. Especially with new evidence.'

Popov lit a cigarette, hunching his shoulders and turning his body away from the breeze. 'All right,' he said. 'Let's examine the evidence. Let's imagine that Kronykin is alive, that I am a prosecutor, that you want an order for Kronykin's arrest.' He sucked deeply at the cigarette as they walked. 'For the prosecution, we have a motive. Dolgov killed Kronykin's father. We have the opinion of this Yedemsky that traces of a cyanide antidote were found in Kronykin's body. We do not know where or how or even if Kronykin obtained cyanide. We do not know if Kronykin, first a soldier and then a maintenance engineer, had sufficient chemical knowledge to devise such an antidote.

'For the defence, we have the statement of Evgenya Kronykina that neither she nor her son bore Dolgov any resentment. We have the psychological probability, that if Kronykin bore such resentment, he would have taken his revenge much earlier, when he was a hot blooded teenager, not a married man in his thirties with a family and a mother to look after.

'We have the fact that Kronykin had recently been rehabilitated by the Fifth Chief Directorate, a rehabilitation that must surely have covered murder as well as political divergence.'

Popov wasn't bending, he was prostrating himself. Aristov had said Dolgov had known where all the bodies were buried, that Dolgov could have brought down the Deryugin government. Which was why Dolgov had been murdered. And that was why Popov was trying to pretend Dolgov had died naturally. To protect Deryugin. 'Kronykin attempted to burgle Dolgov's apartment,' Yuri said, defiantly.

'Burglary is not murder.' Popov crossed the lawn, his gait more relaxed now, enjoying the analytical process that had given him a logical means to refute Yuri's evidence. 'So, what do we have?' he concluded with satisfaction, 'an unsubstantiated motive, and the opinion of an alcoholic Jew.'

Yuri said, 'Yedemsky has some experience in these matters.'

'He is also a drunkard. And drunkards make mistakes. After all, Yedemsky wasn't sure enough of his own opinion to include it in his report. We must weigh Yedemsky's drunken gossip against the expert evidence of Professor Andronov, a member of the Academy of Medical Science and the Sechenov Institute, a man with far greater experience and a much higher reputation than Yedemsky. Professor Andronov confirms that Dolgov died of a heart attack.'

'The symptoms are similar,' Yuri said.

'And would you place your inexpert medical opinion above that of Professor Andronov?' Popov was angry now, his voice rising with temper. 'And would you expect a prosecutor to accept the opinion of Professor Andronov or the opinion of a known alcoholic whom the state does not consider fit enough to treat the living?' Popov stopped, and ground his cigarette beneath his heel. 'No prosecutor would order an arrest on such evidence. You have no case.'

Yuri said, doggedly, 'We have reason to investigate further.'

'Do you realize what you are saying? To investigate further, we must hold Dolgov's body, we must postpone Dolgov's funeral.' Popov pointed vigorously across the river at a concrete water tower jutting into the sky. 'To investigate further, I must go there, to Deryugin's dacha and tell him the arrangements for Dolgov's funeral tomorrow must be indefinitely postponed. That he, the entire Politburo, most of the Central Committee, three companies of the Moscow Regiment, and a number of distinguished Soviet citizens must all be inconvenienced because of the fantasies of one of my officers and the meanderings of an incompetent, alcoholic Jew.' Popov shook his head. 'No, Yuri. I am not going to do that.' He raised himself on tiptoe and brought his face close to Yuri's. 'You will cease your investigation into the Dolgov case. The case is closed. There is no case.' Popov scythed the air with the edge of his palm.

He made for the dacha, stopped and turned to Yuri again. 'That is a direct order, Captain.' His lips were drawn back in a shiny snarl. 'That order comes from the very top. You disobey it, and not even your father will be able to save you from Siberia.' He spat and added, 'Or worse.'

CHAPTER FOURTEEN

When Yuri got home, Rima was there. She greeted him with a brittle fervour and girlishly insisted he wait in the living room, while she brought caviar sandwiches, wine and vodka from the kitchen. From the record player, Boney M went pulsating down the Rivers of Babylon. Perhaps the recent Party directive on procreation had got through to Rima, Yuri thought, half hopefully.

Rima sipped white wine, her favourite sweet Tetra No. 6. Yuri ate a sandwich and followed it with vodka. Rima was wearing her best tailored jeans and an open silk shirt, in total contrast to the baggy sweaters and corduroys in which she usually slouched around the apartment. A new Rima, Yuri thought, or more accurately, an old Rima renewed, and wondered what had caused the transformation. Boney M sang *Rasputin*. Before Deryugin, playing that tune had been an arrestable offence.

Rima's foot beat in time with the music. Awkwardly, she said, 'You must be tired, working all weekend.'

'It wasn't so bad,' Yuri said. 'I played tennis with Popov this morning.'

Rima looked startled. Momentarily she coloured, and bit back a sharp comment. 'I missed you,' she said. 'We all missed you.'

Unlikely, Yuri thought, unless Drachinsky had given the entire Aristov clan a friendly dose of drug therapy. He asked, 'So your father didn't mind my not being there?'

'No, no, of course not.' She fidgeted nervously and lit a cigarette. 'I had a long talk with my father about us.'

So that was it. She was about to enunciate the latest Aristov ukase. 'What did your father have to say about us?'

'My father said that when he was young, there was no such thing as weekends.'

'So in Ryazan they have the secret of eternal life. What else is new?'

'Listen, Yasha. I'm being serious. As a young man, my father worked seven days a week. That's how he got where he is today, and he wanted me to tell you that you're a fine example to all of us, especially to this new generation that is more interested in jeans and record players than consolidating the revolution.'

Up with Stakhanovites, Yuri thought. Down with imperialist jeans.

With an amplified mixture of hissing and crackling, the record changed. Karen Carpenter sang, *Rainy Days and Mondays*. Yuri remembered they'd first heard Karen Carpenter when they'd been meeting secretly at Natalya and Gvishani's apartment. As if prompted by the memory, Rima came and sat by him on the sofa.

'My father says it is wrong for me to complain about your working so hard. He says that you are not working for yourself, but for us. He told me I must make sacrifices for the revolution.'

Yuri had news for Aristov. Enthusiasm was out. Working weekends were out. Deryugin's Russians were required to spend their weekends tending gardens, painting their apartments, producing little Russians, and above all, keeping their heads down.

'I'm not going to complain any more,' Rima said. 'Instead, I'm going to help you. I'm going to share your worries and your problems. I'm going to be a good wife to you, Yasha.'

He could hold his breath on that one, Yuri thought. Inspired by Aristov, and the ideal of a revolutionary heroine, Rima had chosen to play the role of a supportive, understanding wife. He gave her a week.

'From now on,' Rima continued, 'everything will be different between us. I know it's not been good lately but it'll never be like that again. We're man and wife, and we shouldn't have quarrels over stupid, little things.' She took his hand, and said, 'If you get back to the First Directorate and they send you back to London, I'll come with you.'

There wasn't even a hope of putting that to the test, Yuri thought. His only choice now was the Sluzbha or Siberia.

Rima asked, 'Did you find what you were looking for? Have you solved the Dolgov case?'

Yuri couldn't tell if Rima was trying to show an interest in his work, or if Aristov wanted to know. In any case it didn't matter. 'There is no case,' he said. 'Dolgov is being buried tomorrow.'

Karen Carpenter sang *We've Only Just Begun*. Rima's grip on his hand tightened. In Gvishani and Natalya's sparse apartment surrounded by socialist-realist prints and posters of Party Congresses, they had made love for the first time to the sound of that voice.

Rima reached up and kissed him. 'Let's go to bed,' she whispered, 'I want you to make love to me.'

Rima lay beside Yuri, her precise figuring body pressed tightly against his. Yuri caressed delicate threads of muscle and skin as smooth as fine china. Her fingers closed round his hand and pulled it down to her. She was warmly moist beneath his fingertips.

Gently, Yuri stroked. In fifteen months of marriage he had learnt it was the only way she could climax. She moved, sighing softly, her eyes tightly closed, pressing his hand to her, till finally she stiffened and held on to him and heaving frantically went suddenly inert.

When he entered her, she was still moist. Her body stiffened at his thrust, then went limp. She placed her hands defensively on his shoulders. Beneath him, her spread thighs were motionless. After a while she said, 'Yasha, you're heavy. Please be quick.' Her arms tightened mechanically round him.

Yuri pulled her to him, moving faster and faster. Her body vibrated against his, soft as a cushion. Her face was pale glow in the darkness, her open eyes stared vacantly past him. With two massive thrusts, Yuri ejaculated. He felt he had made love to a doll.

Almost immediately she slipped out from under him, and sitting on the side of the bed, began to wipe herself.

Yuri stared past her into the darkness. It would never be like it was before, he thought, wondering why he felt both sad and relieved.

Because he'd worked over the weekend, Yuri had Monday off. He mooched about the apartment. Ordinarily, he would have been glad of a day to himself. Not, today though. Today, Dolgov was being buried in full colour at Novodevichy Cemetery. Today also, Rima's cordiality had evaporated. She'd hardly spoken to him at breakfast and left hurriedly afterwards, saying she might be attending a diplomatic reception with Aristov that evening. *Rainy Days and Mondays*, Yuri hummed tunelessly. He could smell the stew bubbling in the wondrous cooking pot. He slumped before the television and watched Dolgov's funeral with the sound off. At least it wasn't raining.

The camera pulled back from a long line of limousines. Above the fortress walls of the convent, the onion domes of the Gate Church floated. The television cut to a close-up of Dolgov's coffin, an elaborate affair of oak and brass, bright with the glitter of folded dress uniform, cap and crossed swords. They were burying a hero.

A murdered hero! And he, Yuri Gennadovich Raikin was an accessory after the fact. But what could an accessory after the fact do, when to act meant the *gulag?*

The camera pulled back to a platform beside the open grave. Deryugin was speaking. Unlike most Russian leaders, he spoke with lots of gestures. His rimless glasses gave an odd touch of weakness to an aggressive wedge of a face. He was hatless. A coxcomb of wiry, grey speckled hair sprouted. On either side of him were Prime Minister Metkin and Foreign Minister Alexei Grishakov, behind them, other members of the Politburo and Party brahmins, Mikhail Lazarov, the Chief Economics Minister, Schvernik of Gosplan, father-in-law Aristov, Defence Minister Bekhterov. Huddled together on the right of the platform were Interior Minister Vladimir Orlenko, Chairman of Administration & Organs Korsolov, and Soslan Zarev wearing a dark blue Russian tunic, a style rendered unfashionable by Stalin. As Popov had said, too many people to be inconvenienced by fantasies.

Yesterday, Yuri thought, Popov had believed him. Until that

phone call to Deryugin, Popov had been inclined to have him continue the investigation. He stared at the television screen and wondered how Deryugin felt, watching his victim buried. How could he, Yuri thought, a mere captain in the Sluzbha accuse the leader of all Russia of murder? Yet if he didn't, there were others who would charge him with conspiring to hide the fact of that murder.

It was a fine dilemma! He had to act without the power to act. What could he do?

Speak to his father? The Marshal had little love for politics or capacity for intrigue.

Aristov then? A dangerous, double-edged move. Aristov was a man who climbed over corpses. Anything that happened to Deryugin would move Aristov one notch higher. Better keep Aristov, Yuri decided, as a last resort.

Meanwhile, what evidence did he have to take to anyone? The possibility that Dolgov had been murdered. The suspicion that Deryugin had organized it. The opinion of an alcoholic doctor not fit to treat the living. Yuri winced as he recalled how easily Popov had demolished his case.

The camera panned over the gathering. The family mourners stood a slight distance away from the Party leaders, a man in Army uniform with Dolgov's features, younger and softer, a woman with two children, friends and others whom Yuri did not recognize, John Drasen, whom he did. Drasen's face was a rigid mask of mourning.

Yuri went to the kitchen and made tea, came back and threw himself angrily on the sofa.

He needed evidence. He needed a motive. Why had Deryugin killed Dolgov? Over money, over bribes. Dolgov had known too much and had been about to tell all to the Zarev Commission. But Deryugin would never have left a trail of evidence. Fools did not make it as far as the Politburo, let alone to the very top.

A row of Army officers filled the screen, the Marshal in the foreground, ramrod straight. The camera cut to a crowd of men at the rear of the gathering, all of them about Dolgov's age, some in KGB uniform, the others in civilian clothes. As many KGB present as Army, Yuri thought. Strange. He remembered the Krasnaya Dela, went to the study and fetched Simmonds' article.

All Simmonds had written about was Deryugin's connection with the black-marketeer, Lazar, and Zarev and the Krasnaya Dela. There was nothing in the article even remotely concerned with Dolgov.

Yuri paced the apartment. He drank more tea. He couldn't find a connection or a motive. He read the Simmonds article again.

Nothing.

Rifles were being fired silently over Dolgov's grave. There was a rapid cut to a single cannon booming soundlessly. Dolgov was buried. The case was over. And Yuri felt like a goat in a trap for a tiger.

A goat. A trap. Only goats stayed in traps. If there was no way he could convict Deryugin, he had to get out. There was only one way to do that. Find out why Zamyatin had lied. Find out what was in Simmonds' file, and get back to the First Directorate.

He drank more tea and thought, yes; especially if Popov was to be believed and the First Directorate were demanding he be punished more severely. Do it now, Yuri thought, when everyone important was concerned with burying Dolgov. It was a lot better than sitting around and letting his brain overheat.

He picked up the phone and called First Directorate Records. 'This is Major Alexei Zamyatin,' he said. 'Have you had the C23021 file back from Department V yet?'

Quoting the reference was enough. After a few minutes, a woman said, 'Yes, sir. It was returned last Thursday.'

Yuri took a deep breath. 'A Captain Raikin will want to refer to it, before he leaves for London tomorrow. Could you check please if he is authorized?' He waited, hardly daring to breathe. The First Directorate's access system was simple. Only authorized personnel, whose names were attached to the front of the file could read it. Getting names on and off was a procedure in itself, and as the Simmonds' file had only recently been returned, he could still be an authorized accessor.

The woman said, 'Captain Raikin is authorized, sir.'

'He'll be round later this afternoon,' Yuri said. With a sweating palm he replaced the receiver. He was committed. He had done it. All he had to do was drive over to First Directorate HQ and ask for the file. All he had to do? What was it Sudgorny had said about him? That he had no sense of the possible, that he allowed himself to be carried away. All the woman had to do was check with Zamyatin, and there'd be a reception committee waiting to drag him off to Lefortovo.

Wearing uniform with the epaulettes and collar tabs of the First Directorate, Yuri drove up Gorky Street, and at Leningrad Prospekt took the right fork to Sheremetyevo. The uniform felt heavy and close, like an old blanket.

A few kilometres beyond the intersection with the Outer Ring Road, he slowed beside an anonymous building, standing on its own, with powerful looking antennae on its roof. He drove down a narrow side road, turned again and came to a car park at the side of the building. He skidded to a stop two feet from the barrier. His imperious charge, his work pass, uniform and the fact that he was using an entrance known only to the staff, convinced the guard he was legitimate. He raised the barrier and waved Yuri through.

Yuri stopped beside the building and ran down a set of steps, dangling his red work pass as if it were a baton in a relay race. Again, the uniform, the sense of urgency, the fact that Yuri was using a little known entrance, did the trick. The guard nodded him through.

Yuri went into the building, up a flight of steps, along a corridor. Out of sight of the guard he slowed and put away the work pass. He stopped before a heavy swing door and checked his breathing, opened the door and stepped into the main lobby.

In uniform, inside the building, he was safe. He walked purposefully to the stairway beside the row of elevators and went to the basement. Two guards sitting beside wooden railings, stiffened at his approach, half returned his half salute and allowed him past.

The corridor broadened into a small lobby. To the right, a door led to a row of cubicles. The rest of the lobby was screened off by hardboard and frosted glass. Yuri walked purposefully up to the bare counter in the middle of the lobby and pressed a buzzer.

A girl came out, wearing pale blue overalls, her hair gathered under a pale blue surgeon's cap.

'Captain Raikin,' Yuri said. 'I need to look at C23021.'

The girl frowned. 'I don't know. I'll have to check.' And – if you leave a section reference, I'll have it sent –'

'There's no time,' Yuri said. 'I leave for London in the morning.'

'I'll look now,' the girl sighed and disappeared behind the partition.

Yuri released a breath he didn't know he had been holding. He rapped his fingers on the counter and stopped. If the girl cam back, she might think he was nervous.

A few minutes later, she returned carrying Simmonds' file. Yuri showed her his work pass. She checked his name against the list, his photograph against his face. 'Will you sign for it?' she asked, reaching beneath the counter for a pad.

'No, there's only a couple of things I want to check. I'll use the reference room.'

The girl picked up the file. 'I'll bring it to you.'

Yuri took one of the cubicles to the right of the lobby. The girl brought him the file. 'Press the buzzer when you've finished. Do not leave until –'

'I know. I won't be long.'

The file was arranged chronologically and consisted mainly of Yuri's own reports. Yuri riffled through these hurriedly, looking for the dates of his meeting with Zamyatin in Geneva. He found it, stopped and stared. His report of the Geneva meeting had been removed and replaced with a shorter report by Zamyatin. According to Zamyatin, they had discussed everything but Simmonds and the leak of the LASM-Two!

Next to Zamyatin's report was a statement from the Ministry of Defence which stated that the LASM-Two was a satellite mounted, laser offence-defence weapons system using charged particles. It was a magnificent technological breakthrough for Russia rendering all existing offence-defence systems obsolete. The trabsmission of any information about the system to a foreign power was an incalculable loss.

Yuri turned to Simmonds' subsequent visit to America. There was his own de-briefing report together with reports from loyal KGB agents and a summary from Mikhail Krylov, the KGB Resident in Washington. Yuri checked Krylov's report with his own. There were discrepancies, half a dozen meetings which Simmonds hadn't reported and a meeting with Harry Snead.

Simmonds, Krylov's subordinate reported, had met Snead in the bar of the Sheraton-Carlton, a few blocks from the White House. Yuri remembered it as a small, tasteful, discreetly lit place, used mainly by hotel guests. It was not the sort of place for a casual encounter and certainly not the place where one spy would meet another. The reporting KGB agent even had a photograph.

Yuri felt the hairs on the back of his head prickle. In the bar of the Sheraton-Carlton photographers simply did not drift from table to table recording jolly imbibers. In that bar any photographer would have had to use a flash, and if Simmonds and Snead had known they'd been photographed, they would have done something about it, even if it meant Simmonds reporting the meeting to Yuri.

Yuri looked at the photograph. Simmonds and Snead stared white faced at the camera. Before them was a table with glasses and bottles. Yuri studied the bottles closely. French burgundy, red and white, an ashtray and what looked like the remnants of a meal, wine glasses, but no tumblers.

He stared at the photograph, knowing something was very wrong, but not sure precisely what. The table looked as if the two men had been eating together, but if so, where were the glasses of iced water customary in America, the glass in which Simmonds, who drank nothing else, would have had his beer? And why was there no background to the picture? The two men looked as if they were sitting before a grey wall.

Yuri took out his army knife and cut the picture from the file. He put the picture into his uniform jacket, pressed the buzzer and waited for the girl.

CHAPTER FIFTEEN

A neatly printed card by the doorbell at the top of the magnificently curved staircase said, Misha Kuprik. Yuri pressed the bell.

Misha was a photographer. Officially, he worked for Gosplan, photographing tractors, cars, clothes and posters warning against the evils of drink, of shirking work or pilfering State property. Unofficially, he did weddings, portraits, magazine features, and for those lucky enough to get them, passports. Misha was obviously doing well to have set up a studio on the topmost floor of this tall, old house in the Arbat with its magnificent curving staircase and a glass roof like GUM's.

A muffled voice behind the door shouted, 'It's open!'

Yuri entered. A bank of spotlights suspended below the ceiling illuminated a large, sparse room with a harsh brightness. White walls dazzled, as if lit by a desert sun. From behind a closed door at the back of the studio, Misha shouted, 'Don't go away! I won't be long.'

Along one wall were samples of Misha's work, wedding groups on the Lenin Hills, stern looking Party officials, actors, actresses, ballet dancers, a scientist proudly displaying the Order of Lenin. In the centre of the room were cameras mounted on tripods, banks of lights, potted plants and cardboard scenery. On another wall, lovingly mounted and catalogued, were reproductions of post-revolutionary Soviet photographers, Rodchenko's cover for *About This*, Alpert's *Dzhigit Woman*, Khalip's *Baltic Flotilla*, Arkady Skaiket's *Workers Arriving at a Moscow Station*.

There was a time, Yuri remembered, when Misha had wanted to be a painter.

Misha came bustling out of the door at the back, fat like most Russians in their mid twenties, stomach spilling over green corduroy trousers, chest hairs curling from a fashionable, high collared open necked shirt.

'Good Lord! Yasha! I was expecting – never mind. Yasha, what are you doing here?' Teeth flashed under the drooping handlebar moustache. Black eyes gleamed. He swung pudgy arms around Yuri. 'Hey, it's good to see you!'

'Been back just a few weeks.' They hugged and kissed each other on the cheek.

Misha stood back, holding Yuri at arm's length. 'You're looking great, Yasha.' He ran his fingers along the lapels of Yuri's sports jacket. 'I like it. American?'

'English.' Yuri released Misha and looked admiringly round the room. 'Nice place you got here.'

Misha bustled around, opening wine, finding glasses, explaining the studio was partly paid for by Gosplan, who realized he did better work on his own. It was one of those typical Russian ironies that in a society which eschewed the cult of personality, photographers were the only people allowed to freelance.

'I thought you were going to be a painter.'

Misha laughed. 'Painters don't have fringe benefits. I grew up.' He thrust a glass at Yuri. 'What are you doing in Moscow? I thought you were in America or somewhere.'

'I didn't grow up,' Yuri laughed. 'They've brought me back for re-education.'

'Well, the main thing is that you're here!' He raised his glass. 'Welcome home Yasha! May you stay with us forever!' He drank thirstily. 'Now, we must celebrate. Dimitri's giving a party for the publication of his new book. You're invited. Your wife too!'

Rima hadn't been home when Yuri had returned to the apartment to change. He took another gulp of wine and said, 'I think Rima is having dinner with her father.'

'Nonsense!' Misha cried. 'Tell her, her father eats every day. But how often does Dimitri Vostok publish a book? How often does Dimitri Vostok publish a successful book?'

Yuri asked, 'Wasn't Dimitri in trouble over the article he wrote criticising Premier Metkin's literary style?'

'Oh, that was a long time ago. Dimitri's rehabilitated now.

He writes epics about the conquest of Siberia. A new Sholokov, that's what they're calling Dimitri now. Anyway, phone your wife. We mustn't be late.'

Yuri called Rima.

'No,' she said. 'I'm going with my father to a reception at the Hall of Congresses.'

'Have him take your mother,' Yuri said. 'Dimitri's party will be fun. Everyone we know will be there.'

'I don't want to spend an evening with a bunch of drunken artists,' she said. 'Besides, I've promised my father.'

'I'm going,' Yuri said.

'Do what you want. But if you're going to get drunk, I'm staying at my parents.'

For a moment they both held on to the phone. It would never be like it was, Yuri thought, before the receiver whirred in his ear. He put down the phone and said to Misha, 'Rima can't make it. She has to go with her father to a diplomatic reception.'

'Shame,' Misha said, drinking. 'She'll meet a better class of person at Dimitri's.' He refilled their glasses. 'But you'll come?'

'All the Party commissars couldn't stop me.' He reached into his pocket and brought out the photograph. 'Is this genuine, or a fake?'

Misha studied the photograph carefully, ran his finger over the shapes. 'It's made from three separate negatives,' he announced. 'Look at the shadows thrown by the two men. This man,' the finger rested on Simmonds, 'was photographed from the front, the other from the front but slightly to the left. The background has been shaded out and very clumsily, too. The table was inserted afterwards. Look at the line around it.'

Yuri asked, 'Can you break the photograph down into its components and do me a step by step series of prints, showing how it was put together?'

'Take a few days, but sure. No problem.'

'Tomorrow,' Yuri said.

Misha refilled their glasses again. 'For you, Yasha, tomorrow. Now let's go to a party.'

Misha was in a typical Russian hurry to get to the party. So first they had to finish the wine. Then, there were urgent phone calls to be made. Misha remembered a customer who hadn't collected his prints, a school teacher, who arranged for Misha to take photographs of graduation classes. Very profitable, Misha explained. They delivered the prints and drank another bottle of wine with the school teacher. Misha felt hungry. They stopped at a cafe and had greasy pies. They couldn't arrive without vodka. Misha had a friend on the other side of Moscow who'd sell them vodka. They drank some of the vodka on the way to Dimitri's. They arrived late and slightly drunk. Yuri felt as if he'd been riding a roller coaster all evening. He felt happy. At last he was home.

At Dimitri's, the crowd spilled out onto the corridor. A record player blasted Abba, the Bee Gees and Boney M. Misha steered Yuri through the curtain of smoke to a table covered with food and dirty plates, a mixture of bottles and glasses. Voices beat like wings. They moved around, balancing glasses and plates. Yuri greeted friends from MIMO, friends from Psy Math. There were literary critics from *Evening Moscow*, *Literary Gazette* and *Novy Mir*; there were writers, the heads of publishing houses, actors, editors. There were people who'd known Dimitri before he became famous.

A serious looking girl in glasses told Yuri he looked like a poet.

'What do poets look like?'

'Like you.'

She worked in the props department at Mosfilm and was trying to write a screenplay. 'You must be a writer of some kind.'

'No, I work for Glavlit. I stop people writing.'

'You look much too young for such responsible work.'

'They give us new faces with every new set of regulations.'

Couples danced clumsily. A man and a girl were kissing by the door.

A formidable looking woman wearing upswept glasses said she was Dimitri's editor, and that Yuri must be one of his friends. Did Yuri think Dimitri would win the Lenin Prize this time?

'Depends on the competition,' Yuri said, sagely.

'Never mind the competition,' the editor said, 'Dimitri is the best writer Russia has produced since ... since ...'

'Solzhenitzyn,' Yuri suggested.

'Perhaps.'

The voices, a man's and a woman's carried piping through the din.

'Yasha!'

'Yasha!'

Gvishani and Natalya Kirichenko were waving to him from across the room. Yuri pushed his way to them. Gvishani was his oldest friend. They'd been boys together in Sarasovo, Pioneers together, come to Moscow and been classmates at Psy Math, and afterwards at MIMO. They'd run in the same relay teams, gone to jazz concerts at the Bluebird, watched *Hamlet* at the Taganka, and made the same futile efforts to fertilise Komsomol maidens.

'It's great to see you. You're both looking wonderful.' Gvishani and Natalya were the model Party couple, Natalya short and stocky, wearing her usual, dowdy calf length skirt and primly buttoned blouse, Gvishani sagging comfortably over her, his softening frame covered by the standard garb of the Party intellectual, dark trousers, dark jacket, dark turtle neck sweater, horn rims gleaming with ideological fervour.

'You're looking well, too. Abroad suits you.'

They exchanged warm hugs and smacking kisses.

'Why haven't you called?' Natalya demanded accusingly, as she broke free. 'You've been back over two weeks.' Natalya's face had broadened together with her hips, and the extra flesh had added a touch of complacency to her natural primness.

'They've been keeping me busy at the Sluzbha,' Yuri said. The real reason was that Rima was embarrassed by their repatriation from London. But he couldn't tell Natalya that.

'When are you both coming to dinner?' Gvishani asked.

'I'll have to let you know.'

'Where's Rima?' Natalya asked.

'At a diplomatic reception with Aristov.'

Natalya smirked. 'I wish my father were Chairman of Party Organs and took me to diplomatic receptions.' Natalya's father was a journalist on *Izvestia*. She'd always envied Rima's advantages of birth.

Gvishani asked, 'What's been keeping you busy at the Sluzbha?'

'Training,' Yuri said, lightly. 'They're trying to teach an old dog new tricks.'

'And the Dolgov case?'

Yuri fought to hide his surprise. Gvishani worked in the Political Research Section of the Central Committee, analysing data from Russian and foreign sources for the Party Secretariat and the Politburo. It was an important job, but not important enough to know there had been a Dolgov case. 'What is the Political Research Section's interest in Dolgov?' he asked.

'I'm no longer in Political Research,' Gvishani said.

'Haven't you heard,' Natalya interrupted proudly. 'Gvishani is Secretary to the Zarev Commission.'

Yuri set his face in an expression of admiration. 'A step upwards?' he enquired.

'A step forward,' Gvishani said, throwing out his chest. 'A giant step along the path of the revolution.'

Yuri felt his smile grow stiff. Gvishani was the archetypal flag waver, his whole life directed at getting on within the Party. At school in Sarasovo, his bustling officiousness had made him a Pioneer troop leader. At Psy Math, when most of the students found medical excuses to avoid being sent on the harvest, Gvishani had led work brigades; when it was announced that merit points would be awarded for sport, he'd unquestioningly taken up athletics. At MIMO, he'd been a tireless organiser of petitions and member of committees. Yuri wondered what had led his friend to take this unorthodox sideways step.

'Do you know Soslan Zarev?' Gvishani asked, his face radiant.

'I know of him.' Zarev was the boy wonder of Russian politics. Full Party member at twenty-two, he'd become Secretary of Komsomol at twenty-five, been appointed to the Central Committee at thirty-six, and now at forty-three was the youngest member of the Politburo. Though much admired, his rise had been too spectacular to inspire confidence. Aristov

113

regarded him as unserious, and the Politburo still hadn't appointed Zarev to a senior Ministry.

'Zarev's a true revolutionary,' Gvishani carolled. 'Like Lenin himself, he is at once revolutionary, idealist, visionary and philosopher.'

'Not too much for one man?' Yuri enquired. Yuri had once asked Gvishani whether he tried so hard to succeed within the Party for the good he could do, or for the reward of luxurious apartments, chauffeur driven cars, dachas, special stores and trips abroad. Gvishani had looked surprised. Why not, he had muttered, ambiguously, And now, Yuri thought, in Zarev, Gvishani's motiveless ambition, had found a direction and a purpose.

Gvishani smiled thinly. 'We would have crucified Dolgov, if he'd testified.'

Despite himself, Yuri asked, 'How?'

Gvishani brought his head closer to Yuri's. 'We knew about his account at the Staaderbank in Zurich. We were going to make him give us names. We were going to find out whose money was really in that account, and I promise you, Yasha, that evidence would have rocked Russia, all the way to the top.'

Did Givshani know he had been involved in the Dolgov case, Yuri wondered. Or was he merely gossiping to inflate his self-importance?

Gvishani said, 'You should be investigating Dolgov, Yasha.'

'Me?'

'Why not? You're in the Sluzbha, aren't you?'

'I just do as I'm told,' Yuri said.

Gvishani smiled humourlessly. 'A dangerous habit. Especially, these days.' His eyes roved the room nervously, as if looking for informers. He brought his head close to Yuri's. 'Take another look at the Dolgov case,' he whispered, earnestly. 'We know it is not what it seems. Come to me if you need help.'

Natalya grabbed Gvishani's arm. 'There's Grusha,' she said. 'We'd better talk to him.' For Yuri's benefit she added, 'He's deputy to the Minister of Culture, you know.'

Gvishani held on to Yuri's shoulder for a moment. 'Let's

meet soon, Yasha and talk.' Again the humourless smile. 'Our love to Rima.'

'Love to Rima,' Natalya echoed.

Yuri watched them plunge through the crowd, like swimmers diving for coins. Everyone was telling him to look again at the Dolgov case, he thought. Everyone was offering help. He wondered if Popov knew the suppression of the Dolgov investigation was the worst kept secret in Moscow.

Yuri found Dimitri sucking at a cigarette held between the first joints of his fingers and beaming with round shouldered complacency. His thick lips were like rubber bands, his huge glasses glinted. He looked like a proprietorial toad. Dimitri said, 'Yasha, I'm so glad you could make it.' His high pitched voice had acquired a certain pomposity.

Yuri said, 'Tell me about the book.'

'It is above all, a love story.' Dimitri looked melancholic, as if he realized that love stories ended unhappily. The book was multi-faceted, he said, working his lips lovingly around the phrase, a love story set against the building of the Bratsk High Dam. It was also a piece of contemporary history. Did Yuri know how high the dam was? That it produced four point one million kilowatts of electricity? In another facet, the book showed how under the Party's omniscient direction individuals fulfilled themselves and came together in superhuman endeavour to fulfil the greater needs of society.

Yuri said, 'When I left Russia, you were criticising elderly writers.'

'Ah,' Dimitri replied. 'One grows up. Only a fool hasn't compromised by the time he is thirty.' He turned away to talk to the literary editor of *Oktober*.

In the small kitchen, the less famous were crowded around a table, telling jokes. As Yuri entered, a young man with a receding hairline stood up, a smile breaking over his face. 'Yasha, Misha told me he'd brought you. I've been looking everywhere for you.'

'So now you've found me. How are you, Vasili?'

Vasili had been at Psy Math with Yuri. He still carried his head thrust forward nervously and danced on the balls of his feet as he spoke. Vasili said he now worked at the State Bank.

Soon, he was being sent to London. 'You must know all about London,' he began as with much shouting, stamping and shedding of coats, a crowd of boisterous latecomers arrived.

'It's so bloody cold out there, one can't believe it's summer.'

'It's not cold, it's your guilty conscience!'

'Dimitri! Where's Dimitri?'

'Sorry we're late, comrade. Some of us have to work.'

'And don't forget, some of us have to be on the set at seven!'

Vasili thrust himself between Yuri and the new arrivals. 'Is it true we're not allowed more than twenty-five miles outside London?'

'That only applies to certain diplomats. You won't be affected.'

'Dimitri darling, you'll never believe it, but that mad Samoyetkin kept us on set till half an hour ago!'

Her voice sliced his brain. Yuri felt the blood drain from his face, the drink in his hand tremble. He stared dazedly at Vasili. It was she. He wanted it to be so. He didn't want to look and find it wasn't.

'That's Sonya Matsyeva, the actress,' Vasili said.

Yuri peered past Vasili. Her long, oval face was buried in Dimitri's shoulder, her hair spread over his coat. Yuri pushed into the doorway, his heart like a stone in his throat. It was she, Sonya. Talking animatedly, she pulled away from Dimitri, her eyes darting around the room like lasers.

Yuri moved and she saw him. Their eyes locked. His mind completed a stanza from Mandelstam. 'A joy reaches you both across immense plains, through mists and hunger and flying snow'.

She brushed Dimitri away and came towards him, hands outstretched. 'Yasha, Yasha!'

Their hands touched. It was as if a current was passing from her to him, from him to her. He looked into her face, still heavy with make-up from the set.

'I heard you were back in Moscow,' she said.

He clung to her hands, not trusting himself to speak. In Africa, she had been like an ikon.

'You didn't call.'

'I didn't know there was a reason to.'

116

'Idiot. There's always a reason to. How long, how long has it been?'

'Five years,' Yuri said.

They seemed bonded together, like particles stroked by a magnet.

'That long?' She stepped back and looked at him. Their glances felt like caresses. 'You're different,' she said, wonderingly. 'The same, but different.'

The words stuck in his throat. 'You've changed too.'

She said, 'Oh, Yasha!' Then her mouth twisted and her voice broke. 'Let's get the hell out of here,' she said, tears filling her eyes. 'Let's go somewhere and talk.'

In a daze, in a dream, Yuri followed her out of the door.

CHAPTER SIXTEEN

Sonya had a little Fiat sports car, shaped like an aggressive trout, with a large bumper on the front and faired-in headlamps. They drove south past the University. Light from the street lamps scudded over her face turning it into a carnival mask. Yuri felt certain he was dreaming. He'd never thought, never expected – it was so unreal.

In the cramped compartment he could feel the heat of her body. Her perfume and the smell of her made him heady. He looked at her silhouette etched in pale yellow from the glow of the instrument panel, an ikon lit by Easter candles.

How long had it been, how long? Yevpatoriya, nine years ago, then Moscow, then... Like teeth on gear wheels they came together in predetermined cycles. Life was a circle. And he was dizzy from circles. Dizzy, dizzy, giddy. He was giddy with happiness. Circles.

Sonya was saying, '... so much to talk about, so much I have to tell you. You too,' smiling at the windscreen. 'How long will you be in Moscow?'

'As long as they want to keep me.' He could stay in Moscow forever. And then he thought, I've changed in five years. She'd changed. There was no reason why it should be like before. 'What're you doing now?' he asked, surprised at how anxious he sounded.

'Killing myself on *Siege*. I tell you, that Samoyetkin's an idiot.'

Idiot was one of her favourite words, spoken with contempt, with dislike, with affection, with love.

'He takes ages to set up, ages to decide on his camera angles, and then he reshoots over and over again. We're already four weeks behind schedule.' Sonya flicked an errant strand of hair from her eyes, a habit whenever she was irritated. Strange, he thought, how much one did remember.

118

'That man couldn't direct statues in a tableau. I'll never work with him again.'

'You can do that?' he asked, surprised.

She laughed. 'I can choose the directors I won't work with.'

Full circle, Yuri thought.

They went to her apartment in an exclusive, modern block in the Lenin Hills, very different from the single large room she'd had by the Moskva, with its rickety sofa, and a poster of Yevpatoriya tacked to a weeping wall. Sonya's new apartment was small and bright, living room, kitchen and dining room all one vast open plan area separated by pine sideboards covered with trailing creepers. A window ran the entire width of the living room, its curtains matching the cheerful yellow and grey stripe of the walls. The furniture was smooth grained leather and, like the curtain fabric and wallpaper, expensive and imported.

A different circle.

Sonya turned on recessed spotlights, flung her coat over an armchair, went to the kitchen and returned bearing glasses, bottle and corkscrew. 'You still like Mukuzani?'

'I haven't changed.' A statement of hope, perhaps?

She placed the bottle and glases on a low, glass topped table before the sofa. 'I won't be long.'

Now that he had got over his surprise and could see her in proper light, he noticed she was leaner, her face narrower, emphasizing the cheekbones and that wide, curving mouth. She went into the bedroom, walking as if aware of hidden cameras. The walk, the awareness of an unseen audience, that was new.

On the wall beside the bedroom door were framed posters of Sonya's films, her name and face larger in each. *Red Flowers. Winter Loves. Winter Silence. Queen Christina.* Four films and already a star.

Yuri opened the wine. His fantasies about this reunion had always ended with Sonya humble, pleading, on her knees begging forgiveness, crying that she had been terribly, hopelessly wrong. Sometimes, he had been forgiving and taken her back.

What had hurt as much as her betrayal, was the fact that she had neither apologized nor explained. 'It's my life,' she had stormed at him after he'd attacked Kazakov. 'If you don't like it, you can go to hell!' And now, he thought wryly, they had met again, as if Kazakov hadn't happened, as if five years hadn't passed. They were carrying on like strangers in a foreign city who'd discovered they were from the same village.

Sonya returned, wearing an ankle length kaftan, her face shiny and scrubbed clean of make up. She went over to the hi-fi and stared at her collection of records. Then having made a selection, she came and stood in front of him, smiling mischieviously.

Drums beat. Electric guitars thrummed. Hands clapped. Buddy Holly sang, 'Crying, waiting, hoping ... '

'Like it?' Sonya asked.

Five years. Crying, waiting, hoping ... They'd first heard Buddy Holly at a rock and roll revival at the Bluebird, and Yuri had spent a small fortune buying her the record afterwards. 'Is there anything you've forgotten?'

She looked at him calmly, minute yellow circles of spotlights reflected in her eyes. 'I don't think so.' She went and sat on the sofa.

Full circle.

Yuri sat beside her. They poured out the wine. She sighed and said, 'I couldn't believe it when I'd heard you'd gone. I couldn't imagine Africa.' She reached forward and picked up her glass. '*Na zdorovye!*'

They drank.

She placed her hand in his. It lay there limp and warm and fragile, living. She said, 'I kept hoping, one day .... I never dreamed of this.' She turned and looked at him over the rim of her glass. 'Why did you get married, you bastard?'

'It was three years after we'd finished,' Yuri replied and told himself she was being illogical, that there was no need to be defensive.

'You did it to spite me?'

'You had nothing to do with it.'

'And now? Are you glad you're married?'

'I'm not. And that isn't because of you. Things haven't been right between Rima and me for some time.'

'I'm sorry,' she said. Then she sat upright, withdrawing her hand and shaking her head like a swimmer surfacing. 'To be honest, I'm not sorry. In fact, I'm glad your marriage isn't working.' She turned away angrily and refilled their glasses. Then, 'I'm sorry, Yasha. I've got no right to talk about your marriage or your wife. We've got no rights over each other. Remember my saying that?' She laughed, mockingly. 'Oh, shit!' She handed him his glass, took a cigarette from an inlaid box on the table and lit it. 'Tell me what you did in Africa. Tell me how you came to be a hero.'

Africa had been the zap of rifle bullets whipping through banana leaves, gaping bodies with buzzing haloes of flies, bodies swollen with putrefaction and bleached by the sun. Africa had been bones picked bare by marauding dogs. 'You really want to know?' Yuri asked.

'For goodness sake, Yasha, we've got to start again somewhere. Africa was where we stopped.'

Yuri told her how he'd operated in the South with Jonas Nshila's Freedom Army, controlling the railroad that was the only link between the mines and the sea, and the key to control of the whole country. He told her how he'd ridden cargo planes to landing strips lit by kerosene flares, bounced in convoys of ancient trucks, how he'd been shot at by Americans, South Africans, Chinese and Africans.

'Why?' Sonya asked. 'All the time I knew you in Moscow, you wanted to be a diplomat.'

'Mikhail Sudgorny convinced me that in one year in the field with the KGB's foreign service, I could do more for Russia than a hundred diplomats.'

'And you believed him?' She turned sideways to face him and took both his hands in hers.

'Not any more,' Yuri said. Afterwards, Jonas had used Russian arms and material to liquidate his tribal enemies, and Yuri had realized that he hadn't been fighting for revolution, or freedom, or for the African people, but for a small clique around Jonas and a small clique at Moscow Centre.

Sonya said, 'You know something, Yasha? You should have been a poet or a priest.' She told him of her life after he'd left, of interminable hours of work which blocked out whole months interspersed with hectic rounds of guest appearances, parties, premieres and dinners. She was starting a new *Winter* film in six weeks, and as soon as she finished *Siege* she was taping a TV version of Chekov's *Three Sisters*. Next year she said, Mosfilm wanted her to play the heroine in a new Semyonov thriller, and then, the lead in a film version of Dimitri's book. She did not once speak of another man.

Yuri wondered if he should ask her about Dolgov, then decided that if Dolgov had been important to her she couldn't have not mentioned him. 'Tell me about Dolgov,' he said.

She flushed, and frowned angrily. 'Have you been spying on me, you KGB creep?'

'I saw your photograph in his apartment. I was the duty officer when he was – when he died.'

'Dolgov's none of your business,' she said, tersely. She brushed an imaginary strand of hair from her forehead. 'It was after you left and it's over now.'

'But it did matter once.'

'Vyssorian Dolgov never meant anything to me, if that's what you want to hear.'

'I can't imagine you with that ape.' The fact of her relationship with Dolgov reminded him she had never, would never be his. The fact of her relationship with Dolgov hurt. He wanted to provoke.

'You don't have to imagine anything,' Sonya cried. 'He's dead.' Turning irritably, she took her hands away and poured herself some more wine. Drawing her legs up on the sofa underneath her, she sat erect and away from him. 'I suppose you want to know why,' she said after a while. 'I suppose you think you have the right to get married and then come back here after five years and ask me to explain what the hell I've been doing.'

'Just Dolgov,' Yuri said. 'I find the thought of you and Dolgov intriguing.'

'You're intrigued, are you? How perfectly fascinating. I'll tell you why I went with Dolgov. He got me the part of Christina. Satisfied?'

'In Yevpatoriya you wanted to be a great actress. You should have been content with that.'

'None of us become what we choose. At GITIS I discovered

I didn't have whatever it takes to become a great actress. So I became a star instead. You know something, Yasha? To live properly in this country, you have to be somebody. That's the only way you can live your own life. By being somebody. Most people in the theatre are puppets. They play the parts they're given, they interpret those parts exactly as they are told, they do everything they're told, because being an artist is a privilege and no one wants his cards taken away and having to work in a factory.'

'But not you?'

'Dead right, not me. I did what I had to do. And now I'm famous. And I'm free.'

Dolgov, Kazakov, Yuri thought, how many others? Sonya had ridden to stardom on her back, her legs spread like wings. 'How did you first get together with Dolgov?'

'He came on to the set of *Winter Silence*. I saw him a couple of times after that. When I told him I was auditioning for *Christina*, he offered to get me the part. He did, and for three months we went together. I left him when I finished *Christina*.'

'Just like that?' Yuri was apalled at her callousness.

'Why not just like that? He knew I didn't care for him. And I'd told him I would leave in three months. That was the deal. It was nothing more than a business arrangement.'

'There's another word for it.'

'That was the deal,' she repeated. 'I shared Dolgov's apartment for three months. I cooked for him, I kept him company, I went places with him, I allowed him to flaunt me before his friends, I let people think I was his whore. And all the time I lived in that apartment, I never took money from Dolgov, I never took presents, and I paid my share of the expenses. How's that for a whore?'

'You shared his bed,' Yuri said.

'And that worries you, does it? That I slept with Dolgov?'

'You slept with him as part of a commercial transaction,' Yuri said. 'That is a definition of whoring.'

'And what if I didn't have sex with him?' She turned and laughed. 'Let me tell you something, Mr High Morality, Dolgov was impotent. To Dolgov, I was simply an object he needed to show off. I, and all his other women were nothing

123

but virility symbols. The poor man couldn't have sex however hard he tried, which by the time we got together, wasn't very often.'

Yuri stared at her, confused.

'I'll tell you why we broke up,' she continued. 'You might find it even more intriguing, or confusing or whatever the hell you're thinking. I left Dolgov when he got emotional, when he wanted to make our arrangement more permanent. I left then because to have stayed would have been whoring.' She shrugged and grinned and poured wine into both their glasses. 'Also, I'd had enough of being just a pretty face. *Na zdorovye*, Captain. It is Captain, isn't it? Tell me now, Captain Yasha, what do you think, and how do you feel?'

'Crazy.'

'Mmmm. I feel a bit crazy too, meeting like this, sounding off at you, you sitting there grunting and looking like a priest with constipation. Nothing's really changed, has it, Yasha?' She turned to him, smiling. 'Do you still love me, idiot? No, don't say anything yet. Did you miss me?'

'Yes.'

'I missed you too. You know something, Yasha, I knew one day you'd come back and everything would be all right and that's why I could do the other things that don't matter, that never mattered – because I've never loved anyone but you.'

Yuri thought, *And I still love you.* There are no reasons why, because reasons come afterwards. All I know is I feel happier and more complete with you than with anyone else. It's crazy but I feel happy now. I want you more than anything or anyone else. All evening I've wanted to take you in my arms. Just like the evening we'd returned from the Praga, which I had got into on the Marshal's name, and we'd sat by the fire in that damp room by the Moskva and listened to this same music and . . . .

He reached for her. She came into his arms easily, naturally. Their bodies pressed, melting into each other. They kissed, mouth twisting upon molten mouth, their tongues tendrils of fire. They took their heads away and looked at each other in wonder

'So you did miss me.'

In Africa, an ikon, he thought.

Then, with a rustle of clothing, she stepped out of her kaftan and stood naked before him, arms hanging limply by her sides, her breasts with their swollen nipples, proudly erect. She lifted his face to hers, lips parted and smiling slightly, her gaze so rigid her irises seemed to flare.

Circles. Time had come full circle. He stood and fumbled with zips and the awkwardness of sleeves. Dizzy, dizzy, giddy. Circles. He raised her gently and set her down on him, and was immediately enfolded by her moist flesh. Her long fingers stroked his shoulders and back. When he kissed her, she opened her eyes and looked into his face.

Yuri kissed her lips, kissed her tight, pointed nipples. He kissed her throat and the tops of her shoulders, kissed her wide, curving mouth. Her fingers stroked his hair and she pressed his head to her. Slowly, she ran her hands along his body.

Gently, they lowered themselves to the carpet. He felt her tighten around him, hold him, moving in lubricious ripples. He looked into her eyes as they kissed. Sonya. My love, my only love. They'd been away, but they'd never been apart. Sonya. Sonya, darling. She melted around him, and suddenly, helplessly he came, aware only of her, of her body holding him, of her breath sobbing into his mouth.

Afterwards, they lay together in her bed. This is her, Yuri thought, this is me, this is the woman I've always wanted.

She said, 'I've always loved you, Yasha. Always.' She kissed him lightly and asked, 'You remember the day we read Mandelstam in the boat? I wanted you to hold me then. I didn't know what to say to you, because you were Nikolai's friend, and I was frightened you'd think I was crazy or something, and that you'd laugh at me.'

'That afternoon I wanted to hold you.'

'Really?' She looked wide-eyed into his face.

'Really.'

Yuri reached for her and held her. He felt her heart beat against his. Her eyes had the pale glow of a morning star. His dream. His obsession.

When he woke, his head was resting on the curve of her

125

shoulder, her breath fanning his cheek. Silvery light touched her face, polishing a cheekbone like marble. Even in sleep, her face smouldered. Blown up in 70mm it excited millions.

But for now, she was his. His Sonya. For now.

He remembered, they'd gone dancing that last summer at Yevpatoriya. He'd worn a new suit and stiff, uncomfortable shoes. Sonya had complained that he'd stood on her feet, and left him to dance with others all evening.

There'd always been others, he thought. The sensation of remembered pain and rejection was like a knife scraping a wound. He thought of Sonya and Kazakov, of Sonya spread like a pinned insect beneath Dolgov. His breath caught. Anger and jealousy suffocated. He struck out.

Sonya woke. Her glance floated across his face. 'What are you dreaming about?'

'You, you and Kazakov, you and Dolgov.'

She leant over and kissed him. 'Don't.' Then, punctuating each sentence with a kiss, 'That's over. Everything's over. It will never happen again. Never, ever. You're all I want, Yasha. You're all I've always wanted.'

'For how long? Till there's a part you want, something else you want that I can't give you?'

She twisted her fingers in his hair and bounced his head against the pillow. 'You stupid idiot! I've told you that's all finished.'

Angrily, Yuri disentangled her fingers from his hair. 'How the hell do I know it's finished? How the hell do I know that you still don't want to fuck your way to heaven?'

She pinned his shoulders to the bed. 'You insufferable little prig!' she shrilled. 'You with your precious values protected by your father –'

'I've never used my fath–'

'Your special privileges, your special food stores. It's not like that for the rest of us, you know. We can't afford values!' Abruptly, she threw herself face down on the bed, tears filling her eyes. 'What the hell do you think it was like, Yasha?' She beat angrily at the pillow with her fists.

Yuri trapped her flailing hands. 'You should have thought what it would be like before you did it.'

She wrenched her hands from his grasp and sat up. 'Do you know what you're talking about?' she demanded. 'Do you? Let me tell you about the first time. If you're going to judge me, you should at least know why.' She leaned forward, locking her hands around her knees. 'It was just after my parents died.'

Yuri remembered that during his final examinations at MIMO, Colonel and Mrs Matsyeva had been killed in a car crash in Georgia.

'In our society when someone dies the family loses everything. I bet you didn't know that.' Sonya spoke as if she were announcing trains. 'Everyone's privileges go with the job. And when the holder of the job dies, suddenly there are no cars, no special passes, no dachas in Yevpatoriya, no access to special stores, and in my case, no home. When my parents died, our apartment in Moscow was taken over. Nikolai was serving with his unit on the Chinese border, and I was told I was an unattached female without visible means of support, and my Moscow residence permit was withdrawn. They said I had to go back to Orsk, where I was born. Orsk, by the way is on the border with Kazakhstan,' she said. 'I told them I knew no one in Orsk, that I had been born there, because that was where my father had been posted at the time. I told them I'd just graduated from GITIS, that there would be less work for me in Orsk than in Moscow. I told them I had lived in Moscow since I was seven.'

There were yellow flecks in her eyes as she lifted her gaze and looked directly at him. 'You know what they said? They said rules were rules. Unattached females with neither support nor family had to go back where they came from. To Orsk.'

Sonya shrugged. 'The fifth time I went to the Permit Office, this official, this great upholder of the Soviet legal system said to me, *ty mne i ya tebe*. Me for you, you for me.' Sonya stared blankly into Yuri's face. 'It was better than Orsk.'

Yuri gazed at her, horrified. 'But you should have —'

'What, Yasha? Reported him? Refused? Do you know how many theatres there are in Orsk? How many cinemas?' She shrugged again. 'It was easier this way.' She paused reflectively, then brushed irritatedly at a strand of hair. 'When you're out there you learn that we live on each other's backs, that our national anthem is *ty mne i ya tebe*, not all that revolutionary shit about the dictatorship of the proletariat.'

She turned away and stared at the window. 'But not for me,' she said, her voice rising. 'Never any more for me. I've served my time, Yuri Gennadovich, and if you don't like it, now that you've had your fuck, go back to your pristine, fairy wife and get on with your tweeny, privileged life.'

Yuri took her shoulders and turned her round to face him. 'I didn't come back with you just for that.'

'Why did you come back?'

'Because I never left you.' Slowly he leant forward, and kissed her lightly on the lips. 'Because, even when I hated you, I loved you. Because I love you now.' Gently, he pulled her to him and prised her lips apart with his tongue. A nipple sprouted beneath his fingertips.

Sonya said, 'Oh, shit!' She tilted her head back and accepted his kisses. Slowly she took his tongue into her mouth.

Later, much later, an alarm jangled. Sonya stirred drowsily beneath him. Sleepily she said, 'Bloody hell! I should be going soon. I'm due on the set at eight.' She nuzzled his cheek.

Yuri kissed her eyebrows and muttered, 'I've got to get to work too.'

'Mornings,' Sonya said, disgustedly.

They drank tea in the kitchen. Sonya nibbled at a biscuit. He'd forgotten how quickly she could dress. Half smiling she asked, 'Have you thought what you'll tell your wife? Or do you usually spend nights away?'

'I don't. And I can only tell her the truth.'

'Which is?'

'That I've found you.'

CHAPTER SEVENTEEN

'TAKE TAXIS – THE STREETS ARE NEAR.' 'GIVE LIFE TO THE RESOLUTIONS OF THE TWENTY NINTH CONGRESS.' Same lights, same split second change of colour. Same slogans, perhaps even the same people staring at the illuminated Mayakovsky billboard. Yuri sat at the same table in the Yunost Bar, before a fresh bottle of vodka and a plate of salted herring and black bread, Misha's reconstructed photographs in an envelope beside him. They had arrived at the Sluzbha at three that afternoon, proof that Simmonds had been set up.

Furtive in a dark overcoat, Zamyatin came, pausing at the entrance to wipe his glasses and look carefully around at the bar. He sat uneasily opposite Yuri and placed a surprisingly feminine palm over his glass. 'I won't drink,' he said. 'I'm in a hurry. What's your problem, Yuri?'

'I want a meeting with Comrade Director Suslov.' Yuri slid the envelope with the prints Misha had made across the table.

Zamyatin looked at the photographs. 'How did . . . Who got . . . Yuri, how did you get these?'

'That's unimportant. What is important is that I have them.'

Zamyatin pressed himself away from the table with his fingertips. 'I'll have to tell Suslov how you got the pictures.'

'Just tell him I have them. Tell him that unless he agrees to see me, unless he makes arrangements to have me transferred back to the First Directorate and my record expunged, these pictures are going to end up somewhere very embarrassing – the Central Committee or even the Politburo.'

Zamyatin let out a warm breath. 'That may not be wise. You've got to realize there are ramifications, wheels within wheels.' His voice sounded like those wheels, click clacking over an interminable railroad. He reached forward suddenly, poured out a shot of vodka and drank. His eyes watered. Dabbing at them he said, 'The Washington photograph was faked. We had to convince Department V it was necessary to liquidate Simmonds.'

'But why was it necessary to liquidate Simmonds?'

Zamyatin's tongue snaked over dry lips. In a low voice he said, 'We were compelled.'

'Compelled by whom? Compelled why?'

His large teeth glinted perfunctorily. 'Director Suslov will tell you that. I'll arrange for him to see you. I'll call you tomorrow.' Zamyatin hurried out of the bar with the flustered air of a man chasing a hat blown by the wind.

At home, an open can of fish sat before his plate. Rima sat taughtly opposite him, tiny shoulders rigid, mouth drawn tight with irritation. 'You're late,' she snapped. 'Where have you been?'

'I had to see Zamyatin.'

'Zamyatin!' Her eyes flashed darts of anger. 'I thought this Zamyatin business was over!'

Yuri said, 'It'll be over soon. I know now how Simmonds was set up.'

'Stop now!' Rima screamed. 'I won't have you endangering me and my family any longer because of your stupid obsession with Zamyatin.'

'You're exaggerating,: Yuri said. 'No one's in any danger.'

She pressed her lips together, thoughtfully. 'I don't believe you.' Then, tossing her head and tapping the table with her fork, 'You'll never get back to the First Directorate, anyway. My father won't let you take me abroad again.'

Yuri said, 'In that case, I'll go without you.' He pushed away his plate. 'Let's talk about that. Let's talk about living our own lives. Apart.'

'What the hell do you mean?' Rima cried, a tremor in her voice. She stared uncomprehendingly at him. 'You're going to leave me because of this Simmonds business?'

'No, not because of the Simmonds business. Because our marriage isn't working, and neither of us is happy.'

'That's rubbish!' Rima cried. 'If our marriage isn't working it's your fault. Everything was all right till London. In London you left me all alone, without any friends. You never told me where you were going or when you would be back. You made me miserable in London.'

In London, Yuri remembered, Rima had created her own misery. Moody, rude and patronising she'd made no friends. Lazy and temperamental, she'd made it impossible for Yuri to bring friends home. She'd resented his work and his frequent absences. On more than one occasion she'd telephoned Aristov and demanded they be transferred back to Moscow.

Yuri said, 'Let's not discuss the past or who's to blame. What's relevant is that we've become two people who share the same apartment, and who sometimes do the same things. You work. I work. You spend three evenings a week with your parents. I go to the Kodokan, run at the Dynamo, visit my father and sometimes drink with Zamyatin. We do not have a life together.'

'That's not true,' Rima cried. 'It's just that we haven't got used to Moscow yet. We haven't settled down, that's all. Things will get better. You'll see, once we've settled down.'

'Rima,' Yuri said, 'it's not London, and it's not Moscow. It's us.'

'It's you,' she cried. 'You never have time for me. You spend all your time working or going to parties or with this Zamyatin. If you spent a little more time with me, we wouldn't have any problems.'

That isn't true, and you know it,' Yuri snapped. 'Most of the evenings I'm here, you're with your parents.'

'There's nothing wrong with that. I love my family and they love me and they have done —'

'So much for us. I know all that, Rima. But the fact is that if there was anything between us, you wouldn't want to spend so much time with them.' Yuri paused and leaned his elbows on the table. He looked directly into Rima's face. There were tiny lines about her eyes and mouth that he hadn't noticed before. She seemed to be cowering on the other side of the table, as if he might strike her. 'In any case, I want out.'

Her eyes widened, the whites appearing all around the eyeball. Her mouth twisted uncontrollably. Then she screamed, 'No! Never! I'll never let you leave me. Never!' She stopped, staring at him as if stunned by the sound of her own voice.

Then, abruptly she laughed. 'You're being a silly billy, Yasha. There's no reason for us to separate. I'm already forgetting the bad things that happened in London. I'll be all right soon and things will be better. Things will be like when we were first married and lived in that crumbly old apartment on Pavlovskaya.'

'Things will only be right, if we want to make them right,' Yuri said. 'And the fact is, neither of us wants to. You're bored with this marriage, and the routine of being a wife. I'm tired of coping with your moods, I'm tired of your family, I'm tired of us.'

'You're talking nonsense, Yasha. You're just tired from working too much.' She smiled brightly and clapped her hand. 'We'll have a child,' she cried. 'A boy. We'll call him Arkady after my father, and Yuri after you. You'd like that, wouldn't you, Yasha?'

A child who would become the property of the Aristovs, Yuri thought gloomily. A child who would not be conceived in love, but as a reason for staying together. No way, he decided. He said, 'You don't really want a child. You only like the idea of a child, just as you liked the idea of marriage, the idea of going to London, the *idea* of being a wife.'

'That's not true! Things will be different with a child.'

'To have a child we must first have sex,' Yuri said.

'You're obsessed with sex,' Rima observed. 'You're obsessed with everything.'

'Twice in three weeks is hardly obsessional.'

Rima said, 'I'm still adjusting to – All right, I don't like sex as much as I used to, but we can –'

'Rima,' Yuri said, 'why don't you admit what your body is telling you? You don't want me any more.'

'You're talking nonsense, Yasha. There's nothing wrong with me. Nothing, do you hear. Just because I don't like things that are messy and animal and –'

'The fact is that we no longer love each other. The fact is that neither of us are prepared to change enough to stay together.'

'You're the one who won't change,' she cried. 'You're the one who is stupid and obsessional!' She got to her feet and swept the plates from the table. 'I've got some translations to do for tomorrow.' She put the plates in the sink and went to the door.

'Rima, stay and let's finish this.'

'No,' she called over her shoulder. 'There's nothing to finish. As soon as we've settled down, everything will be all right.' She hurried across the living room as if it were haunted.

Yuri went after her. 'Rima, wait. There's something I have to tell you.'

'And I don't want to hear it.' Moving faster as she neared it, Rima ran into the study and pulled the door behind her. The key turned in the lock.

CHAPTER EIGHTEEN

'I felt you in me, all day.'

'All day, I felt I was holding you.'

'You're holding me now.'

'I'm loving you now.'

'And you'll never leave me again. Never. Never. Promise me!'

'Where would I go?'

It was like the old days, when she'd been an out of work actress and he'd played truant from the Foreign Office, and they'd lain together in her damp room by the Moskva making love all afternoon, holding each other close afterwards, talking.

'The night before they showed *Red Flowers*, I stood opposite the October Cinema and watched them put up the posters. I saw my face go up on the billboards and my name in large red letters. I wanted you with me so much, then, so very much. And because I had no one to share it with and I was so alone and wanted you so much, I started to cry.' Sonya smiled and ran a finger along his face. 'A Militia man asked me what was wrong and what I was doing. He couldn't believe I was actually the girl on the posters.' She kissed him lightly on the cheek. 'Now I won't have to cry anymore.'

Yuri found himself listening for the hoarse wails of the tugs on the Moskva. Here there were no tugs. Instead, outside the bedroom window, were rowan trees and a glimpse of the Kremlin above a mosaic of roofs and facades. He asked her about Nikolai, her brother and his friend.

'He's back patrolling the Chinese border,' Sonya said. She sounded relieved.

Yuri remembered that Nikolai had been in Afghanistan.

'As usual,' Sonya said, 'he never writes. But he sent me a basket of lychees last month, through a friend. Nikolai's fine.'

Yurie told her about Rima.

'It's your problem, Yasha. You must find a way to resolve it.'

'I'll have to talk to Aristov.'

'You'll have to talk to him, anyway. Living your life is more difficult than crossing a mine field.'

'That's what the Marshal says.'

'I know. I heard him say it to my father in Yevpatoriya.'

They lay cocooned in contented silence. Sonya's thigh was a milky column, pale as the sky. Naked, she looked small. Her shoulders stood out in creamy spheres. Her legs were long and tapered to fine ankles and delicate feet. Like the claws of a yawning cat, he'd written. He could never have enough of her, he thought, never, ever.

The sun moved across the sky, the sky itself turned a milky white, the light gone from pale gold to silver. To the left of the window, the domes of the Novodevichy Convent, where Dolgov had been buried, turned from gold to pale orange. Even dead lovers didn't leave her, he thought with jealousy. He felt her nipple brush against his cheek.

Five years ago, she'd wanted to get married and have children. Now, would she work less, take more mature roles . . . .

'I'm five years older now,' she said, 'and many times more sure of what I want.'

'What about your career?' he asked.

'You mean what about other men? There will be no other men. Now there's only you and me. You're all I want. All I've wanted. There will be no others. Never. Ever.'

Outside the bedroom window, the rowan trees shook darkening arms and cast thin, gauzy shadows.

He felt her breasts against his chest, placed his hand between them and caressed her nipples. He kissed her closed eyes, her wide mouth. She sighed, 'Yasha,' and pulled his shoulders to her, kissed his eyes and forehead and mouth. He ran his hands along her sides.

Her body spread in pliant offering. Their eyes met as he lowered himself into her. He framed her face with his eyes as he loved her. Sonya. His Sonya.

When she came, her face broke like water rushing over stones. She twisted her head away and gasped. Her thighs drew him deep into her, deeper, ever deeper, sucking him into a

135

delicious, yawning, undulating chasm. He heard his own voice crying distantly in repeated, strangled gasps as he flowed into her in spasm after spasm after spasm.

Rima sat in the living room, smoking a cigarette through a long, white holder and listening to an Armenian group aping Abba. She looked elegantly casual in a collarless needlecord jacket and plaid culottes. Bottles of red and white wine were open on the low table in front of her. Yuri looked around vainly for Aristov.

'I've spoken to my father,' she announced. 'He thinks the best thing for us would be to leave Moscow. As soon as you've finished whatever you're doing at the Sluzbha, he's got a job for you with the Central Committee in Ryazan. We'll have a large house, a Committee car, you'll work regular hours –'

Yuri said, 'I'm not going to Ryazan.'

'Now, Yasha, you will be reasonable.' Rima sounded as if she were reciting a speech she'd rehearsed all day. 'Just think you won't have to work so hard and we'll have more time together.' She tilted her head and smiled up at him. 'And we won't have any more problems.'

Very cute. Yuri flung himself into the armchair opposite her and poured himself some wine. 'Did your father think up all this? Or was it you?'

'What does it matter who thought of it? Ryazan will be a nice place for our child to grow up in. It's clean and fresh, not full of grime like Moscow. As a child, I was happy in Ryazan.'

But his child wouldn't be an Arkady Yurievich, Yuri determined, and he certainly wouldn't grow up in Ryazan. 'We're not going to have a child,' he said. 'And we're not moving to Ryazan.'

Rima tore her gaze away from the wall, looking at him with the surprised annoyance of someone rudely woken. 'My father will be very upset if you refuse this job, Yasha. He's gone to a lot of trouble –'

Yuri waved a hand, dismissively. 'Thanks, but no thanks. Ryazan won't resolve anything. A child won't resolve anything. Our problem is us.'

'It's not us. It's just – just you and – Moscow. In Ryazan –'

'I don't want to go to Ryazan. I want a divorce.'

'A divorce!' Rima leapt to her feet. 'I'll never give you a divorce. Never!' For a moment, she stared at him, wild eyed. Then she brushed a hand across her face, and sat. 'You're talking nonsense, Yasha. You don't mean it. You couldn't leave me. You can't.'

'I've thought about it for a long while,' Yuri said. 'It's what I want.'

Her mouth tightened. The muscles of her jaw stood out like pebbles squeezed against her flesh. 'I'll never let you divorce me,' she said. Her teeth were clenched. Colour washed across her face in waves. 'Never! Never!' She picked up her wine and drank, tipping her head back till she'd drained the glass. She lit a cigarette and inhaled audibly. 'Understand this,' she said tautly. 'If you ever attempt to divorce me, if you ever attempt to leave me, I shall have my father transfer you to some godforsaken hole in the depths of Siberia, and leave you there to rot.'

'The hell you will.' When they'd been meeting secretly at Gvishani's, Rima had warned him of a previous boyfriend who'd ended up chopping forests around Lake Baikal. Given Rima's spite, Aristov's paternal outrage and his own present standing with the Sluzhba, a godforsaken hole in Siberia was a real possibility. 'You mean to keep me with you, even if I don't want to stay?' he asked.

Rima lifted her gaze from the glowing end of her cigarette. 'Siberia,' she said in a strangely high-pitched voice, 'is where people are sent to be punished. If you leave me, you will be punished.'

'And how will you live with the humiliation of knowing I'm staying with you because that's preferable to Siberia?'

'You're my husband. You will stay with me. You will never leave me. You understand that, never.' Her voice broke.

'You're crazy, woman. Simply because your father is on the Central Committee, you can't – Damn it, I'll cut your heart out first.'

She laughed in his face. 'Touch a hair of my head and my father will tear you apart, limb from limb. He's a better man than you, Yuri Gennadovich, and you will do whatever the hell he wants you to. One other thing. You stop this Zamyatin business. Otherwise, I'll have my father talk to Director Suslov.'

Yuri felt the anger rising in him, surging almost out of control. Rima was crazy. His wife, Rima, was mad. 'You go to hell,' he shouted. 'I'll take Siberia.'

The phone rang. They looked at each other in surprise. Yuri picked it up, edging her away with his shoulder. 'Yes,' he grunted. If it was Aristov, he'd tell him to go fuck himself.

It was Zamyatin. The meeting with Suslov had been arranged. He wanted Yuri to bring his car and meet him at the Mars Cafe on Gorkovo, right away.

'At this time?' Yuri asked.

'I'll explain when I see you.'

'I'll be there,' Yuri said. He put down the phone.

'Where are you going?' Rima demanded.

'To work.'

'You see what I mean about leaving me alone? You see why we can't live in Moscow?'

'We can't live together anywhere,' Yuri called, striding to the door.

'Because of your bloody work,' she shrieked after him. 'Go and achieve your bloody revolution single-handed.'

CHAPTER NINETEEN

Zamyatin seemed preoccupied when Yuri collected him from the Mars Cafe. His eyes danced edgily as if blown by the blasts of music from the record player.

'Why all the secrecy?' Yuri asked, as they walked to the car.

Zamyatin walked with a nervous, jerky gait, as if resisting the urge to look over his shoulder. 'Wheels within wheels within wheels,' he replied circumspectly. They climbed into the Zhiguli, and glumly Zamyatin gave directions. They circled around the Kremlin and headed east.

'There are ramifications,' Zamyatin explained. 'You'll understand after you've spoken with Director Suslov. It would be dangerous for Director Suslov to be seen meeting with you.'

'Dangerous for Suslov? Since when is it dangerous for a KGB Director to meet a KGB officer?'

'You'll understand once you've met with Director Suslov. Director Suslov will explain everything.'

They left the centre of the city and picked up the road to Ryazan, long, straight, potholed and empty except for the glow worm tail lights of trucks. The road was lined with straggly trees and anonymous blocks of apartments. Zamyatin looked from a slip of crumpled paper and peered at side turnings.

'Department V has protested about the leniency of your punishment,' he said. 'They want you out of the service. They want you in jail.'

'I heard,' Yuri said. 'Popov told me.'

'You're close to Popov, then?'

'Let's say he knows my father.'

They passed a dimly lit gas station, bounced over a pitted railway crossing. Soon afterwards, Zamyatin asked Yuri to turn off to the right.

They drove past more apartment blocks, nine or twelve storeys high, concrete egg boxes built in the fifties. Washing fluttered from windows. Dismal yellow light from a gastronom seeped across a pavement. They drove past a boarded-up church to where the apartment blocks ended in an area of long grass covered by scrub and small trees.

They turned and skirted the field. At the end of a muddy path the hulk of a half finished construction loomed over a battered fence of rusty sheet metal. Grimy trucks, one carrying a concrete mixer, stood with their wheels buried in the long grass. Amongst the trucks was a shiny Moskvich, its front raised from some previous accident, so that it looked like a praying mantis.

'Here?' Yuri asked.

Zamyatin gave him a pained smile. 'A one time safe house. Just as secure as a one time pad.' He got out of the car and scurried through a gap in the fence like a rabbit.

Yuri carefully locked the car and followed him.

Zamyatin waited on the concrete floor of the block. The construction was a series of immense pillars supporting floors and gaping interior walls. Hoses and wiring snaked over the roughened floor. Barrels and pneumatic drills lay abandoned in the moonlight. A whole corner was covered with tarpaulin sheeted bricks.

Zamyatin groped his way to a wall by the stairway and lit a match. He studied the wall intently and said, 'He's here.'

They went up the stairs, spotted with paint and plaster, littered with builders' debris. The building was eight floors high, each floor a yawning series of dimly illuminated caverns. The sound of their steps and the rustle of their clothing was unnaturally loud. Yuri found he was breathing rapidly.

They reached the top of the stairs and stepped into a broad corridor. Moonlight washed palely over a waist high balustrade, faded into an interior wall gapped with openings for doors. By the third opening, Zamyatin stopped and drew Yuri level with him.

'We're here,' he said into the darkness.

In the darkness, something rustled, something moved. A flashlight beamed into Yuri's face. Behind it he could just make out a looming shadow.

In a high, distorted voice, like a tape run at the wrong speed,

140

Zamyatin said, 'This is Yuri Raikin, a hero from the snow of Tsaritsyn.'

The light seared Yuri's eyes. There was a scuffling movement beside him, a sensation of emptiness. Zamyatin had gone.

Then something large and violent exploded out of the blackness and hurled Yuri against the balustrade.

The narrow wedge of concrete smashed against his pelvis. A bar of swelling, nauseating pain crushed his back. His legs flew upward, helplessly. His hands scrabbled desperately across rough concrete.

He heard Zamyatin's racing footsteps recede. Then a hulking brute of a man loomed into the moonlit corridor, swinging a club.

Yuri curled and pivoted on one shoulder. The club hissed and smashed onto the concrete. The concrete vibrated. The club was pulled back with a sucking sound.

Yuri kicked out at the shape desperately, weakly. His foot was yanked aside without effort. Yuri swivelled off the balcony and fell crouching to the floor, curling his body as he fell, protecting his head with his arms. From eight floors below he heard a car's engine start. It had been Zamyatin's shiny Moskvich parked amongst the muddy trucks. Zamyatin had lured him here and he knew they meant to kill him. Kill him and throw him over the balcony. The injuries from the club would be indistinguishable after a fall of eight storeys.

The club crashed onto his shoulder. He heard his assailant grunt as pain, savage and crippling, flooded over him. His head bounced on the floor. The club glanced off his skull.

He rolled on his back and kicked out at the man, launching himself from the floor. It was pathetic, effective only as a hindrance to the swing of the club. Yuri lunged sideways, grabbed the man's legs, solid as stone. He braced his own legs against the balcony and heaved. His fingers tore through rough cloth. The man lurched. Abruptly, Yuri released his grip and heaved again. The man, stooping to beat at Yuri's hands with the club, went over sideways.

Yuri rolled onto his knees, threw himself at his assailant. Teeth bit through his shirt and clamped in a fiery ring on his stomach. Yuri chopped the side of his palm between the man's legs.

The man bellowed, flung Yuri off him as if he were a bag of feathers. Yuri rolled and got to his feet. The man lumbered towards him, one immense hand flailing the air in front of him, the other clutching his middle. He grunted as he moved, the fierce, warring grunts of an animal.

As Yuri sought to dive beneath the flailing arm, he suddenly hit Yuri with the other. Yuri felt his head jerk back, his teeth snap, blood spout from a torn lip. He spun against the interior wall.

In two steps the man was on him, his bulk crushing Yuri to the wall, fists pummelling ribs and stomach and kidneys. Yuri swung with the heel of his palm, jabbed it hard against the bridge of the man's nostrils. The man grunted and stepped back. Yuri tried to knee him in the crotch and missed.

The man grabbed him by the shoulders and swung him round, began to propel him rapidly backwards to the balcony. Yuri struggled to keep upright. One slip and the man would hurl him over. His feet skittered across the cement. Yuri braced himself, resisted, took firm hold of the man's jacket. As his attacker pushed he took a large step backwards, flexed his rear leg, and took all their weight on it. The edge of the balcony brushed his back as Yuri lowered himself. He raised his arms and lifted his onrushing assailant onto his toes. His left foot shot out, lifting the man by the stomach, as Yuri fell backwards, throwing the man over his head.

He felt the man turn in the air. The lapels tore from his grip, the man cried out once as he fell straddling the balcony, his feet kicking into empty air.

Yuri jumped, turned and tried to grab him. But already the man was over, revolving in flailing cartwheels as he plummeted to the ground.

The pain hit him as he reached the car, a giant, pounding wave which sucked him under. His lungs were rigid as steel mesh. His chest and back were compressed in a mighty vice. The pain was devastating. Somehow he had to stay upright, somehow he had to stay erect. His head throbbed. He could feel his cheek swell. His chin was covered with a crust of dried blood. He swayed and slid against the cold metal of the car as the pain ebbed and flowed.

He had to get away before Zamyatin returned bringing others. He had to get to a hospital. He fumbled for the car keys, with an arm that felt like a sponge.

He couldn't feel the key's coldness. He couldn't find the goddamn lock. The key slithered in his nerveless hand. Don't drop it. Don't drop it. The key scraped and slotted. With an enormous effort he turned it.

Tiny lights danced before his eyes. A chill ran through his sweat-soaked body. He couldn't turn the door handle. He leaned his weight on it and nearly fell. The door opened. He slumped onto the seat.

His breath rasped like sandpaper. The car seemed to undulate as if carried on a high wind. He started the engine and drove one handed, crabbing slowly back the way he had come.

The car heaved ponderously along the muddy track, its lights barely penetrating the darkness. There was endless blackness beyond the lights. A wire fence loomed at him. Desperately, he wrenched the wheel. His shoulder burst with the pain. The car pitched into a pothole. His head bounced against the windscreen. He screamed.

He bounced off the track onto a road. A straggly tree floated in front of his headlamps. Dark buildings with dismal lights undulated past as if borne on an ocean swell. He fought to hold the wheel straight. The car weaved. Light flowed across the road to meet him. Hypnotically he steered toward it, wrenched the car onto the curb and stopped.

A figure moved behind the grimy plate glass of the gastronom. Yuri dragged himself out of the car and staggered across the pavement, threw his weight at a flimsy door. A bell clanged, setting off reverberations in his head. Shelves sparsely filled with greasy bottles and giant packets of soap revolved slowly as if on an ancient merry-go-round. From behind a gyrating counter a man was looking at him, startled. Yuri drew out his workpass. 'Sluzbha,' he gasped. 'Call an ambulance!'

Then, everything stopped.

CHAPTER TWENTY

Yuri heard voices, felt himself carried under crystalline stars to an ambulance. The diesel throbbed dully in time with his head. Pain engulfed him. Faces and voices pressed round him. The wheels of the stretcher creaked.

He stared into misty arc-lights. Eyes over masked faces stared impassively back at him. The heads were rimmed with a phosphorescent glow. Yuri wondered if he was dying.

Gradually the pain receded. He drifted into a warm, comfortable darkness. He woke in a room lit by a blue shaded bulb.

Popov came, looking as if he was going to or from the Bolshoi. His stainless steel teeth had a macabre glint in the cerulean gloom.

'You!' Yuri gasped. 'How did you . . . ' He choked.

Popov smiled, tightly. 'The hospital called the Sluzbha. I came as soon as I could, to show you that we care.'

Vultures showed the same degree of care for carcases, Yuri thought and looked away. Blue walls, blue light, a blue fog in his brain. What could he tell Popov? Goddamn it, he felt too sick to think.

Popov said, 'You killed a man. You could be charged with murder.'

How did Popov know that? Elementary, dear Captain, if only you would think straight. They'd searched the area and found the body.

'What were you doing at that building site?' Popov demanded. 'Who was the man you killed?'

'I was . . . What building site?'

'Don't fuck around, Raikin,' Popov snapped. 'There's a KGB investigator waiting outside. For your sake, you'd better tell me the truth first.'

Like hell he would. But he'd killed a man. He'd have to tell

144

someone something. But to whom could he tell the truth about the photograph, the fictitious meeting with Suslov and Zamyatin's treachery? Yuri turned and looked despairingly at Popov. Popov's eyes were buried in dark blue pits. There was a shiny gleam of pale blue on his forehead. In his dress shirt and bow tie he looked like the owner of a particularly nasty strip joint.

Popov said, 'I've made you talk before and I can do it again. So why not save yourself the trouble?'

Yuri glared at him, too weak to feel hatred.

Popov looked at his watch. 'We don't have a lot of time. So how is it to be? Will you talk, or do I make you?'

Think. Think of a story. His head seemed filled with cotton wool.

Popov's fingers reached for the buzzer beside the bed.

There was no help for it. One way or the other he would have to talk to Popov. 'It's to do with Charlie Simmonds,' Yuri began.

Popov drew a chair to the bed and sat with his elbows on his knees, cupping his chin with his palms. 'Go on,' he said. Father confessor and friendly uncle.

Yuri told him of his meetings with Zamyatin, how he'd suspected Simmonds had been framed; how he'd raided the First Directorate and stolen the faked photographs; how Zamyatin had lured him to the building site to meet Suslov and tried to kill him.

Popov kept looking at him expressionlessly throughout. 'Where are the photographs?' he asked when Yuri finished.

Yuri pointed to the table by his bed.

Popov looked at the photographs carefully. 'There isn't much I can do with these. There is no evidence of how they were obtained, and if I confront Suslov with them, he will deny they were ever on file. Still,' he shrugged, 'it was worth doing. we now know a little more of the truth.'

He stood and stared down at Yuri. 'You're the most stubborn and foolhardy person I know. You're as wild as your father.' He paused and smiled. 'And as big a hero.' For a moment Yuri felt a radiation of genuine affection and concern. Then Popov was advising him to tell the KGB investigator he'd been checking the building site for pilferage when he'd been attacked. 'That should clear you of a murder charge,' he said, and added that Yuri wouldn't be able to return to work until he'd had official clearance from a Procurator. 'Don't worry about that,' he said. 'I'll have a word with Procurator Maslov.'

Why, Yuri wondered. It wasn't because of the Marshal. Whatever he'd done had been something Popov had wanted him to do. So what was Popov's interest in Simmonds and what had happened in London?

The KGB investigator came, a thin, schoolmasterish man with jug ears and wire rimmed glasses. His name he said was Bunin. He wrote down everything Yuri told him in a meticulous hand.

After Bunin left, a nurse gave him a pill. The pain receded. Yuri thought about the man he had killed. He hadn't known he was so close to the balcony. He hadn't expected the man to teeter over. Eight floors. Time to reflect, time to realize what was happening. Yuri wondered if at the end there had been time for pain.

His own pain lingered. He dozed fitfully. He sank into darkness. Out of that other darkness a hulking shape exploded. Yuri woke and screamed.

He lay staring into the gloom.

He had killed a man.

He woke again and found Aristov looking down on him. If he was dead, then he couldn't be in heaven.

'We've all been so worried about you,' Aristov said hoarsely. 'Rima's beside herself.'

Yuri searched for words, wondering what time it was, thinking that the powerful need have no respect for visiting hours. 'I'll be all right,' he managed. 'Tell Rima she shouldn't worry.' He closed his eyes.

'I hear you killed a man.'

Yuri screwed his eyes tight.

'They are going to charge you with murder. If you tell me what happened I could help.'

Yuri opened his eyes and looked at Aristov. Why was everyone being so helpful? Why especially Aristov? 'What time is it?' he asked.

'Twenty past two.

Unusual time for Aristov to have come. Unusual for Aristov to have come at all. He put the thought out of his mind. His pain and the nausea were making him paranoid. Aristov had come because Rima had sent him. Yuri told Aristov he'd been checking the building site when he'd been attacked by a pilferer.

'Was that what really happened? I didn't know you were dealing with industrial security. I though you were doing more important things.'

'Pilferage is an important matter,' Yuri murmured. 'What the state loses, everyone loses.' He closed his eyes and pretended to sleep.

After a while he heard Aristov leave. For one so concerned, Yuri thought, Aristov hadn't enquired how he felt. And he hadn't brought flowers.

Early the next morning a nurse came and drew the curtains. A doctor told him the left side of his shoulder and back were smashed. There would be no permanent damage but it would be a few days before he could move without pain. Also he was concussed. The doctor wrote him a certificate recommending five days rest.

Pasha was waiting in Yuri's Zhiguli. He told Yuri Popov had had him collect the car the previous night, and when they'd heard that Yuri was being discharged, had sent Pasha to collect him.

He looked at Yuri's face and said, 'Asshole, you should have taken me with you. He'd never have done that to a wrestler.' Pasha told Yuri that his assailant had been one Viktor Abyugov, a former member of STF 29, a known consort of criminals, who had worked when necessary as a warehouseman at the Tartarov Wharf.

'Kronykin was in STF 29.' Yuri said. His head still throbbed, and the morning light hurt his eyes.

'So were thousands of others.' Chewing his lower lip mightily, Pasha swerved the Zhiguli round a truck.

'It's still too much of a coincidence.'

Pasha said, 'Zamyatin's dead.'

The shock set off the pain in Yuri's head. White flashes, like short circuiting lamps exploded before his eyes. He leaned his head against the seat and took deep breaths. 'How?' he asked.

'Someone got very close to him and placed a Makarov against his ear.' Pasha said the killing had occurred shortly after midnight, on the embankment between the Novospasski Monastery and the Moskva. The Militia were investigating.

'With what result?'

'Fuck all. No one saw Zamyatin on the embankment. No one saw anyone approach him. No one heard a shot. No one heard the body fall into the river.'

'And the gun?' Yuri asked.

'Yasha, do you know how many Makarovs there are in Moscow?'

They drove to Popov's apartment on Herzen Street. Popov ushered them into a sparsely furnished dining room. In shirt-sleeves and baggy slacks he padded between dining room and kitchen, making coffee in a complicated machine that hissed steam and periodically singed his fingers. The coffee when it came was black and strong. Popov told them the machine was imported from Italy, and the beans from Costa Rica. Mrs Popov loved good coffee.

Leaving Pasha in the living room, Popov took Yuri out to a small balcony crowded with window boxes. They sat on cane chairs on either side of a wooden table, screened from the street by flowers. The glass panes separating them from the living room rattled to the thrum of traffic. Yuri wondered if the Director of the Sluzbha had left the panes deliberately loose to jam bugging devices.

Popov refilled their coffee cups and said, 'It is time we discussed everything frankly.' He looked accusingly at Yuri over the tendrils of steam as if he were the one at fault.

Yuri sipped his coffee, silently. The sun felt pleasantly warm, and a light breeze brought a touch of freshness to the day. His pain had been reduced to a dull ache, and the nausea had gone.

Popov said, 'Let's start at the beginning, with Lazar.'

'Who according to Simmonds's article had made a fortune in

the black market and bribed everyone including Deryugin. Who was a thief, a parasite and an exploiter of the people,' Yuri responded.

'You sound like an editorial from *Pravda*,' Popov snapped. 'Whatever you might think, men like Lazar are necessary.'

'Necessary?' Yuri repeated. He thought he'd injected the right amount of scepticism into the question.

'Yes.' Popov looked sharply at Yuri through a thinning cloud of cigarette smoke. 'The problem is that our great socialist system is too perfect. Our methods of collectivized agriculture do not feed our people. Our factories do not produce goods of sufficient quality, quantity or variety. The fact is our system makes insufficient allowance for human nature, for the fact that human beings are driven not by great theories but by self-interest, by the love of home and family and the desire for a certain standard of living which means a certain quality and quantity of material goods.' Popov shifted in his chair and asked, 'How long do you think this or any government would last if the people were able to buy only officially produced goods? How long do you think the Party *apparatchiks* would support the State, if their rewards were restricted to officially produced goods?' He sighed. 'That's why we need men like Lazar.'

'If that is so,' Yuri asked, 'Why was Lazar arrested?'

'A good question.' Popov smiled, and lit a cigarette. 'Lazar was a very shrewd man. Like everyone in underground business he knew he could operate only if he fulfilled an economic need, only if he was discreet. He knew that whenever there was unnecessary publicity, half a dozen *fartovchiks* would he hauled into court and given long prison sentences, sometimes by the same judges to whom they'd sold unofficial goods.

'Lazar was specially careful not to be one of those *fartovchiks*. If one of his factories was raided, a subordinate went to jail. Lazar bribed lavishly. And each time someone accepted a bribe, he undertook a commitment to support and preserve Lazar. Similarly, each time someone bought illegal Lazar goods, he became part of a conspiracy to protect Lazar. And remember, Yuri, the biggest consumers of Lazar produce weren't workers, but judges and military officers, academicians,

Party high-ups and members of the Central Committee. Every one of these people knew the day Lazar was arrested, they were finished.'

'But despite all this top-level protection Lazar was arrested.'

'Yes,' Popov said softly. 'After the revelations in *Young Guard*, Deryugin had no alternative but to order Lazar's arrest.' The coffee cups rattled as Popov leaned his elbows on the table. 'Now I ask you, why does a magazine specializing in military matters, suddenly concern itself with illegal profiteering? What interest does such a subject have for its readers? And how does such a magazine, with a small staff of specialists in military affairs uncover so much detailed evidence about an underground businessman?' Without waiting for Yuri's reply, Popov continued. 'The answer is that *Young Guard* was *given* that information.'

'By whom?' Yuri asked.

Popov smiled, tightly. 'The more important question is why.' He leaned back in his chair and looked thoughtfully at the sky. 'The article in *Young Guard*, emphasized one thing – the connection between Lazar and Comrade Deryugin. Comrade Deryugin and I grew up together in Dnepropetrovsk. When he was First Secretary in the Ukraine, I was his go-between to Lazar. I know that Comrade Deryugin only used Lazar to obtain materials and goods that were scarce and necessary for the rebuilding of the region. I know Comrade Deryugin never took anything for himself, never accepted gifts from Lazar, never bought goods from Lazar and had never been bribed by Lazar. Comrade Deryugin is the most financially scrupulous man I know.'

A wonderful testimonial from an old friend, Yuri thought. But what else could an old friend say, especially when his job depended upon preserving boyhood friendships.

'When the article in *Young Guard* was published, Comrade Deryugin had to have Lazar arrested, and he had to make a public demonstration of his innocence. That is why he appointed a Commission to investigate every aspect of the Lazar case, and put Soslan Zarev in charge of it, knowing that if Zarev pronounced him innocent, it would be believed.

'Soslan Zarev is a cocksucking son of a whore!' Popov said

and spat neatly on a geranium. 'He knew that he could not investigate Lazar without exposing Lazar's connections. He realized that such an exposure would prejudice his own political future and divert from the real purpose of the Lazar revelations – which was to embarrass Pyotr Deryugin and bring an end to his government. So Zarev began to investigate the Sluzbha, the mainstay of Deryugin's government – and of every government since Lenin.'

Popov paused to light a cigarette from the stub of the first. 'Colonel Turayev, who was then Director of the Sluzbha, resented Zarev's investigation,' he said, exhaling smoke. 'He suspected that Zarev's investigation was motivated by a more sinister purpose. So very secretly, Turayev began a personal investigation of Zarev and discovered that Zarev was being supported by certain important politicians and the Krasnaya Dela; that their objective was to get rid of Deryugin and take power for themselves.'

'Does the Krasnaya Dela exist?' Yuri asked.

'Unfortunately, it does. The Krasnaya Dela was originally a secret association of Chekhist officers committed to preserving the revolution. By the time the revolution was consolidated, they had become addicted to the exercise of power, and under Boris Savinkoff, the Krasnaya Dela grew and flourished and dedicated itself to perpetuating a secret and powerful elite, without whose support no government could survive.

'Not surprisingly, the Krasnaya Dela reached its zenith under Stalin. After Stalin, it helped bring Khrushchev to power. Khrushchev however mistrusted and feared the Krasnaya Dela. As soon as he was able, he divided the KGB into numerous Directorates and diluted the power of the Krasnaya Dela. Every leader since Khrushchev has for that reason kept the KGB divided.

'Now, with the help of certain politicians, the Krasnaya Dela is seeking to regain that lost authority. They are seeking to recreate the circumstances under which they can once again be the secret government of this country.'

'If you know all this,' Yuri asked, 'Why don't you arrest Zarev and the members of the Krasnaya Dela?'

'Because we don't know who they are,' Popov said. 'When

Turayev discovered the Krasnaya Dela was involved, he panicked. He did not know who among those surrounding Deryugin were Krasnaya Dela and who wasn't. He did not know how to warn Deryugin without being betrayed himself. So, when Charlie Simmonds came to Moscow, Turayev leaked the story to him.'

'Why Charlie Simmonds?' Yuri asked.

'Because Turayev was certain that Simmonds was not Krasnaya Dela.'

'But how did Turayev know Charlie Simmonds?'

Popov laughed. 'Turayev was Charlie Simmonds' first case officer. Didn't you know that?'

Yuri shook his head.

'Anyway, by having Simmonds publish that story, Turayev warned Deryugin.' Popov paused to light another cigarette. 'Your friend, Charlie Simmonds was a good journalist. He checked Turayev's story with me.'

'I didn't know you knew Charlie Simmonds.'

'I met him when he was here to interview Deryugin.' Popov waved smoke away, irritably. 'Simmonds wouldn't give me any names. He insisted I got those from Turayev. So, with Comrade Deryugin's permission, I told Simmonds to go ahead and publish the story, and arranged a secret meeting with Turayev.'

Popov's face reddened with anger. 'Turayev never made that meeting. Before we could meet he was summoned by Zarev and accused of corruption. They say that rather than face disgrace Turayev committed suicide.'

No wonder Simmonds had been scared, Yuri thought. No wonder he had run. The moment he'd heard of Turayev's death, he must have known he too would be killed. That day on the embankment, Simmonds had not been crazy. He'd been very frightened. And very brave.

Popov said, 'Comrade Deryugin then asked me to take over Turayev's job. No sooner had my appointment been confirmed than we heard of the attempt on Simmonds' life and your quixotic attempt to prevent it. With Comrade Deryugin's authority I took charge of the inquiry into your misconduct, and asked Colonel Golovkin, an old friend from Special Investigations, to assist me.'

Popov stared at Yuri and shook his head slowly. 'You were quite a surprise. Neither Golovkin nor I could believe you were motivated by simple morality, that you'd done what you'd done simply because you'd believed it to be right.'

'That was the only reason,' Yuri said.

Popov shrugged. 'Golovkin was certain you were working for the CIA. When we were convinced you were telling the truth, I decided to bring you back to Moscow.'

'Why?' Yuri demanded.

'Because with your strong sense of justice, your determination to do what is right and your damnable persistence, I felt sure you would begin your own investigation into the First Directorate, and in that way alarm the Krasnaya Dela and force them to reveal themselves.' Popov smiled. 'Which is exactly what you have done.'

'You were using me as live bait,' Yuri cried, unsure if what he felt was anger or amazement.

Popov looked searchingly at Yuri's swollen face. 'Almost dead bait,' he said. He crushed out his cigarette, fiercely. 'For the present I don't want any more illegal raids on other Directorates. Also, I don't want you taking the Zamyatin matter any further.'

Which meant, Yuri thought, he had to stay with the Sluzbha and the Dolgov case. 'I have to clear myself,' he said, doggedly.

'You won't do that by obtaining evidence illegally,' Popov snarled. 'Be patient. I promise, you will be exonerated.'

What good were promises when he wanted to get back to the First Directorate now?

'If you must do something,' Popov continued, 'Investigate Abyugov. He was with STF 29, the same regiment as Kronykin.'

'We should investigate Georgi Vilna,' Yuri said.

'I see little point in that,' Popov snapped. 'All Vilna can tell us is what was on Simmonds' file.'

'What about Suslov and Zarev?'

Popov shook his head. 'They're more likely to make mistakes if they don't know what we know. Anyway, it isn't Suslov or

Zarev I want, but the men behind them.' He leaned forward, confidentially. 'Through our contacts in the CIA,' he hissed, 'we are trying to get Simmonds to tell us the names Turayev gave him. It's only then we can act.'

'I could talk to Simmonds,' Yuri offered.

'First we have to get to Simmonds. For the present, I want you in Moscow.'

'To investigate the Dolgov case?' Yuri inquired, sarcastically.

'How many times do I have to tell you there is no Dolgov case!' Popov shouted. With an effort he controlled himself, and lowering his voice added, 'Your investigation of the Dolgov case, as you call it, will be restricted to finding out what you can about Kronykin. And that, Yuri, is a direct order. Disobey it and you'll find yourself in Siberia.'

Great, Yuri thought. He was trapped in Moscow, trapped in the Sluzbha, and his only choice was which route he took to Siberia.

Gently Popov placed his hand over Yuri's. 'Do yourself a favour, boy,' he said, softly. 'Leave Dolgov alone. There's no future in being a dead hero.'

Yuri stared perplexedly at Popov. He wasn't sure if he was being warned or threatened.

CHAPTER TWENTY-ONE

Yuri drove home. The effort made his head ache. He felt the nausea returning.

Rima was still in the apartment when he got there. Behind the tinted glasses her eyes were puffy. There were tiny brackets round the sides of her mouth. Her skin looked dry and bleached.

'Oh God!' she said, looking at his face. 'Oh God!' Covering her face with her hands, she turned away.

Yuri stared silently at her trembling shoulders. He felt exhausted. He wanted to lie down. He wanted to close his eyes and obliterate his pain in sleep.

'I can't stand this,' Rima cried brokenly. 'I can't stand this. You look so –' She took her hands away from her face, and stared at the wall. 'I won't stand it. I don't have to.' She whirled to face him. 'My father told me you killed someone.'

'It was an accident,' Yuri said, thickly. It hurt to speak.

'Now there'll be an enquiry, and we'll all be disgraced. Oh, Yasha, how could you? Couldn't you think of your wife, your duty to your family?'

Yuri wondered if Rima would have preferred it, if he had let Abyugov kill him. 'If they were going to charge me with murder, they wouldn't have let me come home.'

She looked at his face in horror. Slowly she began to shake her head, as if in disbelief. 'I can't stand it,' she muttered. 'I can't take it any more. Your goings and comings, your leaving me all alone, and now to know you've killed someone, that I'm living with a murderer.'

She raised her voice as she spoke, screaming the last word. The sudden shout set off triphammers in his head. Waves of red and black washed against his eyes. The recollection of Abyugov flailing into the darkness was like a scene from a movie, endlessly replayed. 'It was an accident,' he shouted. 'Do you hear me? An accident! The man was pilfering building materials and he attacked me!' He felt the room undulate. He staggered to a chair and sat.

Rima followed him. 'My father keeps telling me it is my duty to stand by you. That it is my duty to support you, and help you, because the work you're doing is important. But that's not possible anymore.' She looked quickly away, shuddering as she did so. 'I can't bear to look at you. I can't bear to be in the same room with you. I'm leaving you, Yasha. I'm leaving you because I can't stand it any more. I'm going home to my family.'

He heard her move away. Yuri willed himself to stand, but his body was a dead weight. He could only turn heavily in the chair.

Rima was at the open door of the apartment, already wearing her coat. His head swam.

'I'll stay with my family till you're better,' she called. 'After that you can find yourself somewhere else to live.' The door slammed behind her.

Yuri slumped back onto the chair. His mouth was dry. His head hurt. His back felt as if it had been through a mangle. He wouldn't let her go, he thought. He would. It didn't matter. He felt nothing but his physical pain. He rested his head against the back of the chair. There were things he had to do. Arrange a settlement with Aristov. Find a place to live. Investigate STF 29. His head lolled.

Later.

Yuri slept.

He woke, struggled to the bed and slept again. Woke much later, limped about the apartment and made himself some tea. He slept and woke, thinking about Zamyatin and Abyugov. He sat up and called Army Records.

'Raikin?' a cheery sounding subaltern asked, 'Any relation to the Marshal?'

'My father.'

'A hero. Let me check this on the computer for you.'

Four minutes later, the subaltern was back on the line. 'Sorry, Captain. The computer says STF 29's been Action Invalidated – wiped out by enemy action.'

'Impossible,' Yuri said. 'There are men from STF 29 in Moscow.'

'That's possible,' the subaltern admitted. 'The A I classification only requires a seventy percent casualty rate. Usually when a unit is declared A I, the survivors are transferred to other units. Anyway, STF 29 no longer exists. We have no records under that heading.'

'Try these names,' Yuri said. 'Viktor Abyugov, Sergei Kronykin.'

'Are they still in the Army, Captain Raikin?'

'No, they've been discharged.'

'In that case, I cannot help you. We do not keep records on soldiers once they've been discharged.' He paused for a moment, before adding, 'I'm sorry. Is there anything else I can do to help?'

'No,' Yuri said. 'I don't think so. Not at present.'

'Well if you think of anything, call me. I'd be very pleased to help the son of the Marshal.'

Yuri sat by the phone and dozed. When he woke, he made himself some tea and a sandwich and thought about Popov. Popov had not offered one tiny shred of proof for anything he'd said. True, his story fitted the facts, but then so could any other.

Assume, for instance, that the leak to *Young Guard* had not been made by a seditious intriguer but by a well-intentioned KGB officer. That leak had forced Deryugin to arrest Lazar and create the Zarev Commission.

But the Zarev Commission was impotent. With so many influential people involved there was no way Zarev could conduct an honest or independent investigation. In effect, Deryugin had said, bury me and you'll bury everyone with me.

Suppose then that Zarev, an ambitious and determined man, had diverted his investigation to the Sluzbha, which after all had helped keep Lazar out of jail for so long. Suppose also that he'd found Turayev guilty of corruption and discovered that Turayev, Deryugin and Popov — all Ukranians — were linked to Lazar.

Deryugin and the others would not have been able to take any overt action against Zarev. So they had countered Zarev's threat by giving Simmonds a story impugning Zarev's motives and associating him with a sinister, secret and counter-revolutionary organization.

Zarev had retaliated by confronting Turayev. Turayev, unwilling to be disgraced or betray his friends, had committed suicide. Which had left the problem of Simmonds.

Simmonds would either believe Turayev had been murdered, or that Turayev had been guilty and committed suicide. If the former, there was no problem. But if Simmonds thought Turayev had been guilty, then he would know he had been deceived. If he then talked to Zarev, his story alone would have been evidence of Deryugin's guilt – enough for Zarev to turn his investigation into a humiliating exposure of Deryugin.

So Popov and Deryugin had persuaded Zamyatin to doctor Simmonds' file and pass it to Department V. Georgi Vilna had been sent to London to kill Simmonds.

Then, Yuri had intervened and saved Simmonds. Uncertain of Yuri's motivation or Simmonds' reaction, Popov had come to London and taken charge of the enquiry into Yuri's misconduct.

In London, Popov had found Yuri innocent. He'd known a severe punishment would provoke demands from Aristov and the Marshal for an independent review of the case, which might have uncovered the real reasons for Simmonds' elimination. So Popov had decided to bring Yuri back to Moscow and keep him under his control.

Yuri had then investigated Zamyatin. He'd found out too much and Popov had decided to eliminate him. Popov had Zamyatin set up the meeting at the building site, and when Yuri had escaped, killed Zamyatin.

A credible scenario, Yuri thought. It fitted the facts as closely as Popov's tale had. But which story was true? And which side should he choose? He was too involved not to choose a side. So which side?

When giants cast shadows, Yuri thought, hope for the shade.

Later that evening, he went to Sonya's. He told her he'd been attacked while checking a building site for pilferage. Quite unneccessarily she covered him with blankets and made him sit on the terrace while she made them dinner.

Below him Moscow spread. Beyond the Novodevichy, the massive sandstone hulk of the Foreign Ministry loomed, one of seven massive constructions embedded around Moscow, ungainly castles, their spires crowned with red stars. They had been built by Stalin in what was now termed Socialist Gothic, a confection of architectural styles with an emphasis on the monumental and the atrociously ornate. While Lenin the arch revolutionary lay worshipped in his mausoleum, Stalin's monuments were used as ministries, hotels and apartments. Stalin's towers. Stalin's eyes. Sitting there, Yuri thought how level a city Moscow was, and how gross a distortion the Stalin towers were.

Sonya came on to the terrace carrying a bowl of soup. 'You should be resting,' she scolded, 'not loafing about Moscow.'

While he drank the soup, he told her of his scene with Rima.

'Spoiled little bitch!' Sonya cried. 'How could she leave you like this? You'd better move in here. You need someone to look after you.'

That wasn't altogether a bad idea, Yuri thought.

CHAPTER TWENTY-TWO

The next day Yuri went to the Procurator's office opposite Militia HQ. Procurator Maslov was a bubbly, kindly looking man who looked as if he took Pioneers on camps.

'I didn't expect to see you quite so soon, Captain,' he said. 'Are you sure you're sufficiently recovered?'

'I'm sure,' Yuri said.

Quietly, Maslov took him through the statement Yuri had given Bunin. He sucked a pencil while Yuri talked. It left a grey mark on his lower lip. The lip wobbled as Maslov said, 'I think that will be all, Captain. It's quite obvious what happened. I'll telephone Director Popov this afternoon, and you should be able to resume your duties as soon as you're fit enough.'

At the door he reached up to clap Yuri's shoulder, then shook his hand. 'You acted most courageously, Captain, most courageously. I shall mention that in my report. Obviously, you are your father's son. Give my regards to the Marshal, when you see him. Maslov is the name. Vyaslov Maslov.'

Yuri decided to walk back to the apartment. It was a brilliant morning. Open necked shirts enlivened the street with patches of primitive colour. Halfway up a building men worked on a scaffolding, their russet brown bodies gleaming. Yuri watched as women in dusty grey tunics handed up pails of bricks. His stiffness eased as he walked. He thought of Abyugov, that he had killed a man.

He went up Gorky Street, past the apartment. It was a good day for walking, and as long as he walked no shadows loomed out of his private nightmare. Opposite the Moscow Arts Theatre was the Artisticheskoya Cafe where he had once come with Gvishani to hear Akhmadulina read her poems. He climbed the hill to where the street widened into Sovetskaya Place. He examined the giant equestrian statue of Moscow's founder, Prince Dolgoruky as if he'd never seen it before. He walked on past bookshops and the Beriozka, its windows full of glass and crystal.

Near the top of Gorkovo, he turned into side streets. In a courtyard was a house with tiered rows of arches and tent-roofed towers, its walls decorated with pale green tiles. He looked at statues. He walked. As he walked he relived every moment of the scuffle with Abyugov.

In a side street off the Boulevard Ring he stopped to look at an old building with a steeply pyramidical *shatyor* roof. Its once elaborately painted mouldings were chipped and broken; its once bright tile decorations cracked and gapped. From behind triangular wooden doors came the frail sound of women chanting.

A functioning church in regular use and no *druzhinki* outside to shoo away the faint hearted. Yuri went in. Black garbed *babushki* knelt on the cement floor. Dim yellow light reflected sombrely off brocaded vestments. Brown candles burned smokily before ikons of the Virgins of Kadask and Pechatnik. Yuri felt he had stepped back into childhood.

He went to the back and sat. There were no pews, only chairs with rests attached to their backs. The raw odour of melting wax filled his nostrils. Mechanically he followed the old Slavonic chants and silently mouthed responses. This was how men had worshipped for two thousand years.

It was all superstition, he told himself. Simply convictions instilled in childhood. If he hadn't been brought up by Tanty Sima, this place would be nothing more than a museum where they conducted quaint folk ceremonies. But he felt an ethereal power here, something above and beyond him, something comforting; a sense of belonging and of peace, something that would purge him of his guilt.

He had no reason to feel guilty, he told himself. Abyugov would have killed him, and he had done what he had to do. But still, the fact of having killed weighed on him. He needed to tell someone about it, purge himself. The consequence of believing in absolute right and absolute wrong was guilt, he thought. Damn you, Tanty Sima, I miss you!

The priest turned and blessed the small congregation, a burly

161

man made even larger by his bulky vestments. His bearded face was rigid as if hiding a secret pain. The *babushki* crossed themselves, bowed and bobbed and shuffled with lowered heads to the door.

Yuri waited, unwilling to leave. The lights over the ikonostasis and along the walls went out, leaving the church lit only by the flickering spear points of candles. The whole building became dark and mysterious. Yuri felt an unseen presence permeate the space. Felt all he had to do was reach out and touch it.

A rustle of clothing disturbed him. The priest stood beside him and suddenly all mystery was gone. In a low voice the priest said, 'It is forbidden to keep the church open after service. Come back tomorrow.'

Yuri murmured, 'Father, I am a member of State Security. I have killed a man.'

The priest's hands descended on his shoulders. A finger crossed his forehead.

'The man was attempting to kill me. It was an accident.'

The priest's hands were heavy on his shoulders. 'May God, through me a sinner, forgive you.'

Yuri knelt.

When he got back to the apartment, Gvishani was standing outside, clutching a brown paper bag in one hand and pounding imperiously on the door with the other.

'No one's home,' Yuri said from behind Gvishani. 'Everyone's defected.'

Gvishani turned startled, looked even more startled when he saw Yuri's face. 'Yasha!' he breathed. 'What the hell happened to you? You look as if you got in the way of a sputnik.'

'You should see the sputnik,' Yuri muttered and unlocked the door.

Rima had been back to the apartment while he'd been out. The kitchen looked more sparse. The wonderful British cooking pot had gone. So had the portable television. In the living room two rectangles contrasted pallidly with the walls where Rima's favourite prints had hung. Yuri wondered if Gvishani had noticed.

Gvishani was taking a bottle of Zabrouska, sausages and bread from a brown paper bag.

'I'm not allowed to drink,' Yuri called, going to the kitchen and fetching plates, glasses and fruit water.

Gvishani poured a shot of the buffalo grass flavoured, pale yellow vodka for himself and filled a glass with fruit water. 'What happened to you?' he asked again. 'When the Sluzbha told me you were off sick, I thought you'd come down with the 'flu.'

Yuri told him he'd been checking a building site when he'd been attacked.

Gvishani's face remained rigid.

'Nice of you to bring me lunch,' Yuri finished.

Gvishani looked nervously round the apartment. 'Play some music,' he said, his eyes shifting to the Sanyo record player Yuri and Rima had brought back from London.

'What would you like to listen to?'

'Anything loud. I want to hear what a foreign record player sounds like.'

Yuri picked Rima's favourite Boney M. Gvishani turned up the sound. Yuri wondered if Gvishani knew *Rasputin* had only recently been made legal.

'I wanted to see you,' Gvishani said, sitting close to Yuri on the sofa, 'because the Zarev Commission is beginning an enquiry into the circumstances of Dolgov's death.' Gvishani's teeth flashed humourlessly. 'All the circumstances,' he added.

Yuri felt as if a fist had landed directly on his heart. Willing his hand to remain steady, he reached for a sausage. 'Why?' he asked.

'Dolgov was Red List,' Gvishani replied. 'No one can imagine how an intruder got into his apartment.'

'It happens,' Yuri shrugged. 'Not even the Sluzbha can be everywhere at the same time.' The Sluzbha like every police department in the world operated on the law of averages. Which meant you won some and you lost some. Then he thought, if Zarev was investigating the intrusion he must really have it in for the Sluzbha. He wondered momentarily if Popov might be right, that Zarev was not really concerned with corruption, but with ousting Deryugin.

'It is not only the question of the intrusion,' Gvishani said, his expression remote. 'There is a rumour that Dolgov was murdered.'

'The case is officially one of burglary,' Yuri said. Until he had a good reason to, he could not discuss Sluzbha business with Gvishani.

Gvishani turned angrily, his face flushing. 'Don't piss around with me, Yasha,' he shouted, above the blare of the music. 'I've put my job on the line coming here to talk to you.'

Yuri poured him more vodka. 'Maybe, just for the present, you'd better do the talking.'

Gvishani stared at him, then took the glass and downed the vodka in a single swallow. 'We know the intruder was armed,' he said, chewing a piece of bread. 'We know he got into Dolgov's apartment masquerading as a KGB chauffeur. We believe he knew Dolgov. What concerns us and many other important people, is that for some reason the Sluzbha has made no effort to trace Kronykin's weapon, to find out how he knew Dolgov's schedule or how he got hold of KGB documents and a uniform. You were the officer in charge of the investigation, Yasha. What the hell have you been doing?'

Yuri wished he could tell Gvishani. Goddamnit, he *wanted* to talk to someone! But he had a duty of loyalty to the Sluzbha. He went across and made the music louder. 'Dolgov died of a heart attack,' he said walking back. 'Professor Andronov's report confirms that.'

'We've seen Andronov's report,' Gvishani snapped. 'We don't believe Dolgov died in the car as Andronov's report implies, or as Dolgov's chauffeur confirms.'

'I haven't seen Frolov's –' Yuri began and stopped.

Gvishani raised his eyebrows in exasperation. 'Tell me Yasha, what the hell is going on? Why are you guys pretending Dolgov died naturally?'

Yuri ran his hand over his face and sighed. Gvishani was his friend. Gvishani was taking a great risk by warning him of the Zarev enquiry. He wanted to tell Gvishani it was all to do with Popov. But he had a duty of loyalty, and Igor and the Marshal had taught him never to sneak.

Gvishani said, 'Yasha, we were kids together. You're not a

164

cheat or a rogue or a liar. You're the most honest person I know. Sometimes I think almost too honest for your own good. I know you wouldn't cover up anything unless you were made to. Now tell me, who forced you? Tell me what really happened over Dolgov?'

'I can't talk about that, Vishy.'

'Don't be a fool! You don't owe that asshole Popov anything! I promise you, if the situation were reversed and I were talking to Popov he'd be singing his head off.'

'That's Popov,' Yuri said, glumly. 'I'm me.'

Gvishani sighed, and put the Zabrouska back in the paper bag. 'You're going to have to talk, Yasha. Unofficially to me, or officially to the Commission. It would be better if you spoke to me first. I could make things easy for you.'

Yuri clasped his friend's shoulder. 'Thanks a lot, Vish. But I can't do it. At least not right now.'

'Better do it soon,' Gvishani said pulling his shoulder away. Then, as if realizing he'd been too abrupt, 'Listen. If you talk to us first, you won't have any trouble. No one thinks you're to blame. No one's looking for your head on this.'

'I know that,' Yuri said.

'Then for goodness sake do something! If you cooperate now, I promise nothing will happen to you. But if you delay —' Gvishani stood up and flung his arms out in a gesture of helplessness. He picked up his brown paper bag and asked, 'How's Rima?'

Yuri shrugged.

'You two must have dinner with us soon.'

'That will be nice.' His throat felt dry.

Gvishani ruffled his hair. 'We're still friends, Yasha. Never forget that. We'll always be friends. You can talk to me at any time.' Gently, he pulled Yuri to his feet and embraced him. 'Come and talk to me when you're ready.'

After Gvishani left, Yuri sat wondering what to do. Gvishani was right. He owed Popov nothing. By his own admission Popov had brought him to Moscow as live bait. But one did not rat on one's colleagues. In the KGB one settled differences internally. And one never, under any circumstances, went to outsiders. It was a strange paradox that in an organization whose very existence depended on informers, informing was the most heinous of crimes.

The phone rang. Rima, he thought, wanting more things from the apartment. Or Gvishani with more warnings. Perhaps, even Popov.

It was Yedemsky. 'They've taken Kronykin's body to Pyatnitskoye Crematorium,' he said. 'Is your case over then, boychik?'

So while urging him to find out everything he could about Kronykin, Popov was having Kronykin cremated and wrapping up the Dolgov case. Dolgov, Yuri thought, was the crux of the matter. It was all he could be certain about. Dolgov had been murdered and Popov was hiding that fact.

Which left him with only one alternative. Find out the truth about Dolgov. And once he had the truth ... he shrugged and hoped the CIA were right in their belief that the truth made one free. 'The Dolgov case isn't over yet,' Yuri said.

'The cremation is set for three o'clock.'

'Thanks. I'll be there.'

There was only a man from Army Records at Pyatnitskoye. There was no service. Evgenya Kronykina should have been here, Yuri thought. A man should not be cremated without his family present.

The pale, matchwood coffin trundled. Curtains swished back and forth. Yuri and the man from Army Records looked at each other across the vacant space, like commuters on a train that had made an unscheduled stop.

'His family should have been here,' Yuri repeated aloud as they walked blinking into the sunshine. 'They should have been notified.'

The man patted his notebook, which he had kept open while the coffin was being prepared. He'd worn a stringy, black tie for the occasion. It was wrinkled and had a crusty yellow stain on it. 'We'll notify them right away,' he said. 'We'll send them a telegram saying that Sergei Anatolevich Kronykin will live forever in the annals of his regiment.' For a moment, the man looked as if he might salute.

So even his family would not know how Kronykin had really

died. Yuri turned and walked towards the yellow Troitsky Church. He tried not to think of Evgenya Kronykina, the numbness in that moon crater face when the telegram was received and read. First her husband, in the prime of life, now her son. He tried not to think of Kronykin. Evgenya and Sergei Kronykin were victims. Victims made him want to help.

Meanwhile, he should do something about Dolgov. Might as well start now.

CHAPTER TWENTY-THREE

The KGB man in the lobby said, 'I don't know why you've come. There's nothing left in the apartment. They came with vans and took everything away.' The KGB man had small eyes set very close together. He held onto Yuri's work pass as he spoke.

'Who?' Yuri asked.

'The General's son and some other people.'

Yuri said, 'I have to check that no confidential papers have been left behind. The General was an important man, you know.'

The security man slapped the work pass against his palm, looked from Yuri to the work pass and back again, he handed it back to Yuri. Reluctantly.

Devoid of the giant television set, the bookcase and the Scandinavian sofa, the living room looked enormous. Without pictures or personal possessions it had an air of anonymous, depressing abandonment. Yuri walked past the spot where Dolgov's body had lain to the room Dolgov had used as an office. The photographs had been removed from the walls, but the desk, chairs and filing cabinets were still there.

Yuri went through the files. Factory construction. Sales and purchases of chemicals and synthetics. Business. He meandered through the negotiations concerning the building of a methanol plant in Mogilev, a truck factory in Yauza. Nothing there. Nothing in any of the other files that showed why Dolgov was murdered, that linked Dolgov to Deryugin.

Yuri went through Dolgov's relationship with Amrocontinental. Dolgov had been a commission man, an arranger of complicated business deals, a co-ordinator of plans and ministries, a fixer. Nothing wrong with that. Every foreign company of substance needed a Russian to unravel the skeins of bureaucracy.

Dolgov had been handsomely paid. He'd paid tax on his earnings. His relationship with John Drasen of Amrocontinental had been close and friendly, going back to the mid-fifties when Drasen himself had been a mere consultant to foreign companies setting up business in Russia.

Yuri went and looked around the apartment. In the next room, a pile of torn paper and torn photographs lay heaped in a corner. Dolgov's hoard of *defitsitny* goods were gone. The dining table was still there, covered with an oilcloth. The curtains were drawn. Dolgov's outsize American refrigerator which had been large enough to store food for an army, had been taken.

In the bedroom there was a large, pale rectangle where Dolgov's portrait had been, a smaller rectangle where his medals had been displayed. The bed stood vast and empty, its coverlet gritty with a fine dust. Yuri opened the wardrobe.

Uniforms, suits, and below them shoes and two pairs of glistening boots. The uniforms were the best quality serge. He opened the drawers in the wardrobe. Underwear, socks, shirts. He'd been through all that before.

He took out the suits and the uniforms and laid them on the bed. He went through the pockets. Nothing. Yuri turned and stared at the now empty wardrobe, stared and wondered, then noticed the back of the wardrobe was panelled, remembered that Russian builders backed fitted wardrobes onto walls.

So Dolgov had been meticulous. Dolgov had been concerned about his clothes. Yuri ran his hands along the panelling and tapped. So Dolgov had been clever. The panelling sounded as empty as a used matchbox. He found the catch by the drawers looking like a piece of ornamentation, a wooden knob in the floor partly hidden by the boots. He pulled. It didn't move. He pushed. It didn't move. He tried to waggle it from side to side. No luck. He pressed. A compartment in the rear panel clicked open.

Yuri reached inside. A bundle of letters and signed photographs. Malenkov, Beria, Bulganin, Khrushchev. Stalin. Brezhnev and Andropov. Letters signed, with gratitude, with affection, with respect, with regards. Dolgov had known every Soviet leader since Lenin, and as each of them had fallen from grace or died, he'd hidden their pictures away. Dolgov had been a man with a strong instinct for survival.

Yuri read the letters. Routine congratulations on appointments and routine responses, congratulations on birthdays and acknowledgments. Letters admiring speeches, invitations pencilled, 'Please come'. Dolgov had been close to power, but not intimate with it, a hanger-on, a rider of coat tails.

He pointed a flashlight into the opening. Bare wood. Empty wood. He reached in and tapped the wood with his finger. Not hollow, but not solid, either. He shone the flashlight around the exterior lip of the compartment. Faint lines around the edges showed where it had been fitted into a larger cavity. It was not, Yuri saw, bonded to the wardrobe.

He pulled at it. Nothing happened. He pushed. He pressed his fingers against the sides, against the top, the bottom.

Nothing.

He knelt down and stared at the knob on the floor. Maybe. Perhaps. He pulled the knob. He pressed it. He tried it from side to side. He moved it up and down rapidly.

With a soft sigh of releasing air, the compartment slid forward out of the cavity. Yuri pulled it gently. It was a drawer fitted into the wood. It moved smoothly on oiled rollers. Yuri pulled the compartment to the end of its track, reached behind it and over.

Another cavity. An envelope. He eased it out.

The envelope was brown manila, stained with a stripe of light machine oil. There was no name or address on it. The flaps were sealed with blobs of wax and ribbon.

Yuri opened the envelope. Dried wax crumbled. Paper tore with the sharp sound of a starter's pistol. Inside there was a single sheet of paper, almost as stiff as cardboard.

Yuri read:

February 11, 1953.

INSTRUCTIONS

1. In the event of my death, the Staaderbank undertakes to satisfy itself that the death occurred from natural causes or from a genuine accident.

2. The bank will treat any obstruction or objection to

their investigations by the Soviet or other government authorities as proof that my death occured unnaturally.

3. Should the bank in its sole discretion conclude that my death occurred unnaturally, the bank hereby undertakes to deliver copies of the documents deposited with them this day and identified by my seal and signature across the flaps of the envelope, to Reuters, United Press International, Associated Press, Tass and seven other news agencies of similar standing.

The Staaderbank further undertakes to publish at my expense through paid advertisement, facsimiles of these documents in leading newspapers in Switzerland, France, the Federal Republic of Germany, England, the United States of America and Italy.

4. In the event of my imprisonment for any reason or if for a period of three months the Staaderbank shall not have received communication from me in the form agreed between us, the Staaderbank shall publish the information deposited with them as set out in the preceding paragraph.

5. The Staaderbank agrees that it will not examine the documents deposited with them, nor will it allow any third party access to these documents, except in the circumstances set out in this agreement.

6. All costs of the investigations made by the Staaderbank and the advertisement of the documents shall be paid out of my account at the Staaderbank.

7. In consideration of their services, the Staaderbank shall be entitled to a reasonable fee. It is agreed that such a fee shall not be less than $100,000.

8. This agreement may not be revoked for any reason by either party.

The agreement was signed by Dolgov and Dr Edouard Behr on behalf of the Staaderbank. Yuri sat on the bed, numb with shock. What had Dolgov done? What was in the documents he had deposited with the Staaderbank, that not only revealed his potential murderers, but were of sufficient interest to merit publication throughout the world?

Yuri rushed to the crevice and groped. Another packet,

smaller this time, firmer. He tore it open. Another piece of paper, dried, stiff, disturbingly brittle, and a shiny envelope, much more recent than the paper, containing what felt like small notebooks. Yuri looked at the paper. Fading blue print at the top read, Staaderbank, Zurich. Typewritten figures below showed deposits of $100,000 and $150,000 on February 26th and March 6th, 1953. The account had a number and a name. Vyssorian Dolgov!

So Gvishani and Aristov had been right about Dolgov's illegal bank account. Dolgov had received a quarter of a million dollars in 1953. A quarter of a million dollars, worth twice as much then as now. A fortune! How long would it take to earn a quarter of a million dollars? How long would it take to spend? A lifetime? Half a lifetime? In 1953, Dolgov had not been a general but a major, a simple serving soldier. Now, who would pay a major a quarter of a million dollars, and for what?

Yuri looked again at the copy of the document Dolgov had deposited with the Staaderbank. In 1953, Dolgov had done something that had made him fear for his life. He had deposited that document with the Staaderbank as insurance against being murdered. Had Deryugin been involved in whatever had happened in 1953? If so, why kill Dolgov now? Had Dolgov's blackmail finally become too much, or had Dolgov been killed for an entirely different reason?

He looked in the envelope and found two American passports. The topmost one was in the name of George Smirnin and bore a photograph of Dolgov. The second was in the name of Galina Andersson. Yuri stared uncomprehendingly at Sonya's photograph.

The shock hit him with the staccato force of a trip hammer. Dolgov had wanted to defect! And Sonya had wanted to go with him!

Why, for God's sake! With his contacts, Dolgov could have left the Soviet Union any time he wanted. And Sonya, at last the star she'd always wanted to be, must have known she wouldn't even begin to survive in the very different structure of Hollywood. And how could she have even contemplated sharing exile with the likes of Dolgov?

There will be no other men, Yasha. Now there's only you and me. You're all I want. All I've ever wanted.

Bullshit! Yuri clutched his temples in despair.

'Find anything?' the KGB man asked, when he left.

'Only something that's already been destroyed.'

CHAPTER TWENTY-FOUR

A large black Chrysler stood nudging Sonya's Fiat outside the apartment building. Yuri parked behind them and ran inside. He waved his pass at the security guard and charged the service stairs, his rage boiling and too impatient for Russian elevators.

The violence of his ascent released tension like bubbles. Abyugov's bruises knifed his chest. He shouldered the service door and bounded, panting into a corridor. A row of firmly shut doors like blinded sentinels. Tinted windows at each end of the corridor, turning the afternoon light opaque. John Drasen stepped out of Sonya's apartment buttoning his coat, larger and more solid than in photographs or on television. More vividly coloured too. His face was a suffused red.

Kazakov, Dolgov, and now Drasen, Yuri thought. All it needed was a smell of money, a whiff of influence and Matsyeva's panties rolled down like a flag at sunset. *I've always loved you, Yasha. Always. You remember the day we read Mandelstam in the boat?* He could understand Dolgov wanting to spend his last years with an attractive young woman in the West. But why had Sonya consented to become an old man's mistress, so far from home? Did the silly bitch really think that, with her impotent lover, she'd make it on her back as easily in Hollywood as in Moscow?

He stepped into Drasen's path. With an indifferent glance, the American stepped around him to the elevator. Instinctively Yuri noted: age mid-fiftyish, appearance squarish, grizzled head, rheumy eyes, tiny, red veins in the cheeks. Drasen was wearing an expensive European cut suit. Yuri turned and stared rudely. He wanted the satisfaction of violent physical contact.

With an echoing ping, the elevator arrived. Drasen stepped in. Doors whirred. Just as well, Yuri thought. Attacking important foreigners wasn't the way to resolve Dolgov's murder. He went down the corridor and jabbed furiously at Sonya's doorbell.

She came to the door, her hair tousled and mascara streaking from around her eyes, her lipstick smeared. Her blouse was open as if ripped by passionate hands. There were circular weals on her wrists, and pale blue bruises on her arms where hands had rested roughly.

'Yasha, what are you –'

'Official business,' he said and pushed his way past her.

'Yasha, what's wrong?' She came into the living room after him, massaging the bruises on her arms.

She'd looked just as dishevelled the afternoon he'd found her with Kazakov. Yuri felt the anger inside him seethe. That day he'd had the satisfaction of pulling a wilting Kazakov out of bed and pounding the shit out of him. No such release, today. He stared wildly around the apartment as she moved in front of him. Not yet.

'Yasha, what's happened?'

'This!' He thrust the passports into her face.

She reeled back and took them, looked angrily down at them, then slowly back at him. 'I can see why you're angry,' she said, softly. 'But believe me, Yasha, I've never seen these before.'

'Never seen these before,' he mimicked. 'You lying bitch!' He wanted to split the backs of his knuckles across her face.

'I've never lied to you,' Sonya cried. She flung the passports on the table. 'I've never seen those before.'

'One of them's got your picture.'

'Anyone who sends two roubles to Mosfilm can get my picture. And Dolgov had hundreds of photographs of me. Yasha, have you gone crazy or what? Why should I want to defect?'

'To be famous. To be a star. You said you wanted to be a star in Hollywood.'

'I said I wanted to work in Hollywood. There is a difference.' She went over to the table and picked up a cigarette. 'You don't eat or drink fame,' she said. 'It's something you accept, something you use. If you knew enough about it, you'd know there is no point in being famous if you can't come home. If you can't live where you belong.' She turned to face him. 'I know nothing about those passports, and I never agreed to go to America with Dolgov.'

'He asked you then?'

She nodded and spat a shred of tobacco from her lower lip. 'Yes. A week or so before he died. If you want me to tell you about it, you'd better sit down. I don't like you standing over me like a Nazi interrogator from Samoyetkin's film.'

Yuri went to an armchair and sat.

Sonya perched on the edge of the sofa. 'About a week, ten days before he died, Vyssorian called me at the studio. I was surprised to hear from him. We hadn't seen each other since . . . never mind, he said he wanted to see me and that it was important. When I refused, he pleaded, he asked me to do him just this one favour. He said he was in some kind of trouble and wanted to talk to me. So I agreed to meet him at the Plzen Restaurant in Gorky Park.

'I was waiting outside the restaurant when he came. He looked nervous, worried, uncertain. When he took my hand to lead me inside, his palms were cold. As usual he'd been drinking heavily. Inside the bar, he told me he had no stomach for Czech beer and ordered three hundred grams of vodka.'

'What did you drink?' Yuri demanded.

'Is that important?'

'In an investigation every detail is important.'

'Champagne,' she said. 'Do you want to know the brand?'

'No. Go on with your story.'

Sonya said, 'Vyssorian told me he had to leave Russia for a while, and that he was going to America. He wanted me to come with him. There would be work for me, he said. Drasen had already talked to producers and agents in Hollywood and could guarantee me the lead in a big American film.' She smiled wryly. 'Dolgov told me I would be internationally famous, a real star.'

'And so you agreed to go. And when you couldn't get an exit visa, you and he decided to defect.'

'Yasha, what the devil's the matter with you? I've told you, everything between Dolgov and me was finished. I didn't want to go with him to America or anywhere else. Besides, I'm

Russian. This is where I live. I wouldn't defect for a film part, or anything else.'

Yuri let his gaze wander round the apartment. She sounded convincing. But then why shouldn't she? She was an actress wasn't she? His gaze rested on a gleaming statuette which Sonya had won for *Christina*. Beside the statuette was his own photograph, younger, thinner, and for heaven's sake, did he really look so self-righteous? 'So what happened with Dolgov?'

Sonya ran her hands over her face, streaking her make-up even more. 'It wasn't very pleasant. I didn't mind him getting angry, but then he began to plead. He begged. He told me I was the only woman he'd ever wanted, that he couldn't leave Russia without me. He said he would place no restrictions on me in America. All he wanted was that I should go with him.' She lowered her head and ran her fingers through her hair. 'He wanted to marry me. He told me he was a rich man, that he was much older than I and that one day I would inherit all his wealth.' She looked at Yuri with a pained expression. 'He told me he had money hidden abroad, and that if I came with him, he'd tell me a secret that would make me the most influential woman in Russia.'

'What secret?' Yuri asked, quickly.

Sonya shook her head. 'I refused to go. I didn't want his money, I didn't want to know his secrets, and most of all, I didn't want to marry him.' She lit another cigarette. 'He'd drunk most of the three hundred grams while we talked. He got very angry. He told me I was a silly little bitch who didn't know what was good for me, and I'd have to go with him whether I liked it or not. I walked out of the restaurant and left him. I never saw him again.'

'Was there any way Dolgov could have compelled you to go with him?'

'Only if he kidnapped me.' She picked up the passports and let them slide back onto the table. 'I swear to you, I didn't know a thing about these.'

Given sufficient time, Yuri thought, he could break her. But there wasn't time. What was important was to get as much information as he could on Dolgov. He showed her the bank statements.

'A lot of money,' she said, returning them. 'He never spoke to me about this. He wasn't the sort of person who discussed money with women.'

Yuri asked, 'In the time you were together did he ever talk about 1953? Did he ever tell you about something he'd done then that was very important, very dangerous, something someone might want to kill him for?'

She said, 'I told you, we were not lovers who did things together or shared things. We were not a real couple. We did not share intimacies or memories.' She gave off a laugh that was hardly more than a tiny explosion of breath. 'Except when he made me listen to his stories about the war.'

'What kind of stories?'

Sonya shuddered. 'Horrible stories. How he'd beaten prisoners, how he'd tortured them to make them work. He once told me he'd strangled people with his bare hands. I think he was trying to impress me with his violence. He used to tell me that his violence had earned him great rewards.'

'Was he ever violent to you?'

Sonya nodded. 'Once. After I'd left him, he came here to ask me back. He was quite drunk, and when I refused he started to hit me. Then he tried to strangle me. Fortunately, some friends came just then. Otherwise I think he might have killed me.' She pressed her eyes with finger and thumb. 'That was the end. I never saw him alone again, until that evening in Gorky Park.'

Yuri asked, 'And he never boasted to you about anything he'd done in 1953?'

She shook her head.

'1953,' Yuri persisted. 'In 1953, someone paid Dolgov a quarter of a million dollars. After 1953 he rose very rapidly in the army. He must have told you something about 1953?'

'No.' She frowned thoughtfully. 'No. Except maybe ... oh, about a month before we broke up I went with him to some kind of regimental dinner at the Rossiya. It was a strange affair, with a lot of elderly men, who looked army or KGB though they were in civilian clothes. I felt quite out of place. There were only three other women present, and they were wives. They treated me as if I had leprosy. Vyssorian, I remember, got quite drunk and more than usually boastful. He said he knew where the bodies were buried. A nice man, Guschin, I think his name was, asked where? Vyssorian said, Zurich. He said he could bring down Deryugin's government any time he wanted.'

Yuri put the passports and bank statements away. Whatever Dolgov had done in 1953, had possibly involved Deryugin, had certainly involved money. Large sums of money. Perhaps, Yuri thought, some of the money in Dolgov's account in Switzerland, was Deryugin's. He asked, 'Did Dolgov tell you why he had to leave Russia?'

Sonya shook her head. 'No. But whatever the reason was, I think Drasen had something to do with it. A couple of days after I'd seen Vyssorian, Drasen came to see me here. He wanted me to go with Dolgov to America.'

'But wasn't – isn't – wasn't he a rival for your affections?'

'Drasen!' Sonya laughed. 'Don't be absurd! I've never had an affair with Drasen and never want to.'

'Why did Drasen want you to go to America?'

'He told me there was definitely work for me in America, that his company would guarantee my salary and expenses. He told me that Dolgov hadn't been very well, that he'd been severely depressed by business problems and needed a few months away from Moscow. He told me Dolgov loved me very much, that Dolgov would take good care of me.

'When I told him that I didn't love Vyssorian and didn't want to live anywhere with him, he said, that wasn't important. He said that in no time at all I would be an international star and then I could leave Dolgov.' Sonya laughed. 'I told Drasen an opportunity like that, he should give to his mother.'

'Then today,' Sonya continued, 'He called me at the studio and said he had to see me urgently. He knew we were finishing *Siege* and wanted to talk to me before I accepted anything else.' She threw her arms up helplessly and gave him a half smile. 'I rushed directly back from the set. Drasen still wants me to go to America. He says he's got a part for me in a big movie, that I should make arrangements to leave right away.'

'What's Drasen got to do with you?' Yuri demanded. 'What's his interest in your career?'

Sonya shrugged. 'I don't know. He said, as he'd already

made the arrangements, I might as well take advantage of them. He told me it was an opportunity I'd never have again.'

'So when are you going?'

Sonya looked directly at him and said, 'I told Drasen that you had come back into my life and that I wanted to talk it over with you first.'

What use were discussions, Yuri thought, when she was already sleeping with Drasen and determined to be a star in Hollywood. He got to his feet and put the passports into his pocket. 'We don't have anything to talk about. You go to America, if you want.'

'Yasha, what the hell's wrong?'

'You know what's wrong! I saw Drasen leave. I'm looking at you now. Look at your hair, your blouse, those marks on your arms.'

Sonya let her surprised gaze wander all over his face. Gradually she smiled. The smile turned into a laugh. She looked down at her skirt as if she'd suddenly found herself in a stranger's clothes. 'Idiot,' she murmured. 'Yasha, these are the clothes I was wearing on the set. I told you I rushed straight back from the studio. I haven't had time to change.'

'You look as if you've been tumbled in the back of a haycart.'

Sonya laughed again. 'That's almost exactly what happened.'

'With Drasen?'

'Don't be absurd.' She walked to the table and came back with a script. 'Here. That idiot Samoyetkin insisted on re-shooting this twenty-six times.' She opened the script in the middle and held it so he could read. 'Scenes Ninety-seven and Ninety-seven A.'

'That's not the end of the film,' Yuri said. 'That's from the middle.'

'Yasha, we don't shoot films the way you read a book. See here. Scene Ninety-seven.' Her finger underscoring the lines was smudged. 'Karina – that's me, I'm a farmer's daughter – walks furtively down the street.' The finger halted. She looked up at him. 'I'm actually taking a vital message to the commander of the local partisans.' She looked down at the script and read again. 'As Karina scurries past a parked truck, the cab door opens. Viliu – he's a rich farmer working for the Germans – leaps out of the cab in front of her. Frightened, Karina turns and runs back. Sychev – that's Viliu's brother and also a fascist – leaps from the back of the truck and grabs Karina. Karina struggles fiercely. The two men overpower her. They force her to the pavement, bind and gag her and throw her into the back of the truck.' Sonya lowered the script. 'You have that done to you twenty-six times in one day and you'd look a mess too.' She tossed the script on the sofa and looked amusedly at her hands. 'You should see my back,' she smiled, 'it's as bruised as yours after being tossed so many times into that truck.'

Yuri stared at her. Maybe she was telling the truth. His eyes wandered over the torn blouse and rumpled skirt. Sonya was wearing her own clothes! Brusquely, he pushed past her. 'Sounds like a good film,' he said, 'I'll think of your back when I see it.'

'Yuri, don't be stupid!'

Yuri kept walking to the door.

'Yuri Gennadovich,' she shouted after him. 'You are a stupid, sanctimonious prig!'

As he turned to close the door, her look of angry despair cut through him like a knife.

CHAPTER TWENTY-FIVE

The next morning, Yuri went straight down to Sluzbha Records and asked for Drasen's file. Drasen was a link to Dolgov and a safe area of investigation; a reason why Dolgov had to leave Russia and possibly a participator in whatever had happened in 1953. Best of all, he could investigate Drasen without disobeying Popov's direct orders.

The file clerk was an elderly woman with greying hair drawn neatly to the back of her head in a bun. 'To examine that file you need an authorization personally signed by the Director,' she said.

Yuri felt excitement twitch like plucked violin strings. There was a connection between Dolgov and Drasen, and Popov was doing his best to hide it. 'I didn't know,' he said. 'I'll talk to the Director and be back later.'

'Not without an authorization in writing,' the records clerk said severely. 'What happened to your face?'

'I fell over tying my shoelaces.'

Yuri went to his office, feeling cheerfully defiant.

'What the devil are you doing here?' Pasha growled from behind his desk. 'You're supposed to be off sick.'

'Wanted to make some free phone calls.'

Pasha stood up and ambled around the desk. 'I suppose you want your chair, then. Just as well I've got to go out and check on this *fartovchik*.'

Yuri sat in his chair, still warm from the heat of Pasha's body.

At the door Pasha turned. 'Make your phone calls and go home. Your face has more colours than a cat's vomit.'

Yuri blew him a kiss, and watched the door posts shudder at the passage of Pasha's shoulders.

The Sluzbha wasn't the only organization which kept records. An influential and important man like Drasen had

182

contact with other organizations, and where there was contact, there were always records. Yuri called the Ministry of Foreign Trade.

Yes, they had volumes of information on John Drasen, but to provide that information, even to the Sluzbha, would take months. They could however confirm that Drasen's business was properly and responsibly run, and that it had always complied with the laws of the Soviet Union. John Drasen, they said, was a good friend to the USSR.

And like Dolgov, a hero, Yuri thought sourly. He pondered a while, then called Militia Records and asked if they had any information on Drasen.

Unlikely, he was told. Foreigners were looked after by the KGB. However, the clerk promised to check and call Yuri if he found anything.

Yuri pondered a while longer and called Gvishani. 'I want to talk to you.'

'Of course, Yasha. Come around as soon as you can.'

Yuri left straight away. The Zarev Commission was housed in the Central Committee offices in Staraya Square, a short walk from KGB Headquarters. Flags snapped briskly over the grey pre-revolutionary building, and there were armed guards everywhere. One checked Yuri's work pass and conducted him to a vast lobby. From walls covered with red baize, Lenin looked down, sailors seized Kronstadt and White Russian armies fled in confusion.

Yuri was ushered into a smaller room, whose walls were draped with Soviet flags and pictures of Deryugin. A while later, a dumpy girl conducted him in a cage-like elevator to the fourth floor.

Gvishani's office was spacious, with panelled walls and a heavy mixture of Oriental carpets, revealing a public personality that was rather more flamboyant than his private one.

'Yasha, I'm so glad you've decided to come. If you like, we can go to lunch and talk.'

'I'm meeting someone for lunch,' Yuri said. 'And what I've come for is information on John Drasen. Our file on him is closed to everyone but Popov.'

Gvishani's lips parted in that now familiar humourless smirk.

'And what will you do for us, Yasha,' he asked softly. 'Will you tell us about the Dolgov case?'

'Not yet. But I've taken your advice and re-opened the Dolgov investigation.'

'Obviously without the knowledge of Comrade Director Popov.'

Yuri nodded.

'So what's your interest in Drasen?'

'Dolgov worked closely with Drasen. I think Drasen may have been involved in his death.'

'Interesting,' Gvishani murmured.

'I know that at the time he died, Dolgov was planning to leave Russia. I have the fake passport he intended to use.'

Gvishani came suddenly erect. From behind the thick lenses, his eyes fixed themselves on Yuri. 'Where's the passport?' he asked.

Yuri ignored the question and continued. 'I believe Dolgov wanted to avoid testifying before the Zarev Commission. I also believe his testimony would have endangered many people, and that one of those people was John Drasen. I believe Drasen made arrangements for Dolgov to leave Russia, illegally if necessary.'

Gvishani raised his eyebrows enquiringly. 'How did you find that out?'

'The false passports were American,' Yuri said.

'Who else knows about this?'

'Only you.'

'And so you want to find out what we know about Drasen?'

Yuri nodded.

Gvishani shook his head, ruefully. 'Yasha, you can't expect us to help you, if you won't help us.'

Yuri said, 'You know I can't.'

Gvishani toyed with a gold capped fountain pen. 'We have lots of information on Drasen,' he said, slowly. 'But it wouldn't be proper for me to share it with you.' He flashed a brief, sarcastic smile. 'We too, have principles, you know.'

Yuri looked into his friend's face. Its watchful impassivity reminded him of Aristov. Already, he thought, Gvishani had acquired the soulessness of a Party brahmin. He said, 'In that case, I'd better try somewhere else,' and stood up.

'Wait,' Gvishani said, sharply. He came quickly around the desk. 'Let me have a word with Comrade Zarev.'

Gvishani returned twenty minutes later, accompanied by Soslan Zarev, bigger and more rotund than in his photographs, the familiar wing of black hair swooping low over his forehead. As usual he wore an old fashioned Russian peasant tunic with a short, upright open collar. His flesh had a solid, shiny look.

'Raikin,' Zarev said softly, advancing into the room. 'The son of the Marshal.' With magnificent theatricality he clasped Yuri to his chest. He held Yuri at arm's length and smiled at him. 'I believe you're something of a hero, too.' Warmth and sincerity flowed. 'This is indeed a privilege, Captain Raikin. Let me shake you by the hand.'

Zarev did.

Zarev said, 'From what I hear, you won a whole country for us.'

'It wasn't me,' Yuri replied. 'It was the Stalin Organs.'

'The Stalin Organs? How interesting. What were they?'

'One hundred and twenty millimetre cannon,' Yuri explained, 'with a range of twelve kilometres.' He told Zarev that the Africans were terrified of artillery and that these big guns had frightened them so much that quite often they'd taken whole towns without the loss of a single man.

'I'm afraid you're too modest, Captain.' Above Zarev's smile, a diamond bright sheen masked his eyes. 'From what I heard, you did more than recommend the use of artillery.' His smile became a vivid, white flash. 'Gvishani tells me you're doing something much more heroic now. I have instructed him to give you whatever help you need. Nothing must be allowed to stand in the way of truth or justice. We must seek out corruption wherever it exists and tear it out by the roots.' He raised a clenched fist in a gesture of tearing up roots, and lowere his voice to a dramatic whisper. 'Only then can we build the new Russia.' Zarev stopped, as if suddenly realizing he wasn't addressing a meeting of young Communists. The smile winked like a neon sign. 'If there is anything at all we can do to help, you must tell us.' With a grandiose touching of hands and an extravagant wave Zarev left.

Gvishani turned to Yuri, a rapturous expression on his face. 'Isn't he wonderful, Yasha,' he crowed. 'And he liked you. He wanted to meet you. You know you've really got a powerful friend in Comrade Zarev.'

And a good actor, Yuri thought and said, 'Tell me about Drasen.'

With a gesture reminiscent of Zarev's, Gvishani waved him to a chair.

'It's a love story,' Gvishani said, 'at least at the beginning.' He sounded a little like their friend Dimitri outlining a sequel to his 'multi-faceted' novel. 'Drasen first came to Russia in 1942, assisting in Soviet-American cooperation during the Great Patriotic War. He remained in Russia until the war ended, and during this time fell in love with Valentina Dankova, a sergeant in the Transport Corps. Back in America, Drasen got himself a divorce and came back to Russia as a Third Secretary in the American Embassy.' Gvishani shrugged. 'We and the Americans both disapproved of an American diplomat having a liaison with a Russian. Four months afterwards Drasen was sent back.

He spent the next year on leave from the State Department completing a master's thesis in economics. Then, he was sent to Europe to help administer the Marshall Plan.'

Gvishani fidgeted momentarily with the gold capped pen. 'According to what he told us afterwards, Drasen was an economic idealist. He had hoped the Marshall Plan would help create a world economy in which capitalist and socialist systems would work together for the benefit of all. In fact, all the Marshall Plan did was perpetuate an outmoded economic system by creating American economic colonies for the benefit of American capitalists. So, early in 1950, Drasen defected.'

'Defected?' Yuri echoed, surprised.

Gvishani nodded. 'That's what it says on his file.'

Yuri frowned, puzzled. Drasen was big business. He had built enormous factories and participated in huge industrial projects. He was not an economic idealist, but the archetype of a Wall Street capitalist.

'After the usual de-briefing,' Gvishani continued, 'Drasen was assigned to the State Bank, to work under ...' Gvishani paused for effect, 'Pyotr Deryugin. Deryugin was greatly impressed by Drasen's knowledge of theoretical economics and his ideas of socialist-capitalist cooperation. Together, Deryugin and Drasen began to put those theories into effect.

'At the end of 1950, Drasen married his Russian lover and started work as an advisor to the State Bank. He remained there until November 1952, when he left Russia and went to Europe for three weeks. In January 1953, he went away again, this time for twenty six days. In February 1953, he went away twice, both for short periods, and then, in early March, he left with his wife and took up residence in Switzerland.'

'You mean, Drasen defected back?' Yuri asked, astounded.

Gvishani shrugged and smiled. 'It gets more confusing as we go on. In Switzerland, Drasen incorporated a business consultancy, Drasen Associates SA. Three years later, in 1956, he returned to Russia and with the approval of the Economics Ministry opened an office in Moscow. The Economics Minister at the time was –' Gvishani flourished the fountain pen he was toying with '– Pyotr Deryugin!'

So that was the connection between Deryugin and Drasen, Yuri thought, excitedly.

'And the person Drasen put in charge of that office, and who ran it for many years afterwards was the late and too little lamented General Vyssorian Dolgov.'

And, Yuri thought, the circle was complete. 'What business did Drasen do in Russia?' Yuri asked.

'At the beginning, he was mainly a broker, arranging loans from Western commercial institutions to various arms of the State. Later, he extended his services to Western companies wanting to trade in Russia and needing expertise in dealing with Russian bureaucracy. Then he changed the name of his company to Amrocontinental and became an investor as well as a broker. By the early sixties, Drasen had permanent offices on the Quay Maurice Thorez, and his staff had grown from three to fifteen. In the 1970s when the mad rush of Western investment began, Drasen stood plumb in the forward line. He has been directly or indirectly responsible for at least sixty percent of the foreign investment in this country.'

Yuri whistled softly.

Gvishani said, 'What is significant is that Drasen could not have achieved any of this without Russian help. Since 1950, Drasen's friend and main supporter has been former Controller of the State Bank, former Minister of Economics and present General Secretary of the Party Secretariat, Pyotr Deryugin.' Gvishani smiled and added, 'I suppose you could say Deryugin was demonstrating a Stakhanovite enthusiasm for helping the capitalists provide the rope with which they would hang themselves. I wish that were true.'

He steepled his fingers and stretched his hands out over the desk. 'The truth is that the Drasen-Deryugin axis is only a manifestation of a deeply laid conspiracy to change Russia; a conspiracy of those who want to abandon the principles of Marxist-Leninism for the principles of capitalism, a conspiracy which seeks to exploit Russian labour and Russian skills for the benefit of foreign entrepreneurs, a conspiracy which is turning Russia into a capitalist pig-sty.'

'But why?' Yuri asked. 'We may be less efficient than the West, but we are a young country. Our revolution is only sixty-five odd years old. And militarily we are the equal of the West, if not superior.'

'And given time,' Gvishani said, 'Russian brains and Russian skills could make Russian industry equal to anything in the West. We do not need to prostitute outselves for foreign investment or foreign technology. *Pust khuze, da nashe.* Let it be worse, but let it be ours.'

'In that case why the involvement with foreigners?'

Gvishani's eyes sparkled behind the thick lenses. 'It is profitable,' he said, bitterly.

'So Lazar . . .'

'Was simply a minor instance of how low people will stoop for a small profit.' He pursed his lips as if to spit and thrust his head across the desk. 'Now do you see what we are fighting? You see why we need every bit of help we can get. If we are to survive as Russians we have to stop people like Drasen and Deryugin. Yasha, will you help?'

'If I can,' Yuri said, overwhelmed.

Yuri met Vasili at a *stolovaya* near the State Bank. It was just before noon and the lunch hour crush had not properly begun. Vasili sat at a table covered with cracked plastic, while Yuri collected cabbage soup and fried meat patties from the counter.

'General Vyssorian Dolgov,' Yuri said as he sat.

'Who was buried recently?'

'The very same. We are carrying out a few background inquiries.'

Vasili's face assumed the blankness of anyone faced with a KGB inquiry.

'Dolgov opened an account at the Staaderbank in Zurich on February twenty-sixth, 1953. We want to know if it was authorized. We also want to know if permission was granted for the payment of $100,000 into that account on the twenty-sixth of February, and another $150,000 on March sixth.'

'1953,' Vasili said. 'A long time ago. I'll look into it.'

Yuri said, 'I'll see you here at the same time tomorow.'

Vasili smiled, hesitantly. 'If the KGB are buying lunch twice, it must be important.'

'When do you go to London?' Yuri asked.

'That's been deferred till January.'

'Is there anything we can do?' Yuri asked and thought, *ty mne i ya tebe*.

Vasili smiled. 'If there is, I'll call. I have your number.'

CHAPTER TWENTY-SIX

Beside the athletics track runners bent and twisted, stretching muscles like coiled snakes. Along the track, sprinters exploded, kicked round turns with bodies leaning precariously outwards. Like a persistent fly on a flag pole, a pole vaulter soared repeatedly through the air.

Yuri ran alone, his body automatically geared to a steady, seven minute pace. Two runners surged past him, feet bombing off the track in high lifting strides. Yuri sensed their passage like a distant rush of wind. Three thousand metres into his own run and he was withdrawing into himself.

His mind was passive, aware, a still point in a surging maelstrom of muscle and blood. Already, images of Sonya, Gvishani, thoughts of Drasen, Dolgov and Deryugin had receded.

As he ran, the white lines of the track became walls that enclosed him. His consciousness focused on his breathing and the ceaseless hammering of his legs. Banks of floodlights flashed endlessly over him. He raced with his own burnt out shadow.

Running was endless. Running allowed things to happen. Running was awareness, communion with oneself. When one ran, one was always present and free of the sequence of time.

Five thousand metres. His head throbbed in rhythm with the pounding of his feet and the pounding of his heart. He ran, sucking air deep. He felt himself becoming detached from that straining body and pounding heart.

He floated.

Mechanically his mind clicked off the laps, calculated. Eight thousand metres. He felt strong and full of energy. He could run forever.

Distance running was the pastime of the obsessional, of the individualist. Distance walking too. Endless repetition that reinforced the ability to persist in the direction of the greatest resistance. Lenin had been a great walker. Lenin had been an individualist. And obsessional.

Yuri felt the quiet excitement of a new perception. Lenin had succeeded not through the principles of socialism, but by the imposition of his individualism upon a philosophy of committee rule. Socialism, Communism, all depended on individuals. Marx, Engels, Lenin. There had been no great theorists since Lenin. Perhaps all Russian academics should take up long distance running. Create a nation of individuals. Lenin had been an individual and through the imposition of his individualism, changed history. History was the history of individuals. Without individuals, the masses were doomed.

Heresy!

Yuri ran. He was all fluid motion, his legs stretching effortlessly, almost without sensation. He drew level with another runner, heard a rasp of ragged breathing as he went past. Thoughts speckled his brain like insects darting into water. Air flowed through his body, in and out, out and in, repeated, endless. The lanes became walls, the walls became tunnels. Lights blazed. Between the walls, the track was blue. Light blurred. Sweat cascaded. His body glowed. Pulse throbbed. Thoughts throbbed.

Dolgov. He saw now that what had happened in 1953 was incidental, the first in a series of events that had allowed Dolgov, Deryugin and Drasen to make unimaginable personal fortunes from Russian industry. Dolgov, ever cautious and innately suspicious had wanted to protect himself from Deryugin and Drasen, and so had drawn up that document and left it with the Staaderbank. Perhaps Drasen and Deryugin had drawn up similar documents for their own protection from their so-called friends.

The three of them had been at the top of the dung heap of corruption that permeated Russian industry. For them the hoarding of leather for the manufacture of *na levo* handbags, the payments for dead souls or fictitious industrial projects, had been small change. They had built giant factories, they had directed whole industries. Deryugin had run the country's economy.

Looked at in terms of the Dolgov affair, Deryugin's policies of encouraging Western investment, of political and economic liberalism acceptable to Western public opinion, were not the acts of a Russian leader. They were the acts of a business man, of a self-seeking, unprincipled and corrupt capitalist.

Yuri remembered rumours that Deryugin admired Henry Ford as much as Lenin. They were not rumours to him anymore. They were the truth. Deryugin with Dolgov and Drasen had encouraged the industrial development of Russia in the manner which would best fill their own pockets.

They had been paid by Western businessmen, anxious to exploit cheap and docile Russian labour. They had been paid by Regional Committees anxious to attract new industry to their regions. They had been paid by suppliers, contractors, heads of enterprises, and even Ministers. Very simply, they had been bribed and given bribes. And the amounts had been enormous, and involved numerous others. The names in the vaults of the Staaderbank must have been piled as high as the money.

That had been Dolgov's secret!

No wonder, when Dolgov had been asked to testify before the Zarev Commission, Drasen, Deryugin, everyone had panicked. Dolgov had been depressed, he'd become unstable, was drinking heavily and had become increasingly indiscreet when drunk. Indubitably, they had all combined to persuade Dolgov to leave Russia.

So why hadn't Dolgov gone? Had it been his passion for Sonya, or had he demanded an impossible sum for a lifetime of lonely exile. For whatever reason, he had stayed and they had despatched him another way, trusting Popov to stifle any investigation into his death.

Which only left the question why Drasen was trying to persuade Sonya to leave Russia now. Did he simply want a liaison with her in America? But why go to all that trouble and expense when he could have her any hot afternoon in Moscow? *Could* he have her on any hot afternoon in Moscow?

I've never had an affair with Drasen. I've never lied to you, Yasha.

Yuri ran on. Would Drasen, a businessman and a capitalist, have endangered a long standing business relationship, by playing around with the woman he knew Dolgov loved? Would Drasen, if he wanted her, have attempted to persuade her to go to America with Dolgov?

He ran faster and faster. The answer was obvious. The truth was they feared Dolgov had told Sonya too much, and that the Zarev Commission, knowing of her past relationship with Dolgov, could force her to reveal what she knew. And if that was the truth, Sonya hadn't lied.

I've never lied to you, Yasha. Never, ever!

And if she hadn't lied, he was a prig.

Prig!

The lights blurred. He sprinted. The sounds of desperate breathing filled his ears. Prig! Lights blurred. Walls blurred. He reached the end of his tunnel.

She opened the door to him, her hair tousled, hands pulling a towelling bathrobe around her body. Her legs were bare, her skin seemed burnished. Bare toes gripped the carpet. 'What is this, Yasha? An arrest?' Her voice was low, modulated. Her eyes darted inquiringly.

'Being a prig is also an offence. I've come to give myself up.'

She stepped away from the door and laughed. 'You stupid, silly, sweet idiot!'

In bed, she guided him into her. 'Gently, darling, gently. We have aeons of time.'

'Also, we have a lot to make up for.'

Their mouths joined. She wrapped her legs around him. Yuri moved inside her with a fierce tenderness. Their open eyes scoured each other's faces. Her breasts cushioned his chest. Nipples touched. He was enclosed in her and she was in him. They were part of each other.

One.

One being. One love. Her eyes sparkled with the ferocity of distant stars. The sensation of her gaze was like a caress.

She was all around him. Part of him. He tasted her skin. He was drunk on the scent of her body. He pulled her hair around his face.

She sighed into his mouth, not letting him go, sighed again, and pulled his head against hers, projected her tongue into him as she rose around him, engulfed him, enveloped him.

Their world exploded.

They drowned.

CHAPTER TWENTY-SEVEN

Yuri and Vasili met at the same *stolovaya* near the State Bank.

'The opening of Dolgov's account was authorized,' Vasili said, over his *kotoleta*. 'But I couldn't find any authorization for the payments. However, three days before the dates you gave me, payments of $100,000 and $150,000 were made to Drasen Associates in Zurich.'

'Who authorized the opening of Dolgov's account and the payments to Drasen Associates? Yuri asked.

Vasili lowered his head over his plate. 'The payments were authorized by Comrade Deryugin,' he mumbled. 'In 1953, he was Controller of the State Bank.'

At last, Yuri thought, hard evidence that linked Deryugin, Drasen and Dolgov together. He asked, 'What were the payments to Drasen for?'

'Licences for the manufacture of optical glass suitable for military purposes.'

Yuri remembered how his father had described the race to occupy Germany at the end of the war, a race not to extract vengeance, but to enlarge the buffer zone between Russia and the West and to seize Germany's industrial assets. Wars, the Marshal had said, were not about ideology but economics. Entire factories had been dismantled and shipped back to Russia. In 1945, Karl Zeiss of Jena had been the largest and the most technologically advanced manufacturer of optical equipment in the world.

'By 1953 we knew all there was to know about the manufacture of optical glass,' Yuri said. 'We'd taken the information from the Germans.'

Vasili looked uncomfortable. 'Now you're talking of something I know nothing about,' he said.

A nineteenth century writer had said, once a man indulges in murder, very soon he comes to think little of robbery; and from robbery he comes next to drinking ...

Obviously, the converse was also true. One started with theft, then went on to bribery, tax evasion and murder, a summary of man's essential pre-disposition to anti-social behaviour. A summary, Yuri thought, of the Dolgov case.

In 1953 Deryugin and others had stolen a quarter of a million dollars from the State. They'd got the money out on the pretext of buying false licences and secreted it in Dolgov's name in Zurich. Another instance of how low people would stoop to make a profit. But what had Deryugin and the others done with all that money? How could anyone need so much? How could anyone lie, cheat, steal and murder for it?

Yuri returned to the apartment and started to pack. The previous night he had agreed to move to Sonya's. Already the place where he and Rima had lived felt as anonymous as a lodging house. But then, it had never really been a home, had it?

There wasn't much he needed and there wasn't much he wanted to take. He packed clothes into cases and books into crates. When he'd carried them down to the car, there was just one small case that wouldn't fit. Not much to show for eighteen months of marriage, he thought, but then it hadn't been much of a marriage. He drove to Sonya's feeling as if he'd suddenly been relieved of a burden he didn't know he'd been carrying.

He unloaded the books and clothes at Sonya's and went to KGB Headquarters where he allowed himself to be prodded and poked by a brusque doctor, who made him breathe deeply and put a stethescope to his back and chest and told him he could return to work the next day.

He handed the doctor's certificate to Personnel, and left through the exit on Kirov, joining the five o'clock exodus from the KGB's office that often resembled a mass breakout from the Lubyanka below.

Swept along by the throng, he wondered how much Drasen and Deryugin had stolen. Lazar had amassed three hundred million roubles. But Drasen and Deryugin had been robbing an entire nation. One billion, five billion, his mind boggled at such sums of money. What did anyone do with it? You only slept in one bed at one time, lived in one house.

As he turned into Dzerzhinsky Square, a large black limousine edged onto the curb in front of him. Arkady Aristov was seated in the rear, glowering furiously. Brown fedora jammed across the centre of his head, large Havana smouldering between stubby fingers, he reminded Yuri of the villain in one of those black and white gangster movies he used to see with Gvishani.

'Get in,' Aristov said, swishing down the electric window and beckoning.

Yuri climbed into an interior of leather and soft carpets. A glass screen separated them from the driver, and below it was a complex looking short wave radio. Fitted into the backrest beside the radio was a fold down desk. All the comforts of home, Yuri thought, and wondered if the seats reclined into beds and if there was a refrigerator full of vodka and caviar in the boot.

His head snapped back as the car squealed away from the curb, heading for the centre lane.

Aristov lurched for the intercom, his face livid. 'Slow down, you damned fool!' he yelled to the driver. 'We aren't going anywhere. Just drive around, slowly.' He slammed down the intercom and turned breathlessly to Yuri. 'All Central Committee chauffeurs have this power complex,' he commented hoarsely. 'By instinct they head for the reserved lane at a hundred miles an hour.' Then, frowning, he asked, 'What's all this nonsense about you divorcing Rima?'

'It isn't nonsense,' Yuri said. 'It's going to happen.'

Aristov pulled fiercely at his cigar; its glow seemed to kindle smaller, fiercer fires in his eyes.

'Our marriage isn't working,' Yuri explained. 'Both of us would be happier if we separated.'

'You may be happier,' Aristov grunted, 'but not Rima. That damned fool is in love with you.'

'It isn't love,' Yuri said. 'It's just Rima unhappy at not getting her way.'

Aristov stabbed the air with his cigar. 'You realize you'll

have to vacate the apartment,' he growled. 'I didn't get that apartment for you.'

Yuri said, 'I'm leaving tonight. I'll leave the keys with the caretaker.'

'Where are you going? Your father's?'

Yuri stared pointedly in front of him. There was no reason for him to discuss Sonya with Aristov. The limousine drifted slowly along Marx Prospekt. From the mosaics along the side of the Metropole Cinema revolutionary troops looked down, frozen in stationary advance. Crowds hurried along the broad pavements. Ahead, rows of traffic lights winked.

Aristov asked, 'What kind of settlement are you offering?'

Yuri started. He hadn't thought of a settlement. 'There won't be any alimony,' he said. 'There are no children and Rima is able to work.' Besides, she had a father who would keep her in the style in which she had been brought up, Yuri thought, but he didn't say that.

'I meant your joint property.' Aristov was looking at him with a triumphant gleam in his eyes.

Yuri reached forward and took a sheet of paper from the fold down desk. Carefully, he signed it at the bottom and gave it to Aristov. 'Tell Rima to fill that up however she likes.'

Aristov looked slowly from the paper to Yuri. 'You really mean that? You realize she could take everything that is jointly yours?'

Yuri shrugged. 'I've never been interested in things,' he said.

Aristov looked wonderingly from Yuri to the paper and back again. 'I always thought you a fool,' he snarled. 'I didn't realize till now, how big a fool.'

'Better foolish and happy than clever and sad,' Yuri retorted.

Aristov gave a low, rumbling laugh. They drove majestically around inner Moscow, moving along the Kremlovskaya. Aristov grunted and asked, 'You have another woman?'

Yuri didn't say anything. Ahead the hulk of the Rossiya loomed.

Aristov said, 'Being married doesn't mean you can't have other women. All it takes is organization and discretion.'

'That isn't marriage.'

'So you will go to this other —'

'The basic fact is that Rima and I don't have a life together. We are two separate people, staying in the same apartment. I am unhappy and whatever Rima says, she is unhappy too. You only have to look at her to know it.'

Aristov stared out of the car window. In a low voice he rumbled, 'If you won't do it for Rima, then do it for me.'

Yuri looked at him in surprise.

Aristov said, 'In September, I am being considered for full membership of the Politburo. Any scandal would ruin my chances.'

'Our divorce wouldn't be a scandal,' Yuri said. 'These days everyone gets divorced. Moscow has a higher divorce rate than Los Angeles.'

'That may be true, but it is irrelevant. In my situation everyone is an enemy. And my enemies will use anything to discredit me, even saying my daughter's marriage ended in divorce because I was an improper father.'

'Who would believe that?' Yuri challenged.

'People believe not what is true but what is necessary.' Aristov unwrapped another cigar. 'We Russians are the most conservative people on earth, Yuri. Never forget that.' He rolled the cigar absentmindedly in his fingers. 'All I want is that you stay with Rima for a few weeks. I will speak to her. You will be able to live your own life.'

'And what kind of a life do you think that will be for her, knowing I am with her only to help your candidacy for the Politburo. What do you think that would do to Rima?'

Aristov sat in thoughtful silence till they were back in Dzerzhinsky Square. He gave the driver fresh instructions, then sighed and said, 'Perhaps you're right. But I won't have you divorcing Rima until after September. I insist you do at least that for me.'

There was no urgency for a divorce, Yuri thought, except as proof of mutual relinquishment. He hadn't even spoken to Sonya about marriage. 'All right,' he said.

Aristov got his cigar going, and as if that gave him confidence, said, 'You're a fool, Raikin. Giving up Rima. Giving up my protection. I can be of great help to you. Have you thought about that?'

'I have,' Yuri said.

Aristov squirmed sideways in his seat and eyed Yuri narrowly. 'There are stories about you. In London, you helped a double agent defect. There are rumours that you are a double agent yourself.'

'Those rumours were thoroughly investigated in London,' Yuri said. 'And found to be untrue.'

'We know about that investigation. There is a suspicion, that you were only exonerated because the chief investigator was also a double agent.'

'That's ridiculous! Popov may be lots of things, but he's certainly not a CIA agent.'

Aristov sighed, hugely. 'Who would have thought that Lavrenti Beria was a British agent? They executed him for that, you know.' He drew deeply at his cigar and turned away. Staring straight ahead, he said, 'Popov's in trouble over Dolgov. You too. You're a damned fool to take the blame for Popov.'

'I'm carrying out my own investigation into Dolgov's death,' Yuri said.

Aristov gave him a sharp sideways glance, then busied himself with stubbing out his cigar. 'I can be of great help to you on General Dolgov,' he said. 'You must feel free to come to me at any time. Your problems with Rima,' he shrugged, 'we shouldn't let them come between us. I've always liked you, Yuri, even though sometimes you're a damned fool.'

Sonya had prepared a special dinner to celebrate their reunion. She'd spent all afternoon at Gastronom No. 1, once famous as Yesilevsky's where only the Czarist aristocracy had shopped, buying caviar, bread, rice, wine, chocolate and a fine fillet of beef. She'd peeled onions, sliced mushrooms, cut the meat into razor thin slices. She'd set the table with candles, put Bizet and Vivaldi softly on the record player.

While they ate, Yuri told her everything that had happened in London, and afterwards.

Sonya listened with increasing horror. 'Oh God, Yasha!' she cried when he'd finished. 'I'm so scared. Scared for you . . . for us. I've just found you and . . . and . . . ' she covered her face with her hands. 'If anything should happen to you, I couldn't bear it.'

'There's nothing to worry about,' Yuri said, reaching across and gently pulling her hands away from her face. He looked reassuringly into her eyes. 'Nothing at all, I promise you.'

'I don't believe you,' she said.

'I have powerful friends,' Yuri said. 'Soslan Zarev. Gvishani. Even Aristov.'

'Aristov,' Sonya repeated. 'You've walked out on his precious daughter, you've prejudiced his political career, and you think Aristov is a friend! Yasha, have you gone mad or something?'

'There's still Gvishani and Zarev.'

'Fine friends! A careerist and someone who will sell his mother if it suits him. Yasha, why are these people helping you?'

'Rodina,' Yuri said, confidently. 'For Russia.'

'Russia,' Sonya scoffed. 'People like Aristov, Gvishani and Zarev don't give a fig for Russia. All they're interested in is themselves.'

'You don't know what you're talking about,' Yuri snapped. 'They may be selfish, but they care enough to want to fight Deryugin.'

'Why?' Sonya demanded. 'Do you know that they are more or less corrupt than Deryugin? Do you believe they like power less? Do you think they care more for Russia, more for the Russian people? Let me tell you something, Yuri Gennadovich. When people get power and go behind those big red Kremlin walls, they forget Russia and they forget the people. All they care about is holding on to power.'

'You're talking nonsense, Sonya,' Yuri said. 'These people want to help me.'

'And don't you trust them,' Sonya cried and burst out sobbing.

CHAPTER TWENTY-EIGHT

The next morning, Yuri went to the office, thoughtful and more than a little confused. Pasha came in, grinning over an armful of transcripts. 'Your face is less colourful,' he announced. 'So you must be better.' He dropped the transcripts on Yuri's desk. 'I'll let you sit here and go through those today. Tomorrow, I want you on a stake-out at the Cafe Aramat. Dress like a hippy. We're going to bust a drug dealer.'

'I'll wear bells,' Yuri promised.

He spent the rest of the day fiddling with the transcripts, thinking about Drasen, Deryugin and Dolgov, worrying if he could trust Gvishani and Zarev. Midway through the afternoon, the clerk from Militia Records called. Four weeks ago, he said, the Militia had been called to investigate a burglary at Drasen's apartment. Some money and some jewellery had been taken. Also a gun. An Iver-Johnson .22. The clerk gave Yuri the serial number. The case was still open, he said, though they had abandoned all hope of finding the burglar. The KGB had been notified, and the clerk was surprised there was no record in their files.

Yuri put the phone down. A gun. An Iver-Johnson. His chest felt tight with excitement. He pulled out his notes on the Dolgov case and checked.

The gun Kronykin had been carrying, had been an Iver-Johnson, an uncommon weapon in America; two of them in Moscow was an impossible coincidence!

For the rest of the afternoon, Yuri toyed with the transcripts, unable to work. It was an unlikely coincidence that Kronykin had burgled Drasen's apartment and stolen his gun; an even more unlikely coincidence that Kronykin had bought Drasen's gun from a dealer in illegal weapons. So, Drasen must have given Kronykin his gun, told him to use it if the cyanide didn't work, and afterwards reported its loss to the Militia.

Mentally, Yuri summarized what had happened. Dolgov had refused to leave and they had decided to kill him. Drasen, who had known Dolgov longest, must have known of the accident in which Kronykin's father died. Checking out Kronykin, Popov would have discovered that Kronykin was in trouble with the authorities. They must have thought all their name days had come at once! Kronykin had a separate motive for killing Dolgov. Kronykin was known to be mentally unstable, and had sufficient experience of weapons and physical combat to accomplish his task. By a combination of threats and promises, they had persuaded him to murder Dolgov.

But how to prove it? How to get one of them to talk? There was no way he could confront Deryugin, and Popov would simply order his arrest. Which left only Drasen.

Drasen would be the easiest to get to, the easiest to break. All he needed was one admission of involvement. Then, with the help of Zarev and Aristov, he'd have Drasen arraigned for conspiracy to murder. And the others would follow as simply and inevitably as the links of an anchor chain.

The question was, should he take the risk of going after Drasen? Tanty Sima would have said yes. Tanty Sima would have said the coincidence of the gun was a sign from God. The truth was that privileged and responsible men had abused their trust. Privileged and responsible men had stolen from the state they had undertaken to protect, had committed murder to hide their crimes. There was no doubt that they had to be exposed, that he, with the knowledge he had and a measure of privilege himself, had the ability to do it. Tanty Sima, he knew, would have said it was his duty.

At five thirty the traffic along the Quay Maurice Thorez streamed in both directions, stuttered in sluggish worm trails across the Kammenyi Bridge. Yuri pressed himself against the wall of a building and waited. Beyond the concrete embankment the Moskva was as busy as the streets with darting river trams, bow high pleasure steamers, rows of barges strung together carrying timber. Across the river, stood the Kremlin, palaces and floating domes, massive red walls that had never been breached. Yuri wondered whether if Drasen talked, those walls would come tumbling down.

A faint chime of the clock on the Spassky Tower carried across the water. A black Chrysler edged to the curb. As Drasen came out of the office building, Yuri moved away from the wall.

Drasen walked fast, with the pounding gait of a big man. He carried a briefcase. He looked solid, confident, strong. As he approached the car, Yuri stepped in front of him, holding out his work pass. 'A word, Mr Drasen.'

Drasen stared at the work pass, memorizing its details. His gaze drifted to Yuri, watchful, calculating, a man estimating the strength and weight of an opponent before a street fight. 'What do you want?' His glance gave no indication that he had seen Yuri before.

'The gun that was stolen from your apartment has been found,' Yuri said. 'It was in the possession of a man named Sergei Kronykin, who was shot and killed while breaking into the apartment of your friend, General Dolgov.'

Drasen stepped around Yuri and continued walking toward the Chrysler. As in every good capitalist country, a chauffeur came up, took Drasen's briefcase and put it on the front seat. 'Are you certain it's the same gun?' Drasen asked.

'I believe so.'

'I understand the weapon found on this man Kronykin had no serial number. Mine had.'

'You are extremely well informed, Mr Drasen.'

'Let's just say, I have very good friends.' He bobbed his head sideways and stared at Yuri. 'Very good friends,' he repeated.

Pin him, Yuri thought, pin him about the gun. 'Iver-John-sons are rare weapons. To find two in Moscow –'

'Simply proves that they are not as rare as you think.' Drasen gave him a tight smile and pulled open the rear door.

Stop him. Don't let him get away. 'Did you know Sergei Kronykin?'

'No.' Drasen lowered himself onto the rear seat.

Yuri knew he had to clinch the interview now. 'But you knew Kronykin's father. Kronykin's father was a close friend of

General Dolgov's, and General Dolgov was a close friend of yours.'

'What the hell are you getting at, young man?' The veins in Drasen's cheeks stood out like markings on stone.

Now. Now, If he didn't do it now, he'd lose him. 'Did you know that General Dolgov had been summoned to testify before the Zarev Commission, concerning the bribes you and he had made on behalf of Amrocontinental?'

Drasen raised his head to the level of Yuri's. 'Bullshit!' he snapped. 'Amrocontinental has never bribed anyone.' He turned away.

Yuri lowered himself to the level of the window. 'Not convincing, Mr Drasen,' he murmured. 'I have proof that you and Dolgov were up to your necks in corruption. Let's take 1953, for instance.'

A strained look crossed Drasen's face, as if he had been suddenly afflicted with a severe internal pain. 'What did you say, young man?' he asked, suddenly breathless.

'Nineteen fifty-three,' Yuri repeated. 'The year Drasen Associates was paid $250,000 for licences which never existed. The year $250,000 was paid into the account of your close friend and business associate Vyssorian Dolgov at the Staaderbank in Zurich. Have you dealt with the Staaderbank, Mr Drasen? Did you know of General Dolgov's account there? Do you know what secrets are buried in Zurich?'

Drasen rapped urgently on the glass between him and the drive. 'You're a fool,' he blazed as the car inched away. 'A young, stupid and dangerous fool. Your superiors shall hear of this!'

Yuri watched Drasen's head throught the rear window till it blurred into the traffic. It was done now, he thought. For better or worse he had reopened the Dolgov case. Then he thought, if Drasen was going to report him to Popov, he'd better made his evidence official.

Now.

Yuri inserted two Investigation Report forms into the Underwood and started to type. He began with Drasen's business relationship with Dolgov, then mentioned the fact that Dolgov had been summoned to testify before the Zarev Commission. Allegations of bribery, he typed, were evidenced by the payment of $250,000 to Drasen Associates in 1953, and the transfer, or payment of a similar amount to an account Dolgov had opened at the Staaderbank in Zurich. He set out his reservations concerning the manner of Dolgov's death and described the finding of Drasen's gun in Kronykin's possession. After a brief summary of his meeting with Drasen, he concluded the report by suggesting that the facts be presented to a procurator, that further investigations be carried out into the cause of Dolgov's death, and that permission be granted to have Drasen brought in for questioning.

No sooner had he finished, than the phone rang. It was Popov himself spurning the assistance of messengers and secretaries. 'Get your ass over here,' he bellowed. 'At once.'

Ball stamping time, Yuri thought. He collated his report and went.

Popov stood behind his desk. Unusually for him, he was in uniform. Red stars gleamed on his epaulettes. Red stars above the Kremlin Towers glinted through the window. Popov's face was a shiny red circle. 'What the fuck have you been doing,' he shouted, 'accusing an important foreign citizen of involvement in a murder that never took place!'

Yuri held out his report. 'It's all here.'

Popov snatched the report from him and read it quickly, his jaw muscles clenching and unclenching as if he were chewing gum. 'Rubbish!' he screamed when he'd finished. He tore the report in two. 'General Dolgov was not murdered! The Dolgov case is closed!'

'There is new evidence,' Yuri said, quietly. 'The gun found on Sergei Kronykin was identical to one stolen from John Drasen's apartment.'

'What the hell difference does that make? Dolgov wasn't shot.'

'If the cyanide hadn't worked, Kronykin would have shot him.'

'And if the gun hadn't worked, he'd have dropped Dolgov off the Nikolsky Tower.' Popov was hopping up and down with rage. 'Kronykin didn't shoot Dolgov. There's no evidence of cyanide.' He stopped and stared at Yuri. Beads of sweat stood out on his temples and upper lip. Still staring, he took a cigarette from the pack on his desk and lit it. 'What made you take your investigation back to 1953?' he asked, and sat.

Yuri felt a vivid lightning flash of illumination. Dolgov had opened his bank account and begun his meteoric rise in 1953. Drasen had gone breathless when he'd asked him about 1953. And now Popov, with so much to question him about was concentrating on 1953. 'That's when Dolgov's account was opened,' Yuri said, flatly.

Popov's stare remained impassive and unblinking. 'How did you find out about Dolgov's account?'

'There were rumours,' Yuri said. He mustn't be seen to hesitate. He mustn't allow Popov to think he was making up a story. 'I had a friend do a computer scan of authorizations.'

'What friend? What's his name.'

Yuri met Popov's stare. A KGB officer's contacts were personal. That was the custom of the Sluzbha, the custom of every police force in the world. 'You know I don't have to tell you that.'

Popov reddened. 'I'll damn well make –'

Quickly, Yuri interrupted. 'My contact didn't know the purpose of the scan or its result. Dolgov's wasn't the only account he found.' He stopped, breathless. If Popov thought about it, he'd know it was impossible to run a meaningful computer scan without first knowing what one was looking for.

'And so you discovered Dolgov had an account,' Popov said softly. 'And that it was opened in 1953.'

'That's right.'

Popov scratched his chin. His problem, Yuri thought, was that he wanted to know what Yuri had found out about 1953, but dared not inquire directly, for fear that if Yuri didn't know anything about 1953, he'd become curious.

'And that's the only reason why you concerned yourself with 1953?'

Yuri did not trust himself to speak. He nodded.

'If that was all you knew,' Popov inquired, quietly, 'Why did you ask John Drasen about specific amounts that were paid into Dolgov's account in 1953?'

Godamn it, Popov wasn't letting go. If Popov knew what had happened in 1953, then he'd know the money had not gone directly into Dolgov's account. He'd know that Yuri couldn't have found out what Dolgov had been paid only from the computer scan. 'I ran a check of payments around the time the account was opened,' Yuri said, slowly. He couldn't tell Popov he had Dolgov's bank statements. 'I found a quarter of a million dollars had been paid to Drasen Associates.'

'And ...' Popov was studying him keenly.

'And I assumed Drasen's account had been some kind of conduit to Dolgov's.'

'Why?'

'How else could Drasen have given Dolgov his share of the bribes.'

'What bribes?' Popov sounded irritated, as if he'd expected a different answer.

Play it stupid, Yuri thought. 'The Zarev Commission is investigating corruption,' he said. 'The Zarev Commission wanted Dolgov to testify.'

'The Zarev Commission could ask your grandmother to testify. That doesn't prove anything.'

'I assumed the Zarev Commission wouldn't have summoned Dolgov without good reason. I assumed the payment to Drasen had to do with whatever Drasen and Dolgov were doing. I thought if I confronted Drasen with it he could panic and reveal something incriminating.'

'You're a fool, Raikin,' Popov barked. 'A stupid, obstinate fool. You think Drasen would panic when confronted by a lickspittle little shit like you?'

Yuri relaxed. As long as Popov thought he was a lickspittle little shit, as long as Popov thought he was an idiot, Popov wouldn't think too hard about what he had found out, or suspected.

Popov leaned back in his chair and stretched out his legs. 'You haven't a shred of evidence,' he said, staring angrily at Yuri. 'All you have is a dangerous habit of drawing conclusions from insufficient data. On the basis of pure conjecture you have accused a distinguished foreigner of all kinds of crimes.'

Yes, Yuri thought, happily. Go on. You sound like the

sweetest Tchaikovsky. As long as you keep on like this, I'm safe.

'You have ignored the fundamental principles of investigation,' Popov continued. 'You have flouted departmental procedure. You have damaged the reputation of the Sluzbha and you have disobeyed my direct orders.'

Suddenly, he swung forward onto his elbows. 'Your problem, Raikin, is that you are an individualist. Our society has no place for individualists. In Russia, individualism is a crime. Because you have had certain advantages of birth, it does not mean that you are better than the rest of us or that you are above the law.'

'All I was doing was my job,' Yuri protested.

'And what precisely was that?'

'Investigating the Dolgov case.'

'A matter which I told you was closed. A matter which I formally ordered you to leave alone.' Popov extended his hand across the desk. 'Your work pass, Captain.'

'What? I don't understand.'

'From this moment you are suspended from duty. You will account for your actions to an inquiry which will be convened as soon as possible. You will be notified of the date and place of the hearing in due course. You are no longer an officer of the Committee for State Security.'

Numbly, Yuri reached into his pocket and handed over his work pass.

Popov looked at it and dropped it into a drawer. 'And this time,' he added, grimly, 'no one will save you from Siberia.'

CHAPTER TWENTY-NINE

'What are you going to do?' Sonya cried, when Yuri told her.

'I don't know.' Every night he brought her worse news. He wondered if she saw it that way.

She tossed her head angrily over her plate. 'Can't your powerful friends help?'

'I've spoken to Gvishani. There's nothing they can do. Popov can suspend anyone he wants for any reason. I'll have to wait till the inquiry.'

'Yasha, you fool! You're like a man trying to stop a steam-roller with your bare hands. You're about to get crushed and all those Kremlin-ration sons of bitches will do is tell you to wait till the inquiry!' Angrily, she scooped up their plates and took them to the sink.

Yuri drew invisible doodles on the table cloth. Sonya returned smoking a cigarette and carrying two glasses of Georgian brandy. 'You can't rely on Gvishani and the others,' she said, firmly. 'You must compromise with Popov.'

Yuri took a glass from her. 'Compromise how?'

'Tell Popov you made a mistake. Tell him you were over-enthusiastic. Swear on your father's life you won't investigate Dolgov. Have your father talk to Popov.'

'No.'

'Why the hell not?'

'Because they're wrong.'

'And you're right, I supposed.'

'They've stolen. They've murdered. Someone has to stop them.'

'If someone has to stop them, why you?'

'Because those of us who are given greater privileges, have greater obligations.'

Sonya shook her head incredulously. 'Idiot,' she cried. 'You're in Russia! In Russia, things aren't like that!'

'They could be,' Yuri said.

For a while they sat in silence. Then Yuri said, 'Gvishani tells me the Zarev Commission will begin its inquiry into the Dolgov affair before my hearing commences. If that happens, I'll testify for the Commission. Popov will be finished, and I'll end up a hero.'

'And if it doesn't happen?'

Yuri shrugged. 'It'll depend whether Popov will be able to pack the Board of Inquiry or not.' He rubbed his eyes with thumb and forefinger. 'If the investigators are independent and I tell them what I know, they'll have to acquit me.' He banged the glass on the table in frustration. 'Oh hell, I wish I knew what happened in 1953.'

'You've asked me about 1953 before. What's so special about that year?'

'In 1952, Dolgov wrote his testament. In 1953, he went in a matter of months, from Major to Lieutenant Colonel. In 1953, he got the Order of Lenin. Also, in 1953, Drasen defected back to the Americans, and Dolgov, Drasen and Deryugin stole a quarter of a million dollars. When I spoke to Drasen today I mentioned 1953 and he almost stopped breathing. Then, when I gave Popov my report, all he cared about was what I knew about 1953.'

Sonya pulled him to her and kissed his cheek. 'Leave it,' she whispered. 'You've had a bitch of a day and you're tired. You need to sleep.'

'If I knew what happened in 1953,' Yuri said, 'I'll know why Dolgov was murdered.'

She tugged at his hands till he stood up. 'Bed,' she murmured, brushing her lips against his. 'You won't be able to find out anything if you turn into a zombie.'

'If I was a zombie, I wouldn't need to find out anything,' Yuri smiled. 'And you wouldn't want me in bed.'

He allowed her to lead him toward the bedroom.

'Don't worry,' she said, over her shoulder. 'Tomorrow you'll find the answer.'

Yuri tossed restlessly beside Sonya, unable to sleep, his thoughts nagging him like an abcess beneath a tooth. He felt that if he thought hard enough, if he tried hard enough he'd find the solution. He was like a man running round the corners of a maze, expecting to find the exit at each turning. Rima would have said he was obsessional.

'Can't you sleep, darling?'

'No. I'm sorry, if I'm keeping you awake.'

Sonya murmured, 'Still worrying about 1953?'

'Yes.'

She yawned. 'There's an encyclopaedia in the bookcase, and a chronology of modern history. Why don't you look at them?'

'Whatever Dolgov and the others did wouldn't be officially recorded.'

'No,' Sonya agreed, sleepily. 'But you'll find something. In any case it'll give you a feel for the period, an idea what the times were like.'

He wasn't reading for a part in a film about the 1950s, Yuri thought. Then, what the hell. It was better than lying on his back, staring at the ceiling.

He went into the kitchen and made some tea, carried it with him to the lounge and took out the chronology of modern history.

1953

Jan 6 Asian Socialist Conference in Rangoon.

Jan 12 Yugoslav National Assembly adopts new constitution.

Jan 14 Marshal Tito appointed First President of Yugoslav Republic.

Jan 20 D.D. Eisenhower inaugurated President of the United States.

Feb 12 USSR severs diplomatic relations with Israel.

Mar 5 Stalin dies.

Stalin had died in March. And in March Dolgov had been in Kremlin Security Administration. No, Yuri thought. His obsession and lack of sleep was driving him mad. Dolgov's superior at Kremlin Security Administration, Kronykin's father, Major Anatol Kronykin had been shot on February 25th. The payments to Dolgov had been made on February 26th and March 6.

Yuri stared at the page. *March 5. Stalin dies!* The page shimmered before his eyes. Impossible, he thought, never!

Excitedly, he reached for the encyclopaedia, scattering books off the shelf. He riffled pages rapidly, turning to S. Stalin had been born Josef Vissarionovich Djhugashvili in 1879 and died in 1953. He'd been married twice, widowed twice and fathered three children. According to the encyclopaedia, Stalin had been responsible for the defence of Moscow in 1941–2, and been General Secretary from 1928 to 1952. The entire entry consisted of just five lines!

What the hell was this? Five lines for the man who had ruled Russia for nearly twenty five years, who had ruled Russia for longer than anyone since the revolution! During the period Stalin had been number one man, Russia had fought the biggest war in its history. It had acquired control over countries half as big as Russia itself. And for the man who had led his country through all that, five lines!

Something was wrong. History was being replaced by silence. What had there been about Stalin, about 1953, to require such silence?

For a long while, Yuri sat staring at the encyclopaedia. There had to be a reason for the silence. But he mustn't allow himself to be dominated by his obsession. He mustn't reach conclusions from insufficient data.

Tomorrow, he decided, I'll find the data. Tomorrow, I'll find the truth. He shut the encyclopaedia and tip-toed back to the bedroom.

The Lenin Library fronted four streets, Marx, Kalinin, Marx-Engels and Herzen. A massive light grey building it occupied a whole city block. Its tall columns were faced with black marble and in niches high in the walls were statues of Archimedes, Galileo, Pavlov and Maxim Gorky. Yuri entered underneath the huge gold inscription carved over the main entrance and went to Reading Room No. 7.

There were twenty-two reading rooms in the library, and ten thousand people used it daily for research and study. It had copies of almost everything published in Russia, from Dimitri Vostock's latest romance right back to the early manuscripts of the Rus. In theory anyone could use the library. In practice, well, theory was just for show.

Yuri took his MIMO card to the librarians, sitting corralled behind desks on a raised dais in the centre. He felt like a student again. After the customary ten minutes of inattention, a middle aged woman in steel rimmed glasses snappishly asked him what he wanted.

'Historical and political biographies of Comrade Stalin,' Yuri said. 'Is there any work you would recommend?'

The woman stared at him, blankly. 'Why?'

Yuri shuffled from one foot to the other. 'For my thesis,' he said. 'Foreign Policy and the Economics of Development within COMECON, 1945–53.'

'Comrade Stalin had nothing to do with that,' the woman said primly, and pursed her lips as if to indicate she'd delivered a final judgment.

'Comrade Stalin was General Secretary during that period,' Yuri pointed out, gently. He tried a shy smile. The librarian remained unmoved. 'It was at the direction of my professor,' Yuri murmured. 'Professor Vadim Glinsky, Member of the Academy and biographer of Comrade Lenin.'

The librarian frowned. Then, lowering her voice, she asked, 'Do you have any other card?'

Yuri shook his head.

The librarian reached into a tray beside her and gave him a numbered metal disk. 'Wait there,' she said, pointing to a chair whose number corresponded with the disk.

Yuri waited. Forty minutes later she beckoned him to the desk and handed him a slim volume of forty pages, 'The Speech of Comrade Khrushchev to the Twentieth Party Congress.' As if anticipating his surprise, she said, 'That is all the information we have on Comrade Stalin.' This time it was a final judgment.

Yuri carried the book back to his desk. There were over 200 miles of bookshelves in the Lenin Library, more than 25 million volumes, a library so vast that books were moved on electrified carriers. And they had only one, slim volume on the man who had ruled Russia for nearly a third of its post-revolutionary existence!

He settled down to read. Khrushchev had begun his speech by comparing Stalin to Lenin. Where Lenin had been the soul of modesty, Stalin had been unspeakably vain. Where Lenin had subordinated himself to the Party, Stalin had chosen to dominate it. Where Lenin had used persuasion and reason, Stalin had used terror. And then, the unkindest cut of all. Stalin's proclaimed friendship with Lenin was a lie.

The speech went on, detailing Stalin's crimes. Stalin had mismanaged the war. Stalin had made disastrous mistakes in foreign policy. In the ten years to 1938, Stalin had eliminated all Lenin's lieutenants, with the exception of Trotsky who was in exile. In a single year between 1937 and 1938, Stalin had arrested or liquidated 98 of the Central Committee's 139 members, and 1108 of the 1966 delegates to the 17th Party Congress.

Moscow must have run with blood! Lefortovo and the Lubyanka must have been filled to capacity! Stalin had killed vastly without respect for position or past achievement. Under Stalin everyone had been equally under threat. But that wasn't news. What was intriguing was how the news had been spread.

What had Khrushchev been doing, talking about these things in Congress? Why had the Politburo with its habit of secrecy allowed such a speech to be read? Why had they risked their reputation for infallibility being ruined by such an exposure?

Mystified now, and enthralled, Yuri read on. In October 1952, Stalin had accused Party faithfuls, Foreign Minister Molotov and Trade Minister Mikoyan of unspecified crimes. In his speech Khrushchev had said: 'It is not excluded that had Stalin remained at the helm for another several months, Comrades Molotov and Mikoyan would probably *not* have delivered any speeches at *this* Congress.'

And Mikoyan and Molotov had not been the only members of the Politburo under threat. After the Nineteenth Party Congress, Stalin had proposed replacing the old members of the Politburo with others! And four years later Khrushchev had said, 'This was the design for the future annihilation of the old Politburo members!'

Yuri's mind reeled. Shortly before his own death Stalin had planned to do away with the Politburo!

And what had men like Mikoyan, Molotov, amd Khrushchev done to counter that threat?

Hurriedly, Yuri turned back to an incident described earlier in the speech. In January 1952 a group of Kremlin doctors had been arrested on charges of murder, attempted murder and applying improper methods of treatment. Khrushchev had dismissed the plot as fiction and used it as another example of Stalin's paranoia. But what, Yuri thought, if the doctors' plot had not been a result of Stalin's paranoia, but a device to get rid of Stalin? What if the plot had failed and Stalin had been on the point of discovering who its architects were? And what if the doctors' plot having failed, the members of an increasingly frightened and threatened Politburo had been forced to use other methods?

Yuri carried the copy of Khrushchev's speech back to the librarian. 'Professor Glinsky also suggested I should read *Pravda* for the week of March 6, 1953.'

Pravda was authorized. *Pravda* was truth. The librarian accompanied him to the rear of the building where the stacks were kept in temperature controlled rooms. She described his mission to a uniformed guard, who led Yuri to another librarian, who led Yuri to an airconditioned room with tall desks and high stools. From within a screened area in the room, Yuri heard the sound of files being moved on pulleys. A few minutes later, the librarian was back bearing a huge, bound volume of *Pravda* for the month of March 1953.

'You may only use pencil here,' he said severely.

'Unnecessary,' Yuri replied and tapped his forehead. 'Photographic memory.'

The librarian frowned at him and left.

Yuri turned the pages carefully. News of Stalin's illness had first been published on March 4. In a lengthy communique that named the doctors in attendance and set out in detail the treatment being administered, it was stated that Stalin had collapsed of a cerebral haemmorrhage on the night of March 1. No indication of the time of the collapse was given or its circumstances. All the communique said was that Stalin had collapsed in his apartment in the Kremlin.

A further communique had been issued on March 5, again setting out in the minutest detail the treatment that was continuing to be administered and describing every particular of the patient's gradually deteriorating condition.

A final three page communique on March 6 announced Stalin's death at 9.50 pm the previous night.

Yuri read the communiques twice more. There was altogether too much detail, he felt. If so much detail about the administration of penicillin, caffeine, camphor preparations and glucose, so much information about albumen ratios, white corpuscle counts and blood pressure, why not a little more information about the time and circumstances of the collapse. Was the wealth of detail meant to inform or to conceal, Yuri wondered. And if it was meant to conceal, did it mean he was right?

CHAPTER THIRTY

The Marshal waited in the dining room, flanked by ice buckets of vodka and white wine, the table covered as usual with an array of *zakuski*. 'Where's Sonya?' he asked.

'Rehearsing,' Yuri lied. He went over, kissed his father on both cheeks and sat. Tonight, he'd wanted to see his father alone.

'First your wife and now your mistress is too busy to see me.'

'Next Friday –'

The scar on his father's cheek turned livid as his face darkened with anger. 'What the devil have you been up to?' he demanded. 'Popov came to see me yesterday. He told me he's had to suspend you from duty.'

'That's correct.'

'That's correct.' The Marshal mimicked in a high pitched voice. 'Is that all you have to say? What the hell is wrong with you that you can't take orders? You're a soldier's son. The first duty of a soldier is to obey orders.'

Yuri looked down at the table. 'The first duty of a soldier is to do what's right,' he muttered.

'And how the fuck do you know what's right? You think because you went to that fancy school and had your head stuffed full of crap, you know what's right. You think those asshole professors know what's right? Let me tell you in 1940 . . .'

Yuri had heard the story before. In 1940, the Marshal had been part of a military liaison unit in Berlin. They had observed Hitler's preparations for war and warned of a German invasion. But Hitler would never attack Russia, the diplomats had scoffed. In fact, when the time came, Russia would attack Germany.

'Twenty million lives,' the Marshal said. 'That's the price we paid for listening to assholes who thought they were right.'

'Did you know Stalin?' Yuri asked.

'What?'

'Stalin. Did you know him?'

'What the fuck has Stalin got to do with you and Popov?'

'He may be able to show I'm right.'

Frowning, the Marshal put meat and salad onto the plate and passed it to Yuri. He reached beside him for the vodka and slid Yuri's glass to him. 'You may be my son,' he muttered. 'But I'm damned if I understand you.'

'It's a wise man who knows his own son.'

'Don't you be fucking clever with me! I've kicked your ass before and I'll do it again.'

Yuri raised his glass to his father in a silent toast. They drank, and Yuri said, 'I want to talk to you.'

The Marshal blinked back tears from the vodka and refilled their glasses. 'So talk. But eat something.'

While they ate, Yuri told his father all about Dolgov and how Popov had suppressed the investigation into his death.

'Popov's doing what he has to do,' the Marshal rumbled, when Yuri had finished. 'And you keep out of it. From what you've told me, Popov's suspended you for being too bloody nosy. Now you listen to me. Go and make your peace with Popov.' He tossed back another glass of vodka. 'You can't always do what's right. So better settle for what's possible.'

Yuri shook his head. 'Even if I wanted to, making peace with Popov is not possible. The Zarev Commission is going to enquire into why the Dolgov investigation was suppressed.'

'Zarev,' his father grunted. 'Too bloody big for his boots. Needs to have served under me for six months. Needs a punch in the snout.' Suddenly, the Marshal looked directly at Yuri. 'What's Stalin got to do with this?'

'If I told you, you wouldn't believe me. In fact, I don't believe it myself. Do you remember what it was like in Moscow at the beginning of 1953?'

'1953,' his father mused. '1953. Yes, I remember I was an observer in Korea at the time. I returned in February and found Moscow in a state of great uncertainty. Jews were being rounded up, and even Foreign Minister Molotov's wife, who was Jewish, had been placed under arrest. There were rumours that the purges were beginning again. There was even talk of war against Europe.'

The Marshal refilled their glasses and stretched out in his chair. 'war in Europe,' he repeated. 'Here we were playing an enormous game of double bluff in Korea, and all my superior officers and the brass from the Ministry of Defence were in regular conference at the Kremlin planning a war against Europe!'

'But why?' Yuri asked. 'We'd just finished the war against the Fascists.'

'Stalin,' his father said, shaking his grizzled head in despondent admiration. 'Stalin wanted to invade Europe. He felt that Europe had survived its post-war economic crisis and that it would now be rebuilt and soon be a threat to Russia. Stalin was concerned about NATO and the increasing American influence in Europe. He wanted to prevent America setting up bases in Europe capable of launching a nuclear attack on Russia. Stalin felt we had to act before Europe became too strong.'

The Marshal sat up and looked at Yuri, his eyes burning fiercely. 'That was a war we would have lost,' he said loudly. 'A war we would have lost. I want you to understand that. We had neither the will nor the material with which to fight it. There was nothing we could have done to prevent Moscow being turned into another Hiroshima.' He looked away and leaned back. In a softer voice, he finished, 'Fortunately for Russia, fortunately for Europe, Stalin died before those plans could be implemented.'

Yuri asked, 'In January 1953 was there a plot against Stalin by the Kremlin doctors?'

'There were certainly rumours of such a plot, and I know that a number of eminent doctors were arrested. Ignatiev, the NKVD chief was ordered to beat them until they confessed.'

'Ignatiev?' Yuri asked, surprised. 'But wasn't Beria head of the NKVD?'

'Not in January 1953,' the Marshal said. 'Stalin had fallen out with Beria by then. Come to think of it, Stalin had fallen out with a lot of his close supporters by then. Molotov, I recall was no longer at the Foreign Ministry. Mikoyan wasn't at Foreign Trade. Kaganovich too, I think, had lost his ministry.' The Marshal paused to light a cigarette. 'The story of Stalin is the story of broken friendships.'

Friendships that ended in executions, Yuri thought. 'So by January 1953, Stalin had reduced the powers of those close to him, reduced the power of the Politburo?'

'Oh yes. After the Nineteenth Congress, he'd already begun to replace them with younger men.' The Marshal laughed and pointed a finger at Yuri. 'Your father-in-law was one of the chosen ones.'

'Aristov?'

'Yes. Aristov had been in charge of *agrogorod*. By all accounts he did a splendid job compelling farmers to amalgamate.'

Yuri could picture Aristov fitting in very well with Stalin's young guard. He asked, 'How did the Politburo react to this threat to their position?'

The Marshal shrugged. 'We'll never know. Stalin died before his changes could be implemented.' He pulled deeply at his cigarette. His face was flushed from the vodka. There was a bright sparkle in his eyes. Once again, Yuri wondered if his father did in fact drink too much.

'I saw Stalin shortly before he died,' the Marshal said.

'You did?'

'Yes. He was a demonic worker, was Stalin. He wanted to know everything, had to know everything. He wanted me to report to him personally on what was happening in Korea.'

'How did he look when you saw him? Was he a well man?'

'He looked very robust. And throughout our meeting, he chainsmoked, a sure sign he felt well. He recalled our previous meeting very clearly and without effort. He absorbed the details of my report without any difficulty. In fact he told me he would live to see the end of America. "We Georgians live to be a hundred and fifty," he said.' The Marshal shrugged. 'Six weeks later he was dead.'

They sat in a sudden silence, as if suddenly aware they had nothing else to talk about. It was the first time in years, Yuri thought, that his father had spoken so freely. In future, he would encourage the Marshal to talk about the past. It did them both good, and who knew, one day the Marshal might talk of Igor, his mother and Tanty Sima.

'One thing that may interest you about Stalin,' the Marshal went on. 'Stalin was a compulsive doodler.'

The Marshal had enjoyed talking too, Yuri thought happily.

'All throughout my last meeting with him he kept drawing pictures of wolves. When I commented on the excellence of the drawings, I remember he looked at me very strangely. "I'll tell you something, Gennadi Anatolovich," he said. "The Russian peasant is a simple man, and very wise. When he sees a wolf, he doesn't preach morals to it. He shoots it. That's what he does. He shoots it." '

This time, Yuri wondered, had the wolves attacked first?

Yuri drove to Smolensk. On Temple Hill Marshal Kutuzov rode into the sky. Lose battles to win wars. A message for Generals and obsessive KGB investigators. At eleven o'clock in the morning, despite the bright sunshine there was a hint of Siberia in the air. Yuri shivered.

Her daughter-in-law at work, her grandchildren at school, Evgenya Kronykina was alone in the apartment on Kololkov Ulica. Behind her, candles burned before an ikon of the Virgin of Smolensk. On the table beneath the ikon was a photograph of Sergei Kronykin in army uniform. Single cut flowers rested on the white tablecloth beside Sergei's service medals. The scent of flowers mixed with the smoky odour of melting wax reminded Yuri he was in a house of mourning.

'You,' Evgenya Kronykina said. 'What do you want? My son is dead.'

Evgenya Kronykina seemed to have grown smaller. Her weathered face was pale, the wrinkles seemingly etched into the skin with a scalpel. Her eyes were bleak and stagnant.

'I've come to talk to you about your husband,' Yuri said.

'You still don't know how he died?'

'I know that.'

'So what is there to talk about? My son is also dead. Why is Moscow so interested in what happened over thirty years ago?'

'There is some doubt now if everything was properly investigated.'

'There's nothing more to investigate.' But she moved aside to allow Yuri into the apartment. She was glad of company, Yuri thought.

Evgenya Kronykina pointed to the photograph. 'My son, Sergei,' she said. 'He was a fine soldier, just like his father. He served in Manchuria, you know and in Afghanistan.' She handed Yuri the medals, cold as dead flesh.

'I'm sorry about your son,' Yuri said. 'You must be proud, he died a soldier.'

'I'm glad of that.' For a moment her face was illuminated, as if the sun had passed rapidly through a break in clouds.

She poured them tea, hot, dark and sweet from the samovar and sat heavily on the sofa.

Yuri revolved the glass in his hand. He said, 'The week your husband died, he'd had the Wednesday off because he was working the weekend?'

Sipping her tea, Evgenya Kronykina nodded. 'Yes, at the Generalissimo's dacha in Kuntsevo.' Her ravaged eyes sought Yuri's and held them. 'The Generalissimo was very fond of my husband, you know. He said my husband was the only person who knew his wishes before he uttered them. He always wanted my husband when he was at Kuntsevo. My husband was in charge of all the arrangements there.'

'Tell me about Kuntsevo,' Yuri said, softly.

The dacha had been large, a mansion with seven bedrooms, two reception rooms, a long, panelled dining room, a kitchen, larder and a cellar, each as big as the room they now sat in. In the last years of his life, Stalin had used the dacha to be alone. As Evgenya Kronykina described it, it had been a peculiarly obsessive solitude.

Stalin had travelled to the dacha in a high speed convoy of Zis and Volgas. Sometimes he'd used a bullet-proof Cadillac; sometimes the Cadillac was used as a decoy, and Stalin rode in an armour-plated Zis. He'd travelled with neither friends nor family, not even members of the Politburo. The only visitor he'd received was his confidential secretary, Poskrebyshev, and that had only happened twice.

Stalin had added a wing to the rear of the mansion, three identical rooms, each with a small iron bed, a table and a telephone. The walls had been decorated with pictures cut from magazines, and the only concession to amusement had been a gramophone and a pile of records.

Most weekends, Stalin spent the entire time in these sparse rooms, totally secluded behind an armour-plated door. Four times a day, at 9 am, 1 pm, 7 pm, and 10 pm, food would be placed outside the door to be collected through a slat bolted from the inside. Her husband had told Evgenya Kronykina that in the last months of his life, Stalin had lost his Georgian appetite, and had only rarely ordered his favourite *kharacho*, *chakapuli* or highly spiced *satsivi*. It was as if in his last year, Stalin had sought the simplicity and monastic solitude of his boyhood in the seminary at Tiflis.

'And do you know who took your husband's place at Kuntsevo that weekend?'

'Vyssorian Ilyich.'

'Dolgov?'

Evgenya Kronykina nodded.

'You're certain of that?'

'Yes. I know because Vyssorian Ilyich couldn't come to the funeral. My husband was buried on the Saturday.'

She nodded and sighed. 'That was the weekend the Generalissimo died.' She stared into the space between them as if it was filled with objects of indefinable intricacy. 'I remember thinking how strange it was they should both die so soon after each other. It was almost as if the Generalissimo felt he could not survive without his favourite bodyguard.'

'And that is where Stalin died?' Yuri asked. 'In Kuntsevo?'

Evgenya Kronykina nodded. 'Yes. Alone.'

'I'd always thought he died in the Kremlin.'

Evgenya Kronykina shook her head. 'Not the Kremlin. The dacha. I know.'

She remembered, because it had been the night after her husband's funeral and she hadn't been able to sleep. She'd sat in the bedroom of their apartment near the Nikolsky Tower, staring dry eyed at the persistently falling snow. It must have been about two o'clock in the morning when the cars began arriving at the Kremlin, big limousines, writhing through the snow, their chains grinding like broken bells. There had been an air of hushed excitement, of suppressed urgency, an indefinable sense of tragedy that matched her own.

Early the next day, it was whispered that the great *Vozdh* had died.

'They brought his body back the next day in a baker's van,' Evgenya Kronykina said. 'Without an escort, so that no one would know when and where he had died.'

'You're sure of that?' Yuri asked.

'I helped lay out the body on his bed.'

CHAPTER THIRTY-ONE

Yuri drove steadily back to Moscow. He knew what had happened. He knew exactly why Dolgov had been paid a quarter of a million dollars.

In 1952, Stalin had demoted those closest to him, he had diluted the powers of the Politburo, he had threatened the Politburo with annihilation.

The Politburo had reacted to their potential extermination by conspiring to do away with Stalin. They had used methods that had been successful in Russia before. Poison by the Kremlin doctors.

But their conspiracy had been discovered, and Stalin had used that discovery to speed their extermination.

The Politburo, or those within it who felt themselves most threatened, had turned to more direct means. Dolgov, a friend of Beria's, a man who had murdered before, had been approached.

Dolgov had demanded immunity and $250,000.

The immunity had been given by whatever documentation Dolgov had subsequently deposited in Zurich. The money had proved a trickier problem. Transfers of money were traceable. The payment of such a vast sum would have linked the conspirators to Dolgov. Deryugin, the financial expert had been brought into the conspiracy. He had persuaded Drasen to help, with promises, no doubt, of the fortune to be made from cooperating with the future rulers of Russia. Drasen had acted as a blind and a conduit for the payment of Dolgov's money, and the money itself had been paid to Dolgov in two instalments, the first when he had proved his willingness by disposing of Major Anatol Kronykin, the second when Stalin himself had been disposed of.

Yuri imagined how the act had been carried out. Stalin was a violent, wilful, intemperate man, a man used to absolute power, a man who had murdered by the thousand. What would his reaction have been to a servant who had irritated him by delaying a meal?

Stalin would have summoned him and berated him. Just as that day he had summoned Dolgov who had replaced his favourite, Anatol Kronykin, as administrator at Kuntsevo. In his temper, Stalin would have admitted Dolgov to his private rooms. And once behind that armour-plated door, Dolgov would have attacked Stalin.

Yuri could visualize the scene: Dolgov in his thirties, strong, fit, and experienced. Stalin much older, his body affected by years of chain-smoking, hard drinking and inadequate sleep.

The two men would have grappled. Dolgov, the strangler of Vipuri, would have gone for the throat. Stalin, shorter, stockier, would have fought back. But the physical effort and the rage at being attacked would have been too much. Blood would have spurted to his brain like a fountain. Blood vessels would have burst. Stalin would have collapsed.

Dolgov would have left Stalin where he fell. Later, when Stalin's next meal had remained uncollected, guards and servants would have been called, broken open the door, and found Stalin. Doctors would have been summoned. The Politburo informed.

And Dolgov paid.

That was why the published information on Stalin's death had gone into so much irrelevant detail about Stalin's blood pressure and the treatment administered to him. It was the reason for the vagueness about the time and circumstances of the onset of Stalin's cerebral haemorrhage, and the lie that Stalin had died in the Kremlin. The Politburo had wanted to show the people that Stalin had died naturally, that everything possible had been done for a man whom they knew was dead.

As soon as Yuri got home he phoned Gvishani. Natalya, Gvishani's wife, told him that Gvishani was in Leningrad with Comrade Zarev. He was returning that night and would be delighted to meet with Yuri the next day.

They met the next afternoon, by the fountain in Gorky Park. Though it was a Sunday, Gvishani still wore his Party intellectual's garb, as if to demonstrate the faithful never rested. His Party badge gleamed brightly in his lapel. He hugged Yuri and gave him a toothy grin. 'We opened an office of the Zarev Commission in Leningrad,' he announced. 'They're twice as corrupt there as in Moscow.'

Yuri released himself from Gvishani and in the same motion turned him onto the main path. 'I want to talk,' he said.

'Oh, Yasha, I'm so glad.'

The path leading to the Golitsynsky Pond was crowded with families and groups of teenagers parading with self conscious skittishness. As they walked, Yuri told Gvishani how he had found Dolgov's bank statements and testament, how these documents combined with Dolgov's rapid promotions and the payments to Drasen Associates had made him interested in what had happened in 1953. Yuri described how nervous Drasen had become when he'd been questioned about the payments, and Popov's extraordinary interest in what Yuri knew about 1953. He told Gvishani of his research at the library, his conversation with his father, and Evgenya Kronykina's story. Finally, watching Gvishani's face for an expression of disbelief or suspicion, he told Gvishani how he thought Dolgov had murdered Stalin.

Gvishani whirled and placed his hands on Yuri's shoulders. He brought his face close to Yuri's. 'Yasha,' he breathed. 'Yasha.' Behind the heavy lenses his eyes brimmed with admiration. 'This is the truth I'd hoped you'd find. I *knew* you'd find. You're as big a man as your father. Once we've brought these criminals to justice, everyone will know what a hero you are. It will be Hero of the Soviet Union for you, nothing less. I am proud you are my friend.'

'We have no proof,' Yuri said, and pulled embarrassedly away from Gvishani's embrace. 'Stalin's body is dust. The men who ordered that murder and the man who committed it are dead.'

'But the other conspirators are alive!' Gvishani protested. 'They rule Russia! They cannot be allowed to remain free!'

'We have no proof,' Yuri repeated.

They walked past a garden where people sat silently contemplating chess boards. The ferris wheel soared against the sky.

Gvishani said, 'What we will do is get you an *Odin* Priority and fly you to Switzerland. You will talk to the Staaderbank and bring back the documents Dolgov deposited with them. Those documents will reveal names. It's all the proof we'll need.'

'That won't work,' Yuri said. He walked with his head lowered, his hands thrust deep into his trouser pockets. 'The Swiss wouldn't tell me anything. And there's no way we can compel them. Swiss bank secrecy is protected by law.'

'Tell them what you told me,' Gvishani said. 'Tell them Dolgov was murdered. Have them publish the documents he left with them.'

'Are you crazy? Those documents can never be published! If they were, no Russian government, no Russian leader would retain credibility. Don't you realize what those documents show? That members of the Politburo, representatives of the highest organ of our government, conspired like gangsters to murder the man they had appointed as their head.'

Gvishani thought about that for a moment. 'Perhaps you're right,' he conceded. He told Yuri how in 1956, Khrushchev's speech to the Twentieth Party Congress had caused riots throughout the Eastern Bloc and a revolt in Hungary. 'Khrushchev was wrong,' Gvishani said. 'He told four hundred million people that the rule they had accepted for almost thirty years was nothing more than the ravings of a megalomaniac. We must eliminate the new Khrushchevs. The murderers of Stalin must be brought to justice.'

'Better concentrate on the murderers of Dolgov,' Yuri muttered.

'Same thing.' He gave Yuri one of his humourless smiles.

'The only way we can prove anything,' Yuri said, 'is to make Drasen confess.'

'And you can do that?' There was a tremor of excitement in Gvishani's voice.

'I've thought about it. I'll need help.'

'We'll give you all the help you'll need.'

Yuri told Gvishani how Drasen wanted Sonya to make a film for him in America. On the pretext of wanting to talk about the film, Sonya could invite Drasen over to the apartment. 'Then I'll confront him and force a confession out of him.'

'And how would you do that?'

'With facts. And a Makarov.'

'It's crude, but it could work,' Gvishani said, thoughtfully.

They walked in silence beside the pond. Rowing boats rippled the water. Queues were already forming by a pier on the opposite bank.

'If you're going to talk to Drasen,' Gvishani said, 'There are some things you should know. The money paid to Drasen Associates in February and March 1953 was repaid at the end of April.'

'Repaid! Why? By whom?'

'By the people who ultimately paid for Stalin's murder. The CIA.'

Yuri stopped and looked closely at Gvishani. 'Stop being naive. The CIA may have done a lot of things but –'

'Drasen is a known CIA agent,' Gvishani said. 'You will find confirmation in the files of the First, Second and Fifth Directorates. He is allowed to operate because he only works as a liaison man.' Seeing Yuri's puzzled frown Gvishani explained. 'Sometimes we need to know how the CIA will react to a situation. Or we need to pass certain information to the CIA. We use Drasen for that.'

'I still won't believe the CIA would have got involved in a plot to kill Stalin.'

Gvishani's smile was almost a grimace. 'We had a little problem in Korea at the time,' he said.

They turned toward the embankment by the Moskva. 'I'll need to be wired,' Yuri said. 'I'll also want two unimpeachable witnesses who will monitor the conversation. Can you fix that?'

'Yes. I'll talk to Director Guschin about the body wire. And Director Guschin and Comrade Zarev shall be your witnesses.'

Who better, Yuri thought, and asked, 'What's Guschin got to do with you?'

'He's a friend of Zarev's. Don't worry, Yasha. He's a good man and absolutely reliable.'

They reached the Arctica Ice Cream Parlour. Gvishani pushed throught the waiting queue and emerged with two large cones topped with fresh berry jam and a meringue biscuit. 'Sunday,' he cried, disgustedly, 'and all they have is vanilla.'

'Never mind. It's still the best ice cream in the world.' They walked along the embankment toward the Krymsky Bridge. Music from the Variety Hall mingled with the noise of the river traffic.

Gvishani said, 'You'd better leave the Dolgov documents with me.'

'No,' Yuri said. He'd been taught that both evidence and the chain of evidence always had to be preserved. Documentary evidence was not passed from hand to hand like a pornographic book.

'I'll need something to convince Guschin,' Gvishani said.

'Tell him what you know. Tell Guschin he should treat us like ordinary informers.'

'But how do I convince Comrade Zarev?'

'Tell him the only proof he'll get is Drasen's confession.'

For a moment, Gvishani looked quite perturbed. 'What if something happens to you?' he cried.

'In that case, you'll know what and who to look for.'

'No,' Sonya said. 'I won't do it. I won't invite John Drasen to my home so you can interrogate him.'

'I wouldn't ask if there was another way.'

They were seated in the living room sipping a white Tsinandali. From the kitchen came the appetising aroma of a slowly cooking Georgian pilaf.

'I can't stand you being so damn secretive,' Sonya cried. She carried her wine to the kitchen, checked the pilaf and returned. 'You haven't told me anything since you came back from Smolensk.'

'That's because there are things I can't tell you. Things Drasen was involved with. Things I have to find out more about. That's why I have to see him.'

'I can't know, but I can lend you my apartment.' Sonya flung herself down angrily on the sofa.

'Sonya, Drasen's a murderer. He arranged Dolgov's death. He's been involved in more important killings than Dolgov's.

Dolgov's murder was simply a cover up for what he did before.'

'And you're going to break him! The last time you tried to interrogate him, you got suspended, remember? For heaven's sake, Yasha, you don't even work for the KGB anymore!'

Yuri said, 'When I get Drasen here I'll be working for the Zarev Commission and the Fifth Directorate. I've arranged it all with Gvishani.'

'Gvishani!' Sonya cried. 'Are you crazy or what? You're putting your whole future, maybe even your life on the line, and you're relying on Gvishani Kirichenko!' She came and stood over him, scowling. 'Let me tell you something about Gvishani. You remember when he won the geometry prize at Psy Math? You know how he did that? He threatened to report Nikolai for smoking if Nikolai didn't allow him to copy his answers. That's Gvishani Kirichenko for you. That's the man you're trusting with your life. A liar, a bully and a cheat!'

'Sonya, listen! Please try to be reasonable. Gvishani's past and Gvishani's motives don't matter a damn. What matters is that he is helping me. That he is having Zarev and Guschin help me. What's important is that I break Drasen. Either I get Drasen or I lose. And if I lose, we all lose.'

Sonya went back to the sofa and sat, staring thoughtfully at the window. In a low voice she asked, 'What if you do nothing?'

'Then it's Siberia, if I'm lucky.'

She turned to look at him, tiny pinched lines about her mouth. 'What the hell kind of choice is that?'

'The only choice I have,' Yuri said.

CHAPTER THIRTY-TWO

Drasen agreed to come at two o'clock the following Saturday. Sonya left immediately after lunch to spend the afternoon with Katyusha Asonova, the ballerina. 'Be careful,' she said as she left. 'And call me as soon as you're done.'

Yuri waited in the living room, with the curtains drawn, sitting beyond the halo of light thrown by the single table lamp. The transmitter pressed sharply against his chest. The Makarov felt solid and heavy in his hand. He spoke softly, checking the wire. 'Strelka to Krepost, testing, one, two, three ...'

'We hear you, Strelka. Over.'

Yuri waited, motionless as a statue.

The doorbell pealed, incongruously joyous. Yuri waited for the chimes to die. 'Come in,' he called.

The door opened. Drasen's bulky figure filled the frame, backlit by the light from the corridor.

Yuri thrust the Makarov into the light. 'Don't go away, Mr Drasen.' He sensed Drasen's hesitation, sensed Drasen calculate the chances of darting back along the corridor, Drasen trying to decide if he would shoot. Yuri said, 'The light's behind you, Mr Drasen.' The serrated hammer slid beneath his thumb.

Drasen came into the apartment. Behind him, the latch clicked softly. 'What the hell is this?' he demanded. 'Where's Sonya?'

'Out. But I want to talk to you, Mr Drasen. So sit down on the corner of the sofa opposite me and keep your hands where I can see them, on your knees.'

Drasen remained standing. 'You've no right,' he said, his voice surprisingly calm, as if he looked down the barrel of a Makarov every day. 'You aren't even an officer of the KGB, anymore.'

'But I'm here and you're here. And I'm sure you want to

know how much I've found out about 1953, what I know about the $250,000 you were paid for licences that did not exist, and what I know about the documents Dolgov deposited in the Staaderbank.'

Drasen sat. 'I shall leave when I want to,' he said, pointedly. 'And that gun in your hand won't make any difference.'

Yuri rested the gun on the arm of his chair. Drasen wouldn't leave. Drasen was hooked. 'In March 1953,' he began, 'a man died. A very powerful man. A great *Vozhd*. They said he died of natural causes. But he didn't. He was assassinated.'

Drasen's gaze went rigid. His face was pale and shiny.

'The man was old, perhaps demented, certainly paranoid. He threatened those close to him with annihilation. They acted. You helped them, Mr Drasen. You helped the mice kill the cat.'

Drasen remained absolutely still, staring fixedly at Yuri.

'These other men,' Yuri continued, 'had determined to poison their leader. But their plot was discovered and was about to be turned against them. So they turned to more direct methods. They decided to use Vyssorian Dolgov, the strangler of Vipuri.' Yuri paused. Drasen's face remained impassive.

'Dolgov was promised immunity and $250,000. That was when you got involved, because of your friend, Pyotr Deryugin, and your masters, the CIA. Your sale of licences to the Russian government was a blind. You never had those licences. Your sale was a device to get money to Dolgov without risk of the Russian involvement every being discovered.

'Dolgov did what he was paid for. He murdered Anatol Kronykin. He murdered Josef Stalin at Kuntsevo. That is where Stalin died isn't it? At the dacha in Kuntsevo, not the Kremlin.'

This time Drasen's face was answer enough.

'The rest,' Yuri continued, 'the medical bulletins, the autopsy were all a cover up. Those who knew too much and those who would not cooperate were afterwards themselves, murdered. Those other men, your fellow conspirators were freed from the threat of annihilation. And you got the right to treat Russia like a mining concession.

'The truth was buried, deeply buried you thought, until

Vyssorian Dolgov was summoned to give evidence before the Zarev Commission. Then you had to act. Not because you were concerned what Dolgov would tell the Commission about bribery. What concerned you was that Dolgov was unstable, depressed and drinking heavily. What concerned you was what Dolgov would say about the $250,000.

'You tried to persuade Dolgov to defect. I have the false passport you provided for that purpose. Dolgov couldn't or wouldn't go. So you paid Sergei Kronykin to kill him. You gave Kronykin the cyanide capsule that he burst under Dolgov's nostrils. I have independent evidence that there were traces of a cyanide antidote in Kronykin's body. You gave him your gun as a back-up, and then reported the weapon stolen. And I am certain that if the gun found on Kronykin is tested, the filed away numbers can be raised and will be found to match yours. You see, Mr Drasen, I have all the evidence I need to have you arrested and charged with conspiring to murder Generalissimo Josef Stalin and General Vyssorian Dolgov.'

Very deliberately Drasen selected a cigarette from a battered gunmetal case and lit it. 'Your evidence,' he said, 'is a mixture of supposition and circumstance. As your superiors have already told you, you have a dangerous habit of reaching outrageous conclusions from insufficient data. For instance, do you really think that if Dolgov had murdered Stalin he would have told anyone about it, let alone the Zarev Commission?'

'Dolgov was unstable,' Yuri said. 'That's why he had to be killed.'

'Dolgov's instability is pure conjecture,' Drasen snapped. 'You're inventing facts to fit your conclusions. For Dolgov not to have realized the consequences of publicly admitting he'd killed Stalin, he would have had to be more than unstable. To make such an admission, he would have had to be stark, staring mad.' Drasen paused and stared angrily at Yuri and added, 'Which he wasn't.'

'He was unstable enough to refuse to go,' Yuri said stubbornly.

'Is that why he left me a power of attorney to administer his affairs in his absence?' Still staring angrily, Drasen leaned back on the sofa. 'As for the gun you found on Kronykin, do you imagine that if I'd arranged Dolgov's death, I would have given Kronykin a weapon registered with the Militia in my name and traceable to me? Or are you suggesting that I am as mad as you think Dolgov was?'

'You slipped up,' Yuri said, uneasily. 'You thought that by filing off the numbers, the gun couldn't be traced back to you.'

'You think I don't know about acid etching?' Drasen shouted. 'You think I haven't lived in Moscow long enough to know where to buy a gun?'

Yuri shifted uncomfortably in his chair. 'Perhaps the gun was a mistake,' he said, weakly. 'Perhaps you didn't think about it, because you didn't expect it to be used, or for it to be found.'

'Perhaps,' Drasen said, sarcastically. He thrust his head forward belligerently. 'You said we wanted to kill Dolgov to prevent him talking about 1953, right?'

Yuri nodded.

'In that case why would we have used Kronykin who was a direct link to all that happened in 1953?'

Yuri stared numbly at Drasen. With a few pointed questions Drasen had made nonsense of his theories. And if his theories were nonsense . . .

Drasen said, 'When confronted with a murder, Captain Raikin, the first question an experienced investigator asks is: Who benefits? J. Edgar Hoover told me that. So let us look at Dolgov's killing and ask, Who benefits? Not us, whom you have accused. If we were guilty of what you have accused us of, the last thing we would want was Dolgov murdered and his testament published.

'If that is why we *didn't* kill Dolgov, then it stands to reason that whoever did, wanted that testament published – or wanted to use the threat of it being published. And that person also wanted to lay a trail back to 1953. Otherwise, why use Kronykin?

'So the next question we must ask is: Who had Kronykin murder Dolgov? And then, how was Kronykin persuaded?

'Kronykin, we know, was not a well man. He had been suffering recurrent headaches and amnesia since his return from

Afghanistan. He had been arrested for spreading scurrilous rumours and sentenced to rehabilitation, a psychological process whose object is to permanently alter a man's behaviour. A logical place to begin our inquiry would therefore be the Fifth Directorate where Kronykin's behavioural processes were changed, and where he was probably induced to murder Dolgov.'

Yuri said, 'I have spoken with Director Guschin of the Fifth Directorate. He denies that Kronykin's treatment was improper, or that it had anything to do with his killing Dolgov.'

Drasen smiled, thinly. 'What did you expect? A confession of conspiracy and murder?'

'But why would Director Guschin want Dolgov dead?'

'No reason, unless Director Guschin was part of a larger conspiracy which required Dolgov to be murdered.'

Drasen was standing everything on its head. He was accusing Guschin, one of Yuri's unimpeachable witnesses, of conspiring to murder Dolgov. Yet, there was something convincing about Drasen's reasoning. Yuri reached beneath his shirt and removed the transmitter batteries.

Drasen noticed the gesture and smiled. 'Let us assume a certain group of people wanted to oust Deryugin.'

'Who?' Yuri asked. 'The Krasnaya Dela?'

'If you like. In this country the means of revolution, the possibility of changing a leader are severely limited. A hierarchical, tightly controlled and closely meshed power structure sees to that. I remember, for instance, the machinations that went on at the time Khrushchev was forced to resign – his supporters prevented from returning to Moscow, his opponents brought in secretly, deals made with the Army and even the Kremlin internal phone directory altered – all that to depose a man the majority of the Politburo wanted to get rid of.

'A minority does not have a chance. The only means open to them are assassination or embarrassment. Assassination can only be a last resort. So these men, your Krasnaya Dela and others attempted to disgrace Deryugin by exposing his links to Lazar.

'Deryugin appointed one of the conspirators, Soslan Zarev to inquire into his relationship with Lazar. And Zarev found Deryugin had nothing to hide.

'The truth, Yuri, is that Deryugin is a completely political animal. His highs come not from personal wealth but the exercise of power. He's never taken anything from anyone. He has no Swiss bank account and no secret fortune. So faced with confirming Deryugin's innocence, Zarev broadened the scope of his inquiry and found others that were corrupt, but nothing he could use against Deryugin.

'Zarev and his fellow conspirators were driven to other means. Dolgov. Kronykin. The only purpose Dolgov's death served was to threaten Deryugin with the publication of the Dolgov testament. This fear alone would have compelled any General Secretary to seek an accomodation.'

'Moreso, if he had been connected to the events of 1953,' Yuri said. So far, Drasen had provided a convincing alternative. But the only way to find out if Drasen's story was a carefully constructed lie or not, was to see if Drasen would lie about Stalin's murder. 'Was Deryugin involved with Stalin's murder?' Yuri asked.

Drasen was silent. Carefully he selected another cigarette from the gunmetal case. 'In 1953,' he said, exhaling twin streams of smoke, 'Deryugin was Controller of the State Bank, an important position, but not as important as membership of the Central Committee or the Politburo. In his capacity as Controller, Deryugin was ordered by certain high ranking members of the government to arrange for the secret transfer of $250,000 to Vyssorian Dolgov.'

'Are you saying Deryugin had no idea of why the payments were being made?'

'Not at first. But in the end, he had to be told. No one wanted to take the risk of Dolgov walking off with $250,000.'

'So Deryugin came to you and the CIA? Why?'

Drasen smiled. 'One of the most touching things about the men who conspired to eliminate Stalin was that they could not raise $250,000. They were powerful men, they lived in large apartments, they had the use of cars and dachas, they controlled whole armies and industries worth billions. They had power, prestige – everything but money. So they had to use government funds to pay Dolgov. But even though the payment was being laundered, there was a danger that someone would demand to see the licences that had been bought from my company, demand they be put to use. In an organization as large as the State Bank there were hundreds of ways someone could discover the payment was false and what had really happened.'

'Why did you and the CIA agree to become involved?'

'Ordinarily,' Drasen replied 'we wouldn't have. Stalin's intended elimination of his key supporters was essentially an internal Russian matter and none of our business.' Drasen smiled grimly. 'Not until later, that is. Until 22nd January, 1953 to be precise, when I heard from an impeccable source that Stalin was planning war against Europe. That source was a very patriotic Russian. A gallant soldier who had proved himself many times in battle.' The smile became broader. 'He was, Yuri, a Major General Gennadi Raikin.'

'My father is not a traitor!' Yuri shouted. Yet, as he shouted, he recalled his father's hesitancy at dinner, when he'd told the story of Stalin's plan.

'Your father is not a traitor,' Drasen agreed. 'He was, and is an extremely courageous and honourable human being. In January 1953, he saw very clearly that another war would ruin Russia as well as Europe. So he did what had to be done. Just as we did what we had to do.'

'Did my father —' Yuri began, 'did he have any part in what happened afterwards?'

Drasen shook his head. 'No. But the effect of his information was to compel us to support the conspiracy. We couldn't allow another war to start.'

Yuri thrust his head between his hands. Drasen had not lied. Drasen had admitted that Stalin had been murdered, admitted his part in the conspiracy. And if Drasen had spoken the truth about that . . . He thought of Zarev, of Guschin, Suslov and the Krasnaya Dela. He thought of Simmonds and Vilna, of what had happened in London, and of how Zamyatin had been killed. He thought of Gvishani, his friend Gvishani.

'You chose the wrong side, Yuri,' Drasen said, softly. 'You should have trusted Popov. He is an honest man. Dolgov's murder gave him an enormous problem. He could not acknowledge that Dolgov had been murdered for fear the testament would be published. Yet he had to find out who killed Dolgov. So he tried to use you, in the same way he'd used you to find out the complicity of the First Directorate. That's why he kept pointing you over and over again in the direction of Kronykin. But you were ... over enthusiastic. You kept darting off in the wrong direction. And when you came too close to finding out what you shouldn't, he was forced to suspend you from the Sluzbha.' Drasen put out his cigarette and looked directly at Yuri. 'Do you realize how dangerous you are now to any Russian government? With what you know, you could become another Dolgov.'

'I don't want to be that,' Yuri said, tightly, and looked away. Oh God, how could he have been so wrong! Why hadn't he thought a little deeper? Why hadn't he talked to his father? Why hadn't he accepted his father's evaluation of Popov? And heeded Sonya's warnings about Gvishani? He looked back at Drasen. 'What the hell do I do now?'

Drasen gave him a craggy grin. 'I was hoping you'd ask that. Don't worry. We're still in there pitching, and you may have found out more important information than if you'd gone after Kronykin.' He stood up and stretched, then sat down on the edge of the sofa. 'Popov's at his dacha. We should go there now and you must tell him everything you've found out. Then, maybe you'll have to go to Washington.'

'Washington? What for?'

'To meet with Charlie Simmonds. Turayev gave Simmonds the names of the people behind Zarev, Suslov and Guschin. And Simmonds has agreed to give them to you.'

Yuri got to his feet. He'd got so much wrong, now there was a chance to do something right. 'Let's get the hell out of here,' he said.

The door burst open. Two burly, unshaven men wearing camouflage jackets rushed into the room. Their eyes had a wild, manic look. They carried silenced Stechkin 9mm machine pistols fitted onto wooden stocks.

Yuri dived for the Makarov. The table tilted. The lamp cartwheeled, flashed and shattered. 'Drasen! Down!'

The darkness spat splinters of flame. The frenzied coughing of automatic weapons filled his ears. Fire raked the room. Glass tinkled and shattered.

Yuri saw a figure framed in the lit doorway. He fired, once, twice. A scream. The thud of a falling body. A throaty, wet gurgling by his shoulder.

Yuri pressed himself against Drasen, pressed himself against the sofa. Damp seeped through his shirt sleeve.

One man was down, the other crouching in the darkness. Yuri waited, motionless.

Suddenly, light blazed. Light enveloped him. Yuri raised the Makarov aiming to one side of the flashlight. The pull of the trigger jerked the weapon upwards. He aimed again. A hesitant click. The casing hadn't ejected. The slide had jammed.

In the darkness behind the flashlight, Yuri heard the rustle of clothing as the man lifted the Stechkin. He stared wide eyed at death.

The man was setting the Stechkin to semi-automatic fire. A good soldier, this one. The selector mechanism clicked. Yuri stared at the shadow beside the light. His mouth was dry, his heart pounded furiously. Drasen's blood soaked his arm.

He was going to die. Now! Murdered by a man he didn't know, a shadow behind a light.

Then he remembered another shadow exploding out of the darkness and in the moment of death there was a startling clarity. Tsaritsyn! Tsaritsyn, which Stalin had held and renamed Stalingrad. The snow of Tsaritsyn. Abyugov, who had tried to kill him, had remembered Tsaritsyn. So too had Sergei Kronykin.

He ran his tongue over dry lips, forced himself to speak. 'The snow of Tsaritsyn. Remember the snow of Tsaritsyn.'

He moved. Nothing happened. He was still speaking, still alive. He rose to his knees. The flashlight followed his movements, but no bullets spat out of the shadows. Yuri forced himself to speak calmly. 'Move the selector to position three.'

First silence, then a soft click.

Yuri breathed out slowly. 'Place the gun at your feet.'

The flashlight danced. Clothing rustled. There was a hiss of breath sharply expelled. Something heavy was laid on the carpet.

Yuri stood up holding the useless Makarov. 'Give me the light.'

The flashlight was place in his outstretched hand.

Yuri turned it on the man. A swarthy, unshaven face bathed in sweat. Eyes flecked with red, shiny and bulbous. Manic. A trembling mouth, rimmed with saliva. 'Who are you?' Yuri asked. 'Who sent you?' The flashlight in his hand trembled. In a slow, even voice he asked, 'Where did you come from?'

Suddenly the man whirled away from Yuri, his hand whipping to a pocket in his combat jacket. Too late, Yuri saw the gleam of metal. Too late, he recognized the small TK 6.34mm clutched in the man's fist. Before Yuri could move, the man had placed the gun against his mouth and pulled the trigger.

The man's head jerked back. A dark projectile spun from his head, slipstreaming blood and hair. The man fell clumsily backwards. The gun thudded to the carpet.

Yuri rushed over to him.

The man lay on his back, arms outspread. Broken teeth and splinters of bone gleamed about his head. The head itself was strangely flattened. Blood wept from nose and staring eyes.

Yuri hurried to the door and shut it, turned on the main light. The other man from STF 29 lay crumpled in the doorway, hands pressed to the gaping wound in his throat.

Yuri walked over to Drasen. Drasen lay on his side, his body curled as if to deflect the crazy pattern of bloody holes that riddled his suit.

The blood, Yuri saw, had stopped flowing.

CHAPTER THIRTY-THREE

The dacha basked in dappled afternoon sunlight, its yellow brick seeming to soak up the sun. A breeze scudded across the somnolent Moskva, ruffling the tangled grass on the bluff. Hay seeds floated. On the lawn, sunlight danced off bottles and plates. Yuri got out of the car and shut the door softly, as if any noise would break the spell. He walked lightly up the short drive to the front door.

It was cool in the shade of the porch. Drasen's blood had formed a flaky crust on his jacket and shirt. Yuri pressed the bell. It pealed hollowly.

He hoped Popov hadn't gone to summon other officials. He didn't want to talk to anyone but Popov. Yuri peered round the edge of the house. The garage was shut. Birds swooped low across the abandoned dining table. Flies buzzed. Yuri rang the bell again.

There was no answer. The door, he saw, was slightly ajar, in discreet invitation. Perhaps Popov had gone to summon Deryugin. Perhaps he'd left the door ajar so that Yuri could go in and wait.

Yuri pressed the bell again, and was rewarded by a silence that was absolute.

He pressed gently against the door. It moved and stuck, barred by something soft and heavy. Yuri pressed harder. Whatever it was yielded, with a soft, dragging sound. Not a door stop. A large cushion or pillow. No, something more solid than that.

Yuri leaned his shoulder against the door, eased his head into the resultant crack. The curtains were drawn, the dacha was dark. Something dark and glistening lay on the floor behind the door, a shape stretched out like a shadow. Yuri pushed against the door and went in.

Popov lay spread on his back in the lobby, his arms flung up by the side of his head. His bare, hairless legs protruded from the ends of baggy tennis short. His tennis shirt was cratered with red. Dark, shiny streaks ran from his body and his bald, glistening head. His face was contorted and pale, the mouth twisted in anger.

Yuri eased the door shut. Mechanically he knelt beside Popov. The bullet wounds were like crushed red flowers. He placed his head by Popov's face. Popov was dead.

Yuri stood up, too shocked to feel panic or fear. Guschin and the others had anticipated his visiting Popov and despatched their manic killers.

Yuri walked past Popov into the lounge. Mariya Popova lay on her side on the polished boards, a lambswool rug scrunched up by the force of her fall, spattered with blood as if the floor itself had bled. A hand was thrown over her face, her hair streaked along the floor, her legs spread, so that in silhouette she seemed to be running.

Yuri took her hand. It was lifeless, still flexible. There was no pulse. He remembered her telling Popov not to drink vodka in the sun, remembered her piling his plate with food, remembered her laugh. How could they do this? Popov might have been an obstacle, but his wife had been innocent. She hadn't even been in the way.

All at once he felt the shock recede. He felt anger, like a deep, subterranean explosion, a terrible anger that had no heat, that was like a blue flame.

Gently he laid the dead woman's hand across her face and went out.

Outside, the sun was an angry white light. A bright flash nearly blinded him. Instinctively he cowered, blinked. There was a shiny black Volga drawn up across the end of the short drive, blocking his car. Two uniformed men sat in it, looking at him with a kind of placid menace.

As Yuri walked to his car, one of the men got out, a tall man, walking along the drive with a quietly confident swagger. His cap was pulled deep over his eyes. His hand rested casually on the open holster attached to his belt.

'Captain Raikin?' the voice was low, self assured. 'Please come with us.'

'Why?'

A tight, confident smile, a flash of pearly, even teeth. 'Let us say, you are under arrest for the murder of Comrade Director Popov and his wife.'

Guschin's men. Popov's killers. They wore, Yuri saw, the red and green shoulder tabs of the Guards Directorate. 'I don't know what you're talking about.'

'Come off it, Captain. We heard the shots, we've seen the bodies and you've got blood on your jacket. Don't make it unnecessarily hard on yourself.'

He was holding his hand out, beckoning.

Yuri felt his body grow cold, as if wrapped in a damp winding sheet. He hardly felt the air whispering in and out of his lungs. His head seemed buried in ice. He took one step forward, stumbled and fell against his car.

The man reached out to catch him.

Yuri moved. As the man bent forward, Yuri's hand snaked up, slicing viciously between the man's legs. The man gasped. His head curved down. Yuri stepped aside, grabbed him by the collar and slammed that confident, smirking face against the side of the car.

The man's cap crumpled and buckled. A bloody dent appeared on the Zhiguli's door. Yuri pulled the man back, the face like a sponge spouting blood. In a cold fury, Yuri slammed him into the car again.

The other policeman was getting out of the Volga, easing his head over the roof. Yuri chopped viciously down at the man he held, crushing through the bone and muscle on the back of the man's neck. The man gurgled and went limp. Yuri dropped him face down on the drive and ran.

The second policeman, wedged in the open door was fumbling for his gun.

Yuri sprinted eight, long, lunging strides. Eight strides, and then he leapt high into the air.

He landed feet first on the bonnet of the Volga. The metal vibrated under his weight. His feet slipped and gouged into the paintwork. The second policeman had his gun out, was turning trying to get it aimed at Yuri. Yuri leapt at him, kicking wildly.

His foot glanced off the man's head. He heard a grunt, saw

the cap spin off. Then he was landing on the road, his knees bent to absorb the shock, straightening up again, turning. He grabbed the door of the car, pulled it towards him, then slammed it into the man's body.

The man screamed, twisted, struggled. He tried to bring his gun down to the level of the open window. Yuri hit him with the door again, moved forward, spreading his hands into claws.

No space for a crippling blow to the body. No room for a paralyzing blow to the neck. Yuri jammed his fingers into the man's eyes. The watery softness closed round his fingertips like thick jelly.

The gun clattered to the road. Yuri pulled the door away. The man rolled helplessly along the side of the car, moaning, pressing his hands to his face.

Swiftly Yuri hit him hard behind the ear.

The man stopped moaning and fell.

Quickly Yuri stuffed the man into the back of the car. He moved the car clear of the driveway, then reversed the Zhiguli onto the road and left it with engine running. He reversed the police Volga into Popov's drive, opened the boot and heaved the other man into it.

Then he ran back to the Zhiguli, turned it round quickly and drove for the exit.

The afternoon sun danced brightly through the windscreen.

CHAPTER THIRTY-FOUR

Yuri drove steadily back to Moscow, forcing himself to keep pace with the dawdling Sunday afternoon traffic, his anger refined by violence.

Three people had died because he'd been obsessive, because he'd picked the wrong side. If he hadn't been so arrogant, if he'd done what Popov wanted, if he hadn't questioned and doubted ... but what had Popov wanted him to do? Investigate Kronykin. And where would that have led? And if his investigation of Kronykin had led to the conspirators, would the result have been much different?

The men behind Gvishani and Zarev were playing for the highest stakes of all. They would have killed a hundred times over to prevent being discovered. Whatever he'd investigated, they would have done exactly the same thing.

So what could he do now? Popov would have used his evidence to order arrests and extract confessions. Popov had the power to move against men like Zarev. Without Popov ...

He could file a formal report with the Sluzbha. He could present his evidence to Popov's successor, he could tell all to the enquiry into the deaths of Drasen and the Popovs.

But none of it would be any use. It would take a man with strong convictions to believe him, to challenge other directorates and seek out influential politicians. And what, if Popov's successor, if any of the other officers involved in examining his evidence, were Krasnaya Dela?

So take it to Deryugin. If he could get to Deryugin. If none of those who stood between him and Deryugin were Krasnaya Dela. Turayev's problem.

He drove steadily on, forcing himself to remain inconspicuous by mingling with the other traffic. Even if he did get to Deryugin, how would the General Secretary react to the knowledge that an outsider knew what had happened in 1953?

That a Captain in the KGB could bring down his government? The barricades would be raised, he thought, the nervous Russian political machine go to work. His evidence would be suppressed. More than likely, *he* would be suppressed.

But he had to do something. Gvishani, Zarev, Guschin and those mysterious others behind them, wanted the evidence he'd collected, the evidence which lay in his coat pocket and in his safe at the Sluzbha. They needed that evidence, and they would stop at nothing to get it. And after they had what they wanted, they'd kill him.

He felt his hands tremble on the wheel, a reaction from all the violence. That and fear. He was challenging powerful men, men who controlled vast forces and manic killers. He couldn't do it. Better to run and hide.

Hide where?

He drove to his father's.

The Marshal came to the door, carrying a recently published campaign history of Plotova. His eyes were reddened, his face creased with recent sleep. Tufts of spiky white hair sprouted from his open shirt front.

'Yuri, Yasha – what's happened? Are you hurt?'

'I'm all right. It isn't my blood.' He pushed past his father into the apartment. 'I need to use the phone.' He called Sonya at Katyusha Asonova's apartment. 'Something's happened,' he told her, urgently. 'I can't explain over the phone. Come to the Marshal's straight away.'

He put the phone down and turned to face his father. 'Popov, his wife and John Drasen have all been murdered,' he said. 'Drasen was killed in Sonya's apartment. I was meeting with him there. I need to get Sonya out of the way and somewhere safe for a bit. Can you arrange for her to be flown to Yevpatoriya tonight? Can you get her an escort to the airport?'

'What's all this about?' the Marshal demanded. 'What's –'

'Later,' Yuri insisted. 'Sonya first. Please.'

The Marshal stared at him for a moment. Then he said, 'I hope you know what you're doing.' He shouldered Yuri away from the phone and made two calls. 'Everything's arranged,' he said when he'd finished. 'The men will be here in an hour. Now tell me what the devil all this is about.'

They sat in the living room, on hard leather chairs. Surrounded by relics of another war, Yuri told the Marshal how his investigation into Dolgov's murder had led to his discovery of the murder of Stalin. He told him of Dolgov's bank account and testament, how Gvishani, Zarev and others were conspiring to use that testament and the evidence he had gathered, to topple Deryugin. He told the Marshal of his meeting with Drasen and his visit to Zhukovka. 'And now they're looking for me,' he finished. 'To make me give them what I have and then to kill me.'

The Marshal's face was ashen, his eyes like holes cut in a sheet. 'The sins of the fathers,' he muttered. 'If all those years ago I hadn't gone to Drasen –'

'No,' Yuri cried. 'You did right to involve the Americans. Another war would have –'

'I don't need you to tell me I did right,' the Marshal said angrily.

Yuri said, 'We've both done what we thought was right. We couldn't have done anything else.'

For a long while, the Marshal stared at him thoughtfully. Then he said, 'We must take your story to the proper authority.'

'Who's that?' Yuri asked. 'Who can we trust? All that will happen, is that you will be vilified for what happened in 1953 and my evidence will be suppressed, disbelieved or used against me. The people behind Zarev will go to ground, and emerge later, more secretly and better organised. This is not a job for armies, father. It's for a small group of people, for one man.'

'They will kill you,' his father said softly. 'Yasha, I can't let you do this. You're my only son. You're all I have. Look around you. There are two hundred and fifty million Russians. Let one of them do it. Russia is a vast country, an immensely strong country. It survived the Tsars, it survived Stalin. It will survive these people too.'

Yuri collected a glass of milk from the kitchen and came back. 'Is that what you really want me to do? Is that what you would do, if you were me?'

'I don't know,' his father said. 'I faced German armour. I led raids behind German lines. I fought my way out of Kiev and all the way back to Moscow. I've fought Chinese and Japanese. I've faced knives, bayonets, bullets, canon and bombs. But none of that terrified me as much as this.'

His father stopped abruptly, as if he'd walked into a wall. The thin strands of muscle flanking his throat quivered. Suddenly, there were tears in his eyes. 'Igor,' he said and swallowed hard. He clenched his jaws. Then his shoulders shook. 'For a year – for a whole year –' Tears rolled unheeded down his grizzled cheeks. 'Igor and I harassed the Germans. It was hit and run, but sometimes we stayed. We filled the air with radio messages, so that at times the Germans believed there was an entire army behind their lines. Igor and I ...' Angrily, the Marshal wiped his face with the back of his hand. 'I wish Igor were here to help us, now.'

'Igor taught me a lot,' Yuri said.

'I know.' His father stared pensively into space. 'And sometimes I resented him for that. But I couldn't – I wasn't made that way. I never had a lot of patience.'

'Perhaps it was better the way it turned out,' Yuri said. He closed his eyes, blinking back a sudden stinging. The Marshal and he had spoken as father and son, as two people. The Marshal had reached out to him. And he had finally reached his father.

'What do you propose to do, Yasha?' his father asked.

'Get to Simmonds. Simmonds knows the names.'

'How will you get out of Russia? Shall I –'

'No, you mustn't be involved now. When I get back with the Simmonds' information, then I'll need all your help, all your influence and prestige. For now, just look after Sonya for me.'

'That's taken care of.'

They sat in silence. Yuri wished he didn't have to leave, wished he could stay here with his father and talk. He rested his head against the back of the chair and thought how he would get out of Russia. His father brought him another glass of milk and some biscuits.

'You look exhausted, son. Can I get you something else?'

'No, thank you.'

His father cleared his throat. 'There's something I must tell you,' he said, formally. 'I am proud of you, Yasha. I've always been proud of you. I want you to know that.'

'You've always set me an example,' Yuri said. 'You should know that, too.'

His father sat down. 'You know, when you wanted to go to MIMO I was very disappointed, because I wanted you to be a soldier. You remember, I called you a woman, I told you that diplomats were no effing good.'

'Assholes,' Yuri murmured smiling.

'Worse than assholes,' his father said. 'But it hasn't turned out like that, has it? I was the proudest man in Russia when you came back from Africa with the Order of the Red Banner. And I'm even prouder of you now.' He paused and added, 'Whatever happens.'

Yuri went over and kissed his father on both cheeks. He remained with his arms round his father's shoulders feeling his father's strength, feeling like a little boy again, till the doorbell rang and the Marshal went to let Sonya in.

'I'm not hurt,' Yuri said. 'You were right about Gvishani. They killed John Drasen.'

'Drasen! My God, how terrible!'

'Popov's dead too. And his wife. Sonya, there isn't time to explain. I've arranged for you to go to Yevpatoriya for a few days. The Marshal has arranged for an escort –'

'But I'm staying with you.'

Yuri took her hands in his. 'I'm not staying here,' he said softly. 'And you can't come where I'm going. The best way you can help me, is by going to Yevpatoriya. I don't want you falling into their hands. Sonya, today they killed three important people. They know about you and me. When they can't find me, they'll come after you.'

'But –'

'No buts. There's a time to run and a time to fight. For now, you've got to run. Go right away. Don't go back to the apartment to collect anything. Do you have any money?'

'Yes, but I'm not worried about that. What's going to happen to you?'

'I'll be back in a few days. Then everything will be all right.'

She came into his arms and hugged him. 'Yasha, you will be careful.'

'I'm always careful.'

'You will – will come back?'

'Of course. I'll never leave you.'

The doorbell rang again.

Gently, the Marshal led her away.

CHAPTER THIRTY-FIVE

Yuri abandoned his car near the Paveletskaya station and took the metro to Pasha's modern apartment block near the Dynamo Stadium. When Yuri arrived he was kneeling in the living room, buried up to the forearms in the soil of a window box. Other window boxes lay about the carpet, like minute graves. He looked up as Yuri entered behind Pasha's wife, a dark haired Georgian nearly as large as Pasha himself.

'As you can see, I am gardening. If I had the time to look after it I'd get one of those allotments on the other side of the stadium, grow my own vegetables and become a capitalist.'

Funny, Yuri thought, he'd always categorised Pasha as a city person.

Pasha's wife asked if they wanted tea. Pasha stood up, wiping his hands with a dirty rag, dropping small clods of earth on the carpet. 'What's brought you here on a Sunday afternoon?'

'Popov,' Yuri said. 'Popov's dead.'

Pasha's face darkened. A taut blue tube of vein stood out on his forehead. His hands balled into massive fists. 'Don't say things like that even in fun. It's bad luck.'

Yuri said, 'It isn't a joke. Popov and his wife were murdered this afternoon.'

'I told you, don't make jokes like that,' Pasha looked round the room till he spotted his bleeper on the mantlepiece. 'No one's called me,' he said, belligerently.

Yuri asked, 'Do you have an official car here?'

'In the courtyard.'

'Why don't we go down and listen to the radio?'

They went and sat in the car. Beyond a low fence, children pushed swings, rode a see-saw, dangled from a climbing frame. When he'd lived with Tanty Sima, Yuri remembered, all he'd had was a wooden horse.

The radio babbled. Cars were being directed to one point after another. Radio operators called control, called each other. 'They're setting up road blocks around Zhukovka,' Yuri said.

Pasha stared, frowning, at the radio. 'Those are Fifth Directorate signals. If Popov's been killed, why the fuck aren't we looking for his killers?'

'Because Guschin organised Popov's death.'

Pasha's eyes blazed. His face contorted with fury. 'Fuck!' he cried and flung open the door of the car.

'Pasha, what are you doing?'

'Getting my gun. I'm going to burn that bastard Guschin. I'm going to blast the whole fucking Fifth Directorate.'

Yuri grabbed Pasha's shirt, grabbed one massive arm. 'Pasha, wait, listen. You're not going to achieve anything that way.'

'Fuck achievement! Fuck your mother! Let me get my gun!'

'Listen!' Yuri pleaded. 'Wait! Think!'

Pasha wrenched his arm away. 'There's nothing to bloody think about!'

Yuri said quickly. 'There are too many for you to kill. This whole thing's too big for personal revenge.'

'What the hell are you talking about?'

'If you want to know what happened, you'd better sit down.'

Pasha glowered down at him. Then he said, 'All right, I'll listen. And then I'll get those bastards.' He flung himself down on the seat so hard the car rocked.

Yuri told Pasha that he, Popov and Drasen were working against a conspiracy by the Krasnaya Dela to overthrow Deryugin.

'Why you?' Pasha asked suspiciously.

'Because in London, I stopped them from killing an agent called Simmonds.' He told Pasha briefly about Simmonds. 'Popov then brought me back here to investigate the First.'

'I thought there was something funny about you from the beginning,' Pasha said.

'When I found out too much, the First tried to kill me. They knew I'd got to Zamyatin, so they killed him. Dolgov's murder is part of the same conspiracy.'

The car creaked as Pasha turned in his seat. 'Dolgov wasn't murdered,' he cried.

'Popov couldn't publicly admit to Dolgov's murder.'

Pasha grabbed Yuri by the jacket and dragged him across the seat. 'Don't you dare say things like that!' he shouted.

Yuri pressed his elbow into Pasha's throat. 'Let me go and I'll show you something.'

Reluctantly, Pasha released him.

Yuri reached into his pocket and showed Pasha Dolgov's instructions to the Staaderbank. 'In 1953,' he said, 'Dolgov committed a terrible crime. If the truth about that crime were ever published, Deryugin will fall, Deryugin's government will fall, and those men who killed Dolgov, those people who killed Popov, his wife, and John Drasen, will form the new government.'

Pasha stared open mouthed at Yuri. 'Holy shit!' he muttered.

'That's why Popov had to hide the fact of Dolgov's murder,' Yuri continued. 'That's why Popov had to pretend the murder hadn't taken place and at the same time keep the investigation going.'

'So that's why he didn't close the investigation down when I wanted him to,' Pasha said.

Yuri nodded. 'And why he wanted me to keep after Kronykin. Popov thought Kronykin would give us a lead as to the conspirators. So I investigated Kronykin and the trail led to Soslan Zarev, to Gvishani Kirichenko, to Director Guschin.'

Pasha flung open the door of the car. 'What the hell are we sitting here for? Let's go get the bastards!'

Yuri hung onto Pasha's jacket. 'For heaven's sake, Pasha, wait till I've finished.'

Reluctantly, Pasha edged back into the car. 'Get on with it, then.'

'I met with Drasen today to get more evidence. I was just leaving with Drasen to see Popov at Zhukovka, when we were attacked. Drasen was killed. I got one of them.'

He told Pasha of his visit to Zhukovka, his discovery of the bodies of Popov and his wife, of the attempt to arrest him.

'You should have put out an A10 alert,' Pasha grumbled. 'You'd have had the whole fucking Sluzbha in Zhukovka.'

'To arrest two minions from the Fifth, who were acting under orders? No, Pasha, we need to do more than that. Popov would have wanted us to do more than that. Popov wanted the men behind the Krasnaya Dela. And I want you to help me to get them.'

'Me? How?' Pasha's eyes were orbs of surprise.

'Simmonds has asked to see me. He will give me the names Turayev gave him. I've got to meet with Simmonds. You must help me get out of Russia.'

'You know that's impossible. You might as well ask me to help you get to the moon.' Pasha turned angrily away and stared through the windscreen. He beat his palm against the steering wheel.

It isn't impossible for you,' Yuri said. 'You know the procedure for Agent Priority *Odin*. You can arrange it.'

Still looking ahead, Pasha said, 'I need the authority of the Director.'

'Haven't you had verbal authority before? Authority that was going to be ratified later?'

'Yes,' Pasha said. 'But Popov's –'

'You don't really know that, do you? You only know that, because I've told you.' Yuri paused and added, 'Simmonds knows the names, Pasha. Simmonds wants to talk to me. With those names we'll get the people who murdered Popov.'

Pasha stared silently through the windscreen. The sun dipped behind the building. Shadows stretched across the courtyard. Pasha muttered, 'How the hell do I tell Freddy?'

'Freddy?'

'My boy.'

'I didn't know you had a son.'

'His name is Pavel,' Pasha said, 'and he's twelve years old. He was born with a kidney defect and has to stay in a hospital where they give him a special diet and regular dialysis. It was Popov who started calling him Freddy. Popov and his wife used to go down and see Freddy every other week. Popov even taught him tennis.' Pasha wiped his eyes furiously with the back of his hand.

Yuri looked away.

After a long while Pasha asked, 'How the hell do I know you aren't in with Zarev and the others? How the hell do I know you didn't kill Popov?'

Yuri reached beneath his jacket and took out the Makarov. Butt first he handed it to Pasha. 'Two bullets,' he said. 'Three people.'

Pasha slid open the magazine and checked. He sniffed the barrel and gave the gun back to Yuri. 'Remember,' he warned, 'If you cross me, I'll get an *Odin* Priority myself and come after you, and all your fancy judo tricks won't stop me from breaking your fucking neck.' He looked away and switched on the ignition. 'Let's go.'

While Pasha bustled about headquarters barking into phones and stamping documents, Yuri went through the Dolgov evidence. He kept the passport Drasen had given Dolgov in the name of George Smirnin, the photograph of Simmonds and Snead and Misha's pictures showing how that photograph had been produced. The rest of the dossier, Kronykin's scribblings, the post mortem and ballistics reports, the notes of his interviews with Evgenya Kronykina, Dolgov's testament and bank statements, he put into a large envelope, sealed it securely and mailed it to George Smirnin, Post Restante, K-600, Moscow. The post office would be more secure than KGB headquarters and it was a small guarantee of his safety.

When he got back to his office, Pasha was there with a change of clothing, five hundred dollars in cash, a plane ticket and an impressively sealed document. 'Get changed quickly and I'll take you to Sheremetyevo,' he said. 'They're holding a seat on a British Airways flight to London for you, and we're late.'

'Thanks,' Yuri said, picking up the clothes Pasha had brought. They were the best Russian quality and looked as if they fitted. He peeled off his bloodstained jacket and began to dress. 'Thanks a lot.'

'No trouble,' Pasha said. He grinned and took Yuri's KGB work pass from his pocket. 'Even in America,' he said, 'you might find a use for this.'

CHAPTER THIRTY-SIX

London was three hours behind Moscow. Effectively, Yuri arrived forty-five minutes after he left. Without baggage and with his diplomatic passport, he was in the bustle of Heathrow's Terminal 1 in minutes.

People pressed behind barriers. Chauffeurs stood holding placards for arriving businessmen. The public address system repeatedly asked passengers to go to an information desk. Yuri followed red and blue signs to the Underground.

Standing on the platform, looking at a map of London's subway system, memories filtered back. Every agent assigned to a foreign capital was required to memorise its streets, learn its subway system, know when and where its buses ran. Yuri felt he knew London as well as he knew Moscow. He bought a ticket to Green Park in London's West End.

It was an area between the theatres and restaurants of Shaftesbury Avenue and the gracious sweep of Park Lane. The preserve of luxury hotels, embassies, expensive shops and a few exclusive restaurants, its pavements were empty. A watery sun meandered between the buildings, diluting the weak glow of street lamps as Yuri walked north towards Grosvenor Square.

He hoped George Carpenter would be working this late on a Saturday. But working or not, Yuri knew the embassy would arrange for Carpenter to get in touch. Men in Carpenter's job did not have the luxury of fixed hours or weekends.

In a large square flanked by car showrooms he found a call box, dialled the American Embassy and asked for George Carpenter.

Carpenter was working. 'George Carpenter,' he said.

'This is Mikhail. The friend of Charlie Simmonds.'

There was a measured pause. Yuri wondered if Carpenter was switching on a recording device. Carpenter said, 'Oh yes.'

'I want to talk. Now.'

Again the measured pause. Carpenter was thinking he wanted to defect. Good!

'Let me see –'

'Now!' Yuri was surprised how panicky he'd made his voice sound. 'In five minutes, walk out of the embassy through the Upper Brook Street exit. Walk east along Grosvenor Square towards Claridges.'

In the silence that followed, he wondered if Carpenter suspected a trap. Then he realized that Carpenter knew all about him through Simmonds.

Carpenter asked, 'How will we recognise each other?'

'We've both worked in London and seen each other's photographs.'

Yuri put the phone down and hurried into the street. A taxi! He needed a taxi! He saw a dim yellow light floating above the street and rushed into the road. He was outside a wine bar which flanked the embassy in less than a minute.

Exactly four minutes later, Carpenter slid between the tall glass doors and walked briskly down the broad steps to the street. He was a man of medium height and medium build. He wore a neat blue raincoat and a narrow brimmed brown hat. Underneath the hat, the face was nondescript, wide mouthed, with a hint of cragginess. Carpenter wore circular, horn rimmed spectacles.

Yuri allowed Carpenter to walk past the wine bar, caught up with him halfway along the square. 'I want to talk to Simmonds,' Yuri said, falling into step beside Carpenter. 'I'll meet him anywhere you say, anytime. Your people can be present throughout the meeting. In exchange, I'll give you the names of three companies for your black list. West German companies who supply us with your latest developments in micro-technology.'

Carpenter laughed easily. 'Boy oh boy, you must want to see Simmonds bad.' He turned and squinted at Yuri. 'I wish I could help you, especially if you're going to give me those names. But I can't. Simmonds is dead.'

Simmonds dead! A chill worm of fear twisted his gut. It wasn't true! It couldn't be true! Carpenter was simply following procedure and denying the existence of a defector.

'Come off it, Carpenter,' Yuri cried. 'This is Mikhail, you're talking to. I ran Simmonds. I allowed him to defect.'

'I know all about that. But I can't help you, buddy. Simmonds is dead. If you want proof, his body is being flown back to London tomorrow. I'll give you the address of the funeral parlour. Go round with a wreath and take a look for yourself.'

Carpenter wasn't lying. A dead double was too elaborate a cover for a defector like Simmonds. Yuri felt as if one of Stalin's Gothic monstrosities had fallen on him. Without Simmonds he was lost. He could prove nothing. He was marooned outside Russia. 'You idiots,' he groaned between clenched teeth. 'I gave you Simmonds and you lost him.'

Carpenter said, 'He had a heart attack.'

Heart attack! Dolgov had died of a heart attack. Heart attacks were the likeliest cover for murder. Yuri said, 'Simmonds was young. Simmonds was healthy. What did you people do to him?' Then another, frightening though. 'Who did you allow near him?'

'Simmonds dies at four o'clock in the morning in a hotel in downtown Washington. He was alone. It happened quickly and unexpectedly. If he'd got help –'

'Crap!' Yuri snorted. 'Don't bullshit me, Carpenter. You people don't take a defector and put him in a hotel in downtown Washington. You take him to a safe house, somewhere in Maryland or Virginia. You surround him with guards. You interrogate him round the clock. You don't let him out of your sight until you've arranged for him to disappear.'

'We'd finished with Simmonds. He'd cooperated marvellously. We thought he deserved a reward, a night on the town.'

'In Washington?' Yuri asked in disbelief. The CIA never allowed turned agents nights on the town alone. And not in Washington. Especially not if they were journalists with contacts in Washington.

'That's how it happened,' Carpenter said.

They walked down a small hill. Two gleaming Rolls Royces stood outside a hotel. Yuri glimpsed women in long dresses standing in the lobby. He asked, 'What really happened? Did he collapse under questioning? Did you people kill him?'

'It happened just the way I've told you it did. He was debriefed. He was let out. He got sick and died.'

Yuri stopped. Behind smoked glass and gilt lettering was the glitter of bottles. Barmen in bow ties and close fitting jackets moved discreetly amongst tables. 'Let's go in there,' he said. 'I want to show you something.'

The hotel bar wasn't crowded. They sat in a straight backed booth with red cushions. Carpenter ordered a Martini straight up for himself, a large vodka for Yuri. A barman placed bowls of nuts on the table. Yuri ate hungrily.

Carpenter patted his pockets, then rested his palms on the table. 'Gave up smoking four years ago, but damn it – I still miss a cigarette, at this time of the evening.'

'I've never smoked,' Yuri said.

'You're lucky.'

The barman brought their drinks. Carpenter raised his glass. 'Here's to detente.'

Yuri said, 'Cheers!' Leaving his drink untouched, he showed Carpenter the photograph of Simmonds and Snead in Washington, and those Misha had made.

Carpenter looked at the photographs carefully and returned them without comment.

'That's why they wanted Simmonds killed,' Yuri said bitterly. 'That's why I let Simmonds go to you. I knew he was innocent.'

'I know all that,' Carpenter said. But his expression was interested.

Yuri said, 'The reason certain people in Moscow wanted Simmonds dead, was because he had learned the names of those who are trying to bring down the government of General Secretary Deryugin. Simmonds saw me the day he defected and told me as much. He wanted me to get to Deryugin or to someone close to him. I only half believed him, and in any case I could not get to Deryugin the way Simmonds wanted.

'After he defected, Simmonds got word to us that he wanted to see me, that he would give me the names. And now, suddenly, he's dead of a heart attack. I don't believe that. I don't believe he was brought to Washington for a night on the town. What I do believe is that Simmonds was lured away from your protection, and killed. I believe you've been penetrated.'

'That's absurd,' Carpenter said. 'If you want to defect, there is no need for sensational stories. Just come as you are.'

'I don't want to defect,' Yuri cried, angrily. 'I'm Russian.'

'Have your drink,' Carpenter said.

Yuri shook his head and pressed his fingers to his eyes. He felt exhausted. But he had to think, he had to find a way to persuade Carpenter. In a low voice, he said, 'Simmonds got word to us through John Drasen. You will find confirmation of everything I have told you in Drasen's reports.'

Carpenter stared at him, blankly.

Yuri said, wearily, 'Drasen was arranging for me to see Simmonds. If John Drasen hadn't been killed, I wouldn't be here, talking to you.'

'Drasen killed!' Carpenter looked anxiously around the bar. Then he leaned across the table and whispered hoarsely, 'What the hell are you talking about? I've heard nothing about Drasen being killed. There was an understanding –'

'With the government,' Yuri said. 'Not with the people who are trying to take control. Now do you see what I'm trying to stop?'

Carpenter moved erect. He summoned the barman and ordered cigarettes. 'Even if Drasen was killed, it's got nothing to do with Simmonds' death.' His fingers ripped angrily at the cellophane. He jabbed a cigarette into his mouth and lit it. 'Simmonds was brought to Washington for interrogation by a senior officer at the Russian desk.'

'Who?'

'Harry Snead, and don't you try telling me that Harry is one of yours. I've known Harry for fifteen years. He hates you guys. Your people did something very nasty to a close friend of his, when he was out in Albania. He's one of those guys who's always wanting Moscow nuked.'

In Motumbi, Yuri remembered, Snead had given Sudgorny precise details of the CIA's involvement. Sudgorny's reports had described Snead as a perverse, twisted man, untrustworthy, vicious and an alcoholic, a man with a sense, not of mission, but of revenge. 'Snead worked for us in Africa,' Yuri said.

'That's not true! I don't know what kind of game you're playing –'

Yuri said, 'Snead told us exactly what you were doing in Motumbi. On the basis of Snead's information we brought in more materials and more men and we won. I can tell you exactly what he told us and when.'

'Harry Snead a Ruski agent!' Carpenter exclaimed. 'I don't –'

'Do you have clearance for John Drasen's reports?'

'No.'

'Get that clearance and read Drasen's reports. Then, meet me somewhere in three hours and I'll tell you how we'll get Snead.'

'Why,' Carpenter asked, 'if he is one of yours?'

'Because he's working for the wrong Russians,' Yuri said. 'I think Snead brought Simmonds to Washington so he could find out the names Simmonds had from Turayev. And he wasn't doing that for the CIA. He was doing it for the Krasnaya Dela.'

Carpenter looked at him, warily. 'I don't believe you. But I'll see you in three hours.'

Three hours later, Yuri stood in Curzon Street. People leaving a cinema streamed around him. Yuri looked at glossy stills. A man and a woman escaped across a field. Two men threatened a third with a gun. He turned away. It was too much like reality. People went past with absorbed expressions. He saw Carpenter's hat hovering above the throng.

Carpenter took his elbow and said, 'I've had Drasen's reports beamed through from Langley. If looks as if you may be right.' He looked quizzically at Yuri. 'I've been ordered to give you whatever support you need.'

'I want to talk to Snead,' Yuri said. 'Can we get to Washington tomorrow?'

'No problem.' Carpenter took Yuri's elbow and guided him through the crowd toward a Volkswagen parked illegally in front of the cinema.

Yuri pulled his elbow away and stopped. 'I'll set Snead up for you, but there are conditions. One, whether I'm right or wrong, the information I get from Snead, I keep. Two, I get back to Russia as soon as I've finished. There will be no debriefing and I will make no statements to your authorities.'

Carpenter moved Yuri toward the car. 'All agreed.' He looked closely at Yuri. 'You're sure you don't want to stay on in America?'

'I'm sure,' Yuri snapped.

Two large men were leaning against a white Ford saloon parked behind the Volkswagen. They moved slowly upright as Yuri and Carpenter approached. 'Pat and Mike,' Carpenter said. 'This is Yuri Raikin.'

'How do you do,' they said together. Their eyes followed Yuri as he walked to the Volkswagen.

'They are your personal bodyguards,' Carpenter said. 'From now on, wherever you go, they go.' He opened the car door.

'Where are we going?'

'First to your hotel to collect your things. Then to a nice, comfortable, safe house in Hertfordshire.'

'The house in Hertfordshire will do,' Yuri smiled. 'I don't have a hotel.' As he got into the car he wondered if Carpenter appreciated the irony of the CIA protecting him from the KGB.

CHAPTER THIRTY-SEVEN

From his hotel window Yuri could see the FBI building. When they'd arrived the previous afternoon, Carpenter had pointed it out and said jokingly, 'That's where you go when you defect.' Yuri watched large cars wallow into a basement garage. Young men in blue suits went in and out of the building with a measured, athletic gait. Were all FBI agents young and blond, Yuri wondered. He watched open mouthed as a bus disgorged tourists. He tried to imagine tourists at Dzerzhinsky Square. In Moscow, people crossed the street to avoid passing KGB Headquarters.

Carpenter knocked perfunctorily and came in. He had a room opposite Yuri's. As if alarmed by his entrance, the phone on the bedside table gave a sharp beep. Since dawn, Pat and Mike had been setting up bugs and recording devices.

'Time to get to work,' Carpenter said, cheerily. His cheeks shone, his hair gleamed. Today he wore a grey lightweight suit. The sparkle behind the horn rims was almost scholarly. 'You've learned your script?'

'I wrote it.' Yuri sat beside the phone and rehearsed what he was going to say.

Carpenter was anxious to get going. He reminded Yuri of the horses he'd seen at the Hippodrome, cantering to the start. Carpenter snapped his fingers and said, 'Okay, let's move. We must get to him before he leaves for the office.' Carpenter took out a roll of thin wire with a sucker at one end and tiny earplugs at the other. He pressed the sucker onto the telephone receiver and pushed the plugs into his ears. 'Right, Captain, let's get the show on the road.'

Yuri dialled. The receiver burped rhythmically. A voice said, 'Harry Snead.'

Yuri felt a flash of excitement. His stomach heaved, then he was speaking, fighting to keep his voice level and precise. 'Mr

265

Snead, listen very carefully. I used to work for the First Chief Directorate. I have your complete KGB file. I repeat, the complete file, including Africa. You can have that file, Mr Snead, for twenty-five thousand dollars.'

'You're crazy! Who are you?'

'My name is Yuri Raikin. You can check my background with your archives.'

Snead repeated, 'You're crazy!'

Yuri said, 'Take it or leave it. In twenty-four hours the file will be in other hands.'

Snead said, 'Where can I examine the file? I'm not buying anything on trust.'

'You can check the file when we meet.'

'What makes you think we will meet? What makes you think I want this file?'

'The file contains confirmation of the help you gave in Motumbi, of how Charlie Simmonds died. Now, do we meet or not?'

'I don't have that kind of money,' Snead muttered. 'The company doesn't pay out that kind of money anymore.'

'It's your future,' Yuri said, quietly. 'You have till eight o'clock tonight. I will meet you at the Richmond Motor Lodge.' Yuri squinted at the address Carpenter was holding out. He couldn't believe it. 'It's near Muddy Brown Park. Yes in –' he tried to decipher Carpenter's moving lips– 'Maryland.'

'I'll be there,' Snead said. 'But I don't think I'll have the money.'

'You have many friends,' Yuri said. 'Many new friends. Now, three things. Don't be late. Bring all the money. And come alone. If you breach any of those conditions, you lose the file.'

'I'll have to bring someone,' Snead protested. 'The file is in Russian.'

'In your job, you must read a lot of Russian,' Yuri said.

Carpenter flashed Yuri an approving smile.

Snead asked, 'How will I recognize you?'

'I'll recognize you. After all, we have your picture on file.'

Yuri put the phone down and asked Carpenter, 'How was it?'

He felt strangely tremulous. His palms were sweaty. 'You think he bought it?'

'We will see what we will see.' Carpenter rubbed his fingers together. 'I could really use a cigarette. You ready to start making Harry's file?'

Twenty minutes later, a man came in with a selection of Russian stationery and folders. Someone else brought three typewriters with Cyrillic characters. Pat brought a little machine that typed out facsimiles of Cyrillic telexes. Carpenter brought an old code book.

Yuri worked solidly through the day embroidering recollections of Africa and CIA reports of the interrogation and death of Simmonds. From time to time Carpenter brought him coffee in a paper cup. For lunch he brought a jumbo sized burger and a cardboard box of French fries.

Rain fell in shiny streaks as they left the hotel. They sat with squeaking wipers in stagnant traffic. Pat kept station a narrow bumper's length behind them. Carpenter said, 'If God was all merciful, he wouldn't let it rain in the rush hour.' He kept looking at his watch.

Carpenter said that when they got nearer the motor lodge, he would give Yuri his car and ride with Pat. Yuri was to go into the bar and take the third booth on the left. Mike had rigged up one of the latest electronic news gathering video cameras to cover the booth. It would be activated as soon as Yuri entered the booth.

They drove into Georgetown. Pedestrians darted hunchbacked, over bricked pavements. They went past rows of neat shops and small, colonial town houses. Carpenter said that he would be monitoring everything that happened in the booth from a room behind the bar, that he would move in as soon as the file had been exchanged. 'You don't have to worry about a thing,' he promised. 'We've covered every angle.'

'What if Snead brings in the KGB?'

'That's the first thing we thought of. If Snead's not alone he won't make it to the booth.'

They left Washington and drove along a rain slicked, two lane highway. Through the trees, Yuri glimpsed a meandering canal. Reflections of red tiled roofs broke and bubbled in the water. Carpenter told him the canal was 185 miles long and had been built in 1850. When all this was over, he said, Yuri should take some time to visit the falls.

The motor lodge was a squat, wooden chalet on the fringes of an unkempt park. Light glowed feebly from its windows, a spidery sign in red neon above the door. The rain had stopped. Yuri felt the tyres squelch over mud. He picked up the brief-case and ran, skipping over puddles, into the bar.

Men sat at a counter watching a baseball game on TV. Vast areas of wood were illuminated by pools of dismal yellow brown light. To his left, the booths were in a red shadow. The place smelt of smoke. Yuri saw Mike turn as he entered and walked quickly to the toilet. Yuri went to the third booth on the left. It was gloomily comfortable. Yuri asked the waiter for a beer.

At precisely eight o'clock Snead came, pausing pugnaciously at the door, his square head with its rim of angry, iron grey curls twisting this way and that. Yuri leaned out of the booth and waved. Snead walked with a widespread, shambling gait. He had the build of an overweight prize fighter.

Reddened, bloodhound eyes glared at Yuri. Snead's face was like a worn glove. The crinkled skin sagged. His fingernails were bitten to the quick. He ordered a double martini. He'd already been drinking.

'So you're Yuri Raikin.' The voice strained through successive layers of phlegm. Snead's face had the knowingly hostile expression of a policeman eyeing a suspect.

Yuri didn't say anything.

Snead lit a cigarette and coughed fruitily. He took a long pull at his martini. 'You brought the file?'

'Have you brought the money?'

Snead's hand caressed a small attaché case. 'You'll never be able to spend all this in Russia, you know.' He narrowed his eyes against the smoke from his cigarette. 'I suppose you're going to defect.'

Yuri didn't say anything. He looked past Snead to the bar.

The TV screen showed a figure sprinting, falling. The spectators laughed and pointed noisily.

Snead said, 'You're going to the British, right? You're making yourself a little supplementary pension, right?'

Yuri asked, 'Do you want to check the file?'

'You're a fool,' Snead said. 'The British will nickel and dime you to death and you won't like the climate. If you're going to defect, come to us. I'll find you a hundred G, just for starters.'

'I know what happened to Simmonds,' Yuri said.

Snead's laugh ended in a hacking cough. 'You think the British are different? Kim Philby was British, you know. Real pukka British. He fingered Volkov. He betrayed everyone he ever worked with.'

'Before my time,' Yuri said. 'You want to check the file or don't you?'

'You'd better come over to us,' Snead muttered. He peered suspiciously over the table at Yuri. 'How do I know you won't be back in three months with a copy of the file looking for another twenty-five grand?'

'You don't, but I won't.' Yuri gave Snead a tight smile. 'The British wouldn't like it.'

Snead ordered another martini. He held out a surprisingly small hand, the flesh ridged down to remnants of nails. 'Let's see that file.'

'The money,' Yuri said.

Snead put his case on the table, fumbled with the combination, and opened it. Inside were piles of notes, taped together in separate bundles. 'It's all there,' Snead said. 'Count it.'

Yuri opened his own case and passed Snead the file. 'What concerns you is the confirmatory telex, three documents from the top, and the resident's report attached to it. Also, the directive from Moscow Centre dated two months before that. You'll find it halfway along.'

Snead riffled blearily through the pages. Yuri shut the case. He'd seen what twenty-five thousand dollars looked like. Piles of wadded paper. In America men killed for that! He said quietly, 'There's one thing I don't understand. Why?' He spoke to Snead's bowed head. 'How did they make you do it? Why did you kill for your enemy?'

Snead didn't look up from his reading. 'You wouldn't even begin to understand.'

'What was it? Your drink problem? Your friends in Albania?'

'Asshole,' Snead said.

'It's the only thing that isn't on the file,' Yuri said.

Snead shut the file. 'Simmonds was a little shit. He got in the way. You just remember that, buddy boy. Bad things happen to people who get in the way.'

Yuri looked past Snead to the bar. He didn't see Mike or Pat or Carpenter.

Snead said, 'That's fine.' He threw the file into Yuri's case and shut it.

Yuri placed his hand on the case with the money.

Snead said, 'You could come with me, you know. In two weeks, you could be American.'

Yuri smiled. 'Thanks, but no thanks.' Behind Snead, he saw Carpenter come round the bar. The men seated at the counter cheered. A goal? A try? Yuri didn't understand the game.

Snead said, 'Leave the case alone, boy.' In his hand was the ugly snout of a gun. He prised himself half erect, pressing his shoulders against the back of the booth, then leaned sideways and grabbed the handles of both cases in his left hand.

From behind him Carpenter said, 'Easy, Harry. We've got you on tape and on film. It's all over.'

Snead said, 'Fuck off, George.' His eyes and the gun were still fixed on Yuri.

Carpenter stayed where he was, in the corner of Snead's vision. His hands rested loosely in front of his thighs. He said, 'It's time we had a little chat, Harry. Leave the cases and the gun.'

Yuri hoped Carpenter wouldn't try to be a hero. The gun was pointed unwaveringly at him.

Snead said, 'George, you're being a pain in the ass. You're interfering with a company operation.' He waved the gun at Yuri. 'On your feet, boy. We're going places.'

'There is no operation. I checked with DDI,' Carpenter said.

'The DDI is a stupid jerk. There is an operation. My operation. I am going to stick it to the Russians. I am going to tear their whole fucking government apart.'

'All right,' Carpenter said, reasonably. 'Put away the gun. Let's you and I sit down and talk.'

'Haul ass, George. Go get yourself a beer. I'm taking this creep to meet some of his friends. You try to stop me, you try to follow me, I'll blast his guts from here to Capitol Hill.'

Yuri felt the sweat trickle down the back of his neck. Where the hell were Pat and Mike?

Carpenter said, 'Harry, remember, there's always tomorrow. Tomorrow, you'll have to report to the DDI at Langley.'

'I've taken care of that,' Snead said. 'Tonight, I'm taking this shithead back to his own kind. His friends want to talk to him. They want him back in Moscow.'

Snead's eyes remained fixed on Yuri. The table was between them. The back of his legs were wedged against the bench. He couldn't move fast enough or hard enough to grab the gun.

Carpenter said, 'Leave him. Take the file and the money and go.'

'Go and stand near the bar, George,' Snead said, tightly. 'Stand where I can see you. Don't try anything unless you want your little Russian hero dead.'

Carpenter gave Yuri a helpless shrug. He raised two crossed fingers by his head. He went and stood away from the men seated round the bar.

'You.' Snead gestured with the gun. 'Walk round the table past me, keep walking to the door. If you're thinking of trying anything, remember I'm right behind you.'

Yuri walked. He turned away from the bar. He thought of swinging the door in Snead's face. A latecomer to the baseball game held the door politely open. They walked into the muddy car park.

Snead was canny, walking close enough to shoot and not miss, too far to be grabbed. He guided Yuri to a muddy Pontiac. 'Hands on the roof, buddy boy. Hands on the roof.' He dropped the cases momentarily, opened the rear door and slung them in. 'Now open that door and get in. Very slowly.'

Snead circled round the hood, gun drawn now, held in both hands, pointing at Yuri through the windscreen. He slid in behind the wheel, gun across his chest.

Yuri thought Snead was close enough, but there was no

room to manoeuvre. He thought, with a .38 Detective Special, Snead needed only one shot.

Snead placed the gun against Yuri's head, started the car one handed, lurched out of the car park. Yuri hoped he knew the road, that they wouldn't hit an unexpected bump.

A mile or so further on, he pulled up behind a black Lincoln, turned off the engine and lights. Two men got out of the Lincoln.

'On zdyes,' Snead said. 'Vozmitye yevo.' He's here. Take him.

CHAPTER THIRTY-EIGHT

From low down on the rear seat, Yuri watched the car headlights illuminate trees and roofs and the tops of fences. His hands were cuffed behind him, but his companion leant across his body as if somehow he might escape. The headlamps undulated, fading into the night sky. They might have been flying if not for the hiss of tyres on tarmac.

One thing he was sure of. They were heading for the country, not Washington. Yuri wondered what Carpenter was doing. And his bodyguards. Where had they been, when he'd needed them? The weight of his companion and the gentle heaving of the car made his shoulders ache.

They turned onto an unmade road. Mud swished against the wheel arches. Stones spattered the floor. The lights bobbed and weaved. The headlamps of a second car washed over their rear window. Carpenter, Yuri thought, struggled to look and recognized Snead's battered Pontiac.

The track between them was bordered by tall trees. They were in a forest. The car stopped outside a small house of white brick and dark tile. They pulled Yuri out of the car and pushed him past a lounge with sheeted furniture to a room at the back. It was furnished with a small desk and six straight backed chairs. The windows were battened with steel shutters and the walls were covered with a thick, sound absorbing padding. The door too was covered with the same material. When it opened, Yuri heard the faint hiss of air being released.

The two men pushed Yuri onto a chair and manacled his ankles to its legs. They were both of a type, big, with low foreheads and flattened noses, hands with large, broken knuckles and shoulders like cliffs. They were perfectionists. Having manacled Yuri to the chair, they lashed his body to it with a length of rope.

The door hissed open. Mikhail Krylov, the KGB's Washington Resident, came in carrying a slim attaché case. One of the others placed the cases with Snead's file and the money on a desk in front of Yuri. Snead followed clutching a leather covered hip flask. He sat on the nearest chair, with an anticipatory look.

Krylov walked to the desk with neat, mincing steps. He had a small, precise body and wore a well fitting, pale blue, lightweight suit. A wing of feathery brown hair swept low over his forehead. His face had a quality of exaggeration to it; cheekbones that protruded too far, a triangular chin that was too sharp, a finely arched nose, and olivine eyes that were startling.

He opened his attaché case and took out a manila folder. He looked impassively at Yuri. 'We know everything about you, Raikin,' he said, contemptuously. 'You are an American spy, a murderer, a defector, and now,' he indicated the cases with Snead's file and the money, 'a purveyor of falsified information. I have here your confession. You will sign it.' He made as if to push, the folder towards Yuri.

'No!' Yuri cried.

He was totally unprepared for what happened next. The first man hit him, a swinging open handed slap that rocked Yuri in the chair and made his ears sing. A warm flush washed over his cheek. A second blow caught him on the other side of the head, preventing him falling over. A fist, just below the heart, jarred him. Breath crashed out of his open mouth. A fist, solid as stone, shut it. Teeth gouged through flesh. Blood spouted.

Another blow to the body, another to the head. Yuri fought for balance. The manacles cut into his ankles. Ribbons of pain ran through his hands and shoulders. He was utterly, totally, terrifyingly helpless.

A blow glanced off his shoulder. A gnarled fist found his cheek. Yuri felt the skin split, swell. A blinding flash and his eye was watering. Pain. He lowered his head, protectively. The blows rained off his shoulders and neck. He gasped and groaned.

The men stopped.

Yuri slumped against his bonds, fighting for breath, his body covered with a clammy sweat.

Krylov said, 'Here we do not have the sophisticated tech-

274

niques of persuasion available in Moscow. So that is a sample of what you can expect if you do not cooperate.'

Slowly, Yuri raised his head. One eye was blurring. Krylov appeared distant, vague; Snead, another blurry outline, raised a hand to his lips.

Krylov said, 'We know everything you and Popov did, everything you did with Drasen, Deryugin and Simmonds.'

'I didn't,' Yuri gasped. His head felt as if a brick wall had fallen on it. Blood spattered. He couldn't stop his body trembling.

Krylov said, 'You instructed Simmonds to leak the LASM-Two information to the Americans.'

'I was authorized,' Yuri mumbled.

'I know you were authorized. And I know why you were authorized. You, Popov and Deryugin are American agents. You have been agents of the American, Drasen.'

'That's nonsense.'

'Deryugin did not have that information leaked, because he wanted to use it as a bargaining device with the Americans. He did it, as you did it, because you were paid. Don't waste energy protesting, Citizen Raikin. We know the truth. Director Suslov knows exactly what happened. And when he tried to minimize the damage you had caused by ordering the elimination of the traitor Simmonds, you intervened and stopped it.'

His body had ceased to tremble. His pain was a single, swollen mass. 'That isn't – isn't – how it happened.'

'Then,' Krylov continued, imperturbably, 'Popov intervened at your enquiry and brought you back to Moscow, where you attempted to falsely implicate Director Suslov. You broke into First Directorate Records and stole evidence implicating Simmonds. You replaced the evidence with a doctored photograph, which you tried to show had been planted by Suslov. When Zamyatin, your former control, discovered what you'd done, you and Popov killed him.'

'You're out of your mind!' Yuri cried. 'You're twisting –' A blow to the head rocked him. He wanted to be sick.

'We're not crazy,' Krylov said, softly. 'We're simply cleverer than you. Much cleverer. You see, we know everything. Deryugin, Drasen and Dolgov have been conspiring for years, selling Russian industry to the highest bidder. All of them have made immense fortunes from the prostitution of Russian industry, fortunes which we all know are hidden in Switzerland. Dolgov, however was a little more of a patriot than the others. When he heard how Deryugin and you had betrayed Russia by giving the Americans our defence secrets, he protested. He threatened to expose everything and everybody by going to the Zarev Commission.

'You tried to persuade him to leave Russia. You even offered to give him your mistress, Matsyeva, as an inducement to leave.'

'No,' Yuri cried.

'Then, when Dolgov refused to go, a sick criminal was employed to murder him. And you and Popov suppressed the investigation into his death.'

'I took no part in that,' Yuri muttered. 'That is a matter or record. I saw Gvishani Kirichenko, Secretary of the Zarev Commission –'

'And fed him a lot of lies!' Krylov shouted. 'You went to the Zarev Commission only when you realized that Popov, Deryugin and Drasen wanted to get rid of you, that you were an embarrassment to them. In fact, after you and Drasen had quarrelled over the affections of the actress, Matsyeva.

'You threatened them with exposure. You threatened to reveal the secrets of the Staaderbank. Then, last Saturday, you met with Drasen to negotiate a settlement. Drasen was wired to Popov. When it seemed you would not reach agreement, Popov sent hired killers to eliminate you.'

'But you were lucky. You managed to kill one of the men and then you killed Drasen. Realizing what had happened, you then drove to Popov's dacha and killed him, and because his wife was witness to your killing of Popov, you murdered her. After that you couldn't remain in Russia. So you used a false agent priority to leave and defect to the Americans.

'But you're a greedy man, Raikin. You're used to privilege, used to money. The Americans were not very impressed with you, a cheat and a murderer. You realized that they would not pay for the lavish lifestyle you wanted. So you decided to get yourself a little nest egg, by falsifying a file and attempting to sell it to Comrade Snead.'

'If the information was false,' Yuri asked, 'why did Comrade Snead offer to buy it?'

'To lead you to us,' Krylov replied.

Snead laughed with the humourlessness of a drunk.

A glass of iced water was thrust in front of Yuri's face. He drank. The chill numbed the pain and cleansed his mouth. He swallowed water mixed with blood.

Krylov said, 'You see, we do know everything. So there is no point in prolonging this unpleasantness any longer. Sign the confession. I promise you, you will feel much better.'

'Comrade Krylov, what you are doing here is illegal,' Yuri protested, speaking as much for the two Russians as for Krylov. If they could be made to believe what they were doing was unauthorized, they might leave him alone. 'The proper place for this investigation is Moscow. The proper authority for this investigation, is the Sluzbha. You do not have the authority to interrogate me. Neither do you have the right to use torture.'

Krylov snapped, 'You are no longer an officer in the Sluzbha. You're simply a defector in my territory. I can do with you whatever I like. Let's get it over with. Sign.'

'Go fuck yourself!'

A blow to the side of the head set his chair spinning. He crashed sideways to the floor. His head jarred. Swift, solid currents of pain racked his body. He began to bleed again.

Slowly, he was dragged upright.

Krylov asked, 'Will you sign? Nod, if you mean yes.'

Yuri spat blood at him.

One of the men braced the back of his chair while the other hit him hard to the body. His breath exploded. A paralysing pain stifled him. Open palms stung his face. Blows rained against his head and body. Fingernails clawed at the cut on his cheek. Blood streamed.

One of the men yanked his head back, held him by the hair while the other smashed his nose.

Pain shot to the top of his brain. Breath stopped. His nose filled with blood. He felt the thick stream of it rush down the back of his throat, fill his mouth. An elbow slammed viciously into his stomach. The chair rocked. Yuri felt himself jerked forward as a fountain of blood cascaded from his mouth, and fell with light, slapping sounds onto his thighs and the floor.

He hung limply against the ropes, shook his head in slow reflex as water was dashed into his face. 'I won't sign,' he mumbled. 'I'll never sign. You'll have to kill me first.'

He felt fingers take his chin. Gently his head was lifted. Krylov looked down at him, with the expression of a man who'd found a worm in an apple.

Yuri tried to grin. 'I'm useless to you dead,' he muttered.

Krylov swatted at him, as if at a fly and walked away.

Silence descended.

His head swam. His nose was clogged with blood. He could feel the skin of his face tight and swollen. It hurt to talk, to breathe.

Footsteps. He glimpsed Krylov's polished shoes. Softly, Krylov said, 'Raikin, don't be a fool. You're not the one we want. I'll make it easy on you if you cooperate. We know Drasen and Popov wanted to kill you. We will support a justification of self-defence. But give us the evidence you have. Sign those parts of the confession that implicate Deryugin. It's Deryugin we want, not you.'

His head was pulled back. Water was poured down his throat. 'I couldn't – not true.'

'You don't have a choice,' Krylov said, reasonably. 'Sign the confession or not, you're being sent back to Moscow. Once in Moscow, the Dolgov evidence will be revealed, and Deryugin will fall. There won't be anyone to protect you. You may as well cooperate now.'

Yuri shook his head. Blood spattered on his lap.

Krylov said, 'Think of your father. A hero. An old man. Will you have him die, knowing he had bred a traitor?'

'My father knows me well,' Yuri muttered.

'You know how these things work, Raikin. If you are disgraced, your father will be disgraced. He will have to resign his position, retire from the army. It may even be thought that it was his bad example that led you to this folly. It may be said, that he should have prevented you. He may even be punished along with you.'

'If it will happen, it will happen. Neither I nor my father is a traitor.'

Krylov lowered his head close to Yuri's. 'All right,' he said almost in a whisper. 'I'll come to an arrangement with you. I'll release you to the Americans. You can stay in America and work for them.'

Yuri shook his head. 'I don't want to.'

'Think about it. You will have a nice life in America. The CIA will look after you.'

'I don't want to live in America. I'm Russian.'

'In time,' Krylov continued, 'we will make arrangements for Matsyeva to join you. We know she would like to live in America. She wants to work in Hollywood.'

Yuri shook his head again. 'She doesn't. I don't.'

'Think carefully. Think of others. Think of your father.' Krylov walked back to the desk.

'There's nothing to think about,' Yuri said.

In the silence that followed, he heard Snead slurp as he drank.

From the desk, Krylov called, 'Consider the alternatives, America or Siberia. America or a bullet in the back of the neck. Why don't you sign, comrade, and go free?'

'Go fuck yourself!' Yuri cried, brokenly.

A blow caught him in the face with a hard cracking sound, accompanied by a vivid explosion of pain and light. He couldn't breathe. He sagged against his bonds.

A clout to the side of the jaw sent him to the floor. His shoulder wrenched. Blood, spit and vomit trickled out of the side of his mouth. The two men began to kick him, the sound of their feet like the smacking of wet cloths.

He couldn't breathe, he couldn't think. His nose and mouth and throat were full of blood and mucus, choking him. The floor tilted. He felt it undulate.

Then a bigger wave. A sound of distant canon booming.

The rain of blows stopped. Feet raced across the floor. The floor vibrated. Beyond the curtain of red mist he heard voices shouting.

'Up against the wall!'

'Move, you motherfuckers!'

'Move, now!'

There was a pattering of feet and movement and more shouting.

Yuri felt himself dragged upright. Pat's face swam before his. He heard George Carpenter say, 'Christ, Harry, this time you've really fucked up.'

Water was poured over his head, damp rags pressed to his face. Hands fumbled about his body. People were bending over him, surrounding him. The ropes holding him sprung free. There was a rasp of keys and locks. His hands and legs were free.

George Carpenter was kneeling beside him anxiously, one arm round his shoulders, 'Yuri, are you all right?'

Someone was holding out a glass of water. Yuri drank. It tasted sweet. He looked around. The room seemed to be full of men. Krylov, Snead and the two Russians stood behind the desk, their backs to the wall.

Krylov was saying, 'I am a Russian diplomat. This man is wanted in Russia for theft, espionage, murder and various other crimes. I insist you release us and —'

Someone hit him.

Yuri tried to laugh. It hurt like hell.

CHAPTER THIRTY-NINE

He was a diver rising through layers of sleep. Sleep had colours. It went from black to dark mauve, to grey. Yuri opened his eyes. He was on a high bed in a darkened room. The white walls looked grey, like the last layers of sleep. He felt no pain. Like a diver who had reached the surface, he was floating.

He remembered sprawling across the rear seat of Carpenter's car, followed by a confusion that had nothing to do with him. He recalled people fussing around him, taking off his clothes; he remembered lying in a bed like this one, staring at a ceiling beyond lights like moons. He remembered this room as if from a previous dream; he remembered the drawn blinds, the bedside table, the sharp odour of antiseptic. He closed his eyes. He felt comfortable. He felt safe.

He slept.

The next time he woke, a nurse was looking down at him. She smiled and asked, 'How do you feel?'

A dull pain ran from his shoulders to his ankles. He tried to smile at the nurse. His mouth collapsed in a vacant grin.

He slept and woke. Woke and slept. A nurse held a glass of milk to his mouth. They fed him something that tasted like mashed cereal. Each time he woke, there was a little more pain.

The pain was not unendurable, not sharp, but it was constant. It felt as if each muscle of his body had been stretched out on a board. It hurt to breathe. He slept and woke. Woke and slept.

He woke and watched the rectangle of sun frame the sheeted humps of his feet. They brought him a tray of scrambled eggs, bacon, coffee and orange juice. It didn't hurt so much when he sat up.

Carpenter came in wearing a toothy smile. He placed his hat on the floor beside the bed. Sun filled Yuri's breakfast tray.

Carpenter asked, 'How do you feel?'

'Battered and bruised.'

'You're damn lucky. No fractures, no internal injuries. Just concussion and bruising. You'll be out of here, soon.'

Yuri wondered if they'd give him more coffee.

Carpenter said, 'We goofed. We lost you.'

Yuri spooned up the last of the eggs. 'You told me you'd covered all angles.'

'I didn't expect Harry to pull a gun on you. I never expected him to take you to them.'

'What the hell happened to Pat and Mike? Some bodyguards they were.'

'They were putting away the equipment. We stopped filming as soon as the exchange was made, and I came to get Harry. Honest, I never thought he'd pull a gun.'

Yuri said, 'I'd like some more coffee.'

Carpenter went outside and ordered it. He came back and sat by the bed. 'We thought they were going to take you to the embassy. Hell, we closed off 16th Street and set up road blocks halfway round Washington. When nothing happened, I realized that Harry might have struck cover. I checked with Langley and found he'd borrowed a safe house. Then I summoned the heavy mob and came after you. Jesus, I was sweating bullets. I could have kissed you when we blew that door and found you in one piece.'

'Almost,' Yuri said.

A nurse came in with a jug of coffee.

Carpenter said, 'You order anything you want. Treat this place like a hotel.'

Yuri asked, 'How much does it cost to live like a capitalist?'

'For you, nothing. Compliments of Uncle Sam.'

'Why?'

Carpenter's finger traced invisible circles on the bed sheet. In a low voice he said, 'The fact is, the Secretary of State is dead worried about Drasen's reports. We're all worried about what could happen between our countries if Zarev's people replaced Deryugin.' Carpenter looked seriously at Yuri. 'If things went very wrong, it could mean war. If they didn't go so wrong, we could have another twenty years of Cold War. You know what that means?'

'I studied history. I used to be in the diplomatic service.'

Carpenter poured out some coffee and drank it swiftly. With what sounded like regret he said, 'It isn't as if Russia is some tinpot dictatorship into which we could send the Company and military advisors.'

'Quite.'

Carpenter poured Yuri more coffee. 'Funny about Harry. He'd read Drasen's reports and got some cockamamie idea that if Zarev replaced Deryugin, the Russian people wouldn't stand for it, that they would have rebelled.'

'You don't rebel when there's a boot at your throat,' Yuri said.

'So he joined Krylov and these others.' He sighed. 'Poor Harry. They're holding him in a looney bin.'

'That happens in Russia, too,' Yuri said, and asked, 'Did he talk to Simmonds before he killed him?'

Slowly, Carpenter nodded. 'He was professional enough for that.'

'And did Simmonds give him the names? Did he tell him about the meeting with Turayev?'

Again, Carpenter nodded. 'Turayev, as you know was already investigating Zarev and the others. One evening he followed someone called Guschin to a meeting at a dacha outside Moscow. Apparently the meeting was conducted outdoors, and Turayev was able to listen through a directional microphone.

'Guschin told the others that Dolgov was refusing to cooperate, and that Drasen was making arrangements for Dolgov to leave Russia. Guschin said this left them with no alternative but to implement the Kronykin plan.

'Apparently, the others agreed that Dolgov had to be killed. And they agreed that if Popov suppressed the inquiry into his death, they would uncover that fact and use it to embarrass Deryugin and force his resignation. If that failed, they were going to use the Dolgov testament.

'And if all that failed, one of them suggested they dispose of Deryugin. He described it as the perfect revenge.'

'Who were the men?' Yuri asked.

'Guschin, of course. Vitali Orlenko, your Minister of the Interior and Vladimir Korselov, Chairman of Administration and Organs.'

And political head of the KGB, Yuri thought, recalling the three of them huddling together at Dolgov's funeral. 'Who was the fourth man?'

'The one who suggested that Deryugin should be disposed of? Turayev wasn't able to identify him.'

Yuri sank back onto the pillow. Even if he knew the fourth man, it was all useless. He couldn't go against Orlenko and Korselov and Director Guschin on the word of a CIA agent whose sanity was suspect. With Turayev, Popov, and Simmonds all dead, the information was useless. He told Carpenter that.

'But can't you take it to Deryugin?' Carpenter protested. 'Or to some high up in the KGB?'

'How do I find out who in the KGB is Krasnaya Dela and who isn't?' Yuri asked. 'And even if I got to Deryugin, what could he do? Arrest four important people on my word? On Snead's word?'

'But we know it's true!' Carpenter exclaimed. 'Can't Korselov and these others be made to confess?'

'Made,' Yuri repeated slowly. 'That's exactly what we're trying to get away from.'

Carpenter ordered more coffee.

All the conspirators had to do, Yuri thought, was deny they'd met, and with Turayev and Simmonds both dead, that would be the end of it. That *was* the end of it. No witnesses, no evidence, no meeting. He had to get evidence. Or prove something another way. Prove what? That Dolgov was murdered? *How* Dolgov was murdered? And Drasen... That was it. They'd used the same means to kill Drasen as Dolgov!

How had they done that? Through the Fifth Directorate and Drachinsky. Drachinsky was proof. Drachinsky's files describing in minute detail the treatment administered to Kronykin, Abyugov and the other men of STF 29 was proof. If he could get the files, Yuri thought. If they still existed.

'You all right, Yuri?' Carpenter was looking down at him, concernedly.

Yuri kicked at the sheets. 'I must get back to Russia.'

'You're not going anywhere, son. You can hardly walk.'

Yuri lay back on the bed. 'How long?'

'Two or three days, no more than that. As soon as you can walk, I'll take you to a health farm. That'll help you recover more quickly. What are you going to do when you get back?'

'Finish what I started.'

'How?'

Yuri closed his eyes and turned his head away.

Carpenter said, 'We've got a big interest in this, Yuri. We can give you all the help you need.'

Yuri opened his eyes and looked at Carpenter. 'And precisely how much is that worth in Moscow?'

'We have friends there.'

'And you're going to tell me, a KGB officer, who those friends are?'

Carpenter flinched from his gaze. 'We'll work something out.'

Yuri struggled into a sitting position. 'If you really want to help, get me back to Moscow.' He told Carpenter that Krylov had known how he'd got out of Russia. 'By now they would have invalidated my travel documents. Which means I'll be arrested the first time I'm required to show them.'

Carpenter frowned. 'I'll see what I can do.' Then suddenly he grinned and peered down at Yuri. 'Looks like as soon as you're on your feet, we'll have to get you a State Department haircut.'

Two days later, Carpenter took Yuri from the hospital to a health farm some forty miles from Washington. It was a marvellous place, with luxurious private rooms and saunas, a swimming pool, a gymnasium with exercise bicycles, a running track, indoor basketball and tennis courts, novel weight training equipment attached to the walls and controlled by pulleys.

Yuri swam and worked with the weights. His body went from rich purple to pale blue. He eased his soreness in the sauna, and took massages twice a day. Carpenter, in a pink towelling track suit puffed on the exercise bicycle and jogged determinedly around the track.

'We had to let Krylov go,' he panted. 'He's back in the embassy, but he can't move more than one block from there. What do you want us to do with him? Do you want him returned to Moscow?'

'No.' Yuri jogged easily beside Carpenter. 'Let Krylov stay here and sweat.'

Carpenter visibly shrank. His diet, unlike Yuri's, consisted mainly of lettuce, diced carrots and thin soup. His nose took on a peculiar sharpness. His nostrils twitched at the smell of Yuri's steak. By the end of the week, Carpenter was beginning to look like a rabbit.

A leaner, healthier Carpenter flew with Yuri to London. Apart from an occasional stiffness, Yuri felt recovered from the beating. On his body, all but the worst bruises had disappeared. There was a pale blue mark on his forehead and white strip of healing scar on his cheek. His nose had healed, and now lay squashed in the middle of his face, like a wedge of soft wax. With its neat, American haircut, his head felt strangely light. As they landed, Carpenter said, 'Don't forget, now. If you ever have to get out, call us.'

In the transit lounge, Carpenter introduced Yuri to Philip Adams, an American about his own age. Adams was flying to Leningrad to fill a temporary vacancy at the consulate. Most of the way he read an English translation of *War and Peace*. He told Yuri he hadn't known which modern Russian novelists were banned and hoped Tolstoy would give him sufficient insight into Russian life.

'It's also a good book,' Yuri said.

At Leningrad's Pulkovo Airport they passed quickly through Customs and Immigration. A uniformed chauffeur led them to a black Cadillac Seville outside the terminal. An American flag fluttered from its wing.

They drove around Leningrad to Rzhevka. The chauffeur gave Yuri a plane ticket to Moscow. Adams took back the American diplomatic passport. 'Have a good journey,' he said. As the embassy limousine drew away, he returned to *War and Peace*.

CHAPTER FORTY

The Ilyushin dropped out of orange cloud into darkness, landed with a screaming whistle of engines. As they rushed down the runway the terminal scudded past, a square box of light.

Yuri pushed his way through the crowds at the terminal and took a bus to Moscow. There was a party of foreign tourists on board, huddling together at the back. The Intourist guide counted heads repeatedly. A tourist complained about the quality of the drinking water in Leningrad. One, more knowledgeable than the rest, said that Leningrad had been built on marshes, that even in the days of Peter the Great, the water had caused problems. The bus dropped Yuri and the tourists outside the Hotel Rossiya.

The Rossiya was a towering bank of light. The tourists streamed in. Tomorrow, the Likachev Automobile Plant.

Opposite the Rossiya the swallow-tail battlements of the Kremlin floated. Red stars burned over the Nikolsky and Spassky Towers. Stalin's eyes.

He was home and had nowhere to stay. He felt very alone and vulnerable.

Yuri walked away from the Rossiya, along the narrow Ulica Razina. From the Corinthian columns of the old Gostiny Dvor a fading banner proclaimed: WORK FULFILS THE REVOLUTION! A few dismal lights showed from the interior of the old bazaar. After Washington, Moscow seemed drab and empty.

He moved quickly into Novaya Square feeling like a fugitive. In the five storey Business House, they were still working. Yuri took the Metro to Pavelets Railway Station.

He would see Yedemsky. Work would bring fulfilment and its own release.

Yedemsky said, 'Come in, boychik, come in. You know it's always a pleasure to see you.'

An empty glass, bottle and smouldering cigarette stood by Yedemsky's armchair. *The Idiot* lay behind it. Figures danced silently across the television screen. Yedemsky carried a copy of *The Brothers Karamazov*.

'Overrated,' he pronounced. 'You know, boychik, Dostoevsky never wrote anything better than *Crime and Punishment*. There's nothing he wrote that has such grand simplicity.' He shut the door and turned up the television. The music from Prokofiev's Romeo and Juliet filled the room. Yedemsky brought his head close to Yuri's. 'Are you all right, boychik? You've been in a fight?'

'I'm all right now,' Yuri said.

Yedemsky whispered, 'I've heard rumours that you were in trouble. And what is this new hairstyle?'

'What rumours?' Yuri asked.

'Nothing specific. You know, rumours.' Yedemsky asked, 'You want somewhere to stay for a little while?'

Yuri thought, soon the streets would be abandoned to the law abiding, the privileged, the KGB and Militia patrols. It would be safer to stay with Yedemsky. No one except Popov had known of his friendship with Yedemsky. Yuri said, 'For one night. If you're sure it wouldn't be too much trouble. If you're sure you wouldn't worry.'

'Why should I worry, boychik? The worst they can do to me is a blessing. All they can take is three years. Three years of 200 grammes and sixty cigarettes a day, of finding out that Dostoevsky wrote only one masterpiece.' He took Yuri's case and placed it by the armchair. An expression of craftiness flitted across his face. 'You want a drink?'

Yuri hesitated, 'Well, all right.'

Yedemsky scuttled to the television, turned down the sound, reached behind it and produced a fresh bottle of vodka. His fingers twisted desperately around the stopper. 'Some days I tell myself I should drink less and hide the vodka,' he said, opening the bottle, looking for glasses. 'But it's no good. I always know where to find it.' He poured and held out a glass to Yuri. 'Nice to see you, boychik.' He dabbed at his eyes with the back of his wrist and drank.

Yedemsky insisted that Yuri eat. He fried an egg on a small stove beside the bed. Yuri watched the ballet. Once in London, he had seen the defector Nureyev dance Romeo. This Romeo was less adventurous, different. Patriotically, Yuri thought, just as good.

Yedemsky slid the egg from pan to plate. The room smelled of perspiration and mould, of cabbage, hot oil, soured cream and pepper. A typical Muscovite combination of smells. Home, Yuri thought, he was home and very frightened.

He ate the egg with a slice of stale black bread. He said to Yedemsky, 'You are a doctor. Tell me about the brain.'

Yedemsky flushed. He emptied his glass in an angry gulp, went over to the television and refilled it. 'Eat your food,' he said, his narrow back stiff and erect. 'Talk of something else.'

'I am sorry. I thought as you were a doctor, you would know about these things.'

Yedemsky came back and sat at the small table. 'I only deal with the dead. The dead have no brains.'

'But the brain is something you studied. You must know about it.'

Yedemsky took a fast sip. After a while, he said, 'Yes.' He took another sip and lit a cigarette with furious determination, struggling to control hands that shook, a cigarette that wouldn't keep still. 'Why are you investigating me?' he demanded. 'Why after ... I have helped you? That first day you came to the Pathology Lab, I felt you were different from the others, boychik. I thought you had a soul. But they've got you, haven't they?'

'What's all this about?' Yuri interrupted. 'I'm not investigating you. I've never investigated you. For goodness sake, can't you see I'm in trouble myself?'

'Then why the questions?'

'Because you're a doctor, and I thought you'd know.'

Yedemsky looked down at his glass, sipped, looked back at Yuri. 'Are you sure, boychik, that's all?'

Yuri laughed, shrugged helplessly, flung out his arms. 'What else could there be? I tell you, all I did was ask a question.'

'And you don't know about me?'

Yuri shook his head. 'No.'

Yedemsky gave him a small, placating smile. He refilled his glass. 'Well, let me tell you. Seven years ago I wasn't cutting up corpses. I was a surgeon. Not an ordinary surgeon, a neurosurgeon. I was one of the best.' He looked pathetically at his hands. They vibrated as if shot through with an electric current. Angrily he dashed one hand on the table. The glass and plate jumped. There were tears of anger in his eyes.

Not anger, despair, Yuri thought. A tear brimmed over, glittered and faded into the patchy stubble of Yedemsky's cheek.

Yedemsky jerked the back of his wrist across his face. 'One of the best,' he muttered. He leaned his elbows on the table. 'That's true, boychik. No seamstress could suture as delicately as I could. No sculptor could incise with my millimetric precision. I was very good.' He paused, staring at the table.

'So, what happened?' Yuri asked.

'They took an interest in my work. I was given instructions as to the directions my research should take and what its objectives should be. I refused.' Yedemsky drank and stared resignedly at the table. 'That's when they discovered I was Jewish and sentenced me to work with the dead.'

'It's been seven years,' Yuri said. 'Is there no chance of them letting you back?'

Yedemsky held out his trembling hand. 'Even if they let me . . . .' He let his hand drop. 'My speciality was brain disorders. Do you know anything about epilepsy, Yasha? Epilepsy is caused by a malfunction of the temporal lobe. It is cured by surgical removal. A simple operation, but a very delicate one. On some patients, if you remove the temporal superior gyrus, you could leave the patient without the power of speech. So you have to do it just right. And in order to find out which patients are affected you insert tiny electrodes into the brain and stimulate the gyrus.'

Yedemsky lit another cigarette. 'My work with epileptics gave me a fascination with the brain's control centres. I began to investigate the human brain. I was like a pilot flying in fog. My instruments would tell me there was a mountain, but I did not know its colour or shape or its geological structure. It was only the beginning, boychik, but I was able to arrive at certain conclusions. The brain is a physical organ. All those noble thoughts you have are a matter of electricity and chemistry. Your emotions are electro-chemical.'

'There must be more to a human being than that,' Yuri said.

'Probably,' Yedemsky agreed. 'We are only at the frontiers of knowledge. We are still probing. Perhaps, when we have found out all there is to know about the brain, we will discover that there is something that goes beyond the purely physical. But that doesn't negate anything I've said.

'If I were to stimulate your caudate nucleus, you would cringe from me, yes from me, the drunken ex-surgeon Yedemsky, who makes a living out of corpses. On the other hand, if I were to stimulate the amygdala, you would attack me, attack anyone. The reaction is unavoidable, outside your control.'

'How would you do this?' Yuri asked.

'Oh, that's easy. In surgery, we bore tiny holes through the skull and insert electrodes. You probably wouldn't even feel them on your brain. A lot of the brain has no nerve endings.' Yedemsky grinned crookedly. 'Alternatively, we could inject you with chemicals. Or we might give you a pill.'

'As easy as that?'

'As easy as that to provoke a specific reaction. That's what all the sensory drugs are about. You feel depressed, unable to function, so you drink vodka or take Valium.'

Yuri asked, 'Could you control more complex actions, a series of actions?'

Yedemsky poured himself another glass of vodka. 'You could. What kind of actions are you thinking about, boychik?'

'Murder.'

Yedemsky lit another cigarette. 'That would be more diffi-cult. But with the drugs they have today, and the advances in hypnosis, it wouldn't be impossible.'

Yuri told him about Abyugov and the two men who'd killed Drasen.

'Difficult to be conclusive,' Yedemsky said. 'They could have been rehabilitated, or simply under the temporary influence of a sensory drug.'

Yuri told him about Kronykin's lunatic scribblings and his visit to Dolgov's apartment.

'It seems more likely that this poor man was programmed,' Yedemsky said. 'The scribblings for instance. That was a kind of auto-hypnosis in response to an order buried in his subconscious. The phrase, the snow of Tsaritsyn – to me that seems the trigger, that set him off following embedded instructions. What I think happened was, the whole sequence of the murder was implanted in this poor man. He was like a bomb waiting for a fuse to be lit. At the appropriate time, he was given the activating signal, it may have been a phone call, or a message, anything. He then proceeded to prime himself and go and do what he had been told to do.'

'But Kronykin had never even met Dolgov. Isn't it true that no one can be hypnotized to do what he really does not want to do?'

'Not true.' Yedemsky poured himself more vodka. 'You see, boychik, under hypnosis you can persuade the subject that what is morally repugnant is in fact morally desirable. For instance, you would ordinarily not want to kill your best friend. But if under hypnosis, I persuaded you that your best friend was in fact your enemy, that he planned to destroy you and your family, that unless you killed him you, and everyone dear to you would be destroyed, what would you do?'

'I suppose I'd kill him.'

'You see! And remember, in the case of this poor man, they used both hypnosis and drugs.' Yedemsky upended the bottle over his glass. A few drops trickled out. He drank and looked despairingly at the bottle. 'You know something, boychik? We're all conditioned. We can all be conditioned. Pavlov won his Nobel Prize for the study of digestion, but he should have won it for showing us how easily we can be conditioned. We're all of us puppets.' He raised the glass to his lips and made a sucking noise. 'Pavlov's puppets.'

CHAPTER FORTY-ONE

Yuri slept in the armchair. It wasn't a restful night. Yedemsky snored and tossed in his sleep. Once he called out the name of a woman. Ylena. His wife, Yuri wondered, sitting awake in the battered armchair.

Toward dawn, he slept.

The next morning, Yedemsky woke early. He padded about the flat, coughing, making tea. Yuri sat the table and wrote to his father.

Yedemsky slipped the note inside his jacket. The collar was frayed. There was a small hole in one sleeve. Yedemsky said wonderingly, 'The Marshal, your father. I never thought.'

They went together to the cafeteria in the Pavelets train station. Workers, some in overalls, some in cracked leather jackets, lined up along the counter. A woman unstacked chairs and wiped down tables. There was a warm smell of frying. Yuri ate some meat and potatoes, drank hot, sweet tea. Yedemsky drank tea and looked at him, mournfully.

'Will you be back tonight?'

'I don't know. It depends if it'll be safe.'

'It will be safe. Don't worry, boychik.'

Yedemsky finished his tea and left, a lonely, scarecrow figure loping along the platform.

Yuri took the metro to Dynamo Stadium. He pressed into the compartment against men in overalls, men in jackets and open shirts carrying briefcases, fresh faced girls, hump backed *babushki*, burly women carrying tool boxes, their hair wrapped in bright scarves. At Dzerzhinskaya, a basketball squad got in, wearing red KGB training suits. Yuri pressed deeper into the compartment. He bumped against a girl. She smiled, revealing a gleaming lower jaw of steel.

He spotted Pasha towering above the crowd streaming

between the classical white columns of Dynamo Metro Station. He fought his way to Pasha's side. 'Hello, big boy, I'm back.'

Pasha turned, looked at him heavy lidded. 'You've been beaten up again. What happened to your hair?'

'Scars of war,' Yuri said. He pressed the ticket he had bought into Pasha's hand.

'Did you get what you wanted?'

They allowed themselves to be borne along by the crowd past the ticket barrier. Yuri said, 'Yes. How are things here?'

Pasha preceded him onto the steep escalator and turned. 'Bad. They're looking for you, officially.'

'What for?'

'They say you were connected with Drasen's death, that you and Drasen had an argument over Sonya Matsyeva, that you two, Drasen and the Popovs, were part of a group indulging in decadent sexual practices.'

So Sonya was still at Yevpatoriya. Sonya was still free. They stepped off the escalator and walked onto a crowded platform. Quickly, Yuri told Pasha what had happened in Washington. He said, 'Popov was right. Kronykin is the key to everything. I need to find out where Kronykin was taken for rehabilitation. He was treated by a Dr Drachinsky. I need Kronykin's treatment file. Also, if you can get it, the files of Abyugov and any former members of STF 29.'

Pasha grunted. 'It'll mean sneaking into the Fifth.'

'It's important,' Yuri said. 'How soon can you do it?'

'I'll tell you when I've done it.' The arriving train pressed air along the platform. 'How do I contact you?' Pasha asked.

'Get word to Yedemsky at the Militia Pathology Lab. I'll meet you anywhere you say.'

Pasha heaved into the train. 'Don't go getting beaten up again,' he called, as the doors slid shut.

Yuri waited half hidden behind the columns of the Frunzenskaya Metro Station. He watched the tan Zhiguli drift slowly past the station down 10th Anniversary of October Street. The three military officers in it sat erect, gazing straight ahead of them, like mannequins. The car braked at the end of the street and turned right.

294

Yuri looked around him. People moved in and out of the station. No one was watching him. No one appeared to be loitering.

Three and a half minutes later the Zhiguli was back, gliding slowly past the station. Its brake lights flared before it turned right into Usacova Ulica.

Four minutes later its gleaming radiator grill emerged around the opposite corner. As it drew level with the station Yuri darted out from behind the pillar, ran down the steps, as if to hail a taxi. The Zhiguli sailed slowly by, its occupants rigid as statues. Yuri stood on the pavement, a man about to cross the street, a man unsure of where to go.

A grey Volga darted to the kerb. Radio antennae swayed as it stopped. The rear door swung open. Yuri was hardly in the car, before it pulled away.

'You look different,' his father said.

Yuri looked through the rear window. The tan Zhiguli was keeping station, two vehicles behind. He said, 'I've had my hair cut.'

His father grabbed his hand fiercely. 'You've been hurt.'

'It's nothing. It's all over now. I'm all right.'

From beneath tangled eyebrows, his father studied him closely. 'There's a KGB alert out for you,' he said. 'You should come in and talk to the GRU.'

'Not yet,' Yuri said. 'There are still things to be finalized. How's Sonya?'

'Still safe in Yevpatoriya.'

'Good.' He told his father what had happened in Washington and of Pasha's search for Kronykin's file. 'Did you get the information I asked for?'

His father nodded. 'The computer classified STF 29 as Action Invalidated – the unit was eliminated by enemy action. I had everything re-checked. The computer had made a mistake. The unit had not been destroyed but disbanded.'

He shrugged. 'There's nothing unusual in that. Units are disbanded all the time. I ran a check with Military Postings. Not one of the members of STF 29 had been reassigned to other units. Every single one of them had been discharged. And that is very unusual.'

Marshal Raikin took out a piece of paper from the top pocket of his uniform. 'I had the discharges verified, then checked with Non-Military Placements. Of the twenty-four men in the unit, seven; Kronykin, Abyugov, and five others died violently. Five are in prison for crimes of violence. The rest are under rehabilitation by the Fifth Chief Directorate.

'I don't understand it,' his father said. 'Twenty-four men discharged at the peak of their careers. Not conscripts, professional soldiers, the kind of soldier we need, dedicated, battle hardened, tough. No regiment in the entire Russian Army has had such a record of post combat maladjustment. I have to report this, Yuri. Like it or not you'll have to come and talk to the GRU. I know a Colonel there, a friend of Popov's. He's from the Dnepropetrovsk region. He knows Deryugin too. And inside the Nevsky Barracks not even the KGB will be able to get to you.'

'What can he do without proof?' Yuri asked.

'Perhaps a bigger organization can find it more quickly.'

'Not in this case. The moment they know we're looking for Kronykin's files, they'll destroy them – if they haven't been destroyed already.'

His father asked, 'And if the files have been destroyed?'

'We'll have to see what we can get out of Drachinsky and Guschin. I'll need you and the GRU for that.'

'How much time do you need?'

'A day or two.'

'All right. But after that you'll have to come in. I don't want anything happening to you, and I can't stall the GRU forever.' The Marshal reached under the seat and pulled out a Stechkin. 'I've always preferred these to Makarovs. Don't hesitate to use it if you have to.'

'I won't,' Yuri said.

His father smiled and clasped Yuri's shoulder. 'We make a good team,' he said. 'I could have used you against the Germans.'

'Only the enemy has changed,' Yuri said.

The Marshal turned and looked out of the window. 'If there is a God,' he said, softly, 'may he preserve you.'

They drove across the Moskvoretsky Bridge. In the late evening sunlight, the pink granite seemed stained with blood.

Yuri had himself dropped off at Izmailovskaya Metro Station. Behind the station stretched Izmailovo Park, acres of culture and rest with cafés, a chess and draughts area, athletic stadiums, skating rinks, exhibition pavilions and a concert hall. Yuri bought newspapers and the largest magazines he could find. From a nearby *gastronom* he bought milk and sausage. He walked into the park, hurrying eastward till he came to the forest.

Here royalty had once hunted. The trees grew thick and close together. He moved into darkness. Gradually as his eyes grew accustomed the trees became dark shadows against grey.

He walked deep into the forest. When he came to some undergrowth on the edge of a clearing, he broke off branches and spread them under a birch. He spread the magazines over the branches, sat down, ate some of the sausage and drank half the milk.

He stretched himself over the branches and pulled the newspapers over his body.

He tried to sleep.

Through chinks in the branches he could see bright pinpoints of stars. In Africa, the stars had been like fists. Africa had been warmer than Russia. He had not expected the forest to be so cold. He wished he had some of Yedemsky's vodka. He lay awake, shivering under the newspapers.

The forest was never silent. There was a constant rustling, a constant stirring, a continual sense of stealthy movement. And from time to time, there was a closer, heavier sound. Each time he heard it, Yuri started.

He told himself there wouldn't be patrols in the forest. Drunks, bums, men on the run, all had to come out of the forest. It was easier for the authorities to wait. Still, he took the Stechkin from its holster and kept it in his hand, under the newspapers.

He thought: So far, Sonya was safe. Also, his father and Pasha. Gvishani and Zarev were moving circumspectly. But they were moving. Soon, time and events would force them to act more speedily, act with their accustomed ruthlessness. Then they would kill him, and everyone who had helped him.

He had to act first, and he had to act swiftly. Time was running out.

Which was why he'd been right to refuse to go to the GRU. Army Intelligence, like any other government organization would move ponderously. Evidence would have to be checked and re-checked, decisions submitted for approval; there would be conferences, consideration of alternatives, an increase in the possibilities of betrayal, and most of all, delay.

No, the time to bring in the GRU was afterwards. In forty-eight hours.

He drifted into a light sleep, that was not really sleep but a halfway stage. He could feel the cold as he slept and the effort of his body to remain motionless under the newspapers. Once he opened his eyes and thought he'd been blinded. The stars were blotted out, the space between the trees filled with a ghostly grey mist. His hair and face were damp with it.

He dozed. He woke again to a shrouded world. There was a sudden chittering of birds. He woke, unaware that he had slept. The mist had thinned to wispy trails. The sky was tinged with pink. He slept again. He woke to the rustling of feet.

He sat up clutching the gun. He heard the sounds again. Yes, definitely more than one person walking in the forest. Hurriedly, he folded the newspapers. The sound they made seemed unnaturally loud. He crouched, braced for the shouts, the sight of men rushing to surround him. Somewhere in the forest, a man coughed. Quickly, Yuri finished the milk, crumpled the carton, and put it into his pocket. He walked quietly toward the sound, moving stealthily from one tree to another, stopping, looking, moving again. Then he saw a man, walking stooped with no attempt at concealment. Then another. And another. He almost laughed with relief.

Mushroom pickers!

Stooping himself, he walked past them. No one paid him any attention.

He came out onto Izmailovsky Prospekt and stopped at a cafeteria. It was blessedly warm. He drank hot sweet tea, ate a pie. He walked to the metro station and called Yedemsky.

'Boychik, I missed you.'

'How's everything?'

'Quiet as the grave. How are you?'

'I'm fine.'

'Any news?'

'Not yet.'

He went to the station toilet, washed out his mouth and dabbed water on his face. His eyes were reddened and his face was puffy. There was a heavy dusting of stubble on his cheeks. His clothes looked as if they had been slept in.

So what, he thought. Unshaven men in rumpled clothes were no rare thing in Moscow. He joined a line of workers waiting for a bus. They were rumpled and unshaven too. At last, he thought, I've joined the proletariat.

CHAPTER FORTY-TWO

Yuri returned to Izmailovo. He walked in the park. He played chess. At noon he called Yedemsky. No news.

He returned to the park. An army band was playing. He bought an ice cream sundae with strawberry syrup and ate it while he listened to military marches. He admired examples of Soviet achievement, rockets, space ships, satellites. At three o'clock he called Yedemsky again.

'The Streltsy Church in Zamoskvorechye. In two hours.'

Yuri took the metro to Novokuznetskaya, mystified. Pasha had given him the name of a district, not an address, and the Streltsy had not been churchmen, but pikemen and musketeers. Ivan the Terrible had turned them into Russia's first professional soldiers. Had Pasha meant not a church but an army post in Zamoskvorechye? But it wasn't like Pasha to be so obscure. He must have meant a church.

Swaying with the passage of the train, he tried to recall the churches in Zamoskvorechye. St George near the drainage canal with its five silver domes and yellow belfry. The Church of the Virgin beside the Novokuznetskaya Station. The Church of St John the Baptist, of Saints Mikhail and Fyodor, of St Clement, Pope of Rome. It couldn't have been any of them. The Trinity Church? The huge Church of the Resurrection?

What the devil had Pasha meant? Yuri got out of the station and started to walk. The Church of the Ascension. Nothing to do with the Streltsy there. St Gregory? Again, no connection. An eighteenth-century traveller had described Moscow as a city of forty times forty churches. He could walk forever. The Church of St John the Warrior, planned it was said by Peter the Great. No, not that. Peter had always been wary of the Streltsy.

He walked on, fuming. He would be late. He would miss Pasha. And then he saw it, tucked away in a side street, its windows blocked with boards and thin sheeting, its domes cracked, covered with moss and stained with rust. And above each of the domes, little crosses. Above the crosses, crowns, indicating the church had been built with funds contributed by the Streltsy.

Yuri stepped through a gap in the hoarding. The church was either too decrepit to be restored or of too little interest; too small to be used as a museum or the authorities did not want it known that Russian soldiers had once believed in God. For whatever reason, it stood abandoned, the plan for its demolition, no doubt part of some grander plan of redevelopment, lost, forgotten or indefinitely postponed in some Ministry. Meanwhile, walls crumbled. The small belfry had a pronounced lean. The main door was scarred from numerous, futile attempts to secure it. It stood slightly ajar.

Yuri went in. Light from gaps in the boarded up windows faded into an opaque murk. The floor was slimy from an accumulation of winters. Yuri moved sideways against the wall. Chill like a dead hand pressed through his jacket.

The pews had long since been used for fuel; the aisles littered with broken masonry and the remnants of statues; arms of patriarchs, wings of angels, bearded heads, a twisted torso on what had once been a cross. Niches in the walls stood empty. The walls were patched with mould. An altar gaped.

His foot hit something soft and heavy. He staggered, the Stechkin leaping into his hand. A figure lay sprawled at his feet, curled half across the aisle, jacket pulled awry by the force of the fall, a dark, glutinous stain spreading from throat over the front of the jacket. By the outstretched hands Yuri made out the shattered plastic outline of a radio. Further away the sinister gleam of a gun.

By the broken font ahead of him, a shadow moved. Groaned.

'Pasha!' Yuri cried, half turning, clicking off the safety catch.

'I ... can't ... move.'

Yuri stepped over broken cherubs and the remains of one dimensional faces to the font. Pasha sat with his back to its base, his legs stretched out in front of him. A dark, wet stain soaked the lower part of his jacket and his trousers. A rich, exuvial odour rose above the damp reek of decay.

Pasha gasped, 'I found Drachin ... Kronykin ... taken.'

Yuri placed his hands under Pasha's shoulders. 'Let me help you stand. Let's get out of here.' Pasha's body sagged in his grasp.

'Can't ... walk. Can't ... move. Helpless ... big baby.' Pasha laughed and coughed. Blood frothed from the side of his mouth and dribbled down unheeded. His hand flapped.

Yuri wiped away the blood. 'You have a radio?'

'In ... car. But, wait.' Pasha's head lolled forward. His face was covered with a shiny, clammy sweat. In the opaque darkness, it shone like marble.

Pasha said, 'Got Technical Services ... do me ... work pass. Got to ... Fifth. Kronykin taken to Zartovo ... thirty kilometres from here ... I've been there.' Pasha coughed and laughed again. Blood soaked Yuri's handkerchief and flowed over his hand.

'We can talk, later.'

'No, now. I went Zartovo ... used work pass to get in ... like you ... said Guschin wanted all STF files.' Pasha stopped, breathing heavily. His sweat against Yuri's hand was cold.

'Did you get the files?' Yuri asked, his heart pounding.

'Drachinsky scared like rabbit. Very angry. His files ... very important for science. I say Guschin wants all his files. Feel his collar ...' Pasha stopped and closed his eyes.

'So he has the files?'

'Yes.'

'Wait here. I'll get —'

Pasha's grip on his hand tightened.

'Files no use to ... Guschin. Guschin ... not man of science. Drachinsky will not allow Guschin ... destroy files. I say orders is orders and shove Makarov up his snout.' Somehow Pasha managed a laugh. 'Give me ... twenty-four files ... All STF-29.'

'Where are the files, Pasha?'

'In car ... blue Volga ... on corner.' He screwed his eyes shut in pain. 'Afterwards ... I think ... Drachinsky got suspicious. Called Guschin ... Outside Mosow ... picked up tail ... radio message. Took evasive action ... but one bastard followed me here. Shot him ... before call reinforcements. Bastard got me too ... must be spine ... can't move ... can't control anything ...'

Pasha's voice was fading. The blood from his mouth was a thinning rivulet.

'Your car keys,' Yuri demanded.

Pasha's hand moved, slid the Makarov about on the floor. 'In ... pocket ... can't move.'

Yuri found the key in a damp pocket. 'You wait here, big boy,' he said. 'I'll radio for an ambulance.'

Pasha tried to laugh. 'Where ... can I go?'

Yuri got to his feet.

'Yasha ... you carry ... a gun?'

Yuri looked down at the helpless giant. 'Yes. People kept beating me up.'

'Should have been ... a wrestler.' Pasha coughed again. His head slumped on his chest.

Yuri hurried out of the church. The daylight was blinding. He stopped behind a pillar, checking for any of the KGB men who had followed Pasha from Zartovo.

No one.

He edged his way to the side of the church, looked along the ruined wall.

Again, no one.

No one amongst the weeds and undergrowth between him and the gap in the hoarding. Yuri raced through the gap into the street.

He found Pasha's official Volga parked around the corner, forty yards away. He got in and turned on the radio. There was a babble of voices. He switched to transmit and said, 'This is an AT2.'

Immediately a woman's voice said, 'Come in, AT2.'

The other radio voices were stilled. Quickly, Yuri described the location of the church and asked for an ambulance.

Moments later, the woman confirmed the ambulance was on its way. 'Do you need any further assistance, Comrade?'

'No,' Yuri said. 'Not just at present.'

The place to which Kronykin had been taken was two kilometres outside Zartovo. High walls, topped with barbed wire and illuminated by searchlights surrounded a square, institutional building. Armed guards stood before tall wrought iron gates. Inside, Yuri supposed there were ditches and dog patrols. Three kilometres from the institution he came to the small apartment block where Drachinsky lived.

It stood alone, erupting out of the flat countryside. A few lights showed from its square windows. Beside the block was a parking lot, its entrance protected by a wooden barrier. Beside the barrier was a hut.

Yuri drew up in front of it and wound down the window. 'Escort for Dr Drachinsky,' he said.

The security man took great pleasure in telling him that Drachinsky was at the hospital.

Yuri looked impatiently at his watch. 'I come off duty in an hour. What time is he due back?'

'Anytime now.'

Yuri said, 'I'd better collect him from the hospital. In case we pass each other, what kind of car does he drive?'

'A green Volga,' the security man said.

'Thank you, Comrade.' Yuri reversed onto the road, turned round and drove towards the hospital.

Half way between the apartments and the hospital he stopped, made a U turn and parked. He waited, staring into his rear view mirror.

The files that Pasha had nearly died to get had told him very little. There had been one file for each of the twenty-four members of STF 29, each file marked 'OPERATION PAVLOV 80.' The file on Sergei Kronykin had been the largest.

Yuri hadn't been able to follow the hieroglyphics of drugs prescribed and treatment administered. All he'd been able to glean from the files was that the men of STF 29 had been subjected to some form of indoctrination, which had started shortly before their posting to Afghanistan, and continued after their discharge from the Army.

His rear view mirror brightened with the beam of headlamps. Yuri started the engine. The lights blossomed, filled the interior of his car. A green Volga swept past.

Yuri pulled out after it, switching on the revolving blue roof light as he raced the Volga hard through the gears.

His headlamps dimmed the twin glow of Drachinsky's rear lights. Drachinsky slowed. Yuri pulled past him, swerved and braked. Obediently, Drachinsky stopped behind the police vehicle.

Yuri turned off his lights, got out and walked towards Drachinsky. In one hand he carried the files, in the other the Stechkin hidden beneath his jacket. He turned his face away as he approached the car and kept his head above the line of the roof, as he spoke. 'Dr Drachinsky, we have arrested this afternoon's intruder. He claims to be a patient of yours. Could you come with me and identify him, please?'

'Yes,' Drachinsky said. 'Of course.'

'We'll use your car,' Yuri said. He threw the files on to the rear seat, pulled open the door, turned and slid backwards into the passenger seat. He swivelled, drawing his legs into the car, tucking his arm underneath his jacket. He jabbed the Stechkin into Drachinsky's neck. Yuri said, 'Drive.'

Drachinsky's eyes bulged. 'You! What the devil do you want?'

'Drive,' Yuri repeated and jabbed Drachinsky again with the gun.

Drachinsky drove slowly towards the apartment building. About a hundred yards before it, Yuri made him turn down a side road. They drove past empty fields whose dark earth seemed to absorb the starlight. Yuri made Drachinsky stop, reached forward, turned off the ignition and withdrew the key. 'Now tell me what the fuck you people have been doing to STF 29.'

Drachinsky looked round anxiously. 'You've no right to those files. They're medical records. They're confidential.'

Yuri jabbed the barrel of the Stechkin under Drachinsky's jaw. Drachinsky's teeth clicked, and he gave a little howl of anguish.

'Talk,' Yuri growled.

'There's very little to say. STF 29 was the subject of a properly authorized and controlled experiment necessary to prepare soldiers for battle.'

'And afterwards?'

'A continuation of that same experiment. It was necessary that they be de-programmed in order to adjust properly to civilian life.'

'In that case, why is every member of STF 29 dead or in an institution?'

'That is not correct,' Drachinsky protested. 'Some of those men are currently being treated by us, are still being trained to readjust correctly to civilian life.'

'That's rubbish, Drachinsky! The only experiment you are conducting is changing those men into mindless killers – men who kill to your orders, men who will kill without thought. You are turning them into robots.'

Drachinsky shifted in his seat, looked out of the window. Quietly he asked, 'And what is a soldier, if not a programmed assassin? If our society needs such people, is it not our duty to ensure that they are the most efficient. Efficiency is not only about industrial resourc.s. It is about the effective use of human resources as well.'

'Destroying people's minds is not the most efficient use of human resources,' Yuri said.

Drachinsky turned and looked at him. 'That is how assassins have always been trained. Do you know who the first assassins were? They were Persians, young men brought to a valley in the Alamut. They were motivated by a primitive form of brain-washing. While they were being trained in the arts of killing, every wish they had was granted. Then suddenly, without any warning or reason, they were expelled from the community and left without physical or emotional sustenance. After a suitable interval they were offered a chance to return, provided they carried out the simple task of killing an enemy of the king. Our methods, are simply more scientific. The state needs professional assassins. We provide them.'

'Who did you programme Kronykin to kill?' Yuri demanded.

Drachinsky looked nervously away. 'To be honest, I don't recall.' He sighed. 'So many experiments, so many variations –'

Yuri stretched out his left hand. He pulled Drachinsky's little finger from the wheel and bent it backwards quickly. He felt ligaments tear, the joint dislocate.

Drachinsky screamed.

Yuri grabbed the next finger, and twisted it back. 'You've got nine more fingers, doctor. We are alone, and I have lots of time.'

'You can't do this to me!' Drachinsky cried. 'You're crazy!'

Yuri wrenched the finger. 'Who was Kronykin programmed to kill? Was it Dolgov?'

Blinking back tears of pain, Drachinsky nodded.

'On whose orders?'

Drachinsky's lips formed a narrow line.

'Whose orders?' Yuri repeated.

'I can't tell you that,' Drachinsky muttered. 'You're being very foolish. When the Directorate gets you –'

'When they get me, I'm dead anyway and whatever I do to you, they can't kill me twice. So tell me, whose orders?'

Feebly, Drachinsky tried to wrestle his hand away.

'Whose orders?'

'The Directorate's.'

'Who in the Directorate? Guschin?'

Drachinsky nodded rapidly. 'Yes, yes. Guschin.'

'Drachinsky, you're lying! You're a careful man, a methodical man. You kept Kronykin's files after he was dead, because you believe that records must be preserved, that procedures must be followed.'

'Also necessary for scientific purposes,' Drachinsky muttered.

'So you wouldn't have accepted Guschin's orders alone. You would have wanted a political as well as an executive sanction to murder Dolgov. Who gave you the ultimate authority?'

Drachinsky looked round desperately.

Yuri though he would have to break another finger. Then Drachinsky muttered, 'Korselov.' He turned and looked pleadingly at Yuri.

'How was the order conveyed?' Such an order had to be in permanent form.

'Indirectly,' Drachinsky muttered.

'Where is it?' He released Drachinsky's finger and jabbed him in the stomach with the Stechkin.

Drachinsky gasped. 'In my office.'

Yuri leaned away from Drachinsky. 'Drive,' he said.

Drachinsky's face was white with fear and pain. 'I – I can't.'

'You'll manage.'

Yuri slipped the gun beneath his jacket while Drachinsky laboriously turned and reversed. As they approached the hospital he said, 'Remember, I am much too close to you to miss.'

Drachinsky drove silently up to the guard post. The guards looked curiously into the car and waved them through. Drachinsky stopped outside the front steps.

'Get out slowly,' Yuri said. 'I'll be right behind.'

They got out of the car and went into the building. Drachinsky led him up a flight of bare cement steps to an office. Above a row of filing cabinets was a wall safe. Drachinsky opened it and took out an envelope. He opened it and showed the contents to Yuri. A letter from Korselov, Chairman of Administration and Organs, authorizing Drachinsky to perform Experiment Number 72/6.

'The confirmation is in Kronykin's file,' Drachinsky murmured.

Yuri slipped the authority into his pocket. 'All right, let's go.'

Drachinsky said, 'You'll never get away with this, you know.'

'Walk,' Yuri said. 'Now.'

He followed Drachinsky back to the car. 'Drive me to Moscow,' Yuri said.

Five kilometres from Moscow, Yuri made Drachinsky stop. 'Get out.'

'Here?'

Yuri jabbed the gun hard into his ribs. 'Here.'

Obediently, Drachinsky climbed out. Yuri slid behind the wheel and drove away. In the rear view mirror, Drachinsky's worried image faded.

There was little night traffic around Moscow, because people had little reason for driving about at night. It would be quite a while before Drachinsky found assistance or was able to raise an alarm.

CHAPTER FORTY-THREE

Yuri drove to the Pavelets Railway Station. He circled the block twice. As far as he could tell, Yedemsky's apartment wasn't being watched. He parked and went upstairs.

'Boychik!'

Yuri gave him Kronykin's file. 'Read that. Tell me what you think of it.' He refilled Yedemsky's glass and poured out a shot of vodka for himself. He sat and waited, while Yedemsky read.

When Yedemsky finished, his face was ashen. He convulsed over lighting a cigarette. 'Boychik,' he spluttered, 'boychik. This is worse than murder! This poor man, Kronykin, they've systematically destroyed his brain.'

Yedemsky poured himself a fresh drink. It had started, he said, two years ago, possibly a legitimate experiment aimed at making soldiers more effective. 'It was afterwards that they dehumanised him. After he had been withdrawn from combat.'

'What exactly did they do?' Yuri asked.

'They gave him large quantities of Aminazin. Aminazin is used in the treatment of schizophrenics. It is a powerful drug. It can cause depression, a feeling of exhaustion and loss of muscular control. In large quantities, it interferes with the memory circuits of the brain. This man Kronykin's memory circuits were burned out. I would imagine that when this treatment was concluded, he had no memory.'

'That can't be right,' Yuri said. 'He couldn't have functioned without a memory, and we know he functioned. He worked in a factory afterwards, he lived normally with his family.'

'More or less normally,' Yedemsky corrected. 'The fact that Kronykin had his memory wiped out, does not mean that he had no memory. If a man can live with another's kidney or heart, why not an implanted memory? The only point of destroying Kronykin's memory was to replace it with something else.'

Yuri remembered Evgenya Kronykina telling him that her son had seemed strange after he'd returned from the war, that he'd suffered from headaches, been withdrawn, sometimes looked as if he couldn't remember where he was or whom he was with.

'That wasn't memory lapse,' Yedemsky said. 'Those specific items no longer existed for Kronykin. However,' Yedemsky continued, 'no one knows precisely how memory functions or precisely how it is stored. All people like Drachinsky know is that a drug like Aminazin wipes out large chunks of memory. They don't know how much or what specific memories are erased. They have no knowledge of how long the effect of the drug lasts.

'I think Kronykin was beginning to recover. Hence the headaches, hence the awareness of a loss of memory. That was when they decided to rehabilitate him.' Yedemsky lit another cigarette. 'What they did was unforgivable. They subjected this poor man to electric shocks. They knocked him out for days with powerful mixtures of Aminazin, Seconal, Veronal and Phenergan. In no time at all, Kronykin would have lost what little memory he had. Soon afterwards, he would have lost his sense of identity. We would not have known where he was, why he was there, possibly even who he was. As the treatment progressed, he would have ceased being anxious about his lack of identity, he would have been like a child, living only in the present. At that childlike stage, his mind would have been malleable. It would have been reshaped, re-formed.'

'You mean, he could have been induced to believe that Dolgov murdered his father, that Dolgov had him discharged from the Army, that Dolgov was a threat to his family.'

'He could have been made to believe anything.'

'And so he could have been made to kill Dolgov?'

Yedemsky ran a hand through his hair. In a low voice he said, 'Yes,' and stared silently into space. Then, 'Yasha, tell me again about the notes you found in Kronykin's room.'

Yuri told him.

'It fits,' Yedemsky said, despondently. 'Money, concern for his family, that was the part of Kronykin they kept intact. His fear and hatred of Dolgov was implanted. Was there a candle or a mirror in his room?'

'Yes. Kronykin had a visitor the night before he went to Dolgov's. Soon after the visitor left he asked for a mirror.'

'The visitor must have been this Drachinsky, his control. I suppose he was running a final check. Mirrors, candles, they're devices for focusing the mind. The scribbles were a kind of auto-suggestion. I think Kronykin was programmed to put himself into a trance, and in that trance carry out certain actions which had been previously planted in his subconscious.' He put his hands together and cracked his knuckles. 'Of course, proving all this is something else.'

Yuri picked up the phone and called his father. 'I'm ready to come in,' he said. 'How soon can you make the arrangements?'

His father said, 'The man we should talk to is with Deryugin at Zhukovka. We won't be able to see him till tomorrow morning. What you must do is go to the Nevsky Barracks. I'll make the arrangements. Surrounded by three thousand soldiers, you're going to be safe.'

Yuri said, 'There's someone I want to bring with me. A doctor, whose explanations will be vital.'

'That'll be fine. But Yasha, go now. Please.'

'I'll do that,' Yuri said.

Yedemsky said, 'Boychik, I'm not going anywhere. I'm not talking to anyone.'

'You may not be safe here,' Yuri said. 'And besides, we need your medical opinion.'

Yedemsky laughed. 'My medical opinion! They'll tear my opinion to shreds and your case with it. Find yourself another doctor. Any doctor with any sense will confirm what I have said.'

Yuri said quietly, 'Doctors with sense are no problem. Doctors with courage, are.'

'Courage!' Yedemsky laughed again. 'I have no courage, boychik. I am just a worn out wino. I don't care anymore, don't you see, I don't care.'

'Same result,' Yuri said. 'Get your toothbrush and another bottle and let's go.'

Yedemsky hesitated. He moved round the flat in a daze.

Then he said, 'I've got my toothbrush. I don't have another bottle.'

'I'm sure we will be able to find one in the barracks,' Yuri said.

The door swung open. Yuri grabbed the Stechkin. Gvishani stood in the doorway, arms raised and held away from his body. 'Yasha,' he said, 'I've come alone. I am unarmed. We have to talk.'

Yuri kept the Stechkin pointed at Gvishani. 'Talk about what?'

'Sonya. She was arrested in Yevpatoriya together with the men your father sent to protect her.'

'Shut the door,' Yuri said.

Gvishani shut the door behind him, and stood uncertainly beside the armchair.

Yuri went to the window, looked out cursorily.

'There's no one,' Gvishani said. 'I swear to you, I've come alone.'

'All right,' Yuri said. 'You want to talk. So talk.'

Gvishani smiled and lowered his hands. 'Put away that gun, Yasha. You don't need it. We're friends.'

CHAPTER FORTY-FOUR

For a moment the three of them crowded awkwardly in the tiny room. Then Yedemsky put on a grubby raincoat. 'I think I'll take a walk,' he announced.

Yuri looked from Yedemsky to Gvishani. He looked back at Yedemsky and said, 'Don't be long. Not more than half an hour.' He turned to Gvishani. 'If he's not back in half an hour, you're dead.'

Gvishani shrugged and looked over his shoulder at Yedemsky. 'You heard what he said. Enjoy your walk, but please don't take more than half an hour.'

Yedemsky blinked confusedly at them. 'You enjoy your talk.' Topcoat fluttering about him like a flag, he left.

Yuri lowered the gun and moved close up to Gvishani. 'Raise your hands.'

Gvishani gave him a resigned smile and did so. Yuri ran his hands over Gvishani's body and legs, opened his shirt and ran his hands along Gvishani's chest, stomach and back. Gvishani was neither armed nor wired.

'You should believe me, Yasha,' Gvishani said, stepping back and buttoning his shirt.

They sat at opposite sides of the small table. Yuri placed the gun by his right hand where Gvishani would have to reach across him to get it. They stared at each other in uncomfortable silence.

Gvishani's face broke into a half smile. He raised his hands and dropped them limply on the table.

There was none of the Staraya Square arrogance in Gvishani now, only a friendly submissiveness. It was almost like the old days.

Gvishani said, 'Yasha, we've been friends a long time, you and I.'

'Since boyhood,' Yuri said, flatly. He remembered in

313

Sarasovo, Gvishani and his friends had once beaten him until he'd admitted there was no god and that he was an old woman because he let Tanty Sima take him to church. Yuri remembered too, that Gvishani had only become his friend afterwards, when after twelve weekends of training with Igor, he'd used his newly acquired skill in judo to lay Gvishani and two of his friends flat on their backs.

Gvishani continued, 'And today, I have come to you as a friend. You've seen for yourself, I carry neither weapons nor recording equipment. I have come alone. When Yedemsky returns you will know that.'

Yuri remembered Mariya Popova sprawled on the floor of the dacha. Remembered Popov, Drasen and Zamyatin. Gvishani had murdered them as surely as if he'd held the gun and pulled the trigger. Gvishani had murdered not in self defence, not even in anger. He'd murdered calculatingly, as part of a plan. Gvishani, his friend.

Gvishani said, 'Yasha, I have come to help you. I know how you see things, always black and white, right and wrong. I can understand why you have acted as you have. But you're wrong, Yasha. Terribly wrong. One man cannot stand against the inevitability of history.'

'History is made by men,' Yuri said.

'You know that is not true. History is the inevitable expression of dialectic forces, and you, Yasha, cannot stop that. Our cause, our movement, we, are the inevitable successors to the corrupt Deryugin regime. We shall guide Russia back to the true path of the revolution. Join us, Yasha. Work with us for the Party and for Russia.'

Yuri said, 'I am serving Russia, in my way.'

Light streaked across Gvishani's lenses as he shook his head. 'Yasha, if you have a fault it is your egoism. The individual is always less than the group. A group consensus is the only basis for right decision.'

'Which group to join is still an individual decision,' Yuri said. 'I choose not to choose your group.'

Gvishani reached out and place his hand on Yuri's shoulder. Yuri's shoulder went rigid. 'Yasha, what are we doing here arguing like philosophers? There is a whole new world to be won. It is ours. Join us. Share our future with us.'

Yuri pried Gvishani's fingers away. He said, 'I've seen your future and it is the past. I am implacably opposed to you and your cause. We are enemies, Gvishani. And if my friend, Yedemsky, is not back here in half an hour, I will kill you.'

Gvishani looked pained. 'Yasha, if you weren't my friend, I'd say you were pig-headed. But you are, so I say, please be reasonable, please be less obstinate. Please join us –'

Yuri asked, 'How did you find me here?' His tone was terse, matter of fact. He slapped the butt of the gun for emphasis.

'Drachinsky. He told us what you'd done to him. We put out an alert for his car. When it was spotted outside this building, we checked a list of occupants, and I remembered you telling me about Yedemsky.'

Like you remembered my father had a dacha in Yevpatoriya, Yuri thought. Bastard! He wondered why hadn't they come after him with a squad of men from the Fifth, with guns and manic killers? His mouth was unaccountably dry. Hate, he thought, dessicated before it destroyed. He asked, 'What did you come to see me about?'

Gvishani said, 'First and most of all, to persuade you to join us.'

'What else?'

'To offer you a deal. Sonya for the Dolgov evidence, all the Dolgov evidence.'

Why make an exchange, Yuri thought, when all they had to do was kill him?

As if in answer to his question, Gvishani said, 'And that includes all the files you took from Drachinsky. Also, Comrade Korselov's authorization.'

The authorization that was the direct link to the men behind Zarev, Yuri thought. The authorization that was at once so clear and so damning. They didn't want to take any risks with that, not even the smallest possibility of it falling into the wrong hands.

And after they had what they wanted, what then? The answer to that was obvious. He and Sonya would be shot.

'Let me talk to Sonya,' he said.

Slowly, Gvishani shook his head. 'That's not possible. You see, Sonya was quite upset by her arrest. She's had to be placed under heavy sedation.'

'What the hell have you bastards done to her?' he shouted, his hand blurring as he set the selector of the Stechkin to single fire.

'She's all right, Yasha! I swear on my life she's all right!'

'What the fuck did you do to her?' The gun was trembling in his hands.

Gvishani looked down at the table. Hoarsely, he muttered, 'We couldn't believe she didn't know where you were or what you were doing, that you hadn't been in touch.'

Yuri felt a sudden sinking emptiness.

'We strapped her to a lie detector, but that only confirmed what she said. So we administered sodium thiopentone.' He raised pleading eyes to Yuri. 'We had to Yasha! We had to know the truth!' Gvishani looked down and rubbed the flat of his palm along the table. 'She's simply reacting to the drug. Don't worry, Yasha. Once the effect of the drug wears off she'll wake up with nothing more than a nasty hangover.'

Gvishani was lying, Yuri knew properly administered sodium thiopentone did not produce unconsciousness. What they had done was sedate Sonya after giving her the truth drug, so that escape during or after the exchange would be impossible. 'And was Sonya telling the truth?'

Slowly, Gvishani nodded.

I've never lied to you, Yasha. Never, ever. The words choking him, Yuri asked, 'Where is she?'

'She's in Moscow. You will see her quite soon.' He looked up at Yuri. 'Now put that gun away, Yasha. The sooner we conclude our arrangements, the sooner you'll be with Sonya.'

It wasn't Sonya for the Dolgov evidence, Yuri thought. It was Sonya for the control of Russia. He thought of Sonya helpless, mindless, of Sonya dead! He felt weighed down with responsibility and guilt. He had come back into her life. He had involved her in this. Was there not some way he could exchange himself for her? Sonya, my love, my dearest, dearest love. Through childhood, through youth, throughout the separations, he had loved her. He loved her now. Sonya was all, everything. He thought again, him for her. But that was not the choice. Sonya for Russia. He buried his face in his hands.

Gvishani repeated, 'It is a simple matter.'

Gvishani had seen his anguish, his pain. If you take away all a man loves, what was there left? How could he live without Sonya? How could he live knowing he had condemned her? But there was Russia, millions upon millions of lives. Beside that, his love, his guilt, was miniscule. That was not the way to resolve the problem. He had to find a way out. Come on, man, think. There had to be a way, dear God, there had to be a way, but now, he had to react. He had to plan without arousing Gvishani's suspicions. He took his hands away from his face. 'It is not as simple as that.' His voice was trapped in the back of his throat. It sounded as if he was talking through a megaphone under water. 'There are ... ' Take your time, speak slowly. Think! 'Other matters to be considered.'

'Such as ... ' Gvishani was firmly insistent.

Yuri said, 'I don't believe a simple exchange will be enough. I don't believe that after you have the Dolgov evidence, you will tolerate any witnesses.'

Gvishani said, 'You're talking nonsense, Yasha. All we want is the evidence. After that you and Sonya will be free to do whatever you want.'

Yuri said, 'I don't want to live in your Russia.'

'You're being irrational.'

Good. Yuri injected a note of hysteria into his voice. 'I know how many people you've killed already. I don't trust you or Zarev. There has to be a guarantee of safety.' He got to his feet, whirled round. 'How do I know you have her? And if you have her, how do I know she is alive?'

'The answer to both your questions is yes. Otherwise, I wouldn't be here, would I? Yasha, stop fretting over irrelevancies. The main thing is, do you agree to an exchange?'

Yuri walked to the window. He pressed his face against the pane. The cool glass was like a soothing compress. He forced himself to breathe slowly, easily. Told himself to think, slowly. There had to be a way. Safe passage. An airplane. A deserted airfield. Verification of the objects to be exchanged. Somewhere there was a stratagem he could use both to save Sonya and stop Gvishani.

He screwed his eyes against the glass. Think man, think. An airfield. Plane. Tushino. If Sonya was unconscious she would be brought by ambulance. Verification. An examination. There was a way. It exploded in his brain. He forced himself to keep still, forced his mind to concentrate, to pull the fragments of ideas together. There were risks. Don't think of risks, think of ends, think of objectives.

He turned from the window to face Gvishani. His shoulder slumped in acceptance. 'I'll make the exchange,' he said in a low voice. 'But there are conditions.'

'Conditions?'

'Yes. First, I want exit visas for Sonya and myself to leave Russia. I want to leave immediately after the exchange. Which means I'll need a plane.'

'A plane!'

'Yes, one of those eight seater Yak jets that fly Party bigwigs back and forth.'

Gvishani smiled tolerantly. 'Where will you go?'

'Out of Russia first. The plane must have fuel for about a thousand miles. We'll go to Finland.'

'And then?'

'If you must know, I have my arrangements with the Americans.'

Yuri walked to the table and slumped in the chair by Gvishani. 'The crew should be kept to a minimum,' he said. 'Two. And unarmed.'

Gvishani said, 'Civil pilots don't carry arms. And you'll need a crew of three, two pilots and a steward.'

Yuri pretended to consider that. The steward would probably be a KGB man. Resignedly he said, 'All right.' He raised his head tiredly and looked directly across at Gvishani. 'Can you fix that?' Pleading.

'If you insist. But honestly, Yasha, it's quite unnecessary.'

Yuri said, 'Next, I want to be sure that Sonya is alive, that she is not better off dead.'

'I can arrange for you to see her.'

Yuri shook his head. 'That wouldn't be any good. I'm not a doctor. Yedemsky must see her.'

Gvishani thrust his hands up, helplessly. He had the patient look of a man coping with a drunk. 'All right, Yedemsky.'

'But not now. At the airport. Before we take off.'

Gvishani's sigh had a touch of exasperation. 'All right.'

'Another thing,' Yuri said. 'The airport must be cleared of all personnel.'

'Come on, Yasha, this is ridiculous. We can't close down an airport —'

'We're going to be using Tushino. Tushino is closed after dark anyway. So no guards, no one.'

'I'm not sure —'

'Better do it,' Yuri interrupted. 'Neither of us wants to find out that the guards are really Fifth Directorate men or my father's soldiers in disguise.'

Gvishani saw the sense of that. 'All right,' he said.

Gvishani took a notebook from his pocket and wrote carefully in it. 'Anything else?' he asked, looking up.

Yuri looked thoughtful. He stroked his chin, ran a hand through his hair. 'No, I think that's all.'

Gvishani asked, 'How do I know you're going to give me the evidence you've collected and not a bundle of old newspapers?'

Yuri widened his eyes in surprise. 'I wouldn't give you old newspapers,' he said. 'That's not part of the deal.'

Gvishani gave him a small smile. 'Now it's my turn to be paranoid. I want to examine the evidence before you get on that plane.'

'What good will that do? You're not even sure what you're looking for.'

'I want to make sure everything's there and that there are no substitutions between my examination and your departure.'

'But if I tell you where the evidence is, if I have it on my person, what's to prevent you taking it from me by force.'

'Yasha, we're friends!'

'Maybe that's our problem,' Yuri said and walked again to the window. After a while he turned around and said, 'I've got it.'

Gvishani would arrange for each of them to have a KGB car

fitted with a two-way radio and a special channel for their exclusive use. The ambulance taking Sonya to Tushino would be similarly equipped. Once Gvishani had completed the preliminary arrangements, Yedemsky would be taken to the airfield. Yuri would then take the evidence and by radioing Gvishani from his car arrange where they would meet. Gvishani would come alone. They would both be unarmed.

Yedemsky would examine Sonya and report her condition to Yuri. He would also confirm the presence of the aircraft and the absence of everyone but the air crew and the ambulance driver.

'The ambulance driver will need an assistant,' Gvishani said.

'What for?'

'To drive your car back from the airport afterwards. We must be practical, you know.'

So that gave Gvishani two extra men, Yuri thought. He said, 'All right, as long as they're both unarmed. Yedemsky must check that.'

Gvishani waved a hand in front of his face. 'As you wish.'

Once he'd received Yedemsky's confirmations, Yuri said, he and Gvishani would meet. Gvishani would examine the documents and they would drive to the airfield.

Gvishani made a few more notes, stood up and said, 'Seems all right to me. I'd just better check with the Chairman.'

'Zarev?' Yuri asked.

Gvishani smiled, walked to the phone and dialled.

Yuri listened while he outlined the plan for the exchange, waited till by a series of rapid nods, Gvishani indicated the conversation was near an end. He walked over to the phone and jabbed the Stechkin hard into Gvishani's ribs.

'Yasha, what —'

Yuri held out his hand for the phone. 'There's one more condition,' Yuri said.

Gvishani slapped the instrument into his hand.

'Without this there is no exchange,' Yuri said into the phone. 'Who the fuck are you?'

There was a long silence, punctuated by a soft crackling. Then Arkady Aristov said, 'I should have had you sent to Siberia two years ago, when you first started dancing around

Rima. As Stalin used to say, don't talk to a wolf. Shoot it. Now that you know who I am, go on and complete the exchange. And stay out of Russia. Because, the next time I see you, I shall shoot you like a dog.'

Yuri put the phone down, feeling paralyzing shock and great illumination. Aristov had been one of Stalin's youngest and brightest. Aristov had been deprived of high office by Stalin's death. Aristov had always hated Deryugin.

It explained why Aristov had been so unusually helpful, why he had reacted to the breakup of Rima's marriage with such mature calm, even why he had tried to have Rima come back. He hadn't been concerned about getting in to the Politburo, he'd simply wanted to know where Yuri went and what he did.

Gvishani was standing in the middle of the room, smiling at him. 'I've known you for so long,' he said wonderingly, 'but honestly, Yasha, I don't think I'll ever understand you.' Pocketing his notebook he left.

CHAPTER FORTY-FIVE

Yedemsky returned, looking pale and worried. 'Everything all right, boychik?' He reached behind the television for the bottle.

Yuri carried a glass over to him. 'Drink up. You're going for another walk.'

'But I've just come back.' Yedemsky drank swiftly and looked round the flat. 'You didn't kill him, did you, Yasha?'

'No,' Yuri said. 'Not yet.' He took Yedemsky's shoulder and led him out of the apartment.

As they walked in the street, he told Yedemsky what he wanted him to do.

'But boychik, it's seven years since I've examined a living patient.'

Yuri shrugged. 'So? You're still a great doctor.'

Yedemsky smiled quietly. Then Yuri told him what else he wanted him to do. Yedemsky turned and hurried back to the apartment building. Yuri hurried after him. 'What's the matter?'

Yedemsky was trembling. 'I think I need another drink,' he said.

Outside the apartment, a man in KGB uniform was thumping at the door.

Yuri's hand dropped to the butt of the Stechkin. 'We're here,' he said.

The KGB man, turned, his face red from his exertions. 'Captain Raikin?'

Yuri nodded.

The KGB man saluted, handed Yuri an envelope and a set of car keys with a leather tag. 'The car is in the courtyard, sir. It's a black Volga. You'll find the number on the tag.'

When they got inside, Yuri opened the envelope. There were the exit visas, a radio frequency and a note from Gvishani saying that his arrangements would be completed in an hour and that he would have Yedemsky collected and driven to the air field.

Yuri put the note into his pocket. He told Yedemsky to get himself ready. 'And for goodness sake, try to stay sober.'

Yedemsky pulled ferociously at the bottle. 'Don't worry, boychik. I'll drink just enough to steady my nerves.'

Yuri went down into the courtyard. The Volga was parked discreetly outside, by the courtyard wall. Yuri took a flashlight from the glove compartment, ran it carefully along the bumpers and the underside of the car. No bleepers. He opened the engine compartment and looked. No sign of unusual wiring. Hopefully, no bombs or other farewell messages from Aristov.

He sat behind the wheel and hesitated, his fingers on the ignition key. There was no alternative. He had to turn that key. He did. The engine whirled, caught, exploded, settled down to a smooth whirring of cylinders. He reversed out into the street.

He drove to the Hotel National on the corner of Marx Prospekt and Gorky Street. Music from the late night dollar bar filtered down to the lobby. A party of boisterous diners emerged from the restaurant shouting for taxis. The Post Office was closed.

Yuri spoke to the KGB man in charge of security. 'Get that place open,' he demanded, showing his papers.

A hangdog expression crossed the KGB man's face. He handed the papers back. 'They don't open till eight o'clock tomorrow. You'd better come back then.'

'There won't be a Post Office here at eight o'clock tomorrow,' Yuri said. 'There may not even be a National Hotel. Haven't you heard? There's a letter bomb in there.'

Visions of having to stay on duty while a bomb exploded under his feet electrified the man into action. 'A bomb! Should I call the Army and have them send an anti-terrorist squad?'

'No,' Yuri snapped. 'Just do as you're told.'

Twenty minutes later, a harrassed looking clerk was brought. He opened the office and found Yuri's letters. 'You sure there's a bomb in those?'

'We believe so.'

They directed him out through a side door.

Back at Paveletskaya, Yedemsky was wearing a dark suit which Yuri had never seen before. The knees and the elbows shone. At his feet lay a large medical bag, with a few streaks of dust on the cracked leather where Yedemsky hadn't wiped it. The vodka bottle stood on the table, its level as Yuri remembered it.

'You look like a doctor of the living,' Yuri smiled.

'I feel terrible,' Yedemsky said.

Yuri poured him out a small drink. 'That'll help you, till everything's over.'

Yedemsky gave him a nervous smile.

The doorbell rang. A uniformed KGB chauffeur stood outside. Yuri pressed Yedemsky's bony shoulder encouragingly. 'You'll do fine,' he said.

Ten minutes later, Yuri went down to the Volga and radioed Gvishani. 'Where are you?'

'At Kalinin.'

Fifth Directorate Headquarters, Yuri thought. 'What kind of car do you have?'

'A black Moskvich.'

'All right,' Yuri said. 'Take the ring road to Dobryninskaya. By the metro station turn right into Pavlovskaya. Past the Municipal Hospital turn left into Pavlovsky 1. You got all that?'

'Yes. Have you got what I want?'

Yuri switched off the radio and drove the short distance to Stremanny Pereluok and parked near the intersection with Pavlovskaya.

A quarter of an hour later a black Moskvich drove past. Yuri edged onto the street and watched it turn left into Pavlovsky 1. He waited five more minutes. No other vehicles were following Gvishani, and Gvishani was alone.

He drove back to Yedemsky's and switched on the radio. 'Return along the ring road to Gorkovo. Call me when you get there.'

'Yasha, what is all this?'

'Better safe than sorry,' Yuri said and switched off the transmitter.

He went along the ring road the opposite way, driving anticlockwise along Tchkalow Strasse and all the way round Central Moscow. At the intersection before Gorkovo, he turned right.

Soon afterwards, he picked up Gvishani's call. He ignored it, swung left into the second ring road, and emerged onto the Leningradski Prospekt near the Dynamo Stadium. He was now ahead of Gvishani.

Along Leningradski Prospekt he radioed Gvishani. 'Go straight up Gorkovo and along Leningradski Prospekt. Take the right fork onto the Leningradskoy Highway.'

'Tushino is on Volokolamskoye,' Gvishani protested.

'I know,' Yuri said and again switched off the radio.

He drove along Leningradski Prospekt. Opposite the Dynamo Stadium, the long glass air terminal and the Aeroflot Hotel were columns of speckled light. The road was empty. He passed the dark, utilitarian Palace of Sports, turned right at the huge tower of the Hydroproject Institute.

Leningradskoy Highway was even more deserted. He passed a truck and a taxi. To his left, the land flattened. The vast, gleaming waters of the Kimkinsky Reservoir gleamed. Flood lamps bathed concrete. The navigation lights of ships towered high over the road.

Opposite the reservoir he turned right beside Druzbha Park. Friendship Park. An appropriate place for a meeting with Gvishani.

He turned into a side road by the park and stopped.

Gvishani was going frantic on the radio. Yuri told him where they'd meet. Ten minutes later, Gvishani arrived. Yuri drove out and parked behind him. He walked cautiously up to Gvishani's car.

No surprises. No one crouched in the rear seat, no one leaping out of the boot. Gvishani got out. They checked each other for hidden arms. Friendship.

'Have you got the documents?' Gvishani asked.

'In the car.'

They walked back and got in. Yuri handed over Drachinsky's files on the STF. While Gvishani checked them, he radioed the ambulance. Gvishani spoke and had Yedemsky brought to the radio.

'How is she?' Yuri asked, feeling his heart suddenly accelerate.

'She's coming round,' Yedemsky said. 'Of course I can't be definite. But I think she will be all right.'

Yuri breathed out with relief. 'Are there any guards at the airport?'

'No.'

'How many men with the ambulance?'

'Two.'

'Any other cars nearby?'

'No.'

'Is the aircraft there?'

'We're parked right beside it.'

Yuri said, 'I want you to stay with Sonya until we get there. If there is any change in her condition, any change in the situation that you have described, I want you to radio me. In any case, I'll check again in ten minutes.'

Gvishani looked up from the papers. 'You are suspicious,' he said.

In the dim illumination of the car's interior light, it took him ten minutes to check the Drachinsky material. 'The authorization and the Dolgov stuff,' he demanded.

Yuri reached into his inside pocket and gave it to him.

Gvishani read eagerly, then made to put the documents away.

'No,' Yuri said, and grasping his wrist firmly, twisted it. 'I keep those till we're aboard the aircraft.'

Gvishani stared at him, then gave one of those humourless smiles. 'There's no need for you to be suspicious, but all right.' He released his grip on the documents.

Yuri tucked them inside his jacket and said, 'One more thing. From now on we stay together. We drive to the airfield in this car.'

'But, Yasha —'

Yuri gestured to Drachinsky's files spread over the rear seat. 'That way, you stay with the evidence. And I stay with you.'

CHAPTER FORTY-SIX

Tushino was dark except for lights in a corner of the airfield away from the terminal. The gates were open. There were no guards.

Yuri drove slowly along the perimeter road, his lights illuminating the high silhouettes of parked Antonovs, dumpy Pchelkas and single engine Yak-18 Trainers. The first Soviet jets had landed at Tushino, and for many years Soviet air shows had been held there. Now it was used by flying clubs, Party chiefs, the KGB and would-be defectors.

Yuri edged up the road and bounced over the grass to where a bank of lights illuminated a red and white Yak-40. A ladder extended from the rear of its belly to the ground. Some distance behind it, out of the line of the engines, stood an ambulance.

Yuri stopped beside it. He made out two shadowy figures in the driver's cabin of the ambulance, two more uniformed figures clearly discernible in the brightly lit aircraft cockpit.

Gvishani said, 'You might as well give me the documents and get on board. The men will carry Sonya on.'

Yuri turned to him, smiling. Now that the time had come for action, he felt strangely, beautifully calm. 'I'd better check it's the right woman. Yedemsky's never met her, you know.' Pocketing the keys he climbed out and walked towards the rear of the ambulance. Out of the corner of his eye he saw Gvishani walk carefully to the front, the side further away from the plane.

Yuri rapped on the metal doors. 'It's Yasha.'

Yedemsky thrust open one door. Yuri hauled himself in.

Sonya lay strapped to a stretcher. Her face was pale, her hair tousled, spread over a grey pillow. Yuri looked at Yedemsky. Yedemsky opened his bag and took out the bottle of vodka, while Yuri leaned over Sonya and gently stroked her face.

'You sure she's okay?'

'She'll be all right.'

Yuri reached beneath the blanket, felt under the straps, took out the Stechkin Yedemsky had secreted. As he'd expected no one had thought to check an alcoholic doctor, not considered good enough to treat the living.

Holding the gun behind his back and walking to the rear of the ambulance, he twisted round and shouted above the roof. 'All right, Gvishani. Have your men take her aboard.'

There was a clatter of sliding doors. The two men got out, walked along the sides of the ambulance. Gvishani, Yuri noticed had walked a short distance away.

He lowered himself into the ambulance and stood by the door. Yedemsky stood opposite, still clutching his bottle.

The two men climbed up the steps and walked past them.

'Now,' Yuri breathed.

He swung the butt of the Stechkin at the head of the nearest man. Simultaneously Yedemsky swung his bottle. There were two dull thuds, a single muffled cry, a rumbling thump as one of the men fell.

Yuri lowered the other gently to the metal floor. 'Stay here and lock the doors after me,' he told Yedemsky. He leaped out onto the grass.

Gvishani was a narrow shadow in the darkness.

'It's fine,' he called after Gvishani's retreating figure; heard the sound of movement behind him and whirled.

Three men were moving below the belly of the aircraft, spreading out. The floodlights glinted sharply off the weapons in their hands.

Yuri flicked the selector to automatic and fired. Bright red flashes streaked from underneath the plane. Fire seared through his arm. Yuri twisted, rolled, threw himself down behind a wheel of the ambulance, as bullets screamed off its metal body into the night.

His arm felt nerveless. His sleeve was soaked. He peered through the wheels. A shape lay huddled below the aircraft. So civilian pilots didn't carry arms.

Yuri crawled beneath the ambulance.

Three separate bullets rocked it. He smelt gasoline, felt the deep chill of it over his legs. He crawled to the front of the ambulance.

The two remaining men had separated, one at the front, one at the back. But they had no cover. Gvishani hadn't thought of that. Hadn't thought he'd be armed. He moved the selector to single fire, took careful aim at the figure moving cautiously between the aircraft and the front of the ambulance, then fired rapidly twice.

There was a scream. He saw the man fall.

A shot blazed out from behind him.

Any one of those bullets could ignite the fuel tank, blow all three of them up. He tried to turn beneath the vehicle. His arm collapsed beneath him. The pain almost made him faint.

He gritted his teeth. No way, but to crawl out to the right. He edged forward. Grass brushed his face. The gun was slippery in his hand.

He crawled out halfway. No sign of the man.

There was no help for it. He had to draw the man's fire. He grunted and moved forward an inch, six inches, two feet. His legs were clear of the ambulance. He drew them under him in a trembling crouch.

He waited, watching. Nothing moved.

He forced himself upright, swayed, fell against the side of the ambulance. His legs were like rubber, he was wheeling helplessly.

Then the shots started. He felt them punch into the metal sides of the vehicle, felt his ribs start to burn, felt a knifing pain high on the side of his chest. He slipped, fell.

And falling, swivelled. He saw a figure rise from the ground, move crouched. He jabbed the selector onto automatic and fired.

The gun kicked against his shoulder, each blow sending shuddering, devastating pain through his body. The gun chattered in a wide arc. Clicked. Died.

Yuri waited for the man to return fire.

There was silence.

Slowly he dragged himself to his feet, dragged himself into

the ambulance. He started it, turned on the headlamps, yanked the wheel round, drove.

On the perimeter road, he glimpsed Gvishani's hurrying figure. He lurched over the grass, fighting the lunging wheel, allowing his body to bounce with the movement of the ambulance.

He came to the road, wrenched the wheel round, straightened, trapped Gvishani in his lights.

Gvishani darted off the road, ducked between two parked aircraft.

Yuri stopped, fell out of the ambulance, staggered to his feet, staggered after him.

A fuselage, a wheel. He walked dazedly into the darkness. Something hit his shoulder. Sickening waves of pain engulfed him. He felt his legs sag, his body crumple.

A fist smashed into the side of his head. His head rocked against a metal strut. His legs went. He fell helplessly backwards. His head bounced on the concrete. Pain sliced through his brain. Vomit choked in his gullet. He felt himself sliding, drifting into darkness.

He lay on his back, tried to move. He couldn't. The pain was receding. Everything was receding. He was helpless.

Fingers were clawing at his jacket, reaching into his pocket. Through a misty grey curtain, he heard Gvishani say, 'Yasha, where is it? Where is it?'

He forced his eyes open. Gvishani was sitting on him, his face shiny with sweat. He wasn't wearing his glasses.

Now, Yuri thought. Now. He flexed his right hand. There was no pain. There was enough strength. 'It's here,' he whispered, almost inaudibly.

Gvishani leaned forward, his face looming over Yuri's.

Yuri focused his eyes on Gvishani's neck, concentrated on the one spot. Now. Now. His hand whipped out from under him, fingers folded into a solid wedge. They caught Gvishani precisely on the neck. He felt Gvishani's body stiffen with the shock, lift, then Gvishani's body was rolling over his, shuddering, going very still.

Yuri turned his head and looked into Gvishani's eyes.

Already they were losing their colour. A thin worm of blood crept out of his nose.

Yuri pushed him away.

He heard footsteps, looked up, saw Yedemsky peering down at him.

'I hope to hell you can drive,' Yuri said.

CHAPTER FORTY-SEVEN

Yuri slumped beside Yedemsky. The ambulance jounced. Blood soaked the dressings Yedemsky had put on. Pain striped him in knifing ribbons. He couldn't move his arm. A jagged razor sliced his chest each time he breathed. Headlights washed over the windshield. Blood welled in his throat. Yedemsky drove.

'Boychik, lie down in the back.'

He wouldn't, because he didn't want to pass out.

The Hydroproject Tower loomed. Leningradski Prospekt stretched, a dark, wide ribbon spotted with dismal light. The lights rose into the air like those on an aircraft. The lights revolved and disappeared. Pain bathed his body.

There were red lights above the Aeroflot Hotel, swinging in the darkness. The air terminal was deserted. 'Right,' Yuri grunted, and felt the blood fill his mouth.

The ambulance swayed and bounced. Yedemsky clung precariously to the wheel. 'You want an injection for the pain?'

'That'll ... finish ... the job.' Blood trickled down his chin onto his shirt.

They passed the Hippodrome. Lights swayed and danced. He bunched himself as if the compression would stop the bleeding, as if by holding himself, he would remain alive. The headlamps barely cast light. Beyond them, the road was a void. He slumped against Yedemsky. A great ball of pain exploded. He gurgled and rolled away. The ambulance wheeled. Darkness wheeled. He was falling into a jet black pool. The air was fuliginous. Black water, black blood filled his throat. In the darkness, a diesel pounded. He braced himself against the dashboard with his good hand. He concentrated on keeping still.

Yedemsky said, 'Yasha, you'd better let me take you to a hospital first. Otherwise you'll bleed to death.'

Yuri kept his eyes tightly closed. Rima would never cope

with the fact that the father she idolized was a traitor. And what would happen to her and the family? When someone dies, they take everything away, Sonya had said. Suddenly there are no cars, no special passes, no access to food stores. And when someone was disgraced, it was much worse. He thought of Rima in some village in Ryazan, stripped of position, privilege and wealth.

Yedemsky said, 'We're there. You want me to come with you?'

'No.' Yuri allowed his hand to fall on the door catch, used the dead weight of his body to move it. Blood snaked past his teeth and dribbled down his chin, as he leaned over space, clinging to the door.

Yedemsky half carried, half dragged him to the pavement. His legs felt like pieces of wet string. He was surrounded by a red mist that kept fading and returning, fading and returning, fading . . .

Using Yedemsky as a crutch he moved laboriously across the pavement. Walk, damn you, walk. Put one foot before the other. One, two, now. Move. One, two. Simple if you thought how. He stood swaying before the faintly illuminated row of doorbells. Holding on to Yedemsky, he jabbed the one by Aristov's name.

For a long time nothing happened. He stood swaying, Yedemsky holding him upright. Then a jarring, high pitched squawk followed by Rima's voice, angry, shrill and disembodied. 'Who is it?'

'Me . . . Yasha.'

There was a hiss of annoyance. 'Do you know what time it is?' The intercom clicked. There was an angry buzzing from the door. Yedemsky left him and opened it.

Swaying, Yuri pushed past Yedemsky. A lobby lit by three dim lamps. Vast desk. Large circular carpet. He zigzagged across it to the open elevator. Yedemsky followed him in:

'I'll take it from here.' Yedemsky's face and figure shimmered as if washed by a massive wave. Yuri leaned against the sides of the elevator and pressed buttons, nearly fell as it surged upwards. He closed his eyes. The sides of the elevator closed around him. Darkness, blessed darkness. No. Not yet.

Not yet. He fell against the door as the elevator stopped, staggered into the corridor, turned.

Yedemsky followed him out of the elevator. 'You all right, Yasha?'

'Fine ... Wait outside ... This ... is family business.' He lurched to where Rima stood, pulling a pale green dressing gown around her. Her feet were thrust into pale green slippers. Walls danced. Lights swayed. Rima's face was pale with a mixture of fear and anger.

'Yasha, what —'

He tried to say, 'I want to talk to your father.' Blood frothed and flowed from his mouth as he gurgled.

Rima's eyes went wide with horror. Her face tightened. Her mouth moved. 'Go away! Don't bring your troubles to us!' Turning, she disappeared into the apartment and pulled the door shut behind her.

Yuri staggered to the door, and leaned his shoulder against the bell. Its shrill ring echoed through the apartment, the sound reverberating through his brain. There were sounds of muffled movement, voices, locks. Then Aristov stood in the doorway clutching a dressing gown to him like a flag.

Yuri lurched away from the bell and stood swaying in the corridor. He waved the Stechkin. 'I came to tell you ... it's all over.' Words and blood poured from his mouth. 'Gvishani's dead ... the others too ... I am taking all the evidence to my father and the GRU.'

Aristov's face seemed shiny under the light. 'Come in. You need help. We can talk.'

'Too late ... for ... that.'

Aristov's mouth hardened. 'Come in, anyway.' He stood back from the door.

Yuri staggered through the gap and followed Aristov's bulky figure across the familiar living room to his study, staggered to a chair and sat. He rested the barrel of the Stechkin on Aristov's desk and cocked it.

'You want a drink? Tea? Coffee?' Aristov was a wavering shadow on the other side of the desk. Bookshelves and pictures, a photograph of Rima danced. Yuri tried to focus on Aristov. Slowly he shook his head.

'You have all the documents?' Aristov asked.

Yuri kept staring at him. The longer he stared the more clearly he saw. Aristov's eyes were flecked with red. The stubble on his chin was speckled with white.

'Of course, you do,' Aristov said, answering his own question. 'That's why you've come. You've come to make a deal, isn't that so, Yasha?' He held out his hand. 'Now, give me the documents. I'll take care of everything for you.'

'No,' Yuri blurted.

Aristov frowned. 'Why come here then?'

'Because of Rima ... After you're arrested ... she'll also be punished ... We should spare ... her that.'

'Don't talk nonsense, Yasha. No one's going to arrest me. I'm Arkady Aristov, Chairman of Party Organs, Member of the Central Committee, Alternate Member of the Politburo.'

'Not ... for much longer ... The evidence condemns ... you ... Korselov ... Orlenko ... Zarev. This time ... there's no escape.' He tried to make Aristov's favourite gesture of a knife slicing a throat. Blood spattered on the desk.

'Yasha, do you realize the power of those documents? Do you understand how they must be used? If we do it right, we can have anything we want, do anything we want. You could be Director of the entire KGB, do you realize that?'

'No ... deal.' Yuri felt blood rise into his mouth. He swallowed.

'Don't worry about Zarev and the others. They'll do what we tell them. And they will be grateful for what you've done. I'll make sure they show their gratitude.'

'The plane ... still at Tushino. All crew dead. But get ... a pilot or ask the Marshal. Take Rima ... your wife ... go!'

'Don't be stupid, Yasha! You have in your hands the means to reshape Russia. This is your chance to be remembered in history. Use it!'

'No.'

The flesh on Aristov's face seemed mottled. His features had lost their wary aggression. Quite suddenly, he looked old. 'Where do you suggest I go?'

'Finland ... plane's got enough fuel ... When you get there ... call ... George Carpenter. Tell him ... you want

... defect. Americans will take you ... Never had ... Alternate Member ... of Politburo before.'

'You're a fool, Raikin. A bigger fool than your father!'

Yuri stretched across the desk for a note pad and pencil. 'Call Carpenter ... It's ... your only chance.' He struggled to write. The figures sprawled across the page. Blood oozed from his hand onto the paper. He pushed it across to Aristov and looked up.

Like a huge, empty black eye, the barrel of a Makarov stared straight through the middle of his head. Aristov said, 'Did you think I would let someone like you stop me, especially now, when everything is within my grasp? I shall kill you and claim you came here after Rima.'

Yuri said, 'I have witnesses outside ... Sonya ... Yedemsky.'

'Witnesses can disappear,' Aristov said.

'No one ... will believe you ... I've already been wounded ... by another gun.'

'You think they will execute me for killing you? You fool, don't you realize once I've taken those documents from you, *I* will be the law?'

'No!' Yuri forced himself to match Aristov's shout. 'I'll take you ... first.' He moved the Stechkin. 'This is set to automatic ... It fires twelve rounds a second ... See my finger? ... You have ... no chance.'

'Twelve shots to one at two yards is better odds than you've offered so far.' Aristov's hand tighted round the Makarov. His body tensed for the recoil.

'You bastard, I came here to give you a chance, for Rima's sake.' Anger gave Yuri the breath and strength to speak a complete sentence.

'A mistake, Raikin. Never give anyone a chance.' His finger tightened on the trigger.

Yuri felt his own finger tense on the trigger of the Stechkin.

Aristov's lips curled. 'Fool!'

The door crashed open. Yedemsky stood swaying, waving his bottle of vodka. 'The front door was unlocked, Yasha. I came to see if you were all —' His eyes widened as he took in the scene. With inspired aim he flung the bottle at Aristov's head.

Aristov flung up an arm and ducked. Yuri reversed the Stechkin and swung it, the force of his swing pulling him forward out of the chair. The gun smashed into Aristov's flailing arm. The Makarov thudded onto the carpet.

With surprising agility Yedemsky dived for it. Yuri pulled the Stechkin back and pointed it at Aristov. Yedemsky scrabbled on the floor for the Makarov. Aristov stood clutching his arm, his face purple with rage.

Yuri leaned and took the Makarov from Yedemsky. He gestured to Yedemsky to take the Stechkin. When Yedemsky had got it, Yuri pressed the catch on the butt of the Makarov and slipped the magazine into his hand. With trembling fingers he extracted all the bullets save one, and snapped the magazine back.

'I've had ... enough,' he panted. 'Make ... your choice. The plane ... the Lubyanka ... or this.' Leaving the Makarov on the table, he hobbled to the door. Yedemsky came after him, covering Aristov with the Stechkin.

'You're a fool, Raikin!' Aristov bellowed. 'A fool! You have Russia in the palm of your hand!'

'Better a happy fool —' Yuri muttered, staggering into the living room. Rima and her mother stood there. For a moment his eyes met Rima's. Then she turned her head away. Yuri lurched past them into the corridor. Behind him doors slammed. He heard Yedemsky say, 'Come on, boychik. We'd better get you to a proper doctor.'

The corridor moved. The lights cartwheeled. The walls floated. He stepped into the elevator and groped for the buttons. From his left came the sound of a single shot, followed by women screaming. He lumbered forward. The sides of the elevator dissolved in waves of red and black. Yedemsky's arms caught him. 'Leave it, Yasha, for God's sake leave it. There's nothing more you can do.'

With the sound of Rima's screams and that single shot repeating endlessly inside his head, he plunged relentlessly downward.

Lights blazed. Distant voices shouted. He prised open tacky eyelids. The ambulance was bathed in light. Vague forms solidified. Soldiers.

Yuri fumbled for his work pass, dangled it over the side of the door. 'Get ... Marshal ... Raikin.'

The ambulance rolled forward. Someone stood on the running board and shouted directions. They stopped beneath a dimly lit porch. Men crowded around. Doors opened. Yuri allowed himself to be helped from the vehicle. They let him sit on a hard bench in a grey corridor near the entrance.

Yedemsky sat by him. Sonya was wheeled past. Her face was still pallid, but Yuri thought he saw an eyelid flicker.

Yedemsky stood up, spoke to one of the men crowding round them. Yedemsky said, 'I am a doctor.'

Later, there was a brisk marching of feet, a hurried rustle of clothing. His father's face swam before him. 'Yasha, are you all right? Can you talk?'

Yuri's lips moved. The blood that fell on his legs was frothy.

Later still, there was a roaring, a sound like a frantic beating of wings. It was not inside his head, but outside. His father stood beside another man. A Colonel's stars glimmered on red epaulettes. Yuri made out a round face, eyes like pellets, a fuzz of close cropped hair.

His father said, 'Colonel Rublov. He has just flown in from Zhukovka.'

The flesh of Rublov's neck bulged over the collar of his tunic. 'Can you talk?'

Yuri reached into his pocket, held out the wad of bloodstained papers. 'Read ... talk ... later.'

Rublov's hand took the evidence.

Yuri let himself fall.

Hands caught him. He was placed on a stretcher. He was wheeled along a corridor with grey ceilings.

A voie said, 'A very obstinate man, your son.'

The ceiling danced, dissolved. It went from grey to black.

CHAPTER FORTY-EIGHT

He woke on a narrow bed. Tubes ran to and from his body. A puppet, he thought, and wondered who pulled the strings.

'Try not to move.' His father's face swam over his, lined and haggard. 'They've taken the bullet from your lung. You've lost a lot of blood.'

Yuri tried to speak. 'Sonya?' Blood frothed down his chin.

'She's here.'

Her head loomed over his. There were tiny wrinkles along her brow, tiny lines framing the sides of her mouth. 'I am here,' she said. 'I'll always be here.'

Her face shone. Her eyes glinted. In Africa, an ikon, he thought and closed his eyes.

It was daylight, but how many days? Rublov hovered over him, his badges gleaming. Behind him, men moved. Rublov said, 'Yedemsky, your father and Sonya Matsyeva have told us a lot. We're holding Zarev, Korselov and Orlenko, also Guschin, Suslov and Drachinsky.'

'Aristov?' Yuri asked.

'He shot himself.'

Again, Yuri heard the shot and Rima's scream.

Rublov said, 'We had to cover it up, of course. The official story is that he mistook heart tablets for sleeping pills.'

'He should have taken the plane,' Yuri muttered.

Rublov was looking at him with studied interest. 'The plane hadn't enough fuel to even make Leningrad. In the end, Aristov double-crossed himself.'

Yuri asked, 'What about the family?'

'His wife and daughter will have to go back to Ryazan. Other employment is being found for his sons.'

Poor Rima, Yuri thought.

'We need a statement from you,' Rublov said. 'Do you feel up to it?'

'I think so.' He coughed. There was no blood.

'We'll go slowly, a little at a time. When you are better, Comrade Deryugin wants to see you.'

Traffic parted like water before the gleaming radiator of the Politburo Zil. Yuri sat in the back examining the array of buttons in the arm rest. A radio telephone was recessed into the seat back before him. There wasn't a speck of dust on the plush carpets. He watched, as from their pillboxes Militia men urgently waved them on.

In the nine weeks he'd been in the hospital, Guschin and Suslov had been tried for corruption and disappeared into *gulags*. Drachinsky had disappeared too – into a research institute, Yuri suspected. Zarev, Orlenko and Chairman Korselov had all died in a spectacular car crash on the Moscow-Leningrad highway. The bodies has been burned beyond recognition.

About six weeks ago, an obsequious lawyer had appeared at his bedside with papers for his divorce. 'I understand an agreement has been made with regard to joint property. Given the changed circumstances of the family, the court will understand if a variation –'

'Give me the papers,' Yuri had said, and signed.

The car braked and turned into the empty expanse of Red Square. It raced unimpeded across the cobbles. The deep red battlements soared.

Yuri stared anxiously at his fragile reflection in the window. The stiff uniform collar drooped and made his neck stick out like a cockerel's. His cheekbones protruded. That morning he'd had to spike an additional hole in his belt. In the shadowy reflection of the window glass, his eyes seemed unnaturally large and too close together. His skin had the pallor and texture of a man who had worked underground for a year.

They stopped before the vast, semi-circular arch of the Nikolsky Tower. Flags snapped proudly from the Kremlin's towers. Windows were electrically lowered. Hard eyes scrutinized him. The car drifted beneath the vast arch into the Kremlin. On the roadway in front of the Arsenal a troop of soldiers drilled. From the façade above, Napoleon's cannon sprouted. A plaque read, 'Here the Officer Cadets shot the Comrade Soldiers of the Kremlin Arsenal during the defence of the Kremlin in the October Days.'

They turned past a triangular garden. Beyond a guarded barrier ahead of them, tourists examined the Tsar cannon, walked in loose groupings up the steps of the Cathedral of the Twelve Apostles. The car turned left beneath a magnificent white stone cornice and entered the courtyard of the Senate Building. Above its brilliant green cupola a Soviet flag fluttered.

The car drew up before a flight of steps at the far end of the courtyard. At the head of the steps, Rublov stood, his round face fixed in a smile, his chest bright with medals. With a touch of envy, Yuri saw that his uniform fitted perfectly.

Rublov came halfway down the steps to greet him. The car whispered away. They went through a large lobby flanked with massive paintings of revolutionary triumphs. They walked past guards standing stiffly at attention and took an elevator to the third floor.

On the third floor, more guards, a broad corridor with a wide strip of red carpet running down its centre. On either side of the carpet, polished wooden flooring gleamed.

They walked in silence past more guards, past magnificently moulded doors. Rublov stopped before one such door, knocked and threw it open.

The room inside was vast. Along one side, tall windows overlooked Red Square. To the left, French windows opened onto a balcony. Lush Oriental rugs were scattered over the floor. In front of an ornate Italian fireplace to the right, were sofas and armchairs in green leather. Before one of the windows stood a large desk, handsome and intricately carved, a quarter of its tooled leather surface covered by an armada of telephones. Curling out briskly from behind the desk was General Secretary Deryugin himself.

He was taller than Yuri had deduced from television pictures of May Day parades. His hands were large and workmanlike. There was an unexpected roughness about his skin, and the wiry coxcomb of speckled grey hair seemed more vibrant than in photographs. His rimless glasses, Yuri felt, did not weaken, but masked the shrewd, aggressive intelligence of his wedge of a face.

'Ever since Popov told me what you did in London, I've wanted to meet you.'

Somehow, with no touching of hands or any other physical contact, they were standing before the fireplace. Deryugin sat alertly on one end of a sofa. Yuri and Rublov sat side by side in armchairs.

'Now,' Deryugin said, 'I want to hear all about it. I want you to tell me everything you did.' His grey eyes were bleak as a Baltic squall. 'Take all the time you need.'

Yuri thought: Remarkable. Deryugin had already studied the evidence in detail, read the reports Rublov had made, taken action which had led to imprisonment and death. And now he was devoting an entire morning to hearing it all again.

Yuri began with Simmonds and London. As he was telling them about the attack by Abyugov, secretaries brought in tea. More tea when he told them about the shootings at Zhukovka, and again as he described his meeting with Snead. Deryugin's attention remained totally fixed until Yuri finished describing the shoot out at Tushino.

Then he asked, 'Why?'

Yuri frowned. 'I'm sorry, I don't follow ...'

'What made you do it? What made you perform these extraordinary feats of dedication and heroism? Not loyalty to Popov. You've already admitted that. Hardly loyalty to me. We've met for the first time today. So why?'

'I thought it was right,' Yuri said, perplexed.

Deryugin looked incredulously from Yuri to Rublov. Then he smiled. 'I am glad there are still romantics in the KGB.' Then still smiling, he got to his feet. 'And now ...' Deryugin walked to the desk with precise, measured steps, returned holding a small leather case in his palm.

'Stand up, please.'

Both Rublov and Yuri stood.

'Comrade Raikin, in consideration of your heroic achievements and demonstrated concern for the USSR, it is my pleasure and my privilege to award you the honour of Hero of the Soviet Union.' Deryugin opened the case. The bright gold star shone beneath its scarlet and white ribbon. Deryugin pinned it insecurely askew on the serge of Yuri's tunic.

'Congratulations,' he said and shook Yuri's hand brusquely. They sat.

Deryugin said, 'I very much regret that this honour could not have been accorded to you more publicly. But under the circumstances ...'

'I understand,' Yuri said.

Deryugin's eyes raked his face. Deryugin said, 'After your convalescence, you will return to the Sluzbha. As you know, under Colonel-General Rublov certain reorganizations have taken place, and the Sluzbha now administers several departments formerly controlled by the Fifth Directorate. I shall require you, Lieutenant Colonel Raikin —' Deryugin allowed a wary smile to flit across his face. 'Yes, Lieutenant Colonel. Formal notice of your appointment will be given on your return to duty. I shall want you in charge of a new department responsible for eliminating counter-revolutionary elements in certain levels of our society. Colonel-General Rublov will give you the details. You will be responsible directly to him.'

Yuri couldn't keep the dismay from his face. Counter-revolutionary elements at certain levels of society, meant disposing of threats to Deryugin at Party, Central Committee and Politburo level. It meant midnight arrests and discreet liquidations. Had he opposed Aristov and Zarev for this?

Yuri said, 'With respect ...' he hesitated, looking for excuses. 'My experience in administration is limited. I feel I would serve my country best, if I were transferred to the First Directorate and sent to serve abroad.'

Deryugin glanced swiftly at Rublov. His mouth tightened.

Rublov said, 'I'm not sure that will be possible. You see, you are now too well known to the Americans.'

'Perhaps some country where the American presence is minimal,' Yuri suggested.

Deryugin said abruptly, 'Why don't you discuss all this with Colonel-General Rublov when you return!' He got to his feet and accompanied Yuri to the door, one arm round Yuri's shoulder, Rublov trailing like a waiter hoping for a generous tip. 'The State is deeply grateful to you,' he murmured. 'You are a true hero, like your father. I hope you will always remain a hero, that you will always do what's right.'

They reached the door and Deryugin released him. 'And what will you do with all the information you have gained?'

Behind them, Yuri heard Rublov gasp.

'I've already delivered all the evidence to Colonel-General Rublov.'

'I know that. But what about the evidence inside your head?' Deryugin's eyes had a fixed glitter, as if they had suddenly turned to glass.

'I'm no Dolgov,' Yuri said, but Deryugin was already turning away.

Rublov accompanied Yuri out of the office, along the corridor and down to the ground floor. Summoned by a mysterious agency the Zil waited by the steps, its exhaust silently blowing small puffs of smoke. Yuri pulled his uniform about him. It was the end of September. Already the air had a chill, wintry hardness to it.

As the car pulled away, Rublov turned and walked up the steps.

CHAPTER FORTY-NINE

In Yevpatoriya, it was still summer. Yuri lay on the beach and looked at the scars on the side of his chest. As he had feared in childhood, his body had inherited his father's scars. Across from him Sonya squatted, finishing off a sandcastle.

As children, Yuri remembered, he and Nikolai had taken cruel delight in kicking over Sonya's sandcastles. Once they had buried a crab in one of Sonya's lovingly constructed mounds. He smiled at remembered screams of outrage.

The beach was deserted. Gulls wheeled over an empty expanse of yellow sand. Ruffled waves beat soothingly.

Sonya patted wet sand and said, 'It was a nice wedding.'

'It had to be. It was your only wedding.'

Sand clung to the long thighs of his woman-child, filled the dimple of one knee. Her bronze feet were splayed. Claws of a yawning cat, Yuri thought sleepily and finished his wine.

Sonya said, 'I liked your friend, Pasha. Will he ever walk again?'

'He thinks so, and if he thinks so, he will.' Yuri put the damp glass beside him on the sand. Whatever Pasha thought, he would never wrestle again.

'And that lunatic Misha. He was more excited about the wedding photographs than we were!'

Misha had absolutely insisted that they be photographed on the viewing station across from the Lenin Hills. 'I know every bridal couple does it,' he had cried at Sonya's vibrant protests. 'But it is tradition. And in twenty years time you will be sorry.'

Sonya stuck a small red flag on the sandcastle. Then she found a stick, tied a blue handkerchief to it and placed it beside the red flag.

'What's that?'

'The American flag.' Head on one side, she looked at the

castle appraisingly, turned and gave him a self-satisfied smirk. 'I believe in peace and co-existence.'

'Would you like to live in America?' Yuri asked.

'Work, not live.'

'That wasn't the question.'

'No,' she said, still admiring the sandcastle. 'Neither of us would be happy there. Neither of us would fit.'

'The Americans have special schools that will teach us to be American. They will teach us about baseball and football, how to order in a restaurant, how to book plane tickets. You know you can go anywhere in America without a passport.'

Sonya came and threw herself chest down on the sand beside him. She rested her head on her hands. 'America isn't Russia,' she said. 'We're Russian.'

'In America, we could have a large house. We could take holidays in places like this whenever we wanted. We could eat in restaurants every night. We could go where we liked, even outside America. We could be rich. We would have two cars —'

'And two identities,' Sonya interrupted. 'That would be real wealth.'

'We could adjust to life in America,' Yuri said. 'We could learn to like the life there.'

'What kind of life? Not knowing who we are or who we are running from. Yasha, why are you thinking of living in America?'

Yuri stared at the ceaseless waves. 'When I was in America, the Americans wanted me to stay. They'd still like me to come over.'

'You mean to defect? You wouldn't do that, Yasha! Would you be happy in America?'

'No,' Yuri admitted.

'Then why even think about it?'

Yuri grinned lopsidedly. 'I wanted you to know that we have a choice.'

'The sun is making you stupid,' Sonya said. She reached out and ran a finger over his scars.

Yuri stroked her hand.

346

After a while, she rose to her knees. 'Let's have some more wine.'

She reached for the picnic basket.

Yuri heard her say breathlessly, 'Oh, Yasha!' and opened his eyes.

She was kneeling by the picnic basket, holding the holstered Stechkin away from her. Her eyes were wide and frightened. 'Yasha, why do you still carry this gun?'

Yuri reached out, took the weapon from her and replaced it in the basket. 'Force of habit,' he said.

CHAPTER FIFTY

They came, as Yuri had known they would, two shadows flitting among the trees on the bluff behind the dacha. Yuri yanked the cord controlling the solitary light on the terrace.

'What —' Sonya cried.

'Quick! Down behind the balcony.'

Yuri was already on his knees below the wooden railing, the Stechkin in his hand. He fired two shots into the darkness.

As he expected there was no return of fire. Moscow would have ordered that he be disposed of discreetly. 'The next ones won't miss,' he called into the darkness. 'Come out with your hands raised.'

He stared into the gaps between the trees. In the pale moonlight he could see two of them. He sighted carefully along the barrel of the Stechkin. 'Move!' he shouted.

'Yasha, what is it?'

'Deryugin's killers.'

'Deryugin? I don't understand.'

'Great indebtedness does not make men grateful, but vengeful.'

He watched the figures move between the trees, reached sideways and turned on the floodlights that illuminated the small garden between the balcony and the bluff. Two men stepped into the light with their hands raised.

'Hello, Georgi,' Yuri said and stood up.

Georgi Vilna's simian face was expressionless.

'Drop your guns,' Yuri said.

'We're not armed,' Vilna said.

'What were you going to do? Strangle us?'

Vilna smiled superciliously. 'Only you,' he said.

'How?'

He reached into his jacket and brought out a dart shaped syringe.

'Drop it!' Yuri shouted. 'Him too!'

Both men dropped the devices.

Vilna said, 'Painless, effective and undetectable.'

'And my wife?' Yuri couldn't keep the anger out of his voice.

'A widow.'

Yuri asked, 'Whose orders?'

Vilna's mouth straightened into a narrow line.

Yuri fired once above their heads. 'Next time it's the knees,' he said. 'You can't kill if you can't walk.'

Vilna shrugged. 'Rublov.' His eyes were like live coals. 'Rublov is acting on the highest authority. You're superfluous to requirements, Raikin. You're finished.'

'What reasons were you given?'

Vilna said, 'We have proof that you are an agent of the CIA. We have evidence of your unauthorized visits to London and Washington, of your meetings with George Carpenter.'

'Evidence that is capable of other interpretations.'

Vilna smiled grimly. 'That isn't our concern. We only carry out orders.'

Yuri said, 'Come into the house. Bring your friend.'

He had Sonya cover them with the Stechkin while he checked them for weapons. Both men were clean. They went into the dacha. Yuri had them sit across the room while he called Moscow. The dacha had a priority line to the Army switchboard. Yuri asked for Colonel-General Rublov. They didn't take long to find him.

'It's Captain Yuri Raikin,' Yuri said. 'I have with me Comrade Vilna and an assistant. I have with me the dart guns with which they hoped to kill me. Comrade Vilna says he is acting on your orders.'

'That's correct,' Rublov said. 'Evidence has been placed before us that clearly demonstrates you are an American agent.'

'You know that's untrue,' Yuri shouted. 'You know why I went to London and Washington.'

'But no one else knows,' Rublov said, smoothly. 'Just one moment, Raikin. A friend wants a word with you.'

'A friend? Who?'

'Hello, Yuri,' said George Carpenter. 'The good Colonel and I were just talking about you. It's about time you came home.'

'I am home,' Yuri said.

'Not anymore. You see, Yuri, the good Colonel and his master are very worried about you. They think you are too righteous for your own good. They would like Comrade Vilna to ease their concern. They sent him to you today to show you how easy that would be.'

'What the hell have you got to do with this,' Yuri demanded, angrily.

'Well, Yuri we don't want you embarrassing Mr Deryugin. Or us. Especially after we've all gone to so much trouble to get Dolgov's testament from the Staaderbank and destroy it.'

'I'm not Dolgov!'

'We'll never know that, will we. So it's America for you, my friend.'

'I'm not defecting,' Yuri shouted.

'Be reasonable,' Carpenter said. 'You'll be comfortable in America. Your wife, too. And just think, once you've crossed over, you wouldn't be a threat to anyone. You won't have a thing to worry about.'

'I'm Russian!' Yuri cried. 'I'm staying.'

'Yuri,' Carpenter said, 'think of your father. He retires from the army in two months. He should be allowed to retire with honour.'

Feeling as if he'd touched a live electrode, Yuri realized that the Marshal also knew too much. Only by his defection or death could any of them be silenced. 'He – we – laid everything on the line for Russia,' Yuri said. 'We deserve better –'

'Exactly,' Carpenter said. 'I've been authorized to offer you a resettlement gratuity of $250,000.'

The price Dolgov had been paid! Blood money! Hush money!

'And in six months, the Marshal will be allowed to go abroad, to live abroad if he wants to. And we'll take care of all of you, Yuri. You'll want for nothing, I promise you that.'

Except Russia, Yuri thought. Except home. But they held all the cards. They were the puppet masters. They pulled the strings. 'How can I be sure?' he asked.

'If we didn't mean to keep our word,' Carpenter replied, 'we wouldn't be talking like this. Believe me, it would have been just as easy to have Comrade Vilna perform his job efficiently.'

'All right,' Yuri said. There was no other choice.

'OK, I'm glad that's settled. Our people will collect you and your wife in two hours. Phillip Adams will hand you a cheque for the amount we have agreed. And I'll see you in Washington.'

The phone whirred in Yuri's ear.

Vilna got to his feet. 'Perhaps, next time,' he said, with a hint of regret.

Fontana Paperbacks: Fiction

Fontana is a leading paperback publisher of both non-fiction, popular and academic, and fiction. Below are some recent fiction titles.

- ☐ SEEDS OF YESTERDAY Virginia Andrews £1.95
- ☐ CAVALCADE Gwendoline Butler £1.95
- ☐ RETURN TO RHANNA Christine Marion Fraser £1.95
- ☐ JEDDER'S LAND Maureen O'Donoghue £1.95
- ☐ THE FINAL RUN Tommy Steele £1.50
- ☐ FOR LOVE OF A STRANGER Lily Devoe £1.75
- ☐ THE WARLORD Malcolm Bosse £2.95
- ☐ TREASON'S HARBOUR Patrick O'Brian £1.95
- ☐ FUTURES Freda Bright £1.95
- ☐ THE DEMON LOVER Victoria Holt £1.95
- ☐ THE UNRIPE GOLD Geoffrey Jenkins £1.75
- ☐ A CASE FOR CHARLEY John Spencer £1.50
- ☐ DEATH AND THE DANCING FOOTMAN Ngaio Marsh £1.75
- ☐ THE 'CAINE' MUTINY Herman Wouk £2.50
- ☐ THE TRANSFER Thomas Palmer £1.95
- ☐ LIVERPOOL DAISY Helen Forrester £1.75
- ☐ OUT OF A DREAM Diana Anthony £1.75
- ☐ SHARPE'S SWORD Bernard Cornwell £1.75

You can buy Fontana paperbacks at your local bookshop or newsagent. Or you can order them from Fontana Paperbacks, Cash Sales Department, Box 29, Douglas, Isle of Man. Please send a cheque, postal or money order (not currency) worth the purchase price plus 15p per book for postage (maximum postage required is £3).

NAME (Block letters) _____

ADDRESS _____

_____

_____